The Inverted Banyan Tree

JK ASHER

The Inverted Banyan Tree

Say, 'I seek refuge in the Lord of mankind, the Sovereign of mankind, the God of mankind. From the mischief of the slinking prompter, who whispers evil into the breasts of mankind from among the jinn and mankind.'

Al Quran: 114 Surah An-Nas (Mankind)
Nabi Muhammad PBUH

Atlantis Books

K ARJAN **S**INGH
My brother. My Father. A King
Satnaam Waheguru

No greater love than a man lay down his life.

Our Mother said it best:
The day your father died – the sun eclipsed
Arjan became my light

Thank you Toki Ji
For Vision

Peace and Blessings
Upon your Generations

On the wings of a Dove

Davinder Cumaraswamy

My Muse

And

Kimmy

The Lifter of my Heart in prayer

I could only soar because I was carried

KING JAMES
Psalm 68:13

Nina
Rahim
Shumi
Rabin
Markie

Contents

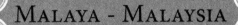

MALAYA - MALAYSIA

↑

NORTH

PORT
DICKSON TOWN

NEGERI SEMBILAN
PORT DICKSON

OPEN
MARKET
LOOKOUT
TOWER
BANYAN TREES

STALLS

PARK

SHOPS

BUS STATION

RUBBER AND OIL
PALM PLANTATIONS

NEW HIGHWAY

CHINESE FARMS

VET

RECLAIMED LAND

PLANTERS INN

DOM
BRICKWALL

15KM

AL-SIJJIN
COMMUNE

TIGER
SANCTUARY

BLOOD FIELD
FISHING VILLAGE

ENGLISH
HOUSE

JAPANESE SOLDIERS
BARRACKS

STRAITS OF MALACCA

OLD COAST ROAD

CAPE RACHADO

SUMATRA

✠ ✝

AL-FUAD MOSQUE

LIGHTHOUSE

CATHOLIC MONASTERY

Prologue
1956
YEAR OF THE INQUISITION

THIS BEING MY LAST WILL AND TESTAMENT –

I, Brother Dom Alfonso Hendrique of the Society of Jesus, bequeath to the *Kristang*, the Christians, my unworldly possessions ... my great hope...

But wait! Something's wrong.

It's unnaturally quiet today. Above the scratching of the pencil lead in my diary, the voices are muffled as if I'm under tons of jello. The harsh clatter of tin cups on metal trolleys, jackhammering eyelids encrusted by barbiturate sleep cures and green mucus – there's nothing.

Not even the screams.

Normally everyone can hear the screams, all the way from Ward C. Through corridors of white tiles and unending fluorescent tubes, like median strips on the ceiling, they wheel you strapped to the iron cot. The gnashing and frothing roils your brain before they can turn the electric current on.

They're going to interrogate me shortly. Break my hope. Lash me down. And nail me with that eternally infernal question – **"Who is your God?"**

Judgement Day – Dies Irae.
Who will save me from the Day of Wrath?
What requiem awaits?

Choking on sulphurous fumes of lime from the latrines and showers -
I'm in hell. Memories flood in. Oh! I can see the British Advisor's
horses, bellies swollen with gas, covered in lime. The vet had to put
them down because of the sleeping sickness. We waited at the edge of
the jungle for all the grown-ups to leave and then we fired sharp stones
with our catapults to cause explosions. The smell was festery and we
had to put handkerchiefs over our faces like cowboys. We got tired of
it when there was nothing left of the horses but slime and maggots.

The doctors say I remember too much, that I don't know past from
present... too many attachment interruptions as a child growing up.
Interrupted by Magellan and the King of Spain's daughter.

The one with the sad eyes, the Lady of the Pierced Soul. She
revealed the deepest thoughts of my heart and ruined me with her
cruelty. This Mother of God.

Pie Jesu domine
Dona eis requiem
All merciful Jesus
Grant Thy eternal rest.

The doctors say they can fix the psychosis but they need something
from me first. Everyone wants a piece of my 'disrupted' selves. Even
Alistair... why else would the Advisor's personal assistant arrange for
me to have my own room. They've shut me in the dhobi quarters. They
don't want me to harm myself... it will look bad for the Order if a priest
took his own life. And for me, the Potter's field, eternal damnation.

As I'm writing, the blood-caked bandage on my hand cracks.

Brownish-red flakes snow over the words I've written. They think I'm doing it to myself... that I'm creating the stigmata. They've started tying me in restraints at night to stop me picking at my hands.

The Monsignors, they want a confession before the delegation from the Holy Office in Rome arrives next month. They want me to renounce who I am, to turn my bloodied back on Him.

For two years I've tried. At the monastery every morning at Lauds and at evening Vespers, my knobbly knees cobbling the granite square, my contemplation is of Him.

> *Recordare, Jesu pie*
> *ne me perdas illa die.*
> *Remember kind Jesus*
> *Leave me not to reprobates.*

With the salted strap, I've killed the flesh but I still can't let Him go, the man who gave us hope. The one who is our Father.

I realise why it's quiet. I'm number one today. They said it wouldn't hurt the first time they put me in the chair. I broke two teeth as I bit down on the mouthpiece and tore a ligament in my knee from the fits. The doctor said it shouldn't have happened. He blamed the war for my powdery bones and teeth.

We were not allowed to have milk during the war.

Babeh Shamoh's cows were seized by the Japanese military. I remember when her son Isher was struck down by an army truck... Babeh Shamoh cremated him with wood and ghee, and washed his bones in buttermilk. Isher always reminded me of Moses.

My memories worry the Holy Fathers. They say the treatment will help me resurface from this miasma of voices from the dead. A resurrection? They want me to forget who I am... Dom Hendrique, son to our ancestral father, Awang Enrique.

Will I become a ghost like the Kristang, my people?

Unseen, not even having the venom of being forsaken.

Awang Enrique took us to Spain, a Malay cabin boy whom Magellan purchased in Malacca. A noble buccaneer in silk stockings and calf boots on the heels of the greatest navigator. What a sight to behold – Enrique, presented to the King of Spain. I fell in love with the King's daughter when Enrique girthed the earth and brought her home to Malacca.

Is this not worth holding onto?

Bedlam over a life without hope and vision.

The outer door's being unlocked and I can hear the grinding of the wheelchair on the cement flooring. It will be Dr Ummah. He's the only one I trust because he doesn't want anything from me. I can see his face so clearly. It's dangerously fierce and tender altogether. Each time after they've put the headband on with the electrodes and before the current is switched on, he leans over and whispers something heavenly –

> *Asyhadu alla illahaill Allah*
> *Asyhadu anna Muhammadar rasulAllah*
> *I bear witness that there is no God but Allah and*
> *Muhammad is the Messenger of Allah.*

He watches over my soul if I should die, Jesu Pie, he watches over my soul.

Last entry in the Diary of Brother Dominic Hendrique
Society of Jesus
Order of Ignatius Loyola

16 June 1956
Tanjung Rambutan Mental Hospital. Perak – Malaya

Part 1

1985 – PRESENT
PORT DICKSON, MALAYSIA

*'... he passed the blade across his face and smelt it, and then said,
"This Kris—good. Has ate a man".'*

The Golden Chersonese and the way Thither – Isabella L. Bird

1

THE GREAT PRETENDER'S DEAD! Cabin servant to Magellan hanged himself.

The inky night smudged the figure on the water's edge. Only the rattling words in his brain kept Alistair Pierce from disappearing altogether. Overhead, the westerly from Sumatra, barrelling down the Straits of Malacca, bowled the clouds, striking the moon. The whisking breakers turned sooty.

'Dom Hendrique, you're nothing but a joke in life and a bigger fool in death.'

Lightning silhouetted bibulous clouds and the shoreline lurched. Alistair felt his feet lift from inside his shoes. The beam from the lighthouse off Cape Rachado scythed through him and he sank backwards.

The floodlit 15th century Catholic monastery on Cape Rachado steadied him. It looked like a fortress, running lights marking the grotto where Our Lady made perpetual succour for the fishermen at sea. A silvery spire pierced the monastery. Hidden on the leeside of the headland was the Al-Fuad mosque. The Kingfisher blue tiles of the minaret with its luminous green grouting filled the night sky over the monastery. It was no longer Mother Mary, whispering words of wisdom, guiding the fishermen. It was Muhammad, the Rasul of Allah.

Drums pulsated in the dark night. A quarter of a mile away, the fishing village was festive with the "Visit Malaysia 1985" gala. Alistair felt nauseous. The answer to Dom's death lay in the fishing village with the Spirit Guide aka Ummah, the village Headman. Dom had been found hanging on the Black Lenggundi Tree in Tiger Sanctuary.

Anger seared Alistair.

'Why the Sanctuary, Dom? You irresponsible bastard! Enough blood has been spilled there already.'

All the snide remarks they thought he hadn't heard came flooding in.

'Typical Dom! Thinks he's a white man...'

'He's got balls, big black ones!'

'That's the *Serani*[1] for you. Just because he's got a Portuguese name!'

'Serani! He's one hundred and ten percent charcoal. I don't see any Eurasian in him.'

'Now, the Serani in Portuguese settlement, they've got blue eyes, and not just the girls.'

'There's one with green eyes – Leverne. He's dolled up every Saturday night for the cultural show.'

'Serani *Gragos*[2]... either shrimping nets or it's dancing time.'

They were especially derogatory about Dom's relationship with him.

'*Orang Putih's*[3] peon. Serani – *Kerani*[4].'

'The white man's lonely, Dom loves to talk, the beer's free. Come on!'

---

1   Serani – a very old term for Eurasians of Malacca's colonial history where Portuguese, Dutch and English bloodlines have given way to a dark-skinned Asian bias as they married locals. The term has a racial connotation as it infers that the person is an outsider ethnically. The term can be endearing; a bit of a joke because there is no trace of European colouring; or it can be disparaging because many of the Serani were poor shrimp farmers. Thus the term Grago (shrimp) which was often interchangeable with Serani or Serani Gragos, Eurasian shrimps.

2   *Grago* – shrimp. Derogatory, alluding to the social and economic status of the Serani, who were shrimp fishermen and had many children.

3   Orang Putih – white man.

4   Kerani – Malay word for clerks in the British administration.

With Dom's death the schadenfreude was terrifying.

'He was wearing women's clothing when they found him.'

'Just like Laverne.'

'That's why the *Katolic*[5] church kicked him out when he was a Padri.'

'No... he became *gila*[6]. He had to have electric shock.'

'He saw Mother Mary! Loco lah.'

'He got kicked out because he's got a Muslim wife.'

'Don't be stupid, look at Dom. Something wrong in that department.'

'The Catholic church won't bury him. He blasphemed Mother Mary.'

'It's because he wears women's clothes! The police have evidence.'

'Always suspected he was a fag.'

'Why hang himself?'

'Maybe he was jilted or maybe someone found out.'

Alistair's eyes slipped off the blue dome of the Al-Fuad mosque and snagged onto the candescent grotto of Our Lady.

They're lynching you again, he thought despairingly.

A bag had been found near Dom's motorbike in the Sacred Forest. Containing a floral kaftan and a long black wig, it nailed Dom to the paranormal sightings in Port Dickson. The simple folk swore it was a female vampire. Some believed it was a prankster; others, a Lourdes-like visitation drawing the crowds. Tragically, Dom was one of the pilgrims.

Between the pounding surf and the drumbeat of the fishing village, Alistair heard his heart crank. The talk about suicide was sacrilegious. Dom savoured life, like an infatuated boy. Friday nights were booked in with Linda Tai, the Chinese Cha-cha-cha dance instructress at the Club. They teased him mercilessly about Linda "Thigh"

---

5   Katolic – Catholic.

6   Gila – insane, mad.

but he was beyond caring about what others made of his conceits.

"I am Dominic Alfonso Hendrique, honourable cabin servant to Ferdinand Magellan, presented in the courts of King Charles of Spain." This was the quintessential Dom, happily pissed, swaying on his feet at the Hunter's Bar, a beer glass in hand. "I do this in remembrance of the Fathers." And with his trademark benediction, he would scull his Tiger beer.

No. Dominic Alfonso Hendrique, cabin servant to Magellan, was in love with the chase. It led to his ex-communication and this time it lured him to his death.

Why didn't I stop you?

His feverish mind came to a standstill.

The Spirit Guide. The Spirit Guide – aka Ummah the village Headman – had seduced Dom. Alistair Pierce's lips curled bitterly, it was a seduction he was familiar with. He could still see Dom in front of him in the living room. He had come to borrow the camera and was practically crowing that he was going with the Spirit Guide to seek out the "woman".

'Do you think I should take some protection?'

He sounded like a pimpled pubescent talking about condoms. Instead, he was looking at the hunting guns and revolver in the antique Malacca showcase. With his dyed black hair and Nat King Cole charm, he looked in his thirties, not someone approaching fifty. He had a surprisingly unlined face for a life of aborted achievements. Alistair watched him wearily. The man could barely pitch a tent let alone wield a gun, but he had such great **hope**. It was ludicrous, a child's magical thinking that never grew cynical or wiser. A part of Alistair envied it.

'Why do you think you need a gun?' Pierce asked guardedly.

'I thought Ummah the Guide said it would be safe.'

'He did, but you know… if there's a tiger or some other animal.'

'I thought tigers were his pets,' Alistair spat out pettily.

Without so much as a "May I?" Dom had unlocked the almirah and was stroking one of the hunting guns. As an antique collector, Dom knew their value but had no knowledge of what they could do. Alistair had bought the guns when he came to Malaya in 1952, as a British Land Officer in the Negeri Sembilan Civil Service. They were for wild animals and the even fiercer communists preying on white plantation managers. The prehistoric forests tamed, the communists withdrew to become traders in precious stones and artefacts from Cambodia, and the guns became showpieces.

'What do you think?' Dom had asked expectantly, gun in hand.

'About what?'

'*The woman!* Is she a divine visitation or a blood-sucking vampire?'

On the wall behind Dom, *"Big Brother"* smirked. Two Victorian paintings looked down on them, portraits of an Uncle and Aunt in ornate oval frames. They were a wedding gift from his mother, a frightful attempt at being upper class. He suspected it was punishment for marrying a "native". Ivy was all peaches and cream with green eyes but she was a Eurasian throwback, her lips all the redder because of her *Cincalo*[7] relish. She embraced the portraits (it was tied up with her need for ancestry) and planted them, dead creatures, on either side of the almirah in the living room. Every evening, great Grand-Aunt Beatrice and Uncle Cedric, distant relatives of the Earl of Doncaster, kept them company until they outlived her.

'This whole business sounds like a bit of a lark. Think about it…'

---

7   Cincalo – fermented shrimp relish eaten with sliced onions, red chillies and lime juice.

Alistair said, aware of the frowning countenance of his relatives.

'Alis, for once don't think! Let your mind go and come to your senses.'

'What bollocks, really Dom!'

'The Spirit Guide said things of the spirit are to be received by the spirit.'

'Ummah should stick to being the Headman and not be off with the fairies and jinn!'

'Don't be unfair Alistair. There are things *you* don't understand.'

Alistair experienced a stab of betrayal. Dom had used the "you" and "us" weapon. In the last three months, a subtle tension had infiltrated their relationship, and it had a name. Ummah aka the Spirit Guide. It began with the sightings of "the woman".

Appearing in the night watches, the fishermen's description tied in with the "lady statue" found in the Catholic churchyard. Dom was hooked. Dozens of times he stood Alistair up at the Club, apologising profusely the next day. He had been with the Spirit Guide, the fountainhead of all things mystical. That he was Ummah the village Headman, with all his foibles, did nothing to unseat Dom's mindless devotion.

As Dom faced him, hunting gun in his hand, Alistair experienced a déjà vu. Fifteen years earlier, Ivy had stood in the exact spot with the same look of hope and defiance. She believed the Spirit Guide could cure her cancer rather than the doctors in Harley Street. Alistair could feel the two portraits behind Dom, coercing him to speak up, to step over "*his line*". This was a line he had drawn in the sand when he came to the Colony. It had kept him sane. If he stepped over it, every truth he had lived would be swept away. That was unimaginable. *What would a man be without himself?* He stepped back. It was effortless, second nature.

'I've nothing against Ummah but this vampire story's a bit rich'.

'It's not just a vampire... there's more to it than the physical realm. Why don't you come along?'

'I gave up hunting a long time ago. If Ummah's going with you, you won't need the gun. Put it back before you shoot yourself,' Alistair said dryly, turning away.

'I need your camera. I'm going to get a photo finish of this nag. Want to place a wager?'

'You mean with Also-Ran?' retorted Alistair snidely. 'And what happens when she turns out to be some old village hag?'

'Oh, folklore says once I've got her soul on film, she's mine. What a way to find a wife, eh?'

'You're a bloody fool...'

'O Carol, I am bloody fool,' Dom crooned, holding the shotgun muzzle up like a microphone. 'Darling I love you, though you treat me croool...'

On the beach, in the dark, remembering, Alistair felt like weeping.

I've got to get to the village, and talk to Ummah. He found the body.

His mind balked. Dom had become "the body". The thickness in his throat swamped him and for the first time since the discovery, Alistair wept, for Dom and himself.

2

PLANTER'S INN WAS SEQUINED with lights from her bougainvillea gables right down to the white petticoat waves. It was a big night for the Club. The Tourism Board had picked her as one of several heritage venues for "Visit Malaysia 1985". The first part of the evening was over, a banquet of Malaysian cuisine "hawker style". Carts and stalls served everything from *satay* to *roti canai* and sticky rice desserts. Guests were then shuttled to the fishing village a mile away where a cultural extravaganza awaited them. Waiters and waitresses had started clearing up the tables, while harried ushers flushed out the stragglers.

Chatter came from the carpark. Lodged in the floodlights were the red lolling arses of chartered Tata buses. Almost every other vehicle was a BMW, Mercedes Benz or Volvo. A group of drivers squatted like ducks, sipping duty-free Tiger beer from the Terendak[8] Army Camp. The tempo of their conversation was faster than usual.

'Three days and they haven't buried him.'

'Bad luck for the town.'

'Tsk... what nonsense.'

'Nonsense! You young people rubbish everything.'

'Same thing happened thirty years ago. When you were sucking milk.'

'Just stories, Uncle.'

---

8 Terendak – army camp in Port Dickson.

'A boy was murdered in the Keramat. His spirit came back!'

'Anybody who dies in the Sacred Forest comes back.'

A night owl hooted plaintively.

'The devil bird agrees.'

Laughter from the waterfront percolated through. On the beach, hostesses in batik, sprouting orchids, waited on the last guests. Rickshaws trussed up in tulle, pink and blue satin, nested nearby like birds of paradise. A ten-seater shuttle van sat under a makeshift tent of palm fronds for the latecomers. The festivities in the village would culminate at midnight, with young turtles being released into the water. What the tourists did *not* know was that the baby turtles would be found dead a few days later. Subterranean pipes from hotels further up spewed contaminants into the sea. It was an open secret.

The stretch of beach from Planter's Inn, past the fishing village to Cape Rachado was called White Sands because of the limestone islands off the coast.

Every year-end, from the 1890s, homesick Colonials congregated here. It would start with joyous carolling, culminating with a Nativity play on Christmas Eve against the backdrop of equatorial "snow". Then another week of carousing, ending in drunkenness and sometimes tears, much to the bewilderment of the captivated fishermen. Before too long the fishermen could sing a risible version of "Auld Lang Syne".

In 1920, rumours of a stopover by Somerset Maugham en route to Singapore skyrocketed Planter's fame. He never came, but "Planter's" continued to roll off tongues like an after-dinner liqueur. The *NAAFI*[9] balls at the Terendak Army Camp brought out nubile Eurasian beauties dreaming of foreign shores. In the sixties, when

---

9   NAAFI – Navy, Army and Air Force Institutes, created by the British government to run recreational programs and sell goods to servicemen and their families.

the Commonwealth forces left for home, there was an exodus of Malaysian brides.

The Ministry of Tourism and Culture wanted to recreate this heyday. Unfortunately, the beaches were rusted with development. *Tanah Merah* (Red Earth) was proposed. Hollywood wanted to collaborate on a film script with a leading lady, wet in an incy wincy bikini, sandpapered against a hunky gunrunner turned saint (not forgetting the turtles). The Ministry of Tourism and Culture found itself in a delicate position. Bikinis were a "no-no". It was an Islamic nation albeit a liberal one. The Hollywood script had to be filtered by forums of people in skullcaps and wimples. Until then, dinner at the Club and traditional drums at the fishing village was the go.

In the Club by the reception console, the Tamil manager stood, his fingers locked in front of him over his coat. Hefty, with a leonine mane, he was listening for the tell-tale creak of the staircase between the reception and dining room. Mr Akiro Kabota, a houseguest, was taking his own "blaady" time and keeping everyone waiting. The manager, however, was in high spirits. He had been employed three months earlier to get the staff ready for the launch. The night had been a great success, and the Club looked "first class". Low, yellow lights splayed the Club with rich hues. He was privately glad because they hid his expanding girth.

'The wife is a damn good cook, man. You should taste her mutton *Varuval*[10]. Come for *Deepavali*[11]... it's open house!'

His hand surreptitiously checked his coat buttons as his eyes settled on the pièce de résistance of Planter's. A magnificent fireplace with a Coat of Arms adorned the large reception area. The fireplace

---

10   Varuval – South Indian mutton stir fry.

11   Deepavali – An ancient Hindu festival celebrating the triumph of light over darkness.

was as cold and as pristine as the day it arrived in 1889. The date and words, "Tunbridge Iron, England" were embossed at the base of the cast. A whim? Nostalgia? Or just English bloody-mindedness? Whatever the reason, the spit and polish edifice, a dead thing, was kept alive by the warm yellow light hugging it.

In front of the fireplace, the Colonial masters faced sudden death. Two rosewood Chinese chairs sat, like club-footed funeral directors to the past. Heavily ornate with jade, the chairs stank of money. Yet again, the soft lights harmonised the eclectic décor, sliding onto a tiger skin on the floor. Sunshine and tar, the marbled-eyed beast faced the entrance. Feng Shui. At the main door, a white planter's chair graced one corner. By its side, an antique oak hat stand looked like a butler in attendance. Devoid of any apparel, it looked castrated. In the other corner, Lennie Xavier, the Eurasian classical guitarist, made hot-blooded music from Catalonia.

That Eurasian pothead's better than José Feliciano, thought the manager grudgingly. *If he stayed clean, he'd be in some five-star hotel in the City.*

The manager's gaze turned to the Coat of Arms over the fireplace. It stirred images from the Robin Hood films made by Americans he had seen as a child.

Sic itur ad astra – This is the way to the Stars. Father Ignatius, who had come for the reunion of the St John alumni, had decoded the motto in Latin. He had also learned that it was the Coat of Arms for the Lambert brothers, two English gentlemen with commanding handlebar moustaches and with grand inheritances. They had obtained a bite-sized parcel of beach from the Sultan in the 1830s in exchange for a stable of pure Arabian thoroughbreds. Henry Edward Lambert died of tropical fever in the Cameron Highlands and James Charles Lambert lived to be an old bachelor in the hill country of

Shimla in India. Heirless, Planter's was bequeathed to the colonial government for British officers and civil servants.

In 1957, with Independence, Planter's went to the highest bidder, the fabulous Bok clan. "Tin Kings", they were Chinese players in the new economy and they needed to make a statement. The bloody race riots in 1969 sealed their fate. By 1975, the entire clan had migrated to Hong Kong, as "Datok" Bok, the patriarch, had his sights set on mainland China. He was positioning the clan for the 1999 hando- ver of Hong Kong by the British. The scion of ancient Manchurian marauders, they fought a new war dressed in cravats and their English public school education, with Commerce as their battle axe.

Planter's fell into disarray and was no longer sought out. In 1980, it was leased for one dollar to the son of the chauffeur who took a fatal bullet to foil a kidnapping of a Bok grandchild. It was a blood debt. The Club was given a facelift as the annex, where the stables once stood, was fitted with a Karaoke lounge and discotheque. The crowd was crass, young moneyed professionals from the city, bringing in huge profits.

The phone at the reception desk trilled and the manager turned hopefully. The receptionist picked up the phone then shook her head at his unspoken query. He studied the portrait of Prime Minister Dr Mahathir Mohamad behind the receptionist.

'Sir', smiled the receptionist, flashing picket-fenced teeth. 'You must be feeling very proud tonight.'

'Shanti, if this keeps up, you'll get a fat bonus,' he said grandstanding.

He reminded himself they were lucky to have her. She spoke good English and was fluent in the national language. Fast-food outlets were gobbling up school leavers. McDonald's was old news. Mama Mia Pizza, Tacos Tex-Mex and Bangers with every imaginable halal sausage, were hives of activity. Globalisation and consumerism – the new gods – were transforming the nation's sensibilities. His own teenage son was a devotee. Wearing an earring, his ambition was to be a DJ at the Hard Rock Café in KL.

'You think *Aneh*[12], I can finish early tonight?'

He frowned. The receptionist had used the respectful Tamil name for "elder brother" to strengthen her request. He disliked working with his own kind because they shamelessly cashed in on the "we are family" number.

'Just before midnight? The estate road is very dark, Aneh, and father's motorcycle lights don't work sometimes.'

Immediately he understood. She was afraid of the strange happenings in the town. The latest incident of the hanging had unnerved him too. Mr Dom had been a regular.

At least twice a week, Mr Dom was a guest of Mr Pierce the fastidious white man, for dinner. Dubbed the "Odd Couple" amongst the staff, the Englishman always wore batik shirts but ate only bland western food, while the Eurasian had chilli-fried anchovies with his beers. The manager was not a nasty-minded man but he *knew* what he saw. In the past three months Mr Pierce had paid all the bills. There was the obvious flirting thing between Mr Dom and Linda Tai, the dance instructress, but women like Linda "Thigh" never gave anything away for free. And Mr Dom was no sugar daddy. There was an emasculation about him that made the manager think "homo".

He felt a little chill run down his back. The receptionist wouldn't be the only one in the town having sleepless nights. There was a

---

12   Aneh – respectful term for elder brother in Tamil.

superstition that until a man was given a proper burial, he would return to his favourite haunts.

'You can leave by ten but on Sunday, you come to the market with me,' he said curtly, turning to the registration ledger on the console. 'Emperor Hirohito...'

'Sorry, Boss?'

'... Our guest, Mr Akiro Kabota, looks like Emperor Hirohito.'

'Who, Boss?' she asked blankly.

'You know Japan?'

'Of course, Boss. Honda Civic is from Japan,' she said cheerfully and then looked contrite at his expression. 'Sorry.'

His thoughts turned back to Mr Akiro Kabota. Interesting fellow. He had asked for the refurbished heritage wing of Planter's. The rooms were highly priced and drew returning Commonwealth soldiers and history enthusiasts. Expensive wallpaper depicting English dales, with four-poster beds draped in mosquito lace, the large bathrooms had antique-style bathtubs and bidets. Locals, however, never asked for a room in the old wing. The manager put it down to the lack of in-house channels, but there were rumours that the old wing was haunted. The Club had been used during the war for interrogation and the cleaners swore they heard screams.

These blaady lazy idiots will say anything to get out of work.

'What's keeping him?' he said aloud.

'Maybe he's fallen asleep. Old people tire easily. He looks like *sotong*[13], Boss.'

Mr Akiro Kabota, with his owl glasses and wooden face, *did* look like dried squid but the manager discovered he was driven. Out by six each morning, he came home only at night.

---

13 Sotong – dried squid.

As if he's running out of time, thought the manager. *Maybe he's dying? But if he were, he'd be at home with his family. Unless he has family here...*

In the old wing of Planter's Inn, Akiro Kabota stood impassively in front of the dressing table. The room was dense with steam from a very hot shower with the bathroom door open. He had taken off his glasses and was staring into the mirror streaked with condensation. Face emotionless, his naked torso was a dried apricot. White hair cut close at the sides, gave him an iced finish.

The man in the mirror appeared and disappeared as the mists coiled around him.

In the reflection, England's green dales on the wallpaper took on fluidity. Droplets shimmied down the mirror and hills drizzled. Akiro Kabota leaned forward. Time shifted with the second hand of the Seiko wristwatch on the dressing table as he waited expectantly. And quietly through the vapours *he* was there, standing behind him in the mirror. The English man with those dead green eyes, a red gaping hole in his left temple. Akiro Kabota stood perfectly still, not even his breath stirred. The English man was looking straight at him through those dreadful eyes... And then those damning familiar words.

'You won't have the honour of Hara-Kiri,' the English man whispered.

White chiffon curtains floated eerily into the room on a cool breeze. With a soft sigh, the curtains sank and he was gone. Kabota's mouth lifted in a sneer as he put out his hand and wiped the condensation on the mirror. He knew how to stand his ground with ghosts, especially in this room.

'General's Quarters.'

General's Quarters and his finest hour...

He peeled back a package in red tartan on the dresser revealing an antiquated Bible in maroon leather. It was not what he was after. From the folds he drew out a slim dagger, slowly unsheathing it. It was a Keris, a traditional Malay dagger. The blade was wavy and viper-like, about twelve inches long, tarnished from lack of care. The damascene of black, grey and silver, was stained with what looked like dried blood. Akiro Kabota lifted the Keris breast high and pressed the tip against his skin. His actions were measured, his face blank as he stared into the mirror.

'Ttrillingggg!!' It was the reception desk.

'Hai? Ahh... Five minutes please.'

He dressed speedily. The wardrobe was empty except for an extra set of clothes, a briefcase and a pair of new Reebok shoes. At the dressing table, he folded the dagger with the Bible into the tartan and put the package into a knapsack. He pulled on a Reebok cap, lying on his dresser, and took a last look in the mirror. The soldier who had served in Malaya stared back at him.

'Kolonel Kabota.'

His hand jack-knifed to his forehead in a salute. He held the pose for a few seconds before his wooden face splintered into a grimace. He was back in the same shit-hole that had cut short his finest hour.

Akiro Kabota would rather have died than return to Malaya but the truth was that he could not die. He had tried to hang himself but the wooden beam with the rope tied to it collapsed, leaving him with a shattered hip. In agonising pain, he crawled into the street for help. He was utterly humiliated. There was nothing worse in Japan than a man who did not know how to die.

In hospital, he had had an epiphany that even Death rejected him. He was seeped in *kegare*[14], defiled and decomposing in impurity.

---

14   Kegare – a state of pollution and impurity in the Shinto religion.

A mother, nursing her brain-damaged daughter, brought him this knowledge. She had tried to abort the baby, the condemned woman confessed, and had brought contamination into her world. There was no reprieve for fifteen years and she had become an abhorrence to all around her.

As she unfolded her story, it annotated his life after his recall to Japan before the war ended.

It had been an ignoble end for Japan and he wanted to forget, choosing to retire in Akita where he was born. And then the dumping started. It began with little bags and boxes of rubbish being left out at the front door of his house. Initially, he would waylay the neighbours and chase them off but nothing deterred them. Not even when he reported it first to the local council and then the police. They took to dropping off their litter after dark. Night vigils proved fruitless and exhausting. He resigned himself to cleaning up before dawn. He could not understand *why* he was an anathema. He had served Japan honourably in the war and was lucky to have escaped a war trial. He had no enemies. Yet putrid garbage continuously found its way to his door.

He and his wife, with their son, packed up and moved but after a few months it started all over again. And it seemed more vicious with each move. There were the midnight forays with explosions of refuse in tin cans and bottles on the roof of the house. Rancid food that should have been pigswill oozed into the house. The stench began to infiltrate his skin and he could not wash it off. He broke out in boils which took months of antibiotics to clear. It dawned on his wife that bad luck followed him like a faithful dog.

Then he contracted cancer of the testes and had to undergo radiation. His manhood was a shrivelled sore by the time it was over. Where he once walked upright, he shuffled about as if he was ready to lay a brick. Children mocked him and he stopped going out during the day. When they took to shunning his son, his wife walked away. After fifteen years of being treated like a leper, she strapped her *kamidana*[15] onto her son's back and left. She would not leave her gods behind.

He became an itinerant. Every six months he moved and only his pension as a soldier saved him from becoming a pariah publicly. The months turned into empty years of just existing until his thoughts turned eventually to suicide.

In hospital, after his failed suicide attempt, he became enlightened. The mother of the handicapped girl had refused the prayers and forgiveness of a Jesuit nun, turning rather to her own *kami* for help. And they had set her free, she was finally at peace. She urged him to seek his *kami*.

Misogi Harai...Water Purification. After all, *Izanagi-no-Mikoto*[16] performed *misogi*[17] on returning from *Yomi-no-kuni*[18] and washed away the hold of death.

Hope rose in Akiro Kabota – like a crane trapped in a frozen lake lifting heavenward as the sun melted the ice. It took him to Southern Honshu to the Nara Prefecture. Beyond Mount Miwa in the hills there was a temple with a sacred waterfall. He stood under the glacial water praying for cleansing from the Death spirit. Then alongside other pilgrims, he chanted and clapped in the *haiden*, the Hall of worship facing the mountain.

Oni wa soto fuku wa uchi

Out with bad luck, in with good luck

---

15 Kamidana – miniature household altar for Shinto deities, called Kami.

16 Izanagi-no-Mikoto – Lord Izanagi visited the underworld to retrieve his dead wife.

17 Misogi – purification.

18 Yomi-no-kuni – the underworld.

Oni wa soto fuku wa uchi

Out with bad luck, in with good luck.

He burnt osenko-incense and with shaky hands, pulled out an Omikuji fortune paper from the box. The words on the yellow rice paper baffled him and he hurried to the temple priest for understanding.

"Crane blackened in flight
Sunlight breaks the green rice stalks.
Spring falls to the earth."

'This is a *daikyo*... great bad luck.'

Kabota watched the agitated priest, the words resonating in his soul.

'The Onryō, the otherworld spirits seek vengeance... You have something the Dead want!'

Immediately Akiro knew what it was. A little dagger and a Bible. He had so few belongings that they filled one brown weathered suitcase. Without even thinking, he would pack them into his suitcase each time he moved. He had secreted them out of Malaya when he was recalled by General Korechika Anami, the War Minister, before Japan's surrender.

'The tormenting demons, they cannot rest,' rued the Shinto priest.

Akiro Kabota felt the fire of truth lick his cold bones. It explained the last three decades. An ill will had pursued him and left him panting for death.

'Return the items and the *Kami*[19] will give you peace.'

Peace... it was like clemency from heaven.

In Nara, as he tied the sacred rice paper to a pine tree in the first step to leaving behind the *daikyo* – the great bad luck – Akiro Kabota

---

19   Kami – Deities worshipped in the Shinto religion in Japan.

felt alive for the first time in years. There was a chance of recon-
ciliation with his forty-five-year-old son Rukiyo and granddaughter
Saruko. He would return to Malaya and rid himself of the Onryo
demons. The dagger and holy book would be reinstated to the foreign
kami and he would be set free.

Hurrying down the corridor of the heritage wing of Planter's Inn,
dread and excitement gripped Akiro Kabota. The van would take him
to the fishing village and the Headman. The Shinto priest had called
him the Soul Eater.

3

DOWN AT THE FISHING VILLAGE, the old Story Teller sat cross-legged on the open stage, lit by fluorescent lights. His fingers drummed his knee to the beat of the Great Drum, the *Gendang*. In a white shirt and black trousers, he was a heap of antiquity, propped up by a blue silk waistcloth. Tucked in the fold was a dagger, a silver Keris, a gift from the Royal Court of Yogyakarta. The Great Drum fell silent. The Story Teller rocked slowly, his face crumpled behind his black bifocals, his eyes, huge white moons. The fire in the loins of his mind leapt.

'Bismillah ilrahman ilrahim.'

His nasal voice drew clucks of approval from the attentive crowd. The Story Teller nodded in agreement but not at the audience. With a flurry of pats, the Gendang began to skip.

"And so the great snake Sakti-muna
broke to pieces,
shattered by the Iron of Creed.
The screaming creature plunged,
scattering the seed of Syaitan,
over the Golden Chersonese.
Woe is me, cried Mother Earth.
I am undone, cried Father Sky.
Lo, for the tail of the beast had break
and escaped into the Navel of the Seas.

> Forever shaken the foundation of the Earth
> the Dragon hath leaped over the fountains of Allah.
>
> Put on the armour of the Almighty,
> O ye faithful Ones... put on the Iron of the Creed.
> Harken the call of Bilal,
> dawning over the Isles of Allah.
>
> Give me the whip of Ali,
> Prepare the steeds of the Wali,
> The Prophet readied Rasul of God
> The Iron of his Sword for Godly men all."

Tall coconut palms crackled as the Java breeze rolled the fat moon over the village.

A baby wailed. To the far left of the audience a batik backdrop hid the womenfolk of the village. A woman cooed out to the child. Brazen young girls spilled behind the seated tourists, where restless youths loitered. Flanking the guests, Alistair scoured faces. Trying to blend in with the crowd that had no seats, he was looking for Ummah Ibrahim, the village Headman. It would have been an advantageous position but not for Alistair. He stood out like a sore thumb. Six foot three, with the deathly pallor of the English, broken capillaries bequeathed him with the robust charm of rosy cheeks.

'Excuse me, Mr Alistair...'

He turned, expecting yet another usher offering a folding chair to the overflowing attendees.

'At the VIP stand, *Tan Sri*[20] Ashman has a seat for you.'

---

20   Tan Sri – a Federal title conferred by the King for outstanding achievement.

Alistair recognised the smart-looking jacketed man in front of him. He ran a security company in town and was a familiar face at the Club.

'Captain Tajuddin,' Alistair said half-heartedly.

'Tan Sri Ashman invites you to join him.'

Shrill screams punctuated the night as a colony of bats strafed through the crowd. Harbingers of ill will! Quick as lightning, the Story Teller sprinkled rose water onto the censer by his side. Instantly, white billows mushroomed onto the audience.

'Back! You wicked spies, tell your master what you see. As long as there is breath in this body, I will boast of the stories of Almighty Allah. Back to hell!'

The smoke of the sweetish benzoin lifted and with the bats, flitted into nothingness.

Sneezes and little coughs were pleasing sounds to the Story Teller. They were an indication of uncleanliness expelled from the bat "invasion". As Alistair blinked his watering eyes, a man from the VIP stand stared straight at him. An oval face, with lidless almond eyes, mouth lifted at the corners in a hint of a smile, the high forehead added to the impression of a mask.

'Ashman... where the body is, there the vultures gather.'

Tan Sri Ashman Lahud was from another life. They had both set sail for Malaya on the *SS Chusan* in June 1952 from the Tilbury docks. For three weeks they shared the luxury of first-class cabins, thanks to Alistair's scholarship, and struck up an intense friendship. Alistair Pierce was heading to the Colony as an agronomist to find an alternative to synthetic rubber with the plummeting rubber prices. Ashman, of English and Middle Eastern descent, was going to Malaya as a representative of Tracton-Atkins, a manufacturing company producing armoured cars and weaponry. Communist insurgency was a national threat.

It was a promising journey with the war behind them and visions of a new world on the horizon. However, when they alighted, destiny pulled them in different directions. Alistair ended up becoming a District Officer and Ashman Lahud, a member of the pre-independence working committee. They both chose naturalisation but it did not close the ranks between them. Thirty years later, Ashman, entrepreneur extraordinaire, was an Advisor to the Finance Minister. He prospered the stock market and those who rode on his coat tails.

In the last three years however, Ashman had started making appearances in Port Dickson. There were the obvious reasons, the "Visit Malaysia 1985" event and plans for a lifestyle marina near Malacca. There was also the private matter of a third wife. Thirty-five years younger than him, she was a stunning model. Pregnant and hounded by his second wife, a psychotic socialite, Ashman moved her to Port Dickson. With the aid of bodyguards, Ashman ensconced Laila Kadir in the English house on *Jabul Musa* – the Shoulders of Moses. His black Mercedes displaying his peerage, or private helicopter hovering over the headland was the only tangible sign of his visits. On the rare occasion their paths crossed at official functions, Ashman was graciously inclusive, but Alistair always came away feeling inconsequential.

The ease with which Ashman sat in the VIP stand exaggerated Alistair's desolation.

'Pa Alistair?' Captain Tajuddin asked expectantly.

'Please tell Tan Sri Ashman not tonight, thank you,' he said stiffly, turning away.

He knew Ashman wanted to talk about Dom. He had seen the look on Ashman's face when they had met a week earlier at the

Headman's house. Ummah was hosting the Story Teller for the week leading up to the cultural evening and Dom was desperate to "interview" him.

'Alistair! Come with me, please!' Dom had begged.

'What do you want from the *Penglipur Lara*[21]?'

'See, you even know the Story Teller's title! This is why I need you. He knows mysteries and I want you to interpret. He speaks with a thick Javanese accent... I think he bungs it on to keep us mortals at bay. He's a nationalist and is very suspicious of outsiders.'

'And I would be perfect,' Alistair said caustically, 'seeing how much I'm an insider.'

'It's reverse psychology. You're a foreigner who chose Malaysian citizenship and speaks the language – he'll be flattered. You've seen it work hundreds of times. It's your gift.'

'Why can't Ummah do it?'

'With the pressure he's been put under to organise the festival at the village, he may not be there.'

When they went to meet the Story Teller, Alistair had been stumped to see Ashman sitting on Ummah's veranda. Then he believed Dom – the Story Teller knew secrets and Ashman wanted them.

Alistair scanned the crowd despairingly. Ummah Ibrahim, the man who had taken Dom into the Sacred Forest, was nowhere in sight.

What am I doing? Dom's dead. It's not going to change anything.

'Peace, peace,' proclaimed the Story Teller magnanimously. 'Sakti-muna the great snake lies dying and should man fear? No! Heaven forbids it!'

Taking the Keris from his belt, the Story Teller lifted it reverently

---

21   Penglipur Lara – a Sage from the courts of the Sultans who brought myth, poetry and history into stories for the larger populace, often endearing subjects to the Sultans.

with two hands to his forehead in salutation. Drawing it out of its scabbard, he drew an imaginary circle, one foot in diameter, on the wooden floor before him. Moving the Keris to the centre of the circle he held it tip down before carefully withdrawing his hand. The Keris, perfectly crafted, stood on its own. The Great Drum began to pulse and the Keris quivered. The Story Teller moved his hand around the imaginary circle.

> 'Oh Guardian of this holy shire, Ho, GrandSire Long
> Claws, Hai one with the hairy face.
> Remember our bones are brittle and hard – there is no
> sweetness in our meat.'

A ripple ran through the local crowd. No one called on GrandSire Long Claws. If they could help it, they didn't say his name at all.

> 'Oh Tok Panjang Kuku
> We beseech you watch over our village,
> slink between the shadows
> and slip through the eaves.
> Walk the line between night and day,
> Watchman of the Nether edge.
> You, Sir LeanShanks, crunch and munch
> All that dare, disrupt this Feast.'

The Great Drum bucked, took a series of jumps and then started cantering.

> 'Putera Langit – the Sky Prince is with us. We salute him.
> He has sucked up the evil ones into his nostrils and cast
> them ocean deep...'

The Story Teller was looking at the sky overhead. The breeze had suddenly picked up and clouds began to roll.

'Ahh... Cousin Monsoon from Majapahit. *Salaam Waalaikum.* Why look you so tired, and why so sullen? What news from the Kingdom and Sakti-muna's revenge? Welcome, welcome, make way for our guest. Come through Cousin, come through! The land Chersonese greets you with a brother's kiss.'

The *Gendang*[22] went wild. The Story Teller was lost to the fishing village. Like a string holding a huge kite in the monsoon winds, his words were the only link with his audience. He had slipped the confines of the disenchanting earth and scaled magical worlds unknown to man.

---

22   Gendang - the largest of drums in the ensemble used for the most solemn or majestic parts of a performance.

4

THE NIGHT HAD BEEN A TOTAL WASTE FOR ALISTAIR.

As he sat in his kitchen, the tick-tocking of the grandfather clock in the hallway sonared through his troubled thoughts.

'Where's Mariam? Something's dreadfully awry.'

Mariam, a Serani, was married to Ummah's son Ismael. Like Dom, they were both outcasts, she, in amongst the Muslims and Dom, because of his ex-communication. They shared a siege mentality, sublimating in each other the things they had lost.

The memory of Dom's fortieth birthday hosted by Mariam, at her brick house in town, loomed in Alistair's mind. It was only the second time he had seen her without her head cover. Brown hair cascading to her knees, cheeks, two little red tomatoes, Mariam and Dom were square-dancing as he sang Portuguese folksongs. Dom looked like a puppet from Thunderbirds trying to do a highland fling. Ummah's wife, Ayesha, kept pretending to wipe her face with her scarf to smother her laughter. Quietly, Alistair watched Ismael's eyes on Mariam. She was in her mid-thirties, untouched by childbearing. Her lissom body still carried the alluring sweetness of youth. If Ismael was jealous of Dom, that day, Alistair's curiosity was laid to rest as Ismael lunged towards Dom and Mariam to move a pouf out of their way. He only wanted for Mariam to be happy and Dom made her happy. They loved each other unconditionally.

Mariam's absence was out of character. She had not contacted him the three days Dom lay in the mortuary. *Ummah's got the family in hiding,* he seethed. He was almost grateful when his sour-faced *amah*[23] of thirty years emerged from the annex adjoining the kitchen. She shuffled to her kitchen god and proceeded to light some candles. It should have been joss sticks, but Alistair had put his foot down at the heady incense. Her steely hair in a plaît, she wore Beijing black trousers and a floral tunic. This morning she lingered at her temple.

'Come back so late, make Ah Lan heartsick,' she grumbled, referring to herself in the third person.

Only Ivy's love for the housekeeper endeared her to Alistair. He weathered her scoldings, ignoring complaints from his houseguests about her choler when they transgressed into the kitchen even if it was to get a glass of water. She was territorial and secretly, he admired her.

'She takes no prisoners,' he once remarked to Dom as they watched her tenaciously unearth a towering rose bush in an attempt to rearrange the garden, undeterred by two-inch thorns.

'A bit like Margaret Thatcher,' Dom agreed in awe.

'... get sick, make trouble for Ah Lan,' she sniffed, clattering the kettle onto the stove. *'Sei leh!'*[24]

Then Alistair realised she was afraid. She had said the "death" word.

Ah Lan was stoical and practical. During the war she had joined the communists in the jungle to escape ethnic cleansing by the Japanese. She promptly abandoned them when the British returned. There was nothing complicated about her. Except that she feared the Devil! Her altar was piled high with oranges to bribe the spirit world.

---

23 Amah – a traditional Chinese female employed to look after a family.

24 Sei Leh – a Chinese swear word which means to die.

Dom's violent death meant unfinished business.

'I thought I'd go to Malacca to see Dom's people.'

'For what?' she spat. 'They chase him away when he was alive. Missy Anna and Boy arriving tonight. You drive here, drive there, make yourself tired.'

She was referring to his daughter Tatiana and his thirteen-year-old grandson Bonny. They were flying in from Adelaide for the funeral. Tatiana had burst into uncontrollable sobbing on the phone. It was such a relief to find someone who cried for Dom.

Sipping his coffee, Alistair could not escape Ah Lan's altar. She was making sure Dom would not go hungry if he visited. Alistair had never cared for her superstitions and they had clashed several times during Ivy's battle with cancer. Ah Lan had tried to bring Devil-chasing charlatans to the house. If Ivy hadn't been so ill, he would have sacked Ah Lan. Now the pile of oranges spoke to him.

Waiting for Godot, he thought.

They were all waiting. For whom, for what... he was not sure. Even Dom in death, was waiting for a funeral.

For three days Alistair saw a trickle of old Eurasians turn up at his gate and was not surprised they did so. The proverbial camel, Dom had, years earlier, taken the liberty of giving Ivy's address as his contact. They arrived in body-panel battered interstate taxis and in cars that had disappeared from production lines. Smelling of Yardley powder and Hazeline Snow cream, the women wore floral dresses over clothes-hanger hips. Several wore hats. The men, tallish over their broad wives, were gallant. Some were in white sandshoes, one in a bow tie, many with hair no matter how thin, Brylcreemed like Dom's.

They looked as if they had come for afternoon tea. Talking quietly, they sipped iced rose water, choosing the cool shade of the big trees. Air fragrant with temple flowers, Alistair had no answers to their hushed queries. As gently, they disappeared, taking with them the guilt of the old when someone young dies.

He knew then that the lot had fallen upon him to bury Dom. He turned to the Synod of St Mary's Anglican Church, where he and Ivy had taken to attending, after the loss of their second child. Prior to that, the Club consumed them. It was in his blood, his father's love for music. Their house in Ravens Hill was the first to have a Kreisler gramophone and His Majesty's Voice would warble Gracie Fields and Deanna Durbin, along with Bing Crosby. And Ivy was born to dance. Saturday nights at the Club with the "Glen Miller" Malay Regiment band was the highlight of their week. On Sunday mornings the mood prevailed, like the afterglow of lovemaking. Strolling along the beach, his trousers rolled up and wearing a boater, Ivy, backless in a red sundress, was a goddess.

Then the baby died, strangled by its own umbilical cord. She was demented for a season. Like a violent thunderstorm it passed, as she took shelter in the Church. In less than six months of their going, he and Ivy had earned themselves a pew. After Ivy died he became a pillar in the church. He was so dignified, they said, in his hour of grief. As if that lent him some sort of spiritual kudos, they made him a deacon. What they did not know was that he was not sure if he believed. He was a man of few words and so his secret was safe.

Alistair was unprepared when the Synod said, 'No!' to a funeral service.

'We don't even know if he was a believer...'

'His ex-communication was a farce. You can't be more of a believer than a Catholic!'

There was a sullen silence in the vestry as the mingy group of clerics avoided his eyes. It dawned on him that they were afraid to bury Dom in case the rumours about converting to Islam were true.

A confrontation with the Muslim authorities was the last thing they wanted. For a church already beleaguered by Islamisation, Dom was jeopardising their peace.

'Wait a while longer. See if *the other side* claims him.'

Sitting in his kitchen, Alistair eyed the altar piled high with oranges. *After such knowledge, what forgiveness,* he thought.

In the hours before dawn, this time wearing a light pullover to appease Ah Lan, Alistair headed for the fishing jetty to intercept Ummah. The Headman would be there with his truck to meet the boats after the midnight catch. Headlights snaked towards him on the coast road, and a black Mercedes "whupped" past him. He nervously gripped the steering wheel.

Ashman, Alistair thought as he followed the flash of taillights in his rear vision mirror. *He's up early. He must be heading for the City... I wouldn't get out of bed if Ivy was in it.*

Instantly Alistair ached for Ivy, the moist heat of her legs high around him and the guttural animal catch in her throat as she fed his hunger.

She hated being touched in the end, he thought dispassionately, killing off his need.

'Unfortunately, it is the last thing on a man's mind before he dies.'

Dom's voice cut into his thoughts. He said that out of the blue, one day, as they were driving to the club.

'What is?'

'Sex...'

'Really?' Alistair responded vacantly, taken aback. Dom was a refined soul, bordering on the ascetic. He did not make risqué jokes, let alone have sexual needs.

'It was on my mind when I died as a priest,' Dom said with the heart-stopping purity of a child.

It was true. Dom had died when he was ex-communicated. As for sex on his mind... there was no mind. Only Ivy saved him from being immured in the mental hospital in Tanjung Rambutan.

I wonder what was on his mind when he died, thought Alistair. *What was he thinking?*

The boats had not come in and there was no sign of Ummah's truck. Parking, he reached for his torch and got out of the car. Under the blanket of dark, the pounding sea with its spume was powerful. Lightning and thunder played tag on the horizon.

How long he waited he did not know. The black moon shifted and the sea sank to her knees. Lightning splintered like a hag's spindly claws and the wind flapped him but he was rooted, like a tragic hero, waiting for a loved one. Only with him, it was two lovers. It was bizarre but he could not think of Dom and not have Ivy come crowding in. He had stopped thinking about her for the last decade.

He became aware of another's presence. Early risers used the beach for Tai Chi and he waited for some sort of greeting. It was not forthcoming. Whoever it was moved closer. Now he could hear the greedy intake of air and almost see the rising and falling chest. The hair on his neck rose as the words brushed him.

Om... I am...Om...I am...Om...I am

Blindly, he turned, the torch in his hand flashing a face. Strong teeth bared in a red open mouth, eyes pus yellow in a dark face, were only inches from his.

'*Gila*',[25] croaked Alistair.

Gila the Madman, threw back his head and cackled, delighted at the fear he inspired.

'What are you doing here?'

It was a senseless question. The Madman owned the town. Defecating in a back street drain in the town or turbaned like a prince in the temple, he was a law unto himself. A Tamil man in his late forties, he was found foaming at the mouth when he was thirteen. The *Swami*[26] divined he was possessed by the goddess Kali and they gave him permanent residence at the temple. Over the years Gila's condition deteriorated. He started leering at and cursing the idols in the temple. Once, at the height of his madness, he chased the God-fearing worshippers out of the temple. Still, they forgave him because *Kali*[27] too was bi-polar. When he climbed onto the roof and threw down the "OM" sign, they barred him from the temple. Gila turned his attention to the town.

Crackling with schizophrenic energy, rapping on lamp-posts with a stone, he was familiar in his dirty Bombay bloomers. When he went missing, always with the full moon, everyone knew Gila was locked deep in the rubber estates to keep him safe. The sea was his friend as he ate bananas and oranges pillaged from Chinese shrines along the coast road. Now naked on the beach, his yellow maniacal eyes narrowed cunningly.

'I say old boy, what are *you* doing here?' Gila teased, breath rancid in Alistair's face.

---

25   Gila – mad/insane in the Malay language.

26   Swami – Tamil priest.

27   Kali – the goddess Kali in Hindu religion, presented as dark and violent and at the same time as a benevolent mother.

The high society falsetto English voice had nothing to do with the demented Asian face. The Madman's bulbous nostrils flared as he devoured the air. Alistair watched him, trapped. Gila's face thickened with lust, eyes slowly closing. The indecency roused Alistair.

'Get out of here!'

Gila's yellow eyes flew open, teeth snapping shut. A strange look came over his face as he pulled back, hand shooting up in a salute.

'Sir Tuan! Club rules, I'm afraid. Sir Douglas won't be pleased! Nobody must know and we mustn't tell. He wouldn't want that!'

Alistair almost fell back, as if released from a tight hug. Gila spun on his heels and walked into the night, laughing like a hyena. Alistair felt his mind cave in as the floodgates lifted. It all came rushing back.

'Tally ho boys! Rimau-tiger steak for tea!'

Hunting horns blast above hysterical yelping as threads of saliva spin from pink rubbery lips. The sun, hard on their heels, hacks through treetops. Jungle rot and the sweetness of rich loam fill the air. Screams of genuine terror from the human dragnet, walloping drums and tins. And that pounding inside his ribs... a shivaree for a killing.

'He's close! The tracks are fresh, not even half an hour,' pants Anak the Orang Asli trekker, running alongside the jeep. They are lucky, lucky, lucky. The new laterite road used by the surveyors and engineers is leading them. All roads lead to GrandSire Long Claws. The earth softened by the rain churns under the jeep wheels. Red, blue and orange thread the dense undergrowth. Garish drumbeaters, Tamils from the rubber estate, wail out to Durga. She who rides the tiger.

Behind them camouflaged in khaki, gung-ho Tuans, hunting rifles cocked, also in jeeps. Pure sensation. No thoughts. The sun burning his neck. Eczema in his armpit weeping from the sting of sweat. The tingle in his crotch with the need to urinate. Images of the beast, gold and tar in jungle green, with each hot breath, chest opening and closing like a giant accordion. A light breeze prickles his damp bush jacket. He shivers. The trekker signals. The jeep comes to a slow stop.

'Let's make a meal of this!' Sir Douglas says aloud with that wonderful blessed assurance. And then quietly, 'Nothing to be afraid of, Alis.'

He is aware of the slippery sensation inside his boots as he steps off the laterite track. And suddenly they are crashing through the jungle macheted by the sweepers. The din begins to crescendo... a tiger trapped in the clearing! His feet are carrying him forward of their own volition. He has never known such exhilaration in his life. A time to kill... a time to kill... a time to kill. Then the expected volley of gunshots gives way to a strange nothingness. Even the dogs are voiceless as he steps into the clearing.

The tiger is already dead. He sees the animal, bloodied and lifeless, the grass and mud still wet with red. The long limbs of the animal are so frightfully vulnerable. Before it can even register, nausea rises. Fearful excitement gives way to horror. It's not a tiger, not the Rimau. The fair hairless limbs are the sweet legs of a boy not yet a man. One hand over the matt of hair to protect his manhood, he is naked, head cradled in one arm in tender repose.

The tiger got to him, he thinks wildly but it does not sit right in his eyes.

The body is intact except for the deep gash below his rib cage. And suddenly he knows the face above the red wet gap. He feels he's falling as he leans forward. A hand grips his shoulder.

'Are you alright Alis?' The voice, strong, steadies him. It's Sir Douglas.

'What's the matter son? Alis?'

'It's Isa...,' he answers from far away.

'Who?'

'Isa... the Headman's son.'

'Damn savages whoever did this.'

'They said there would a price to pay if we built the highway through Tiger Sanctuary.'

'Well yes... dreadful business.'

'They warned us Sir, we should have listened...'

'Get a grip man! This is not the place for maudlin drivel.'

The curtness swings him around. Sir Douglas and all the white faces behind the Advisor, are staring at him. He knows the look. He's seen it hundreds of times at the Club when he has walked in with Ivy. It's a combination of embarrassment and contempt. And he knows what it means.

'You've gone native, old boy. Jungle fever, I'm afraid.'

5

... FIRST ISA AND NOW DOM, thought Alistair.

In the dark, on the beach, Alistair had broken into a clammy sweat. Then he heard the throb of engines. Lights peek-a-booed through misty vapours. Involuntarily he moved towards them. Red and yellow boats streaked to the beach, breasted white by foam. Bronzed bodies hurled over the bows pulling the boats up the sand. Further along, the trawlers throttled up to the jetty. Alistair slipped into the circle of hissing gas lamps, fishermen and boats.

'Pa Ali, you're not in bed?'

The gentle query was incongruous with the unsmiling face, eyes metallic with flames from the gas lamps. It was Ummah's son, Ismael, his head thrown back in a "Do I owe you something?" posture. Over the years he had softened, largely because of Mariam, but the sympathy in his voice was his own heartache for Dom.

'Ismael, old men have no need for dreams,' Alistair answered lightly, steeling himself. Compassion would weaken him.

'Mael, where's Ummah? It's going to rain,' a fisherman said anxiously, holding out a walkie-talkie. 'How does this work?'

'*Rajawali Satu*[28] calling Ummah! Come in Ummah... Come in *Abah* - Father?'

---

28   Rajawali Satu: Eagle one.

The walkie-talkie warbled as a voice cut in and out.

'Use your police scanner. See if there's been an accident – he's never late!'

He will lose his freedom the day Ummah dies, Alistair thought, as he watched Ismael play with his "gadgets".

It was common knowledge in town that Ummah's *ilmu*, the Illumination – *the gift* – would pass to Ismael. Not that Alistair believed what they said about *the gift*.

Thunder erupted and white light seared the beach.

'Where is Ummah?'

On cue, a modified army truck came clunking up. On the bonnet painted in white, from headlamp to headlamp, was a grinning shark. Fastened to the fender, a whalebone stuck out like two horns. The truck pulled up at the water's edge. As the engine died a transistor radio inside the vehicle blared crassly.

'Ray-dee-ohh Onennn! Good morning Malaysia!'

The door of the truck opened and a man got out. Alistair watched him, muscles tensing. His wait was over. Wearing an oversized army raincoat, Ummah Ibrahim lurched on a crippled foot. With the breakers foaming at his ankles, he looked like a creature dragged out of the dregs of the ocean.

'Assalamualaikum.'

'Waalaikum salaam.'

Ummah Ibrahim, the Headman, was a legend in his lifetime, from Ceylon to the Celebes. He was the only fisherman to have surfed the perfect storm, a tsunami that hit the Philippines. He had cheated the Beast at the Navel of the Seas but had to pay for it with a mangled foot. Even the old-timers at the Club reminisced about how he had the Japanese soldiers on the run. He was thirty-five then, a crack shot, and had helped free a young Korean comfort girl. Despite his age and his foot, he was amazingly agile. There was the outer swagger of a gunslinger because of his limp but there was a droop to his head. When he smiled, his dark, gnarled face split open into a white beam. His eyes however, were hot, like a tiger's.

Alistair felt deep rage stir in his breast as Ummah walked up to the circle of fishermen.

'Murderer! You've got Dom killed!' Alistair screamed.

He thought he screamed. The radio filled in the gap where there should have been a greeting.

> "Down the road you see them all
>
> Smiling faces, short and tall
>
> Aaahaaaah..."

It was a traditional Malay tune with English lyrics to promote the "Visit Malaysia 1985 Year". The syncretism evoked fun.

'Pa Ali, this is our *lagu*[29],' Syed, a fisherman sang out in pidgin English.

'It is a good song. *Cikgu*[30] Ivy would have liked it,' Ummah said lightly, his eyes flicking off Alistair.

Cikgu... Che Guru. Teacher! The Guru Ivy.

He's playing with me.

Ummah was taking him to a time when Ivy had home-schooled some of the children from the fishing village. A Kirkby-trained teacher at the Port Dickson High School, her pet project was to get as many of the kampong children into college. Ummah's younger son, Isa, was the most ambitious of her plans. Isa spoke and wrote English well but was torn between an education and the gift, "the Illumination." He was an apprentice to Ummah, the Spirit Guide and Master

---

29   lagu – song.

30   cikgu – teacher.

Craftsman commissioned by the Malay Council of Rulers. It had taken all of Ivy's goodwill and determination to get Ummah to release Isa for night classes at their home. When she secured a promise from the Advisor for a placement in Kirkby for Isa – if she got him through the exams – Ummah acquiesced.

Isa passed with flying colours, the first boy from the kampong with a Grade 1! His placement at Kirkby was deferred until after *Merdeka*[31], Independence.

Six months later, Isa was murdered. His death stained them all and Port Dickson lost her innocence.

He's not talking of Ivy, he's reminding me of Isa, thought Alistair as he felt his throat constrict and he tried to swallow the saliva building up in his mouth. *Don't go there... Stay focused. Don't let him sidestep you.*

'I should have come to Missy Ivy for classes, Pa Ali. I would be working in a bank today,' Syed said regretfully.

'Syed, do you remember when Teacher Nathan caned you?'

Lamps gold-leafed powerful shoulders.

'Ohh... Mr Nathan, *Orang Purba tu*,[32]' Syed said thoughtfully, garnering laughter at his description of the stocky Tamil teacher whose forehead protruded over his eyes.

'He was always saying, "Idiot, you will fail your matter-matic if you don't pull up your sok!" We didn't have money for food, let alone sok, so how was I to pull them up?'

'You didn't have to puncture his Morris Minor!'

'Si-Nathan was always comparing me to Isa.'

A restive silence fell upon them.

Ummah, tiger eyes in a leathery face, held Alistair's gaze as the

31 Merdeka – Malaysia's Independence Day, 31 August 1957.

32 Orang Purba tu – the Neanderthal.

fishermen silently shunted the last baskets to the truck. Like fireworks in a night sky, they streamed away. The radio reprieved the void.

"This is the news, and now the headlines... The Prime Minister, Dr Mahathir Mohamad, has confirmed that Malaysia will buy British last."

'How did he die? What happened?'

'I don't know. I did not go with him,' Ummah said quietly.

'What! ... who?'

'Jihad! Jihad found him.'

'Jihad,' said Alistair faintly, images strobing through his mind of a black-turbaned man in a flowing tunic and a Palestinian scarf.

'Something urgent came up in the kampong. I was late.'

'Where's Jihad? I want to talk to him.'

'I don't know where he is... he came back and reported that he had found Si-Dom hanging from the Black Lenggundi Tree, then he disappeared,' Ummah said, visibly anguished.

'You filled Dom's head with all that nonsense about the woman,' Alistair gritted, disbelief turning into murderous rage.

'I did *not* force him.'

The gas lamp hissed angrily. They were two men held back by the restraint of age and the weariness of death. Alistair trembled with unsprung violence. Ummah leaned on his crippled foot as if the strength in his good leg had left him.

'He trusted you! You did this.'

'Si-Dom chose!' Ummah said hotly. 'You have always treated him like a *budak*, a boy. He was a man. I know him, that's how he wanted to be treated.'

'*You* killed him!' Alistair ripped at the intimacy of the words, "I know him."

There was a dreadful silence. It looked as if Ummah was going to tilt over. Then he caught himself with a jerk and straightened up.

'Abah! Ya Allah.'

They both turned at the lamentation.

'Mael?' Ummah asked concernedly, hurrying over to the fishermen and pools of light by the truck. Gone was the bristling energy, in its place a bewildering torpor.

'Abah, *he* was here.'

In the gaslight, Alistair, who had followed Ummah, saw the set of indentations in the sand and his heart almost stopped.

'Long Claws!'

The name came hurtling from the recesses of his mind. Tok Panjang Kuku... GrandSire Long Claws. The white Sumatran tiger.

From the time he had arrived in Malaya, the Colony was infected by tiger hunting. Every planter, civil servant and spinster aunt from England wanted to ride an elephant and shoot a tiger. Both preferably in one go. And it was the white Sumatran they were all after. The stage was set, not just between Man and Beast but between the Colonial Master and the Natives, when Big Jim Bobson, Plantation Manager, was killed in front of the coolies. Big Bob was, with great gusto, administering a physical castigation when the Sumatran volleyed him to the ground and ate him still alive. Long Claws became the local champion against injustice. Things came to a head in 1953 when the Tiger Wallah, 'Lucky' Sher Singh, was flown in from India by the Advisor to catch the Great *Rimau*.[33] There was umbrage in Port Dickson at the disrespect but when the Tiger Wallah left, empty-handed, Long Claws moved to superpower status.

For Alistair, tiger fever broke on the eve of Independence. Twelve young English civil servants invaded Tiger Sanctuary. It was a parting

---

33 Rimau – Tiger.

gift from Sir Douglas. One hundred beaters, thirty coolies, five cooks and a dozen gun bearers for the hunt of a lifetime. What they found in Tiger Sanctuary was too terrible for Alistair. He never went hunting again. In the years that followed with Independence and the pushing back of the jungle, Long Claws became a fragment of memory.

'Pa Ali, did you see *him*?' Ismael asked anxiously.

'No. I heard... I saw... only Gila the Madman,' Alistair stuttered, eyes fixed on his footprints and Gila's, and behind them, four paw prints. The tiger had only been feet away.

'It's *him*,' Ummah said, on his haunches sniffing the ground. He got to his feet and looked squarely at Alistair.

'He wanted something?'

'What? Want...?'

The fishermen were edging away from him. Ismael turned to Ummah. '*Datuk*[34]?'

"*Datuk.*" Illuminated One. No longer was Ummah, Abah... Father. Ismael had called him *Datuk*. Spirit Guide.

Alistair heard Ivy's voice from the grave. So hopeful and so desperate.

In the tenebrous night, Ummah, the Illuminated One, dawned. His hands, palms together were already lifted to his forehead in a "Salaam".

> '*Dengan nama Allah yang*
>
> *Maha Pengasih lagi Amat Penyayang...*
>
> *Salaam Waalai Kum.*'

A canticle sibilated from Ummah's mouth as he struck out, his army coat flapping in the wind. He grabbed four lamps, his lumbering giving way to buoyancy.

---

34   Datuk - traditional honorific bestowed on an elderly man in the Malay community. In Ummah's case for his spiritual gifts over evil spirits and sickness.

In the name of God Most Merciful, Most Beloved
Who was in the beginning and is in the end
Hear my prayer I beseech thee
O Precious Spirit, Ruah of God
Let these lamps, your shining angels
Hold firm the pillars of this your earth.

Ummah pirouetted, the wind billowing his coat out into full sail. Swiftly he planted the lamps in a square.

'Neraka Hades cannot overwhelm you
Nor a million stars diminish you
Breastplate me with the Firman of Allah
For it is I, Your Steward Ummah Ibrahim.'

Casting off his army coat, Ummah slipped into the burnished square. To the eurhythmics of the vespers, he pulled his sarong off from his waist, plaîting and weaving it. As it transformed into a turban, the Headman placed it on his head, sinking to his knees.

Silently the fishermen extinguished their gas flames. The four lamps in the mystic square blazed and the figure kneeling in the centre leapt into diamond life. Eyes closed, his face beautiful to behold, Ummah, the rickety old fisherman was gone, even down to his misshapen foot. Like an arrow ready for flight, the Spirit Guide – the *Datuk* – glowed.

'Peace be unto you
Master of the Great Sea Anchors
You granted Noah the Rudder of Safe journey
And Moses, Oars that bend the mighty Waters
Grant me your galley of fiery Sea Horses
For I must speed to the Heart of the Earth.'

Alistair watched, his will giving way to an urging. He needed to move closer...

With a thunderclap, lightning split the sky. The iron grip on his elbow propelled him away from the kabbalah to the safety of his car.

Part 2

FOUR DAYS EARLIER

1985 – PRESENT
PORT DICKSON, MALAYSIA

What are the roots that clutch, what branches grow
Out of this stony rubbish? Son of man,
You cannot say, or guess, for you know only
A heap of broken images...

The Burial of the Dead – T.S. Eliot

6

FOUR DAYS EARLIER

APPROACHING PORT DICKSON from the north on the coast road, red and white candy-striped poles created a carnival atmosphere. A power plant with a giant electrical net dashed any expectations. On the south side, an Olympic flame burned, brightly at night and hazily by day. It was a trick, the safety outlet for the oil refinery. Ubiquitous steel drums, looking like Herculean metallic thumbtacks, pinned down the wobbling sea along the coast. On the horizon, oil tankers quietly disembowelled, leaving black gum ribbons to leech onto holidaymakers. And so, a billion-dollar highway smoothly spliced tourists away to the holiday resorts. Fifteen miles out of town, from the headland to Cape Rachado further south, lay the choicest turquoise waters.

People living in Port Dickson were invisible to the frolicking beach invaders. This was evident from the outrageous littering of beaches with bursting plastic bags every weekend, and white styrofoam 'caps' bobbing on the water. Truckloads of Gauguin-faced soldiers, threading the roads in military exercises, struck no chord of loyalty in those who came and left without knowledge.

The town looked as if it needed a whitewash and a stiff drink. It consisted of two elliptic rows of uninspired double-storey shops back to back, a huge marketplace and a railway depot. Only the bank facing the sea, with its glass and marble façade stood out. Shops burgeoning with gaudy beach paraphernalia lent colour to the town, and magazines of Princess Diana, carrying Prince Harry on her hip, added a touch of worldliness.

The bus station – a bald strip of no man's land – faced the sea. Visitors deposited here would, after a cursory look, board taxis for the prettier beaches. Between the bus station and the marketplace was the only charming spot in the town, a park where gigantic flame trees interspersed with magnificent banyans. From the v's of their trunks, wild white flowers ran, like a wedding veil.

It was a Sunday Market morning and the park was teeming with life, where old men watched their grandchildren under the very trees they had once climbed. Tourists, a larger number than usual, sunned in the cobbled square with its fountain and clock tower. In honour of the "Visit Malaysia 1985" a "Mini-Malaysia" had been erected drawing a curious crowd. Alongside the fountain was the "Merdeka Square" in Kuala Lumpur where Independence had been proclaimed. Here, a statue of the first Prime Minister, Churchillian-like, held up a victorious fist. The clock tower with a viewing parapet was converted into a kitsch version of A' Famosa, the Portuguese fort from the Colony's history, propped with plywood and stucco rendering.

Buried alive...

On the stonewall fronting the sea, Dom Alfonso Hendrique sat with his back turned on the town. The Japanese reclamation company, Goyo Kenzo, had lassoed the sea in concrete, and a huge muddy teardrop was all that was left. Little fish gulped desperately, looking for an outlet. A brine-warped boat clung forlornly to the last finger of the sea holding onto the wall.

... Like the Kristang in Portuguese Settlement.

Portuguese Settlement, a precious crumb of twenty-five acres, a hundred kilometres south in Malacca, was the home of his father's people, the Kristang. It was a Creole word for an exotic Christian concoction of Asians and proselytising Europeans in the 16th century.

Portuguese, Dutch and English pedigree ran through the Kristang, their warring colonial history mutating into sibling rivalry. A large, dysfunctional family, they fought and bickered because it was in their blood. The working class Catholic Kristang in the Portuguese Settlement would take umbrage over their educated Protestant city relatives who had become rich and "proud as shit!" Then at some wonderful celebration, like Festa San Pedro, they would all gather at Portuguese Settlement where they happily made up after some gentle roasting.

'Forgot us eh? Big shot living in the city... remember Anti Ursula used to wash your dirty bum?! Now a Dato! Fancy that.'

There was one vagary, however, that could not be rooted out from their hearts even though it was literally skin deep. Secretly, many amongst the Kristang coveted their European bias of light skin and coloured eyes. It generated cruel whispers about "third class" Eurasians who looked Indian, bearing Portuguese names like D'Cruz and Gomez. It was this kink in their psyche that ultimately secured their demise when the British left Malaya.

The boat lolling against the stonewall smote Dom's heart. It reminded him of his father.

The voice of one crying in the wilderness... he thought cynically.

Alfonso, Dom's father, thought he could navigate them out of the darkness in their minds. He was, after all, Alfonso Hendrique, a direct descendant of Enrique of Malacca, who circumnavigated the globe with Magellan.

'We've been chosen boy,' he would say, pointing his finger at his eight-year-old son, 'never forget that!'

How Alfonso discovered he was the direct offspring of Enrique from five hundred years earlier was one of those quirks of destiny. By the turn of the 20th century, the Malacca river was silting and the Catholic cemetery was turning into a bog. A dozen graves had to be relocated. On Easter morning in 1920, after mass by Bishop Olcomendy, the Hendrique clan burst forth with resurrected life. Inez Tatiana Hendrique, Alfonso's blood great-grandmother who died in 1845, was the messenger of God. Her casket, accidentally torn asunder, revealed an ornate silver box, containing love letters. Yellowed and as fragile as tissue, they bore the insignia of high ranking Dutch Coat of Arms.

She was Catholic, and her lover, Van Reuten, who wrote the letters, was a Protestant. They were doomed from the beginning and Van Reuten was recalled to Batavia, leaving her heavy with child. Inez compared her love to that of her "grandmother", Donna Isabella Hendrique, five generations back and her husband, a Muslim convert, Panglima Awang Enrique. History indeed recorded that Panglima "Enrique" accompanied Magellan to the courts of Charles 1st. Romance had it that he brought back to Malacca a Portuguese beauty by the name of Donna Isabella. Her delicate nature was ill-equipped for the tropics and she died after bearing several children. Broken-hearted, her husband went back to Islam, believing Isabella's death to be a sign of God's displeasure. His children remained Catholic and Inez Tatiana Hendrique was a descendant.

The letters were archived by the Crown and the silver box graciously bequeathed to the Hendrique family. Whether or not "grandmother" was a euphemism, Inez Tatiana's broken casket unlocked a grand past. Why the finger of God pointed to the mongrel Hendriques was a question that confounded the Kristang community. They were the least educated, impoverished and were "third class" Eurasians in colour. The Hendricks, not Hendrique (what gall), were only shrimp fishermen. Not to mention old man Hendricks was a compulsive gambler. It was a red herring.

For the Hendricks family, the Inez Tatiana letters brought grace to a dreary existence. The family boat was rotting and half the time at sea was spent bailing water. Hendry Hendricks and Alfonso began to dream of a life that had nothing to do with the stink of fermenting shrimps. And they foolishly talked their dream with everyone they met.

'Oh our lady, Donna Isabella of Portugal a delicate flower... how she managed six children was truly a miracle. And here we are today.'

'We are planning a visit to Portugal to meet up with the family. Alfonso has started looking at shipping newspapers.'

'The letters of our sainted Mother at the Heritage archives...'

'Can you believe it... we're recorded in history! Hee hee hee.'

They were walking a thin line in the community, infringing on the sacrosanct reverence reserved for the first Lady of the Community, the Madonna, but they did not care. They truly believed that fate was on their side and that they could have a better life.

At eighteen, Alfonso began to champion the welfare of Portuguese Settlement and tried to stir the fishermen to form a union with little success. The backbreaking demands of shrimping left no time or energy for inspiration. Alfonso's father, Henry Hendricks, alone cheered him on, but this stopped abruptly a few years later, when old man Hendricks sold the priceless family heirloom. Inez Tatiana's silver box was traded in to pay off gambling debts and an ash-powdered *Chettiar*[35], a moneylender from Madras, took it home to his bride-to-be.

Alfonso was heartbroken and there was a bloody fistfight, leading him to move out with his vivacious wife Rozie and their two children. Continuing to agitate the British crown for trawlers and better housing, he made several trips to Singapore to meet with the secretary to the Governor of the Straits Settlement. Many of the educated Eurasians in government service, like the LaBrooys, had no sympathy for his cause. Their sights were outside of the settlement. The other families, with obvious Dutch heredity like the Koolmeyers and Reincastles, were vicious, almost gloating at the Hendriques's troubles. The "Hendriques" had been hard to digest while the silver box sat like a trophy in Hendrick's old almirah.

'Hendricks, the drunken bum...huh! Pretending to have Dutch blood.'

'They've got *Kling*[36] in their blood.'

'Bloody good-for-nothing toddy drinkers...'

'Ever heard of a Van Reuten wanting to become a Catholic?'

What preserved Alfonso was the love he had for his sultry minx of a wife, with the dancing black mole by her mouth.

'Eh Rozie girl, what you see in this ugly fool, eh?' Alfonso would often say, enjoying the envious looks as they promenaded along the waterfront in the evenings.

'Ah! You got a good heart. Better be an ugly man's darling than a handsome devil's slave.'

Rozie's mole dimpled beside her red, red mouth, fascinating the watching men. When she ran off to Ceylon with a rich Burgher,

---

35   Chettiars are mercantile Hindus from Tamil Nadu who came to Malaya and were traditionally moneylenders.

36   Kling - derogatory word for dark-skinned Tamil Indians. Kalinga was once a great kingdom in India.

Alfonso started drinking. Without a word said, the children took up with different relatives whose hearts softened towards Alfonso. It was not his fault Rozie ran away. She really was too pretty to be a fishermen's wife, what with her *"ta dali kok-kok*[37]*"* tail-swinging style.

> Ozi timpau koza di lonzi,
> Ta tolak prau cuma akeh muleh.
> Ja beng kaza ta buskah kumih,
> Aros ngka kuzeh, muleh ta drumih.
>
> Maridu beng kaza koza kansadu,
> Aros ngka kuzeh, ja fikah fraku,
> Abri boka maridu ta rondadi
> Raskundeh di muleh isti sa verdadi.
>
> Today the tide is far out,
> Like a woman, he pushes his boat about.
> For a meal the fisherman goes home to get
> Wife's sound asleep, the rice is not cooked yet.
>
> Husband comes home, very tired,
> Rice is not cooked and he is weak.
> Shouts to scold his wife.
> But the truth is, says she...
> *I'm tired of this life.*[38]

Dom the toddler would wake up in different homes. When the Unkle and Anti he came with forgot the sleeping child, some other

---

37 ta dali kok-kok – wearing high heels that tap as one walks.

38 Lyrics: Stephen Theseira. Translation: Joan M. Marbeck.

Unkle or Anti would carry him home along with their own brood. In the morning they would all be entwined, heads in armpits, feet in faces, damp with each other's urine.

Alfonso Hendrique did not immediately go into a tailspin because the Colonial Office announced new plans for Portuguese Settlement, in 1938. A retaining wall was put up on the seafront and homes were upgraded from attap roofs and sand floors to zinc roofs and cement floors. Kudos was grudgingly relegated to Alfonso and it overshadowed the loss of Rozie. The long awaited fishing trawlers were going to be a reality.

'Boy, it's out there,' Alfonso would say to Dom when he visited. 'I can feel it.'

'The huge crab Father!' He knew what his father wanted to hear.

'Yes, a Leviathan, with a claw the size of a boat! I'm going to catch it when I get my trawler! And you'll be there boy, to catch it with me.'

Alfonso's euphoria was short-lived. When the British returned after the end of the war, an acre of Portuguese Settlement was given, by the British Advisor, to a Malay chief to build a school. This had never happened in the settlement's four-hundred-year history. When the *Regedor*[39] went to seek an appointment with the Advisor, he was politely turned away.

'The Advisor has pressing matters... Malaya has to be readied for Independence.'

The funds for trawlers never came and the jetty collapsed. The younger fishermen moved away to work in the Public Works Department and the older men walked the beach in silent loss. Alfonso became afraid. The in-coming government wanted to rid itself of all things British, including their illegitimate

---

39   Regedor – Headman of Portuguese Settlement.

cross-cultural progeny. The new government was already calling themselves *Bumiputra*,[40] *Princes of the Land*. Alfonso was frantic.

'We are history's Bumiputras!' he ranted. 'This is our Father's Land! The Land of the Priests. *Padri sa Chang*[41]!'

Then the Advisor made a flying visit. The Settlement would be revamped with a Portuguese food court and a hall for Portuguese folk dancing. The Kristang were flattered and excited but Alfonso was not seduced.

'Performing monkeys,' he cursed, drunk on palm wine. 'Nero fiddled and the Kristang dance. We need trawlers and they give us culture. Bastards!'

When he fulminated into fisticuffs with the male performers, slagging them "*porkas*"[42], the community turned on him. He was given "the treatment". Ostracised, Alfonso Hendrique made the island off Portuguese Settlement, Pulau Besar, his port-of-call whenever he tired of his sea legs. It was here he met Ummah, the Headman from Port Dickson, who regularly visited the gravesite of a martyred Muslim saint. Ummah took him back to the fishing village and gave him the use of a solitary hut at the far end of the village. The fishermen, devout Muslims, let him be, even though Alfonso drank furiously. When he was able, he got into a boat and went out fishing. Dom, a novice in training at the Cape Rachado Monastery, wrote a poem with Alfonso's name on it and sent it to the Governor of the Straits Settlements in Singapore.

40　Bumiputra – a termed coined under a policy designed to help enable the Malay race, as the first settlers of the land.

41　Padri sa Chang – Land of the Priests or Holy Fathers.

42　Porka – prostitute.

Padri sa Chang – Land of our Fathers
Renaissance print on the Archipelago
Now fingered for real estate,
"Lifestyle" to replace Magellan and Galileo.

Padri sa Chang – Light of the East
Drawing galleons and Kings to your dawning
Now in darkness, despised and least
Malacca shrimpers netted in mourning.

Padri sa Chang – Portuguese Settlement
Postal stamp of the Silk Road.
Argonauts, once, riding the Easterlies,
In the doldrums, now sequestered.

Padri sa Chang – Land of the Priests
Nosyora[43] weeps for her children
"they are no more[44]*"*.
Viaticum Eucharist[45] my Malacca.

The Governor wrote back promising that the new government would look into the matter. For a long time, Alfonso carried the reply around with him in a cheap plastic wallet bought for that purpose. Then the wallet got lost, the poem forgotten and Alfonso drowned.

At the age of fifty, his body was brought back to Padri sa Chang,

---

43 Nosyora – Our Lady, the Blessed Virgin Mary in the Kristang language.

44 "they are no more" – Jeremiah 31:15.

45 Viaticum Eucharist – the last rites given to the dying.

where they gave him a wonderful funeral. They were frightfully superstitious and terrified that Alfonso's curses would alight on them.

It was too big, father... for either of us, Dom Hendrique thought, sitting on the stone wall, as he nursed his father in grace born out of self-forgiveness. *The enemy without and the demons within.*

The true tragedy of Alfonso's life was the shadow it cast over Dom. As a child he could memorise scriptures, delighting the Holy Fathers, who earmarked him for the call when he reached sixteen. Alfonso's seeds of idealism and weeds of discontent however, never allowed Dom to be rooted in the normal. He grew up with fantasies of giant crabs, and a patriarch who circumnavigated the globe with Magellan. This was his reality whenever Alfonso disappeared. Dom emerged as a sanguine teenager sublimating on psychic phenomenon. After his Cambridge 'O' levels, Dominic Xavier Hendrique was embraced into the Catholic Church as a novice. The monastery at Cape Rachado became home.

With a "revelation" of the Virgin Mary, history repeated itself. He was idealistic enough to think that the Pope would give him an audience. Like Alfonso, he imagined standing in the shoes of Panglima Awang Enrique before King Charles 1st of Spain.

'God has no Mother,' he declared passionately to the Reverend Father, whom he had to bypass before he got to the Pope. 'It's a spirit of Jezebel, the same one that controlled Ahab.'

The Fathers lovingly embraced him, heaping him with materials, centuries old, validating the Holy Mother. Ironically, it only fortified his thesis and arguments.

This went on for a couple of years, so they extended his tenure as a novice, but he could not be talked into balance. One year after Alfonso's funeral, Dom was ex-communicated.

He remembered only fragments. Cloaks and frocks rustling endlessly down the corridor. Lugging an old metal trunk through Portuguese Settlement, and all the doors of the houses shut to him. And then, finding himself outside Ivy and Alistair Pierce's door at midnight in the rain, chilled and feverish. How he got from Malacca to Port Dickson, he did not know. The night season of his soul eclipsed him. (Later they found out it was meningitis.) And through the nightmares, one memory when he was four, would come floating up, over and over again, to drown him.

MEMORIES

JUNE 25 1940

IT WAS MORRIS LAZAROO's wedding day. Dolores "Dolly" Gomez, daughter of a shrimper was going to marry into the cream of the Kristang community. And what a catch it was, "Green eyes with English skin!" The Lazaroos were the top of the "*upper tens*[46]".

The father, Charles Lazaroo, was an engineer with the Roads Department and it was only a matter of time before he bought his own car, the first in Portuguese Settlement. Rickshaws lined up neatly outside the Christ Church, with an Austin Cambridge and a Chevrolet parked ostentatiously in front. One car had been lent to Bonny Lazaroo, the groom's brother by his English boss. The other belonged to a planter, Cedric Townsend, a good friend of Uncle Rolly, Roland Leembruggen, Charles Lazaroo's brother-in-law.

Rozie had recently run away and Dom, a bow-legged urchin, was dangling on the hip of one of his many "Antis", to keep him out of harm's way. They were waiting for Gwai Eng, his rickshaw deco-rated prettily in pink lace and flowers, to bring the bride. When he returned, carriage empty, and unhappily handed a letter to Charles Lazaroo, no one was prepared. Dolly was calling off the wedding!

---

46   Upper tens – a term for the richer Eurasians.

Like water slipping through fingers, the representatives of the Gomez clan absconded. The groom's party adjourned helter-skelter to Charles Lazaroo's sprawling government bungalow. A search posse in planter Cedric Townsend's car went looking for the bride. In the melee, Dom was transported from the Church to the Lazaroo household, like a little straw in a rushing river. After two hours, by lunch, it was clear that there would be no wedding. Dolores Santa Maria Gomez was not ready to give up her Roman Catholic faith for Morris Lazaroo, a Protestant.

'What are we going to do with all this food?' grumbled penny-pinching Jaffna Geoff Leembruggen, patriarch of the clan, as they sat shell-shocked in the kitchen. He had come to Malaya in 1891 as a surveyor from Ceylon and his first salary was two shillings. The Chettiar gave him a good rate on the black market and every cent was earnt sweating in jungles that had never seen light.

'We'll eat it, Grandpa!' Bonny Lazaroo announced loudly. 'Everyone's hungry!'

Pang susees[47], colourful agar-agar, curry puffs with golden crusts, mountains of spicy prawn sambal sandwiches, and sweets of glutinous rice lay on makeshift tables. Huge serves of Aros Gorda, Portuguese rice decorated with red chillies, begged to be eaten. (Grand-aunt Delphina Theseira refused to share her secret recipe with anyone.)

'You're such a cold fish, Bonny. Morris is crying!' his sister Ivy hissed as tongues clicked in disbelief at his callousness. She was twelve and one of Charles Lazaroo's four children. She and Bonny were spitting images, down to their European skin and unnerving green eyes. They took after their striking mother, Elise Valerie Klyne, an alabaster doppelgänger of her Dutch Burgher *Mamah* from Jaffna. Geoff Leembruggen had had to pay a dowry for her. Absolutely unheard of!

---

47   Pang susees – spiced pork buns.

Bonny and Ivy's similarity ended there. Ivy was fiery whilst Bonnifacio Lazaroo was ice. Gifted with sang-froid, he did not understand the folly of emotions and was condescending in the face of the Kristangs' histrionics. At twenty-one, he was apprentice manager to Humphrey Travers at the Kyle Palmer Printing Press, and had arrived. Enjoying the personal use of a Travers car, he deliberately aligned himself with all things English. Bonnifacio Lazaroo's attitude was becoming the talk of the Kristang community.

'Too good for his own family,' they whispered, and that was the ultimate insult because the Lazaroos were the top of the ladder.

They watched him, a handsome "English man" as he skirted the table laden with food. There were almost a hundred people in the house, all from the groom's side. Half of them were in the kitchen or outside in the back garden peering in. The bride's party, all Catholics, had wisely vanished. The only exception was little Dom, forgotten under the table, chewing on a stump of boiled sugar cane. Everyone was hungry but nobody dared make a sacrilege of Morris's tragedy.

A three-tiered cake whisked from the Church hall was plonked unceremoniously on the table. The doll bride and groom, dislodged, perched precariously at an angle.

'Let's eat this before it turns into Miss Havisham's wedding cake,' Bonny said, as he tried to push the dolls back into place. He had not taken off his coat (even Morris was down to his shirt-sleeves.)

'Heartless!' huffed Anti Philo, cunningly aiming the barb at Bonny, as she flicked her lacquered fan. 'That tail-swinging Dolores better not show her face around here.'

'Dolly changed her mind, it's her right,' Bonny said, picking up a sandwich and biting into it.

There was pin-drop silence.

'Hmmm ... Mama, we need to put some damp tea-towels over the sandwiches.'

'Dolly left Morris standing at the altar. She could have changed her mind earlier. She's humiliated us,' spat Anti Aniow.

A thin dried-up spinster, she was called "Aniow", a childhood abbreviation of "meow" because of her green eyes.

'You're his brother and he needs your loyalty, not Dolly!'

'I think what we all need, is to eat, and you Aunties should have your game of *Chikee*.⁴⁸ And we shouldn't behave as if something bad has happened. Morry doesn't need that,' Bonny said, speaking slowly as if he was talking to children.

It was this patronising attitude that the family so hated. A big dry sob erupted from Morris, with his bouffant hair and tear-stained cherub cheeks. Bonny caught sight of his mother's pinched face and decided to be kind.

'Morry, it was for the best you know. She was probably going to do this at some point... I mean, when the children came. They'd have to be brought up as Catholics, she'd have made sure of that!'

It was the perfect comment. Heckling and venom filled the air.

'No one's going to bring up Protestant children in the Catholic faith!'

'These girls just want to control our boys.'

'It's in their blood, these good-time *Joget*⁴⁹ girls.'

'Good girls brought up in Protestant homes, don't call off weddings,' Grand-aunt Rose Koolmeyer said tartly.

'It's got everything to do with their blasted Pontiff, God bless his hat,' bellowed Jaffna Geoff thudding the leg of the table with his walking stick.

---

48   Chikee – an old Chinese card game frowned upon by the Catholic priests.

49   Joget – lively Malay dance – like the Rumba. There were dance halls where women earned a living by dancing with men for a small fee.

The doll bride and groom slid further. Under the table little Dom squealed.

'What have we here?' Bonny said as he swooped and fished Dom out, eyes saucer wide, drooling with cane sugar juice.

A strapping six-footer, he dangled the scrawny child three feet in the air like spoil after a great battle. All eyes fixed on the dark squirming child. Suddenly, a representative of Dolly's family was there, and questions were going to be answered.

'What have you got to say?' Jaffna Geoff said sternly as Dominic looked down curiously at everyone.

'Well, speak up,' Anti Aniow said in senile distemper.

'Lift up. Swing high... up. Up,' babbled the toddler, kicking happily. 'Dom son of Man... lift Dom higher! Son of man, Son of God. Yeeahh! Through the valley of the shadow of death.'

'Very profound little crow, hmmm, if that doesn't get you crucified,' Bonny said in mock seriousness. 'I'm glad he inherited Alfonso's brains and not Rozie's looks. See what was waiting for you Morry.'

Grand-aunt Rose Koolmeyer sniffed delicately into a linen handkerchief hiding her delighted smile. Anti Aniow's thin shoulders began to bop as several others sniggered. Someone snorted and that was that. People began to laugh openly. Education or colour, it was the way the Kristang pilloried each other. Bonny towered majestically in the kitchen, Dom a little sacrificial lamb, as laughter pealed in the kitchen.

In the delirium of meningitis, Dom clung to this memory after his expulsion. Lying in the folding chair in Ivy's garden, blanket up to his chin, his eyes were black diamonds, shining with unshed tears.

'Ivy, I could see all the family around me laughing and... and I knew that I had united all of us.'

'Dom,' Ivy said gently. 'Laughter doesn't mean unity. And Bonny was being cruel.'

'It's not the laughter! When Bonny held me high up in the kitchen in your father's house, it was a premonition.'

'How? Lift up the Son of Man? The Cross!' Ivy demurred, her heart breaking at his desperation for acceptance. 'Look how divided we are. We can't even take communion together.'

'I just wanted to bring our theologies together.'

'Well, it didn't work. You've been ex-communicated!'

A couple of years later when he was able, Ivy gave him her typewriter and it was the perfect gift. Dom became a petition writer and worked at his own pace. He would sit outside the Identity Card and Citizenship Registry and fill in forms for people who could not read or write. It freed him, giving him dignity with cash in his pocket to rent a room in an old widow's house. He tried his hand at several business ventures from selling herbal Indonesian Djamu and breeding Siamese fish, to panning for gold in Raub but nothing took. And then, organically, he fell in love with antiques, collecting and selling bric-a-brac from Eurasian Uncles and Aunties in the Peninsular. It was not the money. He relished his time in their homes, tenderising in the smells of fish pickle and jackfruit curry. Hours would be spent going through albums of faded photographs, and listening to their stories. It was a hunger for the old things, which was born out of the need for the security only parents can give.

8

I NEED TO SEE MARIAM.

Dom got off the stone wall on the seafront. He was slender, the colour of molasses, with an old-fashioned sartorial elegance. A full head of dyed black hair lent him youthfulness. When working, he looked like a cricketer, typing out petitions. Otherwise he wore button-up-to-the-neck cream cotton shirts over tailored trousers, with his "Lazy man's" shoes. And always his Old Spice aftershave cologne.

Getting onto his Honda Cub, he rode through a side alley to the marketplace. He had an hour before heading out to the fishing village for an appointment with the Story Teller, Ummah's guest. Time for a *teh tarik*[50] and *pikadels*[51] but he dared not be late because he had had to cajole a reluctant Alistair to meet him there.

'Come on Alistair, please be my interpreter. I don't understand half of what the Story Teller says. He speaks Indonesian Malay and you've got the best command of the language of all the people I know.'

---

50   Teh tarik – a Malaysian specialty where tea is cooled by "stretching" it from one cup to another.

51   Pikadel – shrimp patties fried and eaten with sweet chilli sauce. Delicious with beer.

'I don't know what you want to understand, it's a fable.'

'Ummah verifies there's truth in what he says...'

'Let Ummah interpret for you then, if he knows the TRUTH.'

They were standing at the bar at the Club, having a Guinness before a tea of steak and kidney pie. The Club had lost its former glory, but the house specialties had not. Fish and chips served with vinegar, not tomato sauce, and the Ploughman's lunch was excellent. Twice a week Alistair brought Dom to the Club as his guest.

'It's Ummah, isn't it? If the Story Teller were to meet me at the coffee shop, you'd come!'

Alistair's silence spoke volumes.

'You're not still upset that Ivy went to see him?'

Alistair's teeth snapped shut on the pipe in his mouth.

'Ummah helped her, you know. She felt healed and...'

Alistair laughed, cutting him off mid-sentence.

'It wasn't Ummah's fault Ivy died.'

'He filled her head with nonsense! And there's no point to this discussion.'

'So will you come with me to see the Story Teller?'

'Why can't Ummah interpret?'

'He's busy with the arrangements for the cultural evening.'

'What do you want to see this *Penglipur Lara*[52] for anyway?'

'Tok Selamat knows every piece of folklore and history on the Malay Archipelago. The sword of Saint Longinus... Myth has it, it found its way East after the Crusades.'

'We're still at it, then? I remember you wrote to the British Museum accusing the Advisors of filching several Keris.'

---

52   Penglipur Lara – a sage from the courts of the Sultans who brought myth, poetry and history into for the larger populace, often endearing subjects to the Sultans.

'Come on Alistair. I'll get you the best bottle of port you've ever tasted. They've just salvaged the *Fleur de la Mare*[53], from the Straits of Malacca.'

'Pray tell...?'

'The Chief Minister's madly in love with one of our girls, and... er, her grandfather loves port.'

'A Machiavellian Dante...'

'So I'll see you at Ummah's on Sunday morning then?'

'Get there before I do. Let's have some tea before I change my mind.'

The market was bustling. Locals squatted on the ground, haggling like ducks, over fresh produce. Further up, hawker carts served brunch to those caught in the morning rush. Several buses had arrived from Singapore. Tourists with cameras and backpacks meandered through the crowd. Dom pulled up his bike next to the food stalls. With a light heart he walked towards the Portuguese food stall and Mariam. She was not there. A young lad was manning the stall. He plonked himself on a plastic chair and looked across to the stalls where clothes and cosmetics were sold, away from the pungent food. Mariam was talking with a sales girl.

'*Pikadel*[54] *dengan teh tarik,*[55]' Dom said to the boy who came to take his order.

Waiting for Mariam to finish, he watched her. She had her head wrapped up in a greenish turban. A white lace trimming with pearls

---

53 Fleur de la Mare – a Portuguese carrack, that sank in 1520 laden with treasure for the King.

54 Pikadel – shrimp patties fried and eaten with sweet chilli sauce. Delicious with beer.

55 Teh tarik – a Malaysian specialty tea, cooled by "stretching" from one cup to another.

framed honey eyes, passionately kholed. She looked like a Palestinian in her long lime tunic, nipped in over a soft bosom at the waist by an exotic leather belt. Under her head cloth she hid knee-length, soft brown hair.

Something moved in Dom. He couldn't help but compare her to Ivy. Ivy had been exciting and beautiful. Mariam, on the other hand, glowed as if lit with a thousand candles on the inside. She turned and met Dom's eyes, breaking into a delighted smile. Dom took a deep breath. He was home.

Mariam Sybil Serani, a Kristang, had no blood link with Dom, but theirs was a bond stronger than family. They were both castoffs. She was married to a Muslim, Ummah's son, but was not wholly accepted by the Islamic community in Port Dickson. There were the obvious reasons. Her liberal behaviour was not a good example for the womenfolk. She was never at home, and ran not one but two stalls at the market. The food stall was tolerated, but there were jokes about *pikadels* and *gragos*[56], from the children. Still, the menfolk would ask their wives to cater from her for special occasions, like weddings.

The second stall, however, drew their sullen misgivings. 'Ya Allah!' She was selling and promoting, cosmetics and perfume for the womenfolk. That they were alcohol-free, *halal*[57], gave her no credibility.

The real reason she was suspect however, was that she went openly to Church for Easter and Christmas. Ummah and Ismael had been asked several times amid long sighs and silences, to censor her actions. Whilst Ismael refused to humour them, keeping stonily silent, Ummah patiently expounded the Koran.

---

56   Grago – shrimp. The Eurasian shrimp fishermen were called gragos, denigrating their social status.

57   Halal – Kosher under Islamic law.

' "*Al Shiddiq Allah*, there is no compulsion, God will lead the faithful." '

With more sighs and even longer silences, Mariam's behaviour would come under the grace of the *Surah Al-Baqarah, the Cow*. The matter would go away for a season, until the flesh again corrupted grace. Secretly they believed she was not blessed because she was childless and they waited for Ismael to take a second wife.

'Mariam, come and sit with me. I've got to go soon.'

'Dom, give me a minute.'

A few tourists had found their way to the food stalls. An elderly Asian man in his seventies, seated a couple of tables across, caught Dom's attention. Khaki shorts, knee high socks and Reebok cap, the deep nod to the boy taking his order gave him away.

Japanese... he's not with a tour group.

He had to keep his mouth from falling open as the old man ordered a meal in perfect Malay.

'*Tolong bagi satu kopi dengan roti kahwin*[58]. Kopi-o lah.'

('Please may I have a coffee with toast. Black coffee.')

He's no stranger to Malaysia, he thought intrigued as he became aware of a pair of eyes boring into him from the side.

'Jihad!' Dom said good-naturedly.

Jihad, Ummah's nephew, lifted his eyebrows lordly in acknowledgement before averting his face. He was in his early thirties, well built and tall. Bearded and turbaned he cut a striking figure in a black flowing tunic. He would have been handsome, except for the disdain on his face. A fundamentalist, he belonged to a sect called the Al-Sijjin. The Al-Sijjin would not deign to socialise with non-Muslims but were a thorn in the flesh of their Muslim brothers of a more tolerant ilk, waylaying and lambasting them at every opportunity.

---

58   Roti kahwin – Bread toasted with egg and coconut jam.

Dom Hendrique took in the insolent side profile and Ummah's words about Jihad came flooding back.

'*Macam katak di-bawah tempayang*[59]...' Like a frog living under a coconut shell.

As he turned back to his breakfast, a middle-aged Malay woman selling condiments for betel nuts chewers, came into the direct line of his sight.

Ibu Latah[60]! *I better change seats before she thinks I'm ogling her*, he thought, hurriedly moving chairs.

Ibu Latah, educated at the Sacred Heart Convent, was notorious in the town. She would startle into fits of Tourette's, manifesting in a verbal barrage the locals called "*latah*"[61]. Anything from a "boo" to something titillating could set her off. Once, an old man, sarong hiked to his thighs to assist him to squat, had unwittingly exposed his nakedness. Ibu Latah had gone bonkers. Picking up a bunch of areca nuts, she tried to cover his shame. The horrified old man had run around the market to get away from Ibu Latah, who played hide and seek with him, areca nuts in hand.

She could only stop when she fell into an exhausted sleep. When she woke she would not remember anything and others would kindly forget. Cruel as the malaise was, she provided great entertainment for children and teenagers who would happily startle her and then watch the fun.

---

59   Macam katak di-bawah tempayang – like a frog under a coconut shell thinking it is the vault of the sky – i.e. having a narrow worldview.

60   Ibu Latah – Mother Latah.

61   Latah – A malaise common to Malays where there is momentary Tourette's, triggered by shock. It results in verbal outpouring and can verge on the obscene. The victim will also mimic the actions of people around him / her.

'Did you try the stuffed eggplant?' Mariam queried as she walked up to Dom's table.

'You're busy today,' he said pulling out a chair.

She declined the chair, slanting a quick glance sideways before sitting with her back to Jihad's table.

'You're having breakfast late?'

'I'm going to see Ummah, to talk to the Story Teller. So I thought I'd better be ready for a long session.'

'Ummah's really busy. The Sultan's youngest, Raja Adnan, is getting married.'

'Arranged or love marriage?'

'They met at the Massachusetts School of Computer Technology...'

There was a short silence, then they burst into laughter.

'I'm not ready for this new technology,' Dom said ruefully.

'No one's ready in Port Dickson. People are so blooming narrow-minded.'

Dom looked at her knowingly.

'Is Jihad still there?' she asked quietly, her eyes darting sideways.

'No. He's gone. He's taken the posse with him.'

'Something's brewing, Dom. It's this vampire woman...'

'Yeah?'

'What have you heard about her?'

'She sucks blood, seduces men and is beautiful with long hair.'

'Stop it!' she said sharply.

'What's up! Why so emotional?'

'Because it is! People are getting wound up.'

'Okay. Everyone's excited. Ummah said it's spiritual.'

'He didn't say anything to us when we went for dinner last night.'

'You know Ummah...'

'I'm his daughter-in-law! Especially when family members are making remarks.'

'What's Jihad been saying?'

'The usual! I've got Ummah and Ismael in my pocket... And guess what? I've got long hair and the Vampire's got long hair!'

'He's not serious... what an idiot!'

'I don't want to involve Ismael. There's going to be words and unhappiness. I thought Ummah would sort him out.'

'Ummah *is* taking this seriously. He wants me to go with him to the *Keramat*[62] tomorrow.'

'The *Keramat!*' She was clearly shocked. 'He doesn't allow anybody there...'

'I've just finished fasting for a week, and when I eat, only Halal food.'

'Hmm. It must be something spiritual then. You're blessed!'

'Relax, you're looking tired.'

'Try being me, I'm veiled by all this and I'm still in trouble. I'd better get back to the cosmetic stall.'

Before she could get up, a shrill scream startled them both.

'Get this psycho off me!'

Ibu Latah was at it again. This time the catalyst was Stella Loh, the Chinese Madame of the Lucky Lady Karaoke Lounge, in her famous "hot pants".

'Hot! You naughty girl... You go home right now... Hot shame... hot flesh... oh what shame,' chattered Ibu who had literally clamped Stella at the wrist.

Stella Loh looked like a film star. A crown of hair with red highlights, pearly skin, and long legs, she looked thirty. The tell-tale marks

---

62   Keramat – a sacred site for the Malays.

of a cosmetic surgeon's knife could only be felt by her hairstylist. She had a rhythm in her body, like the sea on a lazy afternoon slapping against the town wall. Rumour had it that she was once a mistress to a tycoon who would have made her a film star in Hong Kong if he had not died in her bed. As she swayed through the marketplace she was accompanied by *Towkay*[63] Lee, a wheeler-dealer from the city who owned the video outlets in Port Dickson. Lee was talking loudly into a handphone the size of a brick, as they headed for the stewed pork knuckle stand.

Stella made the cardinal mistake of stopping in front of Ibu's stall and lighting her cigarette. As Ibu looked up Stella's long legs, every sense of decency she was accustomed to, was breached.

'Adoi! My God, flesh. Why your mother let you wear this?'

'Huh... what?!'

'Naughty girl. Hot! Hot! Fire... Look at this trousers! Mortal sin. Shameful must go to confession.'

'She's crazy! You stupid bitch, get off!' Stella screamed, trying to shake her off.

'Crazy bitch... Fire... hot... 999,' spasmed Ibu, the word "bitch" setting her off deeper into the malaise. '999, where's the fire brigade?'

Towkay Lee rushed over and began to pry open Ibu's fingers. That was the worst thing he could have done. It was not acceptable for a man to touch a Muslim, unless she was married to him. Ibu went ballistic.

'Don't touch... don't touch me. Haram! *Haram*[64]. He's going to rape me... Rape! Help this crazy bitch. Hot pants, take off your pants. Rape... he wants to take off my hot pants!'

Mariam hurried over to the older woman. Ibu had released Stella

---

63 Towkay – a colloquialism in Chinese for a man often denoting a businessman.

64 Haram – not kosher.

and was posturing like a Kung Fu fighter, lunging and kicking at Towkay Lee, who had dropped his handphone in the fracas.

'I *silat*[65] you. Die, hah...*Kung Fu Chow*[66], hieee!'

Towkay Lee abandoned the handphone and backed as far away as possible from Ibu.

'*Mati engkau*[67]... *Enter the Dragon*[68]! Eeee yah!'

Ibu was now fighting off an imaginary rapist, speaking in bits of English and Malay, punctuated with Chinese obscenities. She looked like a wind-up doll. Suddenly, the handphone on the ground burst out into ringing and Ibu triggered off into yet another level of latah. She stopped her choreography and turned her attention to the phone, not ever having seen a handphone. Going down on her hands and knees, she eyed it with a child's interest. The phone continued to ring, and she picked it up.

'Hello? Hello, yes, this is the Sacred Heart Convent. I am me speaking. How can I help you?'

People started tittering. The phone continued to ring, Ibu having no idea how to turn it on. Mariam was by her side, and had got down on her knees.

'999? Emergency! This is a Malay Dilemma... look East, look East! The Yen is very strong. We *dah jual buntut*[69]. Ringing... ringing! Why you not stop? Ah stop already. Eh! Ring again? Tring Tring Tring...'

Mariam gently put out her hand and cradled Ibu's, clutching the phone.

---

65 Silat – Malay martial arts.

66 Kung Fu Chow – Chinese noodles.

67 Mati engkau – you die.

68 Enter the Dragon – Bruce Lee movie.

69 Dah jual buntut – sold our backsides.

'Got *hantu*[70] in this phone,' she said, turning to Mariam.

'Yeah Mak,' Mariam said gently, and put her arm around the befuddled woman, all the while reciting prayers under her breath.

Ibu looked at Mariam as trusting as a baby. Tiredness came upon her. Mariam continued to pray and blew softly onto Ibu's forehead. She sagged against Mariam and closed her eyes.

Suddenly everyone was moving. Towkay Lee took his phone from Mariam, daring not even to look at her lest Ibu woke up. Someone brought her a glass of warm water and people went on with their marketing. The old Japanese man on the next table had stood up and was watching Ibu.

'She's alright,' ventured Dom.

'Yessh, is a latah. She wake, is okay,' said the old man bowing politely, his parchment-like face giving nothing away.

He was here in the war! thought Dom suddenly. *He's come looking... Someone he left behind. Probably one of the local girls.*

He searched out Mariam in the crowd and spotted her still nursing Ibu Latah. Dom got up reluctantly, fully aware that he was running late for his appointment with the Story Teller. Alistair was going to be unhappy.

---

70   Hantu – an evil spirit.

9

Fifteen miles out of town, the emerald headland of Port Dickson basked under a sapphire sky. A handful of lucky people owned property here, reverently called *Jabul Musa*, the Shoulders of Moses, by the fishermen.

One of the stunning homes on the headland was the "English" house, in Tudor architecture. It once belonged to the East India Company.

Tan Sri Ashman Lahud, entrepreneur extraordinaire, had bought it for an undisclosed figure, and it was common knowledge he would leave it to the State as a national heritage.

The face of the headland, a harsh stony outcrop, fell a few hundred feet to the beach. Underneath Moses's Shoulders, the fishing village nursed like a child. Steep steps had been incised into the stone outcrop along an old dry waterfall. It took the hardy fishermen up onto the coast road, to a bus stop. On the other side of the road stood the world's oldest rainforest. This was Tiger Sanctuary or *Keramat Rimau*[71] and it was owned by the fishermen. Desperate developers had tried to court the fishermen who obdurately refused to negotiate. It was their Keramat, holy place. The *Nenek Moyang*[72] lived there. The village was only truly accessible from the beach via the Planter's

---

71   Keramat – Sacred ground. Rimau – Short for Harimau which means tiger.

72   Nenek Moyang – ancestral spirits.

Inn on the seafront, one mile from the village.

On the coast road, Alistair was driving past the English house. A twelve-foot ivy-laced wall secreted a spectacular view. On the grounds was a conservatory with a grand piano, an in-ground swimming pool and a heli-pad.

He can't have it all, Alistair thought meanly, in self-commiseration.

Thoughts of Ashman's many attempts at marriage flooded his mind. His first marriage was annulled, with the French woman being deported. She was arrested for attempting to empty his Swiss account. His second ex-wife was a diagnosed sociopath who had employed hitmen, and his third wife, who was pregnant, had to be kept hidden from her. Ashman had had abysmal luck in love.

He pulled in at the parking lot of the Club. He planned to take a leisurely walk to the village to keep his appointment with Dom. Next to the Club was a huge field, called *Padang Darah* or Field of Blood by the locals. A woman lumbered slowly across the field towards him, her dogs bounding ahead of her. With a dowager's hump and a hefty bosom, she looked like an overstuffed scarecrow with straw-white hair and cotton floral dress.

'Hello Maude,' said Alistair, patting the dogs as they sniffed his ankles.

'Alis,' she replied, her voice grating like a rusty gate.

'Taking the dogs for a walk?' he asked politely, knowing exactly where she was heading.

'Hardly, I need a drink,' she said bluntly. 'Care to join me or will it cost you your precious respectability?'

Maude MacKeerne was the wife of an English geologist with BP in Port Dickson after the war. Living in a big company bungalow, she had a young Malay servant girl, Aini. "Servants". It was such a wicked indulgence after England. No more washing sheets in winter with buckets of boiling water, knuckles frozen and drained of blood. Aini turned out to be invaluable. The girl learnt how to cook lamb chops "reah" just the way her husband loved them. Before too long, Maude was always at the Club playing bridge.

Coming home unexpectedly one day, she found her husband with the Malay maid in their bedroom. Shocked, she turned away quietly and went back to the Club. The next morning, she sacked Aini and when her husband came home in the evening there had been a huge row. The day after, he moved out to the rest house. She turned to the expatriate wives at the Club who were full of sympathy for her. They too feared the lissom cocoa girls who served them. Maude MacKeerne hated her life in Malaya yet she could not get herself to return home to England without her husband. When he died suddenly of a heart attack, leaving her with a huge insurance pay-out, she stayed on in Port Dickson.

Standing before Alistair she was a washed-out alcoholic. She only kept a semblance of respectability because of her housekeeper, Sook Lin. The faithful servant would come to the Club after lunchtime and take her home for a siesta. By six in the evening Maude would be at it again.

'So! Will you join me?' Maude challenged, as she reached out to leash the dogs, hands shaking visibly.

'No, thank you, Maude, I've got an appointment down at the fishing village.'

'Surely they're not still using you as Master of Ceremonies for weddings? I'd thought they'd have found fresh meat by now.'

'I've got to hurry, I'll be late,' he said, wanting to get away from her ugliness.

'Beware the "Blood Field", you might lose your soul.'

Alistair cut across the green fields which ran into the start of the stony outcrop on the headland. The wind buffeted the undulating fields, whistling and whispering on normal days, and screeching like a banshee during storms. The locals called this acreage *Padang Darah* or Field of Blood after the war. It was here that the Japanese soldiers slaughtered over three hundred Chinese. Entire families and four generations from a great-great grandmother to a three-month-old baby girl were wiped out. It was a warning to the community in Port Dickson. They would not tolerate disseminators of pro-British pamphlets.

Part 3

1944
JAPANESE OCCUPATION, BRITISH MALAYA

As a Christian I have...
Through clever and constant application of propaganda...
people can be made to see paradise as hell and also the other way
around, to consider the most wretched sort of life as paradise.
I believe today that my conduct is in accordance with the will of
the Almighty Creator – I am fighting for the Lord's work.
Terrorism is the best political weapon, for nothing drives people
harder than a fear of sudden death.
Any violence which does not spring from a spiritual base, will
be wavering and uncertain. It lacks the stability which can only
rest in a fanatical outlook.
In boundless love as a Christian...

Excerpts from speeches and *Mein Kampf* – Adolf Hitler

10

THE RISING SUN FLAG was flying high in the courtyard of the King George the Fifth School (KGV). His Majesty was on his knees, face down, with Kolonel Akiro Kabota's feet on his head. Japanese soldiers had hauled down the five-ton statue of the monarch and it lay, kow-towing to all who came and went. The building housed the Propaganda Office of the Japanese Military Administration (JMA). Here they ran an invaluable asset, the printing press.

Kolonel Kabota, Head of Psychological Warfare, was deep in thought. He had just returned from a hushed meeting at the Imperial headquarters at King's House. All was not well with the Japanese in Malaya. Pamphlets heralding Allied success in Europe had been mysteriously surfacing in the peninsula. They contradicted the heady stories put out by the JMA, stirring the locals and demoralising their homesick soldiers. Under penalty of death, radios had been sealed with smelted tin on the Radio Nippon frequency. *Someone* had a receiver tuned in to the BBC, and *somewhere* there was access to a printing machine.

In the crackdown, there was an unfortunate incident in Port Dickson. A huge *Pathan*[73] by the name of Fateh Khan, had been

---

73 Pathan – a Pashtun originally from Afghanistan.

brought down in a hail of bullets in violation of the curfew. The Pathan, with shivery breaths, laboured to live, the soldiers taking bets, only to jubilate or curse as Khan's powerful lungs kick-started his body. It took six hours for Fateh Khan to die, his family and neighbours forced to watch.

There were no spies, no collaboration and no radio. Fateh had gone to visit his ailing father in Seremban on a bicycle hidden in the jungle. Kolonel Kabota knew it had been a bad call. It had been unwise to kill Fateh Khan. He was a local hero saving two children from drowning, volunteering to kill cobras that invaded homes and was the specialist cook at wedding parties. The people in Port Dickson were seething. Kabota's job was to smooth over the present agitation.

There was also a second, darker reason for Kabota's critical intervention. His soldiers were indulging in the unholy. Bodies of Chinese women attired in garters and lingerie were found dismembered. Used as whores, they were favoured by the soldiers because of their oriental similarities. Initially the reports were that these women were killed trying to escape but depraved details infiltrated to the top. The soldiers were venting their deep-seated hatred for the Chinese through sadomasochism, some even indulging in necrophilia.

Before it compromised the Nippon plan of garnering the support of Malay Leaders, the JMA turned to importing women from Korea. And Kabota was given the job of creating a diversion.

Kolonel Kabota had masterminded some brilliant strategies to foster goodwill and had the attention of Tokyo. He managed the two most powerful tools in the hands of the JMA. These were the printing press and the JMA Hockey Association.

The printing press from Kyle Palmer Printers had been left intact because of the hasty British retreat. The "English man", an apprentice with Kyle Palmer was now working for Kabota. Even though he was a Eurasian, Kabota insisted on calling Bonnifacio Lazaroo "the English man". With European looks and an amazing ability to keep his upper lip immobile, he was more English than the British Kabota had encountered at the School of Social Studies in London. The English man was cooperating wholeheartedly, on the promise of the release of his family interned at Changi. They had rushed after the British trucks in the midnight evacuation, when petrol and luck ran out on them in Muar. Lazaroo worked with Kabota on JMA propaganda, preparing the headlines and editorials. It was Kolonel Kabota's sweetest acquisition, a white man dogging his heels.

The JMA Hockey Association was the other feather in Kabota's cap. When things had settled down in Malaya, the JMA encouraged locals to get into ball sports and field events. The first time Kolonel Kabota witnessed the English man play a hockey game, a lightbulb went on in his mind. There would be two teams. The Emperor's team comprising Japanese soldiers, and the National team of local boys. They would play each other in different towns creating public relations exercises with the locals and at the same time, prepare a team for the Emperor when the war was won. The *Tiger of Malaya*[74] gave his approval.

Through the English man, Kabota appointed Roland Leembruggen, his uncle living in Malacca, as manager to source the best players. From these, Kabota personally handpicked the National team. They in turn were to train selected Japanese soldiers for the Emperor's team. The two teams, along with Roland Leembruggen were housed in a huge bungalow off Jalan Bellamy in Kuala Lumpur. They did their centralised training there and when the need arose

---

74 Tiger of Malaya – General Tomoyuki Yamashita, responsible for the invasion of Malaya and Singapore.

they were deployed as trouble-shooters. Kolonel Kabota was a master strategist. A good game, where the National team "battled" the Emperor's team, would be cathartic. The grand finalé would be when the Emperor's team presented hockey sticks to young hopefuls. It worked every time.

A game had already been scheduled for the weekend in Port Dickson. Roland Leembruggen had been dispatched to Malacca to source reserve hockey players for the National team because several of the boys had malaria. Nothing was to stop the game. The English man would cover the game in the *Malai Baru*,[75] a branch of the Dōmei News Agency of Japan, but the main story would be another rehash of Pearl Harbor. Kolonel Kabota looked forward to his stay in Port Dickson at Planter's in the plush General's Quarters and some time spent horse-riding. The Advisor had left his horses in the care of the local vet.

Inside the KGV School at the printing press, the English man cut a strange figure amongst the Japanese workers. Eyes averted, there was an atrophy about him as he scurried around. Not one day passed where Bonnifacio Lazaroo did not curse himself or his boss, Humphrey Travers. Travers had called him into the office at noon on the 10 January 1942.

'We're pulling out in a couple of hours. Just watch the shop. It won't be for long and we'll be back in a jiffy.'

'You're evacuating! Shouldn't you stay and fight... I mean the army?'

'It's only to realign from Singapore. Be a good fellow, dismantle the press and dump it into the river. And you can have the Austin.'

Bonny refused to heed the warning that he was not one of them. His parents, Grandpa Jaffna and Morris were visiting him in the city in their new Hillman Minx. It was his idea that they follow the

---

75 Malai Baru – the *New Malaya*, a local newspaper.

trucks. He would then pick Ivy and Cuthbert up from Malacca in Travers's car. Unfortunately, he could go no further than Malacca. A boatload of soldiers arrived by sea up the Malacca river and cut the road off going south. It was Kolonel Kabota who relayed how Charles Lazaroo's car, hot on the heels of the British trucks, had spluttered and died as it ran out of petrol. They were sitting ducks as the trucks disappeared down the blackening road.

That was two years ago and Bonny still could not get over the vomit feeling in the pit of his stomach. The only way he could assuage his sense of self-loathing and guilt was to work for his family's release. Stationed at the JMA Propaganda Office, he was privy to the "mood" of the establishment. He had sensed Kolonel Kabota's disquiet but he was unwilling to risk his family by snooping around. They kept a very close watch on his movements.

The typeset locked into the bed of the press, he was finished for the day. Only the Japanese staff were allowed to roll the printers. He needed to release his angst and headed straight to the field, shouldering half a dozen hockey sticks tied up with jute. It would be the teenagers who played with him, hoping to get into the National team (the older folk kept a contemptuous distance). The English man's love for the game was pure. The best players were already taken but he still gave the ragged group a fair go. It was the one place he was truly free.

There was one particular fellow, a Chinese youth of about sixteen who called himself Henly, a corruption of Henry. He spoke terrible English, looked like a pig farmer's son and was an appalling player. He brought extra drinking water in a tin, ran after the ball and offered to carry Bonny's hockey sticks. The fellow was becoming an irritant, hanging around after everyone left.

'Sir, water! Sir drink?' Henly enquired obsequiously.

'Shouldn't you be heading home?' Bonny said coldly on his haunches, in the process of tying his hockey sticks.

'Water velly good for your thirsty.'

'I said go home!'

'We need your help. I belong to the underground movement. Please listen, don't say anything.'

The diction was perfect and something inside Bonny shook. Instinctively he looked in the direction of the soldiers.

'We need information on the deployment of army personnel. You work inside, you...'

'Get away from me or I'll call the guards,' Bonny cursed softly, cutting Henly off.

'Take the water! They've lied to you about your family,' Henly said calmly, holding out a tin cup of water to him.

Bonny stood up, the hockey sticks sliding off his shoulder and clattering onto the green.

'Uncle Rolly told me to contact you. Don't put Ivy and Cuthbert in danger.'

"Uncle Rolly", Roland Leembruggen's family name was like ice water on Bonny.

'Act normally. Pick up the sticks!' Henly commanded quietly, like a snake about to strike.

Mechanically, Bonny obeyed. He needed to centre his mind. A word came springing into consciousness like a frog. He saw it land, then it leapt and disappeared from his mind's eye, then it landed and leapt again.

Fornication Under the Consent of the King. F...U...C...K. King George's given us his permission to fornicate... His Royal permission, he found himself thinking.

'Uncle Rolly's sent you something. You'll find it inside your sports bag. The soldiers! See you tomollow... I play tomollow.'

Then he was gone. Bonny picked up the sports bag, heart thudding, and bowed to the soldiers who were upon him.

'Good game (in Japanese).'

'Thank you.'

'Get home before the curfew.'

"Home" was the government yards near the railway station in Brickfields, a forty-minute walk from the KGV School. The place stank of urine where barefooted, worm-infested children ran around. It was one of the areas designated for locals working for the Nippon government. He rented a storeroom with a back entrance from an Indian engineer who had five nosey children. Inside his spartan room, heart in his mouth, he carefully put his sports bag on the bed. Stoking his paraffin lamp, he closed the windows and bolted the internal door that led to the kitchen and bathroom. Then he sat on the bed and with sweating palms opened the bag. As he took out a package wrapped in brown paper, he knew it was a book. Fearfully he untied the string.

As soon as he saw the Bible, Bonny knew. Jaffna often gathered the grandchildren and told them his childhood adventures in Ceylon. It always ended with "Jaffey" reading from the Bible. Bonny coveted it because he loved books. In maroon leather, it was inlaid with a silver Celtic cross. It had belonged to Greer John Kerr, a Scotsman who was Jaffna's grandfather.

'You'll get it, when I'm ready to give it to you,' Jaffna would say, slapping off Bonny's hands as they fingered the leather.

'You're going to live for another hundred years, Jaffey,' Bonny said cheekily, taking liberties with the old man no one else would dare.

'You'll get it when I smell the fear of God on you, boy.'

'I'll wait then.'

Even though he refused to laugh, Jaffna delighted in Bonny. Everyone knew he would get Jaffey's Bible. The old man had written Bonny's name after his.

With trembling hands, he opened the front cover. There, in blue ink, were the words, "Jaffey Geoff Leembruggen. Called to His Service. January 12 1942" It was like a fatal crack in the wall of a dam. His body heaved, with sharp intakes and grunts for air. Strangled cries erupted from his throat as he clawed at his chest.

'Jaffey...' Bonny groaned, but they were lost to him. Porcelain-skinned Elise Valerie Klyne, barrel-chested Charlie Lazaroo... Morris, cursed with his father's stoutness. And grand old Jaffna Jaffey, "The Pioneer". He had laid down the milestones from the Kra Isthmus to Singapore on a bullock cart when there was only jungle in Malaya.

Morning found Bonny hollow-eyed and exhausted. He had struggled all night with emotions, something he was not accustomed to. By daybreak he had weighed up his options. He could wait till evening, meet Henly and join the underground movement or he could go to the factory, look for Kabota and bludgeon him to death. The second of the two options was going to be hard to execute. Kabota was surrounded by guards and the chances of him being shot first were great. Bonnifacio Lazaroo chose to kill Kabota.

As he shaved, he looked at the man in the distorted mirror in the bathroom. He looked almost grey, eyes sunken. His lips curled with self-contempt.

'We are the hollow men,
we are the stuffed men.'

Without warning, he smashed his fist into the mirror. It shattered and broke, shards falling into the sink.

'Mr Bonny! Are you okay? Everything alright?' the landlord called out urgently knocking on the bathroom door.

'Mr Bonny! Sir... Mr Bonny, Sir!'

'Yes! Yes, alright.'

After he got dressed, he sat down at the table in his room and opened Jaffna's Bible again. For the first time he noticed a verse penned under the entry. *John 12:24*. He turned to the verse.

Unless a grain of wheat falls into the ground and dies, it remains alone; but if it dies it produces much fruit.

It was a message for him. With that, he got up and headed for the JMA Headquarters. When he got to the KGV School, the guards looked at him in surprise. It was Sunday, and no one was working. His resolve broke. He staggered home and fell into a deep sleep without opening his shutters.

He woke with a start. He could hear someone crying in the darkness. As his eyes adjusted, he saw a boy of about six.

'Huh? What is it?'

Confused, he thought it was the landlord's son. The boy walked towards him sobbing uncontrollably and caught his arm in a claw-like grip.

'She's not coming back Bonny. She's gone! Something's happened to Mama.'

'What... who?'

And then he recognised him. It was Dom, little Dom Hendrique.

In terror, Bonny saw the colour fade from the boy as he became pale, ghost-like with green eyes. He was staring at himself. He woke up drenched in tears, sweating in the sun-baked afternoon. As he had a cold shower he knew that whatever Henly wanted him to get involved with, it meant Kabota was going to live.

11

ONE WEEK LATER, army trucks carrying the two hockey teams with Kolonel Kabota's car in the forefront, headed south for Port Dickson. Bonny sat in front with the driver while the Kolonel sat behind with one hand on the hockey sticks to be given away as souvenirs. It was a quieter trip than Kabota had expected and he put it down to the English man being unwell. He had not reported in to work after the weekend and the soldiers had found him in his room unshaven and sleeping.

'I have received a report that your family is well.'

Then Bonny turned and looked at him. They were the most lifeless eyes Kabota had ever seen.

'I'd like to go down and see them soon. You could arrange that.'

Kabota was unprepared. The English man had never spoken or looked at him with such directness. An alarm went off in his head.

'I will telegram the headquarters in Tokyo and recommend your visit...'

Hara-Kiri: disembowelling oneself. A highly honourable act, Bonny thought as he looked at Kabota.

'I had a dream about death,' he said aloud.

'So you want to see your family?'

'Yes, before someone dies.'

'Ah, you are sick... Transference of anxiety,' Kabota counselled, relaxing. 'As soon as possible I will arrange a visit.'

Bonny forced himself to look away from Kabota. The white mile-stones reminded him of Jaffna Geoff and gravestones. He had to leash his mind. As a young child he had invented a game. He would retrieve words in alphabetical order from memory.

... *murder, mush, must, mutation, mutilate, muzzle*..., and on it went, until they reached Port Dickson.

People were already gathered at the field next to Planter's Inn in Port Dickson. As the Kolonel was greeted and whisked off by Japanese officials, Bonny carried the hockey sticks out of the back seat, his eyes on the faces in the crowd. He was looking for Uncle Rolly who was coming up from Malacca with some replacement players. It took everything that he had, not to break down as Roland walked towards him.

Uncle Rolly's grown old... he looks like Jaffey, Bonny thought as he stiffly put out his hand.

'Son, are you alright?'

They struggled with silence, half nods and shuffles, all the while gripping the other's hand.

'It's really yours... Jaffna's Bible. You're the next...'

'We all knew he wanted you to have it.'

'How did you get it? I mean... could it be... they could still be alive.'

'The underground got it from a Chinese Headman who escaped into the jungles near Muar. They started walking when they ran out of petrol but soldiers caught up with them the next day...'

Bonny nodded, as he looked around. It was one of those rare moments when no one was watching him.

'The Headman remembered Jaffna from the days he laid down those milestones. He was a witness to the... God-damn their souls! He got the Bible from the abandoned Hillman and passed it on through Alfie because they know he's from the Settlement.'

'Which "Alfie" do you mean?'

'Alfie... Alfonso. Little Dom's father.'

'Alfonso... and the underground!'

'He gives them fish when he can.'

'He's a better man than I.'

'Don't do this to yourself son.'

A couple of soldiers walked towards them.

'I'll need the boys to help with the hockey souvenirs,' Bonny said loudly.

Roland turned around and wolf whistled at the hockey players from the National team.

'O'Hara, give us a hand.'

Several players dressed in bright yellow jerseys emblazoned with a red sun, obediently marched over.

'Lads, these are souvenirs to be given away by the Kolonel. Don't manhandle them! They're gifts.'

'Relax Uncle Rolly, the hockey sticks won't break. Really! They're well made.'

'Ehmm! I'm sure they are. Well, I've got a surprise for you too. You'll never guess who...'

Roland was cut off in mid-sentence as a big whoop of excitement exploded behind Bonny.

'Ivy!'

A tousled-haired girl of about fifteen, wearing dungarees, white shoes and socks came tearing up to him. With total abandon, she leapt the last few feet into Bonny's arms, wrapping herself around him.

'Bonnyface, I thought I'd die if I didn't see you soon!'

'I convinced the Kolonel that the boys needed to meet with family to lift morale. We got a lift up on a tanker.'

'Baby girl, you're all grown up,' Bonny said in disbelief, as he stood her on her feet.

With unnerving green eyes, her beautiful face was too young to be so haunted. It was his face. He gathered her in a hug unable to meet her eyes, looking at Roland Leembruggen. Roland shook his head and Bonny nodded.

'Where's Cuthbert? Did he come along?'

'He wanted to stay for the Feast of St Peter. He's hanging out with the Catholic girls. Jaffey's not going to be happy. Have you got any news? Do you know where they are?'

'Slow down... breathe. They're in Changi and I'm trying to see if we can get them home soon.'

'Hurry up! I can't be bringing up Cuthbert all on my own. He drives me to distraction and he's getting too big to cane,' Ivy said bossily and then burst into tears.

Bonny felt his self-control slip. Roland Leembruggen stepped forward and put his arms around his niece.

'Come on girlie, now's not the time to break down. You've been so brave. Elise is going to be so proud.'

A whistle sounded calling for the players onto the field.

'We'd better let Bonny get on with his job. The game is about to start,' said Roland as he extracted a weepy Ivy from her brother.

The hockey match between the National team and the Emperor's team was nail-biting. As the National team battled the soldiers of the Emperor's team, no one mentioned Fateh Khan but he was on everyone's mind. Kolonel Kabota especially knew the importance of the game. This was one time the National team of local players *had to* win. There was no shouting, only grunts and groans. Arms folded tightly to lock in cheers, rocking in agitation, the locals watched their sons in the National team work out the murder in their hearts. As the Emperor's soldiers were spun around like tops by the mercurial

Eurasians, sullen anger gave away to quiet gloating. And with that came a fragile sense of dignity and honour.

Inwardly smug, Kolonel Kabota congratulated the National team. The PR exercise had been a success. It was all smiles and goodwill as the Emperor's team gave hockey sticks to young hopefuls in the crowd. Looking on from the grassy verge of the field, Bonnifacio Lazaroo disgraced himself publicly. He threw up.

12

Roughly three miles south from the fishing village, the Japanese Army barracks backed onto a cliff that plunged into the sea. The goings-on there were privy to the children from the fishing village, who had been warned under threat of beating by their parents to stay away. Isa, Ummah's younger son, was one of them.

'Abah, she was crying like *Cantik*[76],' Isa said as they sat on mats eating their meal.

Ismael choked, his eyes almost popping out of his face.

'Don't eat so fast,' Ummah cautioned.

He was father and mother to his two sons, his wife having died from smallpox. Isa was nine, a fair, gentle-looking boy, like his mother. Ismael, a teenager, was muscular and darkly handsome, with a faint trace of a moustache.

'Who was crying, Isa?' Ummah asked, scooping a handful of rice into his mouth. Ismael spluttered and Ummah reached out and thumped him firmly on his back.

'Drink some water.'

By this time Isa was receiving the message clearly from his brother. He was in grave danger if he divulged their day's adventure to their father.

'Did you want Abah to kill us?' Ismael whispered angrily as they

---

76   Cantik – "pretty", a pet name for their monkey.

lay down to sleep. 'You know he forbade us to go near the barracks.'

'I was only going to tell him about the girl that we saw at the Japanese barracks, that we should help her.'

'Are you stupid? If Abah doesn't kill us, the soldiers will,' Ismael said, slapping his brother with his pillow. 'Go to sleep!'

Isa could not sleep. He kept seeing the androgynous eighteen-year-old girl standing against the wire fence looking out at the sea, crying. At first she had not seen them because they were on a narrow ledge below the rim of the precipice. When she did, she reacted strangely. She put her face in her hands and squatted down as if she were hiding.

'That's one of *them*,' Ismael said excitedly, pulling Isa down onto the ledge.

Isa was very disappointed. The older boys had whispered they were going to see the *perempuan malam*[77], and made it sound as if they were blood-sucking vampires. She was just an *Ah Moi*, a Chinese girl like the daughters of the vegetable farmers who bought fish from them. And Isa knew she was *malu*, ashamed. The teenaged girls in the kampong reacted in the same manner when the boys stumbled upon them by the river as they bathed in their sarongs. She was "malu" even though she was fully clothed.

When the girl finally removed her hands from her face, four brown faces gaped up at her. Looking around to see if there were any guards, she said something unintelligible.

'What did she say?'

'I don't know. Zainal, you speak Chinese, you ask her name!' Ismael ordered.

Nobody could understand the girl. As she realised that, she

---

77   Perempuan malam – night women, a code word amongst the elders for prostitutes.

bunched her hands on her knees and started sobbing. She was tiny, with her thick-cropped hair and a flat chest. The four boys watched, curious and helpless. She had the same look as Cantik, the village pet monkey, whose baby had been savaged by wild monkeys until Ummah put a newly born kitten into her arms.

That night, Isa resolved to free the girl. And he knew his audacious brother would help him.

And so, after many visits to the barracks, communication starting with *cikkus* and *rambutans*[78], they found out her name was Kim. A few months later, a plan was hatched. Kim would escape via the latrine before dark. They would have the advantage of the darkness because no soldiers ventured into the tiger-infested jungles at night. The latrine was a wooden structure with two planks jutting out over a ravine. Several hundred feet below flowed a river, which was notorious for crocodiles. A soldier had slipped and his sorry remains were found downstream. Isa argued that the soldiers would presume the same about Kim, who they would hide at one of their durian groves. Ismael, not wanting to appear the lesser man and secretly amazed at Isa's resolve, found himself leading the rescue.

Armed with an old bald tyre and sixty metres of rope, just before dusk, they waited on the ledge.

'Why isn't she here?' Ismael said, clearly agitated.

'Steady! We're early. I told her we'd be here at dinner time.'

'And how did you tell her that?'

'I pointed at the sunset and showed her the sign for eating, like this,' demonstrated Isa.

'I hope you're as clever as you think you are.'

'I hope you're as brave as you think *you* are.'

---

78   Cikkus, rambutans – tropical sweet fruit.

'What's that supposed to mean? You want to climb up and get her?' Ismael asked testily.

'Getting her out is not the problem. Anybody can do that,' Isa said quietly, as he unfolded the belt of his trousers. 'Have you forgotten Old Ugly Face?'

'*Aai Seh*,[79] did you bring the prayers?' Ismael asked contritely.

'Yes. And this.'

'*The* sacred Keris! You took it without Abah's permission...'

'We need protection. Abah only warned us not to use it *wrongly*. We're using it for good, not evil, aren't we?'

Ismael looked at Isa, knowing his younger brother was challenging him.

'It's been in our *keturunan*[80] for hundreds of years. Abah said if anything bad happened to the Keris, our family name will be cut off.'

'Nothing's going to cut off our family name,' Isa said confidently. 'Let's read the *Surah*[81] from the Koran.'

'The Illumination's yours. You know how to *Doa*[82] like Abah. Just pray against Old Ugly Face, this river is his sanctuary.'

'Don't fidget, we've got to be respectful.'

Ismael nodded submissively as they got on their knees. Digging a hole, Isa put a strip of paper with a Koranic verse into it. Then he covered the hole and placed the Keris on a red cloth by the little mound. Heads bent, palms open to heaven, Isa prayed.

---

79 Aai Seh – I say.

80 keturunan – ancestral line.

81 Surah – chapter in the Koran/Quran.

82 Doa – the Muslim word for prayer.

>Ooi Old Ugly Face of the Thick Hide
>Grandfather Crocodile of the Muddy Waters
>Offspring of the Serpent Sakti-muna
>Severed by the Iron of Allah.

>Servant of Iblis. Thooi! Thooi! Thooi!
>Be off, get lost, don't linger near
>We speak unto you fear, Fear, FEAR
>Of the Almighty Allah!

>Ooi Tok Buaya, Old Ugly Face
>Regard you these two good men here
>Not for your dinner, not for you maw
>But for the pleasure of Allah forever more.

'That was good.'

'Not as good as Abah though,' Isa said earnestly, as he rewrapped the Keris in red cloth and fastened it into his belt.

'Don't talk about Abah now. We should ask God for protection from him, not Old Ugly Face.'

Kim appeared well before six, clutching her sides in an exaggerated manner to indicate she needed to relieve herself. The two boys felt a thrill rush through them. They were on the last foothold of earth on the rocky outcrop before it right-angled into the ravine and latrine.

'She's coming. Get going! If anyone comes I'll whistle,' Isa said, heart beating fast.

'When I let her down, be there! Swim her out to the sea.'

Ismael took the rope and slung it over his shoulder. The old tyre strapped onto his back like a knapsack, he scaled down the side of the rock. In less than a minute he was down on the sliver of mud and rock that took him to the elbow of the river directly below the latrine. Here the water was swirling and eddying rapidly. Then he started up the slippery face of the rock to get to the latrine. It was easy for him, having climbed coconut trees from childhood.

Isa watched anxiously as Kim reached the latrine and disappeared into it. A minute later Ismael climbed into the wooden structure from the rock face below. As Isa looked back again at the barracks, two soldiers had come out and were having a smoke.

Mael hurry up, he thought, suddenly feeling afraid. Then to his horror, he saw one of the soldiers walking towards the latrine. Without hesitation he whistled their signal birdcall, and started clambering down the side of the rock face. He was not as dexterous as Ismael and the jagged rock face tore into his hands and knees.

In the latrine Ismael, sweating profusely, heard the whistle. He had tied one end of the rope around the leg of the structure but he was fumbling with the rope around the girl, not ever having come up so close to a female before. It was the girl who grabbed the rope and knotted it. They could now hear the soldier, shoes crunching, barely twenty feet away. Ismael thrust the tyre over the girl's head, gesturing to her to be quiet. He pressed himself against the side of the wall where the door hinged open slightly. The soldier put his rifle down against the outside wall of the latrine, and started unbuttoning his trousers.

From inside, Ismael saw the rifle leaning against the wall, bayonet attached to the muzzle. Without hesitation, he pounced. He stepped out and picked up the rifle. The soldier, taken by surprise, barely had time to drop his trousers.

'Offf...' was all he managed as the bayonet sliced into his liver.

Throwing down the rifle, Ismael rushed into the latrine and shoved the girl onto the planks to hoist her down. The other soldier standing near the barracks had not noticed the drama. He was savouring his rationed cigarette, eyes on the horizon. Glancing casually in the direction of the latrine he saw the figure lying prone outside the latrine. The cigarette fell from his fingers as he started running towards the outhouse, cocking his rifle.

Isa had reached the elbow of the rivulet and was desperately yelling up into the latrine.

'Mael! Mael, get out of there fast!'

In response, Kim came whizzing out of the dark shadow of the wooden frame, clinging to the tyre around her waist. Isa jumped into the water, fighting off the strong current as he readied to dive into the gushing river to get hold of her.

Ismael gritted his teeth as the rope seared through his hands. The girl's weight was too much for him. At the same time, he could see the soldier heading for him. She was half-way down and he let the rope go. She fell like a weight and when the length of the rope ran out she jerked to a standstill in mid-air, screaming in fear. Whipping out a knife from his belt, Ismael cut the rope, and she plunged down into the river.

'Isa! Take her and go!' he roared.

The soldier burst through the door as Ismael dived off the plank into the river. The tyre saved Kim's life as she fell against the rock, bounced off and buoyed on the water, lacerating the side of her head and neck. Isa hooked his arm through the tyre and looked up to see Ismael diving down.

Then the shot rang out. Blood sprayed the air. The next second they were being catapulted down the river. When they hit the back surge of the water from the sea, the river changed gears and they slowed down. Swimming to the riverbank, Ismael and Isa pulled the tyre-draped girl out of the water. She was bleeding from the side of her head and her ear was hanging on her neck, but she was conscious and alert. As they raced through the jungle running parallel to the beach, Isa saw the blood trailing down off Ismael's thigh. He had been shot in the buttock. They had to get to Ummah. Subconsciously, Isa put his hand on the Keris in the back of his belt. His legs buckled. The Keris was gone. He must have cried out because Ismael turned around sharply.

'What's wrong?!'

'Nothing! Nothing... Keep moving, you're bleeding. We have to get to Abah!'

But Ismael's words rang in his heart.

'If anything bad happens to the Keris, our family line will be cut off.'

A deathly silence was upon the village even though it was only eight o'clock. Torches blazed on Ummah's veranda, crammed with villagers sitting on the floor. As the two boys and young woman stepped over the threshold there was a mixture of shock and dismay on faces. The fishermen made a little passageway for them that led to Ummah. He got up slowly, his face formidable.

'What have you done? Tok GrandSire Long Claws has been prowling the village. Where is my Keris?'

'We took it to rescue the girl from the barracks and...' The words were cut off with the crack of Ummah's hand across Ismael's face.

'Abah it was my idea,' Isa said shakily, stepping forward, 'beat *me* not Mael.'

'Yes, it is you I will beat! How *dare* you touch my Keris? You think you can take your father's place? I'm not dead yet!'

Wordlessly, everyone watched as Ummah unbuckled the belt from around his sarong and started whipping Isa. It was the girl who stopped him. She ran to Ummah and tore the belt out of his hands, sobbing wildly. Ummah took a deep breath and stepped back, his eyes red with anger. For the first time he looked at the girl.

'Enough, Ummah, enough! The boy's been shot and we've got to hide the girl,' said Pa Jo, an elder of the village.

'First we must ask Tok GrandSire to protect the village and cover the boys' tracks in the jungle. It will lead the soldiers to us.'

Kim was bundled off to the village *Bidan*[83] who specialised in traditional medicine. She had secret hiding places in the forest where she gathered herbs for her poultice. Ismael's bleeding had ceased but he had broken out in a fever. It was a long and terrible night for the fishermen as they waited for the crunch of soldiers' boots and torches that would plunge their village into an inferno. For the first time in the history of the fishing village, nobody went out to sea in the midnight hour. The strongest fishermen, along with Ummah and Isa, put a shivering Ismael in a litter and went out into the night to look for help. Ismael was going to die if the bullet was not removed.

---

83   Bidan – Malay midwife.

13

Dr Masalamani Azariah, an Indian with thick, premature silver hair and olive skin, was of Brahman origin. The Azariah had crept in, thanks to Doubting Thomas who had made his way to India. He had an equally handsome wife, Alice, with a cord of black hair in a big *kondeh*[84], always in Banarasi silk saris. They met when he went to study at the University of Manipal in India. It was a love marriage and blessed, their two sons studying medicine in India. The good "Doctor" however, was a vet and the darling of the English community all because of his devotion to animals. (He was invited to all of Lady Hill's parties.) Before the British evacuation, Dr Azariah was entrusted with Sir Douglas's precious stable of horses. The noble steeds endeared Azariah to the Japanese Generals. On his part, he was charming and effusive; he attended Japanese classes, and sang their songs. They harboured great plans for Azariah with the ridding of the British from India.

The doctor lived on a rambling property near the headland. The front of the compound was fenced up to keep in the dogs, with the back running into the jungle. At 3.00 am in the moonless night, with hearts hammering, Ummah, Isa and the four men carrying Ismael, slunk out of the jungle to Azariah's house. Ummah, lugging a sackful

---

84   Kondeh – doughnut-like hair bun on top of the head.

of seafood, tapped lightly on the backdoor.

The doctor himself opened the door. He had already received a message that a boy had been shot and needed urgent surgery.

'Come inside! Quickly!' he ordered. Turning to the servant girl behind him, he said something in Tamil. She nodded and slipped out nimbly.

'Indra's gone to release the dogs, so that if anyone comes we'll know,' he said to the fishermen, who had been half expecting the dogs to attack.

Azariah ushered them into his kitchen where a manservant, Rajan, was boiling water over a wood-fire stove. On the floor of the kitchen was a six-foot by four wooden timber board covered with a rubber sheet. Over it lay thick jute sacks with a top layer of sheets of paper. On the paper, heavily sedated, lay an Alsatian dog. The fishermen looked nervously at the animal.

'He's asleep,' Azariah said reassuringly, patting the fisherman closest to him.

The kitchen had a huge door through which you could see the living room with a staircase leading upstairs. Across from the stove there were two rooms, both with their doors shut. Azariah walked over to one of the doors and opened it. It led into a large storeroom, which was empty except for a wooden table and a long shelf on the opposite wall. The shelf was lined with a neat row of steel kidney trays, knives, scalpels, bottles with disinfectant, bandages, cotton and scissors. Each of the corners of the table had a hole drilled into it and an eighteen-inch iron rod lay by each hole. There was one high window, with a stool under it that looked out onto the side garden. Outside the dogs yelped, frisky in their freedom.

The four men bundled a delirious Ismael in and laid him down on the table. While they did that, the doctor walked around the table and fitted the rods into the holes, screwing them in firmly. Isa watched puzzled. Ummah was busy in the kitchen. He had strewn papers all over the dining table, and was ready to display his fish. He and Azariah had not exchanged a single word.

'Hide in the jungle,' Ummah said to the fishermen. 'When we're finished I'll signal.'

Rajan took a pot of boiling water to where Ismael lay. He put it on the shelf and began to quietly sterilise instruments. Azariah put on a clean white apron and a pair of gloves and without any fuss the operation began. He poured chloroform onto a cotton pad, which he placed over Ismael's face. For the first time that night the incoherent boy fell silent. Dr Azariah reached out for the glass bottle of disinfectant. The smell curdled Isa's tongue. Ummah walked over to the stool under the high window and stood guard. Azariah blocked Isa from the scalpel that cut into Ismael's buttock.

Obstructed from watching the procedure, Isa turned and walked over to the dog lying on the kitchen floor. Tentatively, he put his foot on the dog's tail. It was taboo for a dog's saliva to touch a Muslim. He became aware that he was being watched, and turning to the living room he saw an *Orang putih*[85] girl of about seven. Light-brown hair floating to her waist, in a white cotton nightdress, she looked like the doll on Tuan John's tree when they delivered lobsters for Christmas. She walked over to the dog, knelt down and started stroking it. Isa sank to his haunches beside her.

'The soldiers killed my family,' she said in perfect Malay. 'Did they do that to your brother?'

'Yes... We went to their barracks and we rescued a girl.'

'Isa,' Ummah said in a cautionary tone.

He was standing at the door, afraid that Isa was giving too much

---

85   Orang putih – a white person.

away. The doctor too, had half turned at Ummah's words.

'It's all right Ummah,' Azariah said. 'Mariam's my goddaughter.'

Ummah nodded and went back to his lookout. It took over an hour, with Rajan mopping up after the doctor and dropping bloodied cotton and gauze into a pail.

'I'm afraid my needlework's a bit rusty,' the doctor said apologetically, removing his gloves.

Before Ummah could answer, the tyres of an army truck screeched noisily outside. The dogs started yelping.

'We've got visitors,' Azariah called out calmly to Indra. 'Open the gates before they shoot the dogs.'

Isa started trembling. Outside, the soldiers shouted for the dogs to be restrained. Isa saw Ummah check the back of his belt where a Keris was concealed. Rajan moved quickly to the wooden board on which the dog was lying. In unison, Ummah and the doctor went over to him and wordlessly, they carried it to the room where Ismael lay. Swiftly they mounted the board with the dog onto the iron rods, creating a false top. Underneath on the table lay Ismael, unconscious. Rajan checked to see that the rubber sheet dropping around the table to about three feet, had not been caught in the iron rods. Then he started scattering the bloodied cotton in the pail from Ismael's operation, around the dog.

'Mariam, go upstairs!' Azariah said sternly to the girl lingering in the kitchen, 'and get into the hidey-hole.'

Outside, Indra screamed at the excited dogs, slapping them with a leather strap for effect to calm the angry soldiers. As Mariam walked up the stairs, Mrs Alice Masalamani Azariah came sweeping down in a dressing gown. Eyes soft from sleep, black tresses plaîted, she stepped barefooted into her kitchen. Ummah walked over to the kitchen table where the sack of fish lay and spilled its contents. Alice Azariah stepped up and began to pick and prod at the fish before her.

'Don't say a word. Bow! We've come here after the night catch to sell fish.'

'Yes, Abah,' Isa said feebly.

Dr Azariah moved back to the room where he had operated on Ismael and pulled on a pair of gloves. Only this time, the dog lay in front of him. Picking up a scalpel he made a quick sharp incision on the inside of the lower flank of the dog and blood spurted out. When the soldiers burst into the kitchen, Alice Azariah and Ummah bowed deeply.

'What are you doing here? Why are your lights on?'

'They always bring fish to us first,' Alice said gently in Japanese.

'You, what are you doing?' demanded a second soldier who had charged up into the room where Dr Azariah had stopped operating and was also bowing.

'The dog, it's very sick. Kolonel Kabota said he wanted this animal as a watchdog,' Dr Azariah said cunningly, as he held out bloodied hands. 'If I don't operate on it immediately, it will die.'

Kolonel Kabota's name had an immediate effect on the soldier. He turned his attention back to the kitchen. Azariah bustled as he started stitching up the dog. A third soldier prowled around Ummah and Isa, poking at the empty sack with his bayonet.

'Would you like some fish?' Ummah asked in a servile tone.

'Take some fish back for Kolonel Kabota,' Azariah said grandly, fully aware that Kabota was in the capital, his fingers slipping on the needle.

The soldiers said something in Japanese, enticed by the crabs, prawns and fish. On cue, Ummah started filling the gunnysack. Isa, eyes down, clutched the kitchen table.

'Rajan, I've finished. Give me a hand,' Azariah called out, walking out to the big sink in the kitchen. With aplomb he removed his apron and gloves before proceeding to wash the blood off his hands.

And then Ismael groaned, thudding the false top of the table. The soldiers simultaneously turned, guns trained at the room where he lay.

'What was that?'

'What?! Oh, the dog, it's waking up,' Azariah said lightly.

The soldiers looked at each other, uncertainly. Holding up the bayonet of his gun in front of him, one of them moved carefully towards the room. Isa could see the whites of Ummah's knuckles. A quavery moan trickled clearly towards them. The two soldiers near the kitchen table cocked their guns, pointing them at Ummah, the doctor and Rajan.

'It's the dog. When they have an operation they have bad dreams,' Azariah said, talking quickly.

The soldier outside the room where the dog lay, looked in cautiously. Nobody in the kitchen breathed as he stepped in, and quickly checked behind the door. Then he almost tiptoed up to the dog, head cocked.

'Uncle.'

Everyone including the soldiers almost jumped out of their skins. Mariam was standing at the doorway of the kitchen. The soldier from the room where Ismael lay came charging out. Suddenly all guns were pointing at Mariam.

'Inggerish girl! Inggerish girl,' the soldiers chattered in nervous excitement, waving their guns from the girl to Azariah.

'No, no, she's not English! She's my godchild. Mariam, why aren't you in bed?'

'I heard noises, Uncle, and I got frightened,' Mariam said in Tamil.

The soldiers who had lived in Malaya long enough to discern an authentic slang were stumped. Azariah walked up to Mariam and put his arm around the girl.

'She's my cousin's daughter. She's not English, her father is Bengali, very fair,' he said placatingly.

The soldiers stood their ground, guns cocked.

'*Ammachi*[86]!' Azariah bellowed. Isa buckled and would have fallen over if not for Ummah's hand gripping his shoulder. The soldiers jumped back, guns cocked, ready for an assault.

'Ammachi, come here!' Azariah's voice boomed through the house. 'Rajan go and bring her.'

Rajan began to move very slowly to the other door in the kitchen, next to the room used for the operation. Fear and pandemonium broke out in the kitchen as the guns waved frantically back and forth from Rajan to Mariam to Azariah. All the while, Rajan continued his slow walk.

'You get back.'

'It's alright...'

'Stop or we'll shoot!'

'Tell him to stand back from the door.'

'Don't shoot!'

'Stop!'

A soldier rushed up to Rajan and hit him in the back of his head with the butt of his rifle. The manservant flew against the door and fell to the floor groaning. Isa felt the blood drain from his face. He expected to be shot any minute.

'What's inside the room?'

'Come out with your hands up! Or we'll shoot everyone!'

Slowly the door opened, creaking as it did. An old woman in a pale blouse and yellow sarong appeared in the doorway. She was totally limestone white.

---

86 Ammachi – used in South India to represent mothers or old ladies.

'My Aunt,' Azariah explained, 'she's deaf.'

The soldiers watched as Azariah walked over to her and put his arm around her. The woman was suffering from vitiligo, a depigmentation disease, but the soldiers had never seen it before.

'My Aunty. Mariam come here, *slowly*,' he said, talking all the while to the soldiers. 'Mariam's white like her grand-aunty.'

A soldier stepped up, commando style, into the room from which Ammachi emerged. He checked the cupboard, underneath the bed and then stepped out niftily. He nodded an all-clear sign to the other two soldiers, who had guns trained on Azariah, arm around his Aunt and Mariam.

As the three stood together, Ammachi, a pure leprous white, olive-skinned Masalamani Azariah, with his silver hair, and fair English-looking Mariam, there was a distorted similarity.

Slowly the guns went down.

After the soldiers left, Ummah watched Mariam and Isa playing with some kittens.

'Who's her father?' he asked Dr Azariah, as he put his coffee cup down.

'Emanuel, my best man. The Serani family from Penang,' Azariah said quietly. 'They buried them alive.'

'I owe her. My people are her people.'

Kim's escape from the barracks shrouded Port Dickson for a week. The soldiers believed it was master-minded by Chinese insurgents. Kolonel Kabota, who was sent to Port Dickson to investigate, was given an antique silver Keris found in the mudflats near the river.

After seven days, when there was no trace of the woman, Kabota had to make a decision. The Keris pointed to the Muslim Malay fishing village, but the woman was, in appearance, a Chinese. The Malay leaders being groomed could care less about the Chinese, but the Keris told its own story.

Kolonel Kabota was in a hard place as he looked at the beautifully crafted dagger in his hand. Punishing the fishermen would turn the rising Malay goodwill against them. Action, however, was imperative! The escape of the woman, whilst embarrassing, was the least of his worries. A soldier had been killed and a lesson had to be taught to the Malayans. Kolonel Kabota made a calculated decision. The soldiers rounded up three hundred men, women and children, all Chinese. Four generations from a great grandmother to a three-month-old baby girl were executed in the field next to the Club and the Malays from the fishing village were deliberately selected to dig a mass grave.

Overnight, the field was renamed, *Padang Darah*, Field of Blood.

In Tiger Sanctuary, Ummah the Headman gathered with the elders. A solemn fast was proclaimed by the Spirit Guide, to cleanse the village of bloodguilt. Three days later a cow was slaughtered. In the evening doa, Ummah, Ismael, Isa and the men of Tiger Sanctuary, bowed down in the direction of Mecca and completed their atonement.

One year later, several months before the Japanese surrendered, Bonnifacio Lazaroo was executed in the same field. An informant named him as the disseminator of the pamphlets. "The English man" was tortured to reveal his sources. The rumour that circulated for years after, was that Kolonel Kabota got his answer. It so incensed him, that he blew the English man's brains out.

After the war, the bodies buried in the Field of Blood were exhumed and reburied in new graves.

Part 4

FOUR DAYS EARLIER

1985 – PRESENT
PORT DICKSON, MALAYSIA

*"When Lucifer and the Trinity began to war, those who did not
take sides, worthy, noble angels, had to descend to earth to that
Stone which is forever incorruptible.
Since that time the Stone has been in the care of those whom
God appointed to it and to whom He sent his angel.
This, Sir, is how matters stand regarding the Gral."*

Parzival – **Wolfram von Eschenbach**

14

THE FIELD OF BLOOD veered off to the beach, a good seventy-foot drop. Erosion left natural footholds making for an easy descent. Standing on the escarpment, the wind sounded like half words and sighs to Alistair. The locals swore they could hear the dead from the Japanese execution talking, sometimes even wailing. Ivy had become unhinged when the cancer metastasized to her brain. She would demand that he take her to the field.

'They're calling me Alis. Mummy and Bonny... can't you hear them?'

He heard laughter and turned, expecting to see children from the commune of Islamic zealots at the forest end of the Field of Blood. The Al-Sijjin were only kept in line by the Prime Minister's crackdown on fundamentalists. In the marketplace they sold Islamic accoutrements from beads and Palestinian scarves to portraits of Ayatollah Khomeini and Yasser Arafat. There was no one there. The wind sniggered.

The blood of Abel, thought Alistair cynically, as he started his climb down.

In front of Alistair, on the shore, was the jetty for the fishermen of Tiger Sanctuary. Half a mile back lay the Club and half a mile ahead was the fishing village. The road that ran past the Club ran up to the jetty. Here it stopped short, like an amputation. The water around the fishing village was silting due to commercial development on the headland, and the government wanted the village to relocate. The tenacious fishermen improvised with scooters, old jalopies and vans. Three-wheeled motorcycles, side carriages loaded with squealing children was a common sight. Nearing the village, the pungent smell of dried fish assailed Alistair. The beach dazzled with sweetened milk tins, beaten out and embedded like pavers. They were used to dry salted fish, a condiment to meals in most Malay houses in the country.

'Pa Ali, good morning *Che Gu*[87], how are you?' a fisherman called out in English, in one sing-song breath.

They called him Che Gu, even though it was Ivy who was the teacher. She was Kirkby trained in Liverpool, England. An elite group of Malayans were flown to England in ex-military York aircraft to be trained as teachers, after the war. She gave evening lessons in their home to fishermen's children who could not go to school because they helped with the midnight catch. When Ivy fell ill, it had been Dom's suggestion that Alistair continue with her evening classes; it was only until the 'O' level exams, a short six-month stint. She was forty when she died, but her success was immortalised in the kampong boys who went on to college and univeristy.

Except for Isa, Alistair thought, pained. *She was so ambitious for him.*

'Alis, *you* go and ask Sir Douglas for a place at Kirkby for the boy.'

'Ivy, you can't do that... it's not ethical.'

'Isa's special, I feel it. He's bigger than the fishing village.'

And she was right. The first time he had laid eyes on Isa at the forge, Alistair had been struck by the youth's gentility, which was out of place in the fiery furnace. He was fair, with such light-coloured eyes they were almost orange. Dom's explanation for Isa's *sui generis* was so typical of Dom's Catholic malarkey. He had to make it all

---

87   Che Gu – Che means Mr. or Mrs. Gu is an abbreviation of Guru, which means teacher.

sound so mysterious.

'Do you know, he was born "in the veil", set apart.'

Isa had been born en caul, with the amniotic sac intact. The baby had to be delivered a second time by the midwife outside of his mother's womb. In the village, that was a special sign and it heralded Isa for a great destiny. And Ivy was determined to chart his stars.

'If *you* don't ask Sir Douglas, I will!'

And she did.

'If you can get him ready my dear, and he passes the 'O' Levels, I'll get him the place,' Sir Douglas said graciously.

Convincing Ummah was like pulling teeth. Isa was "called to be a Master Craftsman." Ivy would not take "no" for an answer. Reluctantly, Ummah agreed to the evening classes. At the age of twenty-one, Isa passed his Cambridge 'O' Levels with a Grade 1. Four months before he was due to leave for Kirkby, he was murdered. It was the biggest blow the fishing village had ever suffered, he was their son of promise.

Ummah's house was situated at the far end of the village and there were no secrets in the kampong. Visitors had to cut through the hundred something Malay timber houses on stone posts. Halfway to Ummah's, a black Mercedes crunched slowly towards Alistair. The peerage badge mounted on the front was a dead giveaway. The car was empty as it went past, the chauffeur saluting respectfully.

Ashman, what's he doing here?

Vines and creepers from beyond the rainforest draped Ummah's roof in a green web. His old Cortina with its patchwork paint, and Dom's motorbike were parked outside. There was a second bike, a Norton Commando, alongside Dom's. Alistair wondered if Ismael was there as well. He had to pass a small brick structure, the forge, to get to the steps of the house and he heard raised voices coming from the brick annex. He recognised Ummah's voice.

'What are you doing here?'

'I'm opening the forge, Old Man!'

Alistair was taken aback. Nobody talked to Ummah like that. It was not the Malay way.

'You're not clean and you've not observed any of the *pantangs*[88]! You'll bring harm upon the kampong.'

'My father was the first born. I have rights.'

'You have to be *born* into these rights. Like Isa!'

'Isa's dead and gone. My father's right is mine!'

'Jihad be careful!' Ummah's voice was dangerously quiet. 'Not even Ismael, my first born, would touch the forge without my blessing.'

Untying his shoes at the bottom of the stairs, as was customary in Malay homes, Alistair's ears pricked up at the name. He knew Jihad.

'I want to make my own Keris!'

'Not in this forge! We make Keris for the Kings and the Sultans here. Why do *you* need a Keris?'

'The season of *D'Ajjal*[89] is coming. Everyone who is a true Muslim knows that. I want to be prepared.'

It was *only* a harmless twelve-inch dagger but Alistair felt alarm. Jihad had been instrumental in his decision to shut down the English classes after Ivy's death when he had filled in for her to prepare the kampong students for the exams. Jihad, then seventeen, was one of the pupils and had turned the lesson into an ugly religious incident.

It was an exercise on 'punctuation', with three boys and four girls

---

88   Pantangs – cultural and spiritual prohibitions.

89   D'Ajjal – The Dark Messiah, very much like the anti-Christ who will deceive the world.

listening attentively, as they sat at the dining table in Alistair's house.

' "Would you like a chicken sandwich?" ' Alistair said, pointing to the sentence on the blackboard.

'You drink beer?' interrupted Jihad.

Alistair, accustomed to his disruptive and sometimes morose behaviour, chose to cajole him into cooperation.

'Yes, I drink beer. That's good Jihad, you've just asked me a question,' he said encouragingly and wrote the question down. He was oblivious to the shift in his students.

' "Do you drink beer?" ' he asked. 'Close inverted comma here.'

'You eat pig.' This time Jihad was not asking a question.

'Sit up Jihad, put both your feet under the table. Someone could trip and fall,' Alistair said firmly, ignoring the statement. 'Let's do an exercise shall we?'

The youth stared insolently at Alistair before reluctantly obeying. After that, Alistair was painfully aware that Jihad's eyes were on the buffet where crystal decanters held port, scotch and brandy.

At the next class, none of his students turned up. By eight pm he was worried to death. It was the time of the monsoon. Putting on his raincoat and armed with a torch, he drove to the Club and walked to the village. His students were all there, safe, and he was invited into one of their homes for sweet black coffee and *kueh*[90]. Knowing the Malay way, he asked no questions. He wondered if there had been an incident in the kampong. The next class they all turned up except for Jihad, and everything was back to normal.

A week later however, Dom brought a discreet message from Ummah not to use any non-halal symbols. Jihad had maligned him and told the elders that Alistair had offered them beer. The elders

---

90   Kueh – Malay cakes.

were upset, but when Alistair had gone looking for them in the rain, all their misgivings melted away. They were an open people but a new season was being ushered into the village, a season of suspicion and fear.

Fifteen years on, Jihad had grown into an ultra-religious man. Often seen in the company of Al-Sijjin followers, he was a thorn in Ummah's side. Belligerence in the face of the Chinese vegetable sellers who reared pigs, led to his poisoning their water in a drinking pond. Fortunately, it was a disused pond but the fishermen were terribly ashamed. Ummah's goodwill prevented a bloody punch-up.

One Chinese New Year, when fireworks were abundant, Jihad and several youths spent hours unravelling the paper to get a large milk tin's worth of gunpowder. Deep in the jungle, they blew up a wooden durian lookout. Nobody would have known had it not ended with one of them losing two fingers.

The acrimony from inside the forge volleyed out to Alistair on the steps of Ummah's kampong house.

'Jihad, you will bring a curse upon the family!'

'Your family *is* cursed Uncle! Isa died because he lost the family heirloom. A four-hundred-year-old Keris that should have been my father's!'

'Your father was not appointed, as you are not. And the Keris does not belong to anyone, not to your father or to me. When it returns, it will go to the next chosen.'

'When it returns! *Dah nyanyuk*[91]! You're talking as if the Keris is going to walk back into your belt. It will *never* return. It's gone and with it, your family line.'

---

91   Dah nyanyuk – You've gone senile.

'The Keris *will* return. It is looking for us.'

'*Mimpilah!*[92] You've become soft in the head.'

To have Jihad literally cross swords with Ummah over the Keris was absurd. Alistair suspected there was a bigger issue between them. Stacking his shoes to the side neatly, he lingered on the steps.

'Your heart is not clean...'

'Not clean!' Jihad laughed. 'What about Mariam?'

'Don't touch things you don't understand.'

'Why? Mariam can't even bear you grandchildren. God has cursed her. Everyone in the kampong knows.'

'Your talk is stirring people and if I have to banish you from this village, I will.'

'Banish! People want that *kaffir*[93] out of this village.'

'She's *our* family!'

Alistair almost jumped out of his skin as Jihad came crashing out of the forge. Face contorted, he jumped onto his motorbike, and took off, revving the engine furiously.

Alistair hurried up the stairs two steps at a time, nearly colliding with an elderly woman on the veranda. She too had been listening to the altercation.

'Ah! Kak Ayesha...,' Alistair managed, face reddening.

Ummah's wife, Ayesha, smiled graciously. She was almost sixty, with the roly-polyness of a broody hen. Wearing a headscarf, colourful cotton tunic and sarong, her face was remarkable. It was like the clear still waters of a lake. It drew Alistair because it was a face that had seen the violence of war, and yet she had triumphed.

---

92 Mimpilah – In your dreams.

93 Kaffir – Arab term for those who read and rejected the Quran.

———◆

Kak Ayesha, Ummah's wife, was no other than Kim, the Korean woman whom Isa and Ismael had rescued from the Japanese entertainment barracks in 1944. She was one of many Korean sex slaves recruited by Japanese officers under the guise of lucrative employment in their colonies. When the English doctor, Dr Kendrell, returned after the war, he removed her uterus without delay. When the time came for her to be repatriated to Korea, Kim, riddled with shame, hid in the jungles of Tiger Sanctuary unable to face returning to her family. The tender-hearted villagers had already accepted her as one of their own in the year she lived secretly amongst them and they screened her from the Civil Affairs police.

For many months the effete girl struggled to live. Relentlessly she combed the shoreline of the village, unable to escape the confining sea. The only person she allowed into her world was Isa. From his veranda Ummah watched them. He had never seen Isa so happy and confident. He had come into his own with having rescued Kim. Ummah's heart was strangely moved by the girl too. She reminded him of a mouse deer caught in one of his traps, trembling itself to death, and he wanted to set her free. Using any pretext to talk with Isa, Ummah started weaving into the twosome walking on the beach.

He was ruggedly handsome and the Headman, but he was invisible to the girl. For months in the eventide he would try to walk with them but she ignored him, much to the delight of the spiteful hopefuls in the village (the whole drama being enacted before their eyes). Then one day, as Isa skipped off to find shells, she stopped in her tracks.

'*Mau apa?*[94]' she spat.

He was beginning to stir feelings of anger and fear, which distracted her from her cocoon of self-absorption. Even though a shawl concealed her head and her neck, her hand involuntarily went to the side of her face where she had lost her ear after her escape from the barracks.

'I don't want anything,' he said gently. 'I want to give you a home.'

'Give me *what?*'

'A home... a family.'

'Family!'

'Yes, a family.'

'There is no family without children,' she said bitterly.

'You will have two sons, Mael and Isa.'

She looked at him in disbelief. He turned away to the setting sun, as Isa came running up.

'Kimmy,' Isa said, holding out a beautiful mother of pearl conch, 'look at this.'

She took it in her hands, turning it every which way, to look into the conch. Then she shook it vigorously.

'Where's the crab gone? It's empty!' she said a little wildly. 'You've taken its home. It's not going to find its way home!'

'Kimmy, there are millions of empty shells on the ocean floor. The crab will find a new home. It'll crawl into another shell, find a bed and go to sleep.'

She was looking at Isa who had taken the shell back and was following the markings on it with his finger. His words cut the darkness in her heart.

'Isn't that true Abah?' Isa asked, looking at his father.

'Yes,' Ummah answered, looking at her, 'there are many empty

94   Mau apa? – What do you want?

shells under the sea and they're all beautiful.'

'It's for you Kimmy,' Isa said placing the conch into her hand. She looked at the boy, then the conch and slowly she closed her fingers over it. As Isa ran off, Ummah stood alone with the young woman in the twilight.

'I... hate...' she choked as she clutched the conch to her heart.

'There's much love in this kampong.'

Then she started crying. Without touching her, Ummah stepped forward, cutting her off from curious onlookers and drew her into his quietness.

It was not long after that Kim embraced the name Ayesha, after the wife of the beloved Prophet. She became a "tiang", a pillar, in Ummah's house. When Isa died she took his place in the forge. She was perfect because she had no issue of blood and was considered clean. She became a female *empu*[95].

---

95 Empu – a craftsman of a Keris.

15

'AH, KAK AYESHA. How are you?'

'I'm good Pa Ali,' she said shyly in English, adjusting her scarf over her ear. '*Alhamdulillah* - Praise God. Coffee?'

'Yes please.'

'I'll have some coffee too,' Ummah sang out behind Alistair, coming up the steps.

There was no sign on his face to indicate that he had been in strife. Ayesha nodded and walked into the house.

'Pa Ali,' Ummah said warmly, as they shook hands, 'we haven't seen you for a long time. I thought our "visitor" would have brought you here. Everyone in the state has been here since the excitement started.'

For a fraction of a second Alistair did not understand, then in a flash he realised Ummah was alluding to the female apparition.

'Oh, I don't believe in these things.'

On the veranda, Dom, the old Story Teller and Ashman were already seated. The Story Teller was conspicuous in his soft white bedroom slippers, clearly from a hotel where he had been a guest.

'Alistair, this is Tok Selamat who I was telling you about. He's here for the cultural celebrations.'

The Story Teller remained seated as they shook hands, looking at Alistair slowly from the top of his head to his feet. There was no guile in his gaze and Alistair took no offence.

'You know *Tan Sri* Ashman of course...'

'Yes, yes of course.'

'Alistair, put away that infernal pipe and try one of these cigars. Hand-rolled from Nicaragua – the very best.'

'Tan Sri Ashman, how are you?' asked Alistair struggling, not knowing if he should call him by his title.

'I was telling Si-Dom, that when I was a boy spinning tops, Tok was in the Spice Islands collecting the folklore for his father, who was going blind,' Ummah said, plonking himself beside the Story Teller on the settee.

'During the first war I was visiting the Borobudur and in the second war I was protected in Langkawi by the Sultan,' Tok Selamat said gleefully, his toothless mouth an empty cave.

He spoke with a heavy nasal Indonesian accent and Alistair immediately understood why Dom had asked for him to be there. Quietly he turned to Dom and interpreted *sotto voce*.

'Have you been back to Langkawi lately, Tok?' enquired Ashman.

'No, but I hear you've been buying up all the land there in the last ten years,' Tok said knowingly.

Good for you, thought Alistair, looking fixedly at the *kueh*[96] offered to him by Dom who was playing host.

'The locals were happy to sell. The land was barren and we gave them fair prices,' Ashman said smoothly.

'Yes, now there's big development going on.'

'May I keep one of those for later?' Ummah asked, reaching out for a cigar.

'Please Ummah, have the whole box. I've got a crate from the Trade Commissioner, compliments of Daniel Ortega.'

---

96   Kueh – traditional Malay cakes.

'Make sure you respect the Spirit of Langkawi or *Mahsuri*[97] will curse the land again. They've put up a hotel next to the Borobudur... beside a sacred site. Disgraceful.'

'The Borobudur was built by the Sailendras in the 9th century in Java, wasn't it?' Alistair asked, by way of linking in Dom's purpose for being there.

'You're a historian and speak *my* language.' The Story Teller was looking at Alistair with interest and nodding approvingly. 'Are you an *Orang Belanda*[98]?'

'Sorry, English, and I'm a scientist.'

'A scientist!' Tok exclaimed, twisting his whole body stiffly. 'One of those people who send rockets up to the moon? The Americans, they're very clever. The atom bomb, then synthetic rubber... almost destroyed our country.'

'Pa Ali used to work with the Research Division of the Land Office,' offered Ummah.

'*He's* the clever one Tok. He can help us to find oil but he prefers retirement,' Ashman said pointedly, as he reached out and slapped Alistair on the knee.

'Retirement has its benefits. Dom's looking for a special sword and I've got the time to help him.'

'That's right.' On cue Dom pulled out a little *555*[99] notebook and pen from his breast pocket.

'You're not a reporter, are you?' Ashman asked, turning to Dom.

---

97 Mahsuri – a young beautiful woman who lived in Langkawi and was falsely accused of adultery. She was executed by stabbing with a Keris and white blood, signifying her innocence, flowed. Langkawi was cursed for seven generations by the dying Mahsuri.

98 Orang Belanda – person from Holland, referring to the Dutch rule in Indonesia.

99 555 – a ubiquitous notebook of that time, commonly used by small provision shops for IOU's.

'You're a reporter!' Tok was ramrod-straight, even though Ashman had asked the question in English.

'No! No, I'm not a reporter,' protested Dom. Reporters, especially the TV3 crew, were persona non grata in the village because they were attracting strangers to the sacred grounds.

'He's not writing a book about me is he?' Tok asked Ummah preciously.

'Dom's my *Anak angkat*[100]. He just wants to ask you a few questions.'

Just then, Kak Ayesha came out with a tray holding a pot of hot coffee, cups and more food. The veranda was flooded with the delicious smell of freshly fried banana fritters.

'Dom, did I hear you say something about reporters?' she prompted. 'That reporter's been back again.'

'Why? Has the woman been seen again?' quizzed Dom excitedly, a banana fritter arrested inches from his mouth.

Alistair was irritated at his "wide-eyed, tongue-hanging" pose.

'Does this story have any truth, Ummah?' probed Ashman, his tone belying his scepticism, as he rolled his cigar on wet lips.

'A female's been appearing around the Keramat, the Club, even up at Cape Rachado. Usually very late at night. And always there's some animal sacrifice. Chickens, a baby goat... different people have seen her over a dozen times,' Ummah said lightly.

'We haven't!' Ayesha attested. 'But people *are* frightened.'

'There's talk that... er... GrandSire Long Claws is no longer guarding the village,' Ashman stated carefully.

'This woman, there's got to be a reason. Maybe there's a message,' Dom declared earnestly.

'Maybe Si-Dom should check out this *vision*, there could be an answer in the Keramat,' Ummah said, thoughtfully studying his cigar.

---

100   Anak angkat – a child taken or adopted into one's family.

'I thought only Muslims could enter the Keramat,' Ashman said pointedly.

'Oh, Si-Dom is one of the *Ummah*[101].'

Tok lifted his little face out of his shoulders like a turtle, as if he was about to say something. He was not only a devout Muslim but the quintessential Malay, a "Prince of the Land", a *Bumiputra*[102]. Ummah had called Dom a citizen of a supranational Muslim community. If he had reservations about Dom, Tok swallowed it. He trusted Ummah implicitly.

'Who is he? Do I know his people?' Tok asked Ummah quizzically. Alistair translated quietly.

'Tok, Dom is a *Sufi*[103]. It's in his blood. His ancestor is our Panglima Awang Enrique of Malacca. The cabin boy who sailed with Magellan around the world.'

The slipper that had been dangling on Tok's foot leapt off quietly onto the floorboard of the veranda. The old man blinked a couple of times and then he reached out a gnarled hand and caught Dom's wrist.

'Panglima Awang! Magellan's boy! Yes, his name was also Dom Enrique. He was my hero. I wanted to stow away on one of those ships in Bencoolen when I was ten. They had to tie me up and pray for the Restless sea spirit, to leave me,' he said, eyes wide. 'And *you* are his ancestral grandchild, this is good *rezeki*[104].'

Alistair squirmed as he translated. Dom's quixotic accounts of 16th century connections were all too familiar, yet Ummah and Tok

---

101   Ummah – Muslims, Jews and Christians who were brought within the fold of one community to be protected by Prophet Muhammad.

102   Bumiputra – a termed coined under a policy designed to help enable the Malay race, as the first settlers of the land.

103   Sufi - a Muslim who believes in the Spiritual realm and supernatural phenomenon.

104   Rezeki – Blessings from God.

were regaling Dom with genuine appreciation. From the eye contact between them, it was clear that Ummah and Dom had a great rapport.

'So what is it you want, *Anak*[105] *Panglima Laut*[106]?' the Story Teller asked Dom, peering at him closely with great marvel.

'What is the Iron of the Creed? Is it a sword or is it gold?'

'According to ancient scriptures, the Iron of the Creed fell on the *Golden Chersonese*[107],' Ummah volunteered.

'Suvarnadvipa... the Isles of Gold. That was the ancient Sanskrit name of the Malay Archipelago. *Sulaiman*[108] came looking for the gold of *Ophir*[109] but Ptolemy's map was not accurate,' the Story Teller mused.

'What do you think Alis?' directed Ashman. 'You've studied geology. Is there gold in the Peninsula?'

Alistair was gobsmacked. Suvarnadvipa, the Golden Chersonese and Ptolemy were facts he had studied in his youth at Cambridge University. The old man, without any formal education, was mouthing the wisdom of scholars.

'What I know of the Iron of the Creed...'

The old Story Teller was ready to talk, as he released Dom's wrist and took out a cigarette. Dom picked up the matchbox lying on the table and lit it for him, as he put it in his rubbery mouth. Alistair noticed that he had dropped his dialect, speaking in a more commonly used Malay language. Dom was going to get his story.

---

105   Anak – child (of).

106   Panglima Laut – the Sea Warrior, Magellan.

107   Golden Chersonese – ancient name for the Malay Peninsula.

108   Sulaiman – King Solomon.

109   Ophir – a biblical-era land,

The sound of waves chomping in the midday tide, ate into the quiet on Ummah's veranda. Coffee drunk to the dregs, fritters cold and limp, with cigars burnt to little stubs, the convivial mood had fizzled into a languor.

'Tok is saying *it*, the Iron of the Creed, fell from the sky in fragments? A meteorite! And the only existing piece is part of the Kaaba in Mecca?' Dom asked, disappointment etched on his face.

'Not just a meteorite. When Iblis was cast out, it was with this heavenly rock. One third of *Syurga* – Paradise – was destroyed and the serpent Sakti-muna that Iblis was riding, fell into the sea to hide.'

'I thought the Iron of Creed was a sword from the Holy Land.'

'Abang,' Ayesha whispered urgently to Ummah, 'you're late for your appointment with *Tuanku*[110].'

'*Aai Seh*[111]! Okay, I better get going.'

'I'll walk with you Ummah.' Ashman stood up. 'Good luck Dom with your hunt, for your... er... lady friend, this apparition.'

'Thank you Tan Sri, it won't be a hunt, it'll be a *journey*.'

'We've held several doas but she won't go away,' Ummah said with a big sigh.

Several prayers! One's usually enough. It was with Ivy. She believed she was healed, Alistair thought spitefully.

'I've told you Ummah... you won't be around forever,' Ashman said quietly.

There was an unspoken tension between Ummah and *Tan Sri* Ashman as they looked at each other.

---

110   Tuanku – Title for Royalty e.g. the Sultan.

111   Aai Seh – I say.

'We'll talk next week *Tan Sri*, after the cultural night,' Ummah said with a great sigh, heaving himself out of the rattan chair.

'Good. Come to the house... I'll see myself out.'

After shaking hands with all, he was gone, his black shiny Mercedes purring quietly.

'Is there something on Tan Sri's mind?' Dom asked Ummah in his unique busybody style.

'Oh, he's concerned about the bad publicity. The "Visit Malaysia 1985" celebrations in Port Dickson kick off in three days at the village and he's organising some business investors next week.'

'It's nothing more than childish nonsense.' Alistair had meant for it to sound friendly, but even to his own ears, it was impatient.

'Oh, I think it's more than a child's trick. This woman vampire, vision, she's real. Dom's right, there's a message,' Ummah said politely.

The warmth on the veranda evaporated. Neither Dom nor Tok noticed the subtle shift.

'We're going to the Sacred Forest tomorrow to get some answers,' piped Dom.

'Well, I think I should be going,' Alistair said neutrally.

'Why?' Tok demanded. 'You should stay and chat.'

'You and Dom don't need me to interpret Tok. You seem to be getting along quite well.'

'It's true,' Tok agreed happily, 'we understand each other.'

'Si-Dom is a dreamer of God's dreams. A Sufi,' Ummah gushed with open affection.

'I'll see you in a couple of days Alistair, when I'm back from the Sanctuary,' Dom said importantly, eyes bright and shiny, as Alistair shook hands first with Ummah and then the Story Teller. 'Ummah and I need to discuss the protocol for the Sacred Forest.'

'You're a secretive man,' Tok mused, grasping Alistair's hand with both of his, and looking into his face, '... with many secrets.'

'What do you mean? I mean I'm not, not really.'

'*You are.* You speak wonderful *Bahasa*[112], you know ancient history and you're hiding in little Port Dickson. Why?'

'I've lived here half my life. It's my home.'

'One day you must tell me why you *really* came to Malaya. The secret reason, the one in your heart.'

'I came looking for a wife,' Alistair quipped, drawing laughter from Ayesha.

As he cut through the Field of Blood to get to the Club where his car was parked, the Story Teller's words shuttled through his brain.

'One day you must tell me why you *really* came to Malaya, the secret reason, the one in your heart.'

---

112   Bahasa – Malay language.

Part 5

DECEMBER 1953
BRITISH MALAYA

"And Alexander wept,
for there were no more worlds to conquer."

Alexander the Great – Plutarch

16

ALISTAIR ROBERT PIERCE, 27, officer of Crown Property, peered dubiously over the rocky edge of the headland. He was feeling nettled. In his clenched fist was a list with names and directions from the British Advisor's office. The instructions, like everything else in the Colony, were fallacious.

'At the twelfth milestone, there'll be a little footpath. Duck through.'

The path was an ankle-twisting thicket swarming with black mosquitoes, which jutted without warning hundreds of feet into the air.

'The villagers use it every day... a shortcut, halves the time getting there.'

The "shortcut" was a number of roughly hewn steps down a now dry waterfall. They cascaded dizzyingly to the fishing village below and he sank to his haunches. He could see the edges of kampong houses closer to the beach and boats lolling in the shallow waters. Easing backwards into a hollowed rock, he smoothed out the crumpled paper in his hand, folding it before stuffing it into his shirt pocket. Then he lit a Wills and took in the panoramic view of the coast and rainforest. The gable of the "English" house, property of the East India Company, in the black and white Tudor style, made him think of strawberries and cream in a curry tiffin.

'Ashman's got what he wanted. A warm bed in the company house and I'm just a goddamn dogsbody.'

In his eighteen months in Malaya, sitting under a cobalt blue sky was a luxury, but that was how he preferred it. It disallowed an inventory on his life. Alistair Pierce smiled in self-derision.

'I wonder if Ashman ever knew about *Brave New World*? Or that it's been disavowed?'

His mind went back eighteen months earlier to the day he met Ashman Lahud. They had set sail from Tilbury in June 1952, two young men who had survived the war, heading for a new world. The esprit de corps was as palpable as a hug. He was joining the Negeri Sembilan Land Office as an agronomist to fight synthetic rubber. Ashman was heading to Malaya as a representative of Tracton-Atkins, an arms manufacturing company. With the communist insurgency in the Colony, the British had a new fight on their hands.

On the very first day of their journey, Ashman had invited him to his first-class cabin.

'New play fields, Alis, to be harvested. The world's been reborn!'

Alistair was not convinced. For him, the world had aged prematurely with the war, like his father.

'MacArthur's a visionary. You're in the right place, Crown Property and all!'

There was a keenness about Ashman that made Alistair think of shrapnel. Yet he was inordinately warm and generous. His grandmother, Sarah Schaffer-Marrick, had been a governess to a wealthy Middle Eastern family living in London. The patriarch from Lebanon, entitled to four wives, was besotted with the flame-haired Sarah, and he married her. Ashman, her grandson, was the godson of James Schaffer Temple who belonged to the Bletchley Park intelligentsia, which had decoded the Enigma encryption. Ashman Lahud

146

grew up pressed against the bosom of the elite.

'I'm the only representative for Tracton-Atkins. The *old boy* owed my Uncle one.'

Alistair knew he was alluding to Churchill. Ashman's loyalty to England was entrepreneurial. It was a new experience for Alistair. He knew only men like his father, Jack "Blackie" Pierce, who served the country to the detriment of their families.

'What does your father do? You haven't said a word about Pater.'

'He was a bomb aimer... Lancasters. Shall we get some air before dinner?'

'He didn't die in the war, did he?' Ashman asked concernedly, noting the change of subject.

'No, actually he went on to be decorated. He was one of the path-finders over Dresden.'

'Sterling! We need good pilots and bombers. Too many went down with the Spits!'

They stood on the deck watching the setting sun amidst people laughing and lovers stealing kisses. A hat flew off, ribbons flapped in the wind. Screams and more laughter erupted. Alistair sensed the excitement Ashman felt, but he could not enter in. He was trapped between his father, blighted with post-war psychosis, and his mother, cold and unloving.

By the time they disembarked at Port Swettenham three weeks later, Alistair was desperate for his own company.

'Captain Soames said he'd be here himself to pick me up,' Ashman said, preening as they waited at the terminal. 'Will you be needing...'

His words were arrested as the Advisor's Bentley slunk up, flags fluttering like the wings of doves. Behind it, two army trucks followed, with a team of Ghurkhas pushing through the crowd.

'Mr Pierce! Alistair Pierce?' an English civil servant called out.

'Yes! Yes. Alistair Pierce. Crown Property.'

All eyes were on him as he sweated in his black suit, hat and freshly acquired moustache. (It had been specifically grown for his new life in the Colony. He had since shaved it off due to tropical itch). Ashman watched quietly as containers, the size of garden sheds, were loaded onto the army trucks.

'Alis? You dark horse. I've been rabbiting on about the old man and here we've got his nibs, a personal friend of Sir Douglas.'

'Oh, he's not a friend, it's just work...'

'That's interesting baggage for *work*.'

'It's stuff I'll need.'

'What sort of stuff? And what's the army got to do with it?' Ashman persisted, the irises of his eyes gold-flecked with inky pupils. They were the eyes of a raptor.

When they said goodbye at the port, Alistair did not dream that he would see Ashman again in less than a month. They met at a state luncheon hosted by the Sultan in Negeri Sembilan. Eighteen months later Ashman was ensconced as a guest in the English house, while Alistair was still without a permanent desk in the Colony.

Alistair pulled on his cigarette, his eyes on the English house.

That old bastard... thinks he can buy dreams.

"That old bastard" was none other than the philanthropist, Lord Giles Hallingworth of Cumberland. He had the ear of Whitehall and was the Patron of *Brave New World*. Lord Giles came from a family owning iron mines and steelworks in Furness and opium concessions in China, with money to burn. Spurned by not being included in the atom bomb race by the Americans, he turned his attention to herbicides and biological warfare. Secretly approved by Whitehall, it was codenamed *Brave New World* in honour of Aldous Huxley. Malaya was the perfect site for research and experimentation with her dense jungles and the rising communist threat in South East Asia.

Alistair was completing his doctorate on plant microbes and soil types affected by chemical contamination, at Cambridge's Department of Plant Sciences. He was one of eight, handpicked for interviews. The psychological test he underwent, placed him high on the Humm-Wadsworth Temperament Scale, of "Introverted".

'He has a "Fear of Intimacy",' the Board was told. 'A young man who can keep secrets.'

He was perfect because he had the advantage of studying the Malay language, which *Sir R.O. Winstedt*[113] had deemed compulsory for those wanting to work for the Civil Service in the Colony.

In Malaya, he was to source a suitable location for a greenhouse away from prying eyes. A fully equipped research laboratory, with a centrifuge and generator, was shipped with him. Once the engineers got it operational, his team of geneticists would arrive. With a jeep of gun-toting trekkers he went deep into the jungle. The rains made his work tortuous and he was exhausted, listlessly burning leeches from his body with his cigarettes. Only the geckos chiming to Cole Porter on his father's gramophone kept him company as fireflies lit the veranda. Under a mosquito net, pinned by bloodcurdling screeches, he drifted between Malaya and England.

When a well-drained piece of land was found, piling stopped as soon as it started because it was loaded with tin. Exciting as it was, they had to move on. They were forced to go further into the jungle.

---

113 Sir R.O. Winstedt – a British civil servant who was an Oxford scholar and wrote 'A Dictionary of Malay Language.' Decorated for his achievements, his papers are archived at the School of Oriental and African Studies.

Alistair contracted malaria and for a month he was desperately ill. By the time he was well enough the monsoons brought the work to a stop. Ten months to the date of his arrival in Malaya, Alistair saw the completion of the greenhouse. The day the centrifuge thundered into life, he could not tell which was louder, his heart or the machine.

When Sir Douglas summoned him for dinner, Alistair was ready for an evening of congratulatory toasts. Sir Douglas did not even wait for him to finish his aperitif.

'I'm afraid Alistair, I've got a spot of bad news. Lord Giles wants an end to *Brave New World*.'

Alistair's mind went blank as he watched Sir Douglas pick up a pair of steel clippers and circumcise the tip of a fat cigar.

'What do you mean? I'm sorry... I beg your pardon, Sir!'

'Lord Giles is under some pressure, son, from Whitehall.'

It was the word "son" that bolstered the shock.

'I didn't mean to delay the project.'

'My boy, don't flagellate yourself,' Sir Douglas ordered mildly. '*Brave New World*'s been leaked and the London papers are waving the Geneva Convention.'

'Lord Giles? What's he saying, Sir?'

'Oh, he's moved on to cryonics.'

'Cryonics?'

'Cryobiology, coming back from the dead after being frozen! Lord Giles is enthralled. He's a bit of a child you know.'

Lord Giles's face, with his orange hair, deep-set eyes and lips pulled over large yellow teeth in a grin, flashed before Alistair. He had been invited to a cocktail party to discreetly meet his patron. Lord Giles was bound to a wheelchair, but what a wheelchair! A technological wonder. Propelled by an engine, it was a prototype from Canada on trial and not even on the market yet. As it zipped around, the crowd applauding, Alistair could clearly see the rapture on Lord Giles's face as he manipulated the joystick. Before anyone could tire of the exhibition, the motorised chair spirited the mischievously smiling Lord away.

'Chin up!' Sir Douglas ordered kindly. 'You're still an officer of Crown Property. There's work to do, what with the Supremo's bloody directive.'

"The Supremo" was Sir Gerald Templer, High Commissioner of Malaya. He had replaced Sir Henry Gurney, assassinated by communists and was a man on a mission. Wearing a permanent wicked glint, he had no qualms about putting his best foot forward, up somebody's backside. After only eight months in Malaya, he had the communists on the run and the Advisors walking on glass because of his razor-sharp tongue and extensive powers.

The "bloody directive", involved moving Chinese farmers, squatters, from communist-infested "black" areas into new "white" villages. These were acreages literally wrenched out of the hands of the unhappy Sultans and allocated to the Chinese to foster loyalty. It was a brilliant strategy because the Chinese farmers no longer needed the communists to fight for them.

In the blink of an eye, Alistair found himself reassigned to the Land Office, Negeri Sembilan. He had to filter the Crown's master plans against a quagmire of ancient land deeds. It was a battlefield. The Malays were unhappy about giving away indigenous land to Chinese pig eaters but his command of the Malay language gave him leverage. A month before Christmas, all the newly mapped deeds and titles lay on the Advisor's desk. He looked on as Sir Douglas signed off next to his scrawly signature. When Captain Rutherford stamped the deeds with the hot vermillion sealing wax of Crown Property, a strange sensation came over him. The wax, congealing like blood, rose off the paper and he resisted the urge to press his finger into its warmth.

'You're tied to the land Alistair,' Sir Douglas said welcomingly. 'I hope you're not in a hurry to go back to England... take a break before you decide.'

17

THINGS HOWEVER, were never predictable with this man Templer. Barely had the ink dried when a barking order over the phone to the Advisors put an end to a happy Christmas in the Civil Service.

'Get cracking on a round of parties for Her Majesty's Malayan friends. Teas, dinners, jamborees... whatever it takes to show our appreciation!'

'Excellent idea Sir Gerald. The new year would be perfect, with...'

'Now!' growled Gerald Templer. 'I want them at the Christmas parties.'

'The boys have worked hard and it's a special time for them.'

'This is no time for sentimental claptrap.'

'... but the printers will take...'

'Forget the blasted protocol! Use jungle vines, drums! And I mean *all* Her Majesty's friends. FIND OUT WHO THEY ARE!'

'Click!' went the line and that was that.

The story behind "Her Majesty's friends" was a pique on the part of the Malay leaders and Sultans. Smarting over having been forced to give *their* land to the Chinese settlers, they needed endorsement in the eyes of their subjects. They brought up an old gripe. There had been very little acknowledgement of local heroes fighting the Japanese.

Whitehall acquiesced because they wanted a move on Independence, in four years. The Supremo put his boot in and kick-started the process. Clubs' "members only" policy was relegated to the rubbish bin. The entire committee at the Lake Club in the capital resigned in protest. Templer happily accepted. The Civil Service was up in arms. It was the Yuletide season and they wanted nothing more than their tiger hunts and watering holes. Moreover, no one was in the mood to pander to the Malay leaders. They had made the land concession program excruciating with their toing and froing, and "*buat ta tahu* – make as if you don't know*," passive aggression.

Sir Douglas himself was "most put out". He had a prior engagement. The Advisor was hot on the tracks of a white Sumatran. The Sultan's permission was only obtained after Sir Douglas persuaded the Crown to allocate several million dollars to building the *Yamtuan Besar*[114], a new palace in *Seri Menanti*[115]. Further, 'Lucky' Sher Singh, a Tiger Wallah from India, had been issued with a ticket on BOAC. Sir Douglas had to strike. Once the tiger crossed over into the next state, the Sultan of that state had his own Advisor and there were new players with bigger concessions. Sir Douglas appointed Alistair Pierce as his Personal Assistant. The very same reasons that qualified Alistair Pierce for *Brave New World* under the Secrets Act, now drew him into the Advisor's charmed circle.

Sir Douglas was already in "civvies" when Alistair arrived at his office for the briefing. Gone was the royal blue coat and trousers with his trademark silk cravat. In its place a white shirt, flicked open at the collar and beige jodhpurs. A silver-tipped cream topee lay on his table.

'Alis, I'm depending on you. Follow up on Her Majesty's... er... friends. Rutherford will see to the office.'

Alistair noted the "Alis". It had such intimacy to it, that the dossier Sir Douglas slipped him could have been a billet-doux.

---

114 Yamtuan Besar – the Sultan.

115 Seri Menanti – the royal capital of Negeri Sembilan.

Her Majesty's "friends" were a motley crew. This was a list compiled by frazzled District Officers, who had to go back a decade to the war. Shoeless freedom fighters, to a hybrid team of hockey players, Alistair found himself on a strange trail. In Rembau he found out that the names on the list had no connection with persons alive or dead. Everyone had a nickname and it would have been comical if it had not been in earnest.

'Mr Hussein? Ali Bin Hussein! You mean Mr Ali... Hussein's his father. Or is it Mr Hussein you want? Hussein Bin Ali?'

'There are three Ali Husseins... Which one is it you want? Black Ali or Cigarette Paper Ali or Deaf Ali?'

'Cigarette Paper died before the war.'

'God rest his soul, he fell asleep smoking.'

'Er... where can I find Mr Black Ali?'

'In school.'

'No, I'm looking for someone in his forties, who served in the war.'

'Black Ali's in school. He's the gardener... I don't know about the war.'

'Didn't Deaf Ali plant the bomb on the Jepun submarine?'

'Yes... it exploded while he was in the water.'

So the trail leading to His Majesty's friends disappeared geographically and surfaced over the map of the human heart. It took him outside the state to Malacca where he had to flush out some hockey players at Portuguese Settlement. And for the first time he saw Malaya, driving through her main range with heavenly vaults, the sunrise, stained glass through them. Green paddy fields with diamante dewdrops, the hand of an Eastern princess, regally waved to him.

He was rudely catapulted out of his reverie by the scrum of human bodies plugging the bridge over the Malacca river. Frantically pulling on the brake handle, the screeching tyres got their attention, with half-naked boys torpedo-ing themselves into the water.

What on earth...? he thought, getting out of the car.

Across the bridge, a procession was winding its way through the street with a cross licking heavenwards in pyromaniacal glory. Resplendent in costume, it looked like a scene from the courts of 14th century Portugal. Behind the cross, a grand triumphal arch radiated with hundreds of candles and was supported by shoeless Jesuit priests. Under this twinkly lunula, European Monsignors in silk chasubles, swept the road. In the centre of this ecumenical vanguard, a Papal Nuncio in white gloves, reverentially clasped an ornate monstrance at eye level.

The sea of faces that phalanxed them though, contrasted starkly with the beatific expressions on the Monsignors. With a mixture of European and Romany features on umber skin, there was a defiance. It was the ardour of a regiment of golden sunflowers proudly resisting a Mediterranean sirocco Apart from a few dozen who were altar boys, the Irmang de Igreza, all the rest were dressed as Portuguese and Spanish nobleman and ladies-in-waiting.

'Eurasians!'

The sudden burst of excitement around him cut off Alistair's thoughts.

'*Ibu Nabi Isa!* Jesus mother! Si Mariam! It's Mary!'

The "Madonna" was a lass of about sixteen in white robes, an ivory vision of purity. Head inclined, palms in prayerful repose; the rosary through her fingers moved as the float was pulled along.

'Statue of Our Lady, Tuan'.

Alistair turned around. A trishaw had pulled up behind him. The driver, a Chinese man of about forty with a rubicund face knew he was addressing a potential client.

'*Seranis*[116],' the trishaw driver said, a toothpick sitting in one corner of his mouth, 'bringing back the relic of St Francis Xavier.'

He had never seen Seranis, Eurasians, like these. Most of the Seranis, he knew were *Keranis*[117], clerks in the Civil Service because they spoke good English. The word upgraded them from the unschooled locals and they gloried in the privilege of their colonial heritage. Amongst the civil servants however, there were mixed emotions for the "half-Tuans".

'Where's the rascal, Serani Kerani?' the District Officer would bellow. 'If he's gadding about organising a lottery, he's fired!'

Nobody used the name Clarence, but everyone knew "Serani Kerani". A washed-out watercolour picture, Clarence had pale blue eyes, light brown hair and milky skin. The fellow had the luck of the devil and had more lives than a cat. He always seemed to escape accidents, falls and terrible illness, being reasons given for not appearing at work. And there was always one whey-faced Serani Kerani in every district office. Cruel jibes surfaced at the work place. Lickspittle... yellow fever... brown noses...

'Tuan, see the relic? The Fathers brought back from Macau.'

'Relic?'

'Saint Francis's arm... in the glass box'.

Alistair's eyes were riveted on the glass case being carried reverentially by the Nuncio.

'Tuan, they open the tomb and St Francis's fingernails still growing. When they cut off his arm... real blood. Still fresh after 400 years'

---

116   Serani – a colloquial term for Eurasians in Malaya.

117   Kerani – a Malay word for clerks and often stenographers.

The trishaw driver must have seen the look on the Tuan's face.

'Gwai Yee swear Tuan, on the Mother of God... blood, a miracle!'

I'm in a rabbit hole, Alistair thought incredulously.

'Today publick (sic) holiday, Tuan. Gwai Yee take you sightseeing...?'

It was not a public holiday but clearly St Francis Xavier's arm had seized the day and town. Wisdom told Alistair that he would not find any hockey players at home. He hesitated. In normal circumstances he would gravitate towards the "Tuans". The only white faces were the long-bearded pontiffs and envoys in Portuguese livery. He fished out his watch from his trouser pocket. If he got to the District Office and delegated the invitations, he would be able to get back to Port Dickson in the afternoon. He had an invitation for the Headman of a fishing village at Jabul Musa, fifteen miles out of the town. Sir Douglas had stamped "priority" next to the name.

'Could you take me to the District Office and back?'

'*Lalu!*[118]...Out of the way! LALU!' Shrilling his bell between stentorian calls, Gwai Yee acquired a new power over the crowd. Alistair observed the pageant from a vantage position and noted the dark-skinned Indians at the tail end of the pageant.

'*Indian* pretending to be Serani, Tuan. Become Catholik, speak English and get promotion...,' sniggered Gwai Yee.

It was a cruel jibe but it rang true. Despite their costumes, it was in their body language, a lack of bravura.

'Look Tuan! Look!' Gwai Yee urged, furiously pumping his wormy, veined legs.

There, in the monstrance behind a glass face, was a fragment of an arm severed from the elbow, upright on a red cushion. It was clearly

---

118   Lalu - out of the way. Move.

recognisable, albeit being waxy. As the trishaw swung off Fort Road for the District Office, Alistair turned inside the trishaw to the oval window in the hood behind his head to have a last look. Unwittingly, his shifting weight lobbed the trishaw off the ground. Through the opening, as the pageant of Eurasians defied gravity and lifted away, Alistair had a déjà vu.

'Gypsies!'

He was standing at the green around the corner from Notting Hill Gate tube station and the Rumanian circus was pulling out. It was the spring of 1940, he was only fourteen and on the way to school. Passing the "Big Top" every day for three weeks, it was an exotic assault on his senses.

He fell instantly in love with the aroma of coffee Arabica in enamel pots over wood fires. And he could not get his eyes off the unshaven men, groping rambunctious women – pink nipples peeping from dressing gowns – in their laps. In the background, a gramophone defrosted the morning with Caruso's hot-blooded caterwauling.

In the afternoon, the women would still be in their dressing gowns. Only this time they flashed fishnet stockings and sequined plump breasts. Faces flawless, hair slick with lacquer, they were loquacious in a deep-throated language. And almost always a man-boy plucked a flamenco guitar. Sometimes a woman would jump onto a crate, hoist up her dressing gown to her crotch and dance. The camp would resound with stomping and clapping. Once they caught him rubbernecking and one of the women winked and thrust her hips out. Red-faced he turned hastily away, their whistles and raunchy calls pursuing him. At night he dreamt that he was unshaven, and cavorting with the women in lustful embraces.

The morning the circus pulled out, the "green" now a barren patch, he felt a sadness he had never experienced before. It was as if *he* was being left behind. And yet strangely, he had not *once* made an attempt to go to the circus. It was as if he was afraid to realise his feelings. He followed the caravans for a mile. After the war, it was in the *London Times*, that the Rumanian circus had been gassed at Krakow. Loss rampaged his soul for years.

Half twisted, as he glanced backward in the trishaw, Alistair Pierce was sentient, the pageant of receding Eurasians were his gypsies, heading into oblivion.

An impulsivity, alien to every fibre of his being seized him as he flung his leg out of the moving vehicle. Instead, he backfired into the seat as Gwai Yee, the driver, braked and simultaneously counter-tilted the listing trishaw expertly with his gluteus maximus.

'Sorry Tuan,' he apologised with a winning smile to Alistair, scooched unceremoniously in the carriage. 'We go to the District Office now!'

It snapped Alistair into the moment.

'The List! It's top priority. Sir Douglas is depending on me. I've got to get to Port Dickson this afternoon.'

18

PERCHED ON THE CLIFF high above the fishing village, Alistair struggled with a dysphoria that he was familiar with from after the war. He was not given to reminiscing because it took him to dark places, to his father... and death.

He had been triggered by his morning encounter with his Malacca "gypsies" and the audit of his squandered months in the Colony. Ashman Lahud's coup with the East India Company exacerbated his despondence.

Lord Giles was right. We're just sacrificial pawns for the greater good... whatever that is, he thought morbidly.

Wrenching his eyes off the gables of the English house, he gingerly began his descent down the cliff face with the help of the rusty railing drilled into the rock. It was easier than he thought. Half-way down, through a break in the foliage, he found himself looking into the porch of the English house. By sheer coincidence, the front door opened and a man and a woman came out. They embraced and the woman walked to a yellow Sunbeam-Talbot, by the banana fronds. There was only one person who owned a car like that.

Barbara... Soames's wife.

He averted his face and continued his descent. Laughing, naked children playing on the waterfront rushed to him.

'Tawfee! Tawfee please... thank you.'

'Sorry, no toffee today! *Di-mana rumah Encik Ummah Ibrahim?*[119]'

'*Penghulu*[120] Ummah? Penghulu Ummah...'

Alistair followed the screaming children to the Headman's house. A good twenty metres from Ummah's house, the children stopped and quietly pointed at Ummah's house. Metallic clanging noises rang out from the brick forge next to the house.

Walking up to where there should have been a door, he found himself looking through a window. A man was wielding hammers in both hands. Lightning strikes, on a red-hot piece of iron held in pincers by a teenage boy, threaded the room with silver needles. A hunk, naked to the waist, worked the bulging billows. The whole room was an orchestration of light and power.

'Ya Allah!'

A young woman had come out of the house and seen him standing at the window of the forge. Like a child she escaped behind a wooden beam even though it was not broad enough to hide her.

'I'm sorry I didn't mean to startle you. I'm looking for Encik Ummah.'

'*Abang!*[121]' she called out urgently.

The noise stopped and a man in his forties came walking out from the back of the brick cubby. Strong and hawkish, he unwound a waistcloth and wiped his hands and face. Behind him followed a clone, except he was twenty years younger. Hands on his hips, his head was thrown back with defiance. Last out was a teenager of about eighteen who looked totally different from the two men. He was almost elegant, with eyes that arrested Alistair because they were uncanny. The pigmentation of his irises made them look glassy with

---

119   'Di-mana rumah Encik Ummah Ibrahim?' – Where is Mr Ummah Ibrahim's house?

120   Penghulu – Headman.

121   Abang – respectful term for husband or the elder male.

gold circles around dark pupils. Tiger's eyes, fearless.

'Encik Ummah?' Alistair queried politely, as he extended his hand. 'My name's Alistair Pierce.'

'I'm sorry,' Ummah said, holding his hands back, palms up, not taking his hand, 'we're ritually clean... for the work on the Keris.'

'Oh!' Alistair said awkwardly. 'I've come to invite you, on behalf of Sir Douglas Hill, and your sons for dinner, at the Planter's Inn.'

'Ah, Sir Douglas, is he well?'

If Ummah was surprised that he spoke Malay, he did not show it. The two youths looked at each other, the elder with eyebrows lifted.

'The Advisor's very well, thank you. He's away at the moment.'

'These are my sons, Ismael and Isa.'

On cue, the two teenagers raised their hand respectfully to their foreheads in "Salaams". Alistair lifted one hand limply.

'Pleased to meet you. Sir Gerald Templer, the Honourable High Commissioner will be the Guest of Honour. I'm sorry the invitation is at such short notice.'

'The best invitations are when someone makes a difficult journey to your door,' Ummah said evenly, his eyes sliding off the mud skids on Alistair's Bombay bloomers and knee-high socks. 'But when is this dinner?'

'Oh, I beg your pardon, dinner's at seven at the Club on New Year's Eve.'

'The funfair will be on Abah,' sniffed Ismael, the older of the two.

Alistair was shocked. In his short time in Malaya, he saw civil servants clamber over each other in the Land Office for invites to dinners and cocktails. Lawn teas were ambrosia for aspiring locals. It was very niminy-piminy with gloves, hats, blazers and tea in China cups with delicate cucumber sandwiches.

Ismael was choosing the *Pesta*[122] over dinner with the High Commissioner.

The Pesta was a night of celebration for locals, organised by the District Office to usher in the New Year. The venue was the field next to the Planter's Inn. It was the bane of the civil servant, because the local staff would start playing silly buggers. The normally quiet workplace would erupt with flurries of chatter. Officers would look up sharply only to catch the word "Pesta" bob away like a mischievous imp. By the middle of December, a lotto cum tontine for the New Year would be drawn and lots cast. The organiser was always the Eurasian clerk, Serani Kerani, who had the Organisers' draw. This was to pay off all his Christmas debts, money spent before he even got it. The carnival mood grated on the nerves of the cold fish from the Atlantic.

The Pesta, however, was the crowning glory of the year for the estate labourers, the vegetable farmers and the kampong fishermen. A budget allocation would allow Ferris wheel rides, ice cream, candy floss, bottle drinks, film shows and a packet of poppers and whistles. The whole caboodle, with coconut mats and pillows for children, turned up for the fireworks at midnight.

Alistair had never been to a Pesta. He was in bed with malaria, in his first year.

'We'll be happy to have dinner with Tuan Douglas and then we'll join the Pesta,' Ummah said to Alistair but it was directed at his son.

'If *Tok Rimau*[123] doesn't eat him first,' Ismael said softly in Malay, aside to his brother.

Quiet as it was, Alistair heard the remark. Ummah looked

---

122   Pesta – funfair.

123   Tok Rimau - Grandpa Tiger.

poker-faced at his sons, who were wise enough not to meet their father's eye.

'Can I get you a drink, some coconut water?' Ummah asked Alistair.

'Yes please. Water would be good, it's so hot.'

The girl on the top of the stairs moved silently into the house.

'I'm sorry I can't invite you in, but when we are making a Keris, we have to observe strict ritual.'

'It's quite all right. Er, is that why the children are not coming into the compound?'

'Yes, they know that they will have strange dreams if they disturb the spirit of the Keris.'

'I hope that I'm not causing any problems.'

'You did not come with bad intentions,' Ummah said, eyes narrowing. 'The Keris... *it knows.*'

'Isa,' the young woman called from the veranda.

In two easy strides, Isa swung over the cement balustrade of the steps. As he took the glass of water from her, he said something to her. She giggled. Isa brought the drink down the stairs solemnly and offered it to Alistair, short of bowing.

'Sir, please do have a glass of water,' he said in English, enunciating each word clearly. 'Truly, it is very hot today.'

The young woman chortled, retreating hastily into the house.

'Isa,' Ummah said, putting his hand on the teenager's shoulder, 'likes going to school but I need him at the forge.'

'What about you Ismael?' Alistair asked curiously, challenged by the young man's indifference.

'I want to be a soldier, to use a gun,' Ismael said without hesitation.

'The Malay Regiment is looking for soldiers to fight the communists.'

'At the right time. Mael looks after the fishing boats.'

'Mael will make a good soldier, Abah. And we can easily get one of the girls in the kampong to work the billows.'

'Isa would like that Abah, for one of the girls from the kampong to work in the forge... now that he's finally growing a moustache.'

Isa was red in his cheeks as he threw himself nonchalantly on the ground and leaned against the wall of the forge. Ummah reached out and strapped the cloth he had unwrapped from around his waist over Ismael's neck like a scarf.

'Get me a fresh sarong and some water,' he said quietly, his tone requesting Ismael to stop his teasing.

'Yes Abah,' Ismael said obediently.

Alistair was not accustomed to brawny submissive men. Even seeing Ummah touch Ismael was odd. He moved his gaze from the bronzed torso as the young man walked up the stairs.

'Tuan Douglas has gone hunting?'

Alistair tried to keep a straight face, as Sir Douglas's words ran through his brain.

Neither confirm, nor deny my whereabouts! Change the subject!

'I hear there's a tiger, a white Sumatran in the Sanctuary... they say it's been around for a while. It killed a couple of Japanese soldiers near the old garrison.'

'There are many stories...'

'Have you seen it?'

'GrandSire Rimau,' Isa said in English from where he was sitting. 'GrandSire is sacred and his Keramat must not be defiled.'

'I have never seen Tok Long Claws. Only those who have an appointment with death meet him,' Ummah said philosophically.

'The pure-hearted have nothing to fear.'

'Two farmers were killed. They stole land from their cousins. They deserve to die.' This was Ismael coming down the stairs with a clean towel and water. He gave the items to his father, then leaned against the steps of the house, arms akimbo.

'The tiger has killed about twenty people in the last eight years, some of them children,' Alistair said in disbelief.

'Tok Long Claws kills for a reason. None of the bodies were eaten. NOT ONE!' Ismael declared defiantly.

'So, why does it... er... Tok Long Claws kill?'

'Tok is our guardian. He walks the line between heaven and hell,' Isa said leaning forward, head noosed by sunlight. He looked yellow, separated from his darker body in the shadows. As he put his hand out over his eyes to block out the sun, they were wet from the glare as if he were crying, he looked touched. On his exposed forehead, Alistair noticed a tuft of white hair, like a birthmark below his hairline.

'He does not kill without a reason.'

They're not talking about the tiger. They're angry about Sir Douglas's hunt, Alistair thought.

'The great hunter they've brought from Punjab... they say he's got a special gun?' Ismael asked, the gun clearly the focus of his question.

'Bro, no gun can kill GrandSire... the Jepun couldn't.'

'I know! I just hope Tok Rimau won't swallow the gun along with the *Bai-Ji*[124] from Punjab.'

The brothers exchanged goofy grins and Alistair wondered if he was dealing with yet another variation of the cobra theme. A few weeks in the Colony and he had found out how steeped in superstition the locals were. A cobra had ventured into his bungalow. Alerted by his Alsatian, he had rushed for a club while the dog cornered the spitting reptile. Before he could kill it, the Tamil guard had come running in with a sack, all googly-eyed.

---

124   Bai-Ji – respectful term for 'brother' in the Sikh religion.

'Tuan! Tuan! Today Friday. No good to kill *pambae*[125].'

Alistair watched dumbfounded, as the fellow danced around the escaping cobra. With a courage that defied intelligence, he scooped up the cobra by its tail, shoving it into a jute sack.

'Tuan,' the guard said smiling broadly, forehead red from the temple ash. 'Tuan buy lottery... sure strike! Snake very good luck.'

Alistair believed he was dealing with the same pantheistic nonsense.

'The tiger hunter... his name is Lucky - Lakhvir Sher Singh. He's been shooting tigers from a teenager. He's killed about thirty,' Alistair attested to the unimpressed faces around him.

'Will he be at the dinner?' Ummah enquired.

'Yes he will, he's a guest of Sir Douglas.'

'Good, we will be happy to meet him.'

'Inshallah. If God wills it,' Ismael said with a straight face as Isa smiled in the shadow.

Alistair hoped Sir Douglas and Lucky Sher Singh would display the dead beast at the Club.

'I've got to be going. Thank you for the drink and I do apologise again for the short notice.'

With a choreography of "salaams" and limp wrist salutes, Alistair walked away from the forge. From the corner of his eye he saw Ummah take his towel and crack it at his sons' shoulders. Amidst laughs and protests, Isa and Ismael like agile bucks, leapt towards the door at the back of the forge.

It's going to be an interesting party, Alistair thought, suddenly looking forward to New Year's Eve.

---

125   Pambae – snake in Tamil.

Part 6

DECEMBER 1953
TIGER HUNT – BRITISH MALAYA

The last shaman to be left unburied in Upper Perak was "stuck up" in a tree with purple flowers (Lagerstroemia floribunda) *between 1870 and 1875 and became a tiger with a white patch.*

The Malay Magician – Sir Richard Winstedt

Lend me thy coat, Shere Khan. Lend me thy gay striped coat that I may go to the Council Rock.

The Jungle Book – Rudyard Kipling

19

'KRILL! KRILL! KRILLING... KRILLED!' The Devil Bird, *Burung Hantu*, came out at dusk, signalling the hour when Abomination stalked. Mothers, hearts trembling, gathered their children, smearing faces with ash to hide their countenances. If the Abomination looked upon you, you lived forever, the unholy half dead.

The sun began to dip over the dinosaur-back range, casting the first long shadows over the ancient rainforests. Near the river, virgin rainforest had been felled to cater for the three hundred-odd hunting party. The jungle trekkers had chosen the campsite well, settling for the lee side of the hilly terrain, which was well drained. The stranglehold of giant trees, palms, vines and ferns had been sawn and macheted by thirty Negerito rangers, experts in trekking communists. Logs were laid down to make walking easy.

An impenetrable bamboo grove backed onto the campsite. The Advisor's entourage camped here. Every precaution was being taken to protect his party because the tiger was not the only danger lurking. Tin tycoon Bok Kai Seng and TK Abdullah, popularly known as Teak, who owned timber concessions in Pahang, were worth a fortune in ransom if the communists seized them. For all their money they were bankrupt in one thing. Youth. Necromancy and the Chinese zodiac pointed to the White Tiger. The elixir was in the blood, which had to be drained before rigor mortis set in. It would renew an old man, filling him with the virility of a stallion.

There was life in the blood.

The tiger lay on the ground, lifeless, bathed in the last rays of the sun. It was as if the Hunter of the East lingered for One He admired. The tiger burnt with fire. The Tamil sweepers and drumbeaters tee-tered between ecstasy and dread, expecting the magnificent creature to lunge at any second. It was not the White Sumatran but a female with milk-filled teats. Dead as she was, the elephants could not be cajoled with bananas or vicious spikes, into settling down.

A little gasp ran through the sweepers as Sir Douglas placed a boot on the tigress, the barrel of his Paradox in his hand. Lady Hill was down on her knees. Hair falling around in unruly curls, her starched trouser suit bore the tiredness of the hunt. Her hand lay gently on the tiger's head but her smile was elated. It was she, who had killed the tigress, the loaded gun placed in her hand by the Tiger Wallah.

'Shall we take the photograph then... before the sun goes down?'

Patriarch Bok and TK Abdullah posed with fixed smiles. The tigress held no excitement for them. The photography session was quickly over and the aboriginal trapper moved in to skin the tigress. The sweepers surged upon the tigress, hemming in the trapper. They knew of the tiger's prowess, now they wanted some of its power. A claw to hang around a scrawny neck, the liquid jelly of the pupils to improve eyesight, bones to be boiled into a broth to give strength, the hard parts in the centre of the eye to be set in gold as rings and the gall for a health tonic. It was all a promise of abundance.

'Ayoyo Kadavullah!'[126]

Screams and vociferous cheering erupted at the first incision. It was a deliberate spectacle to debunk the legacy of GrandSire Long

---

126   Ayoyo Kadavullah – 'Oh my God' in Tamil. – A lamentation.

Claws, the white Sumatran who they were out to capture. Then the scramble was on. The liver belonged to Patriarch Bok and the Advisor was to be given the skin. TK Abdullah was interested only in the Sumatran. For the rest of the camp, there would be tiger steaks, a feasting on the body to partake of its great fearlessness.

'Gentlemen, we'll see you for dinner,' waved Sir Douglas, ushering his wife to their tent.

A chain of servants ferried buckets of hot water for the bathtub brought in for the Advisor and his wife. Every indulgence was shamelessly catered for, thanks to Bok and TK. The only one who picked up on the real fear of the stomping elephants was Lucky Sher Singh, the Tiger Wallah. The Shikari from India, like the elephants, could smell the tiger. Not the one being skinned but the one *stalking* them.

'Sir Douglas, I'll have a look around if you don't mind. The trekkers will see you back to camp,' he reported uneasily, after the tigress had been gunned down.

The aboriginal trekkers were thunderstruck that the Tiger Wallah was going it alone.

'Oh, Lucky's a big boy,' said Sir Douglas, outwardly blasé, waving aside their concern. Internally he was chuffed that ten minutes before the tigress attacked, Lakhvir Sher Singh had positioned them for the kill. The Tiger Wallah was proving his mettle.

"Lucky" Lakhvir Sher Singh, was the greatest Shikari – game hunter – in India. Baptised at the Golden Temple in Amritsar, his name, Lakhvir, oracled that he would be "Brave as a Hundred Thousand". And indeed he was. His grandfather, Dada Bhag Singh Tugal, was a Sikh Jatt who owned vast tracts of forest at Amrita Nagar in the north of Rajasthan. His playmates were tiger cubs, whose mothers had been killed. He would swing the caterwauling cubs in the air by their tails, to stop their sharp teeth from tearing at him. Just as easily, he would be fast asleep with them, curled up like a little ball amongst their furry bodies.

Lakhvir's fearlessness led him to tiger hunts at the age of ten, and it soon became evident that he had the "magic eye". He would be able to "see" his prey ahead of the other hunters and his gift was so uncanny that the white Sahibs christened Lakhvir "Lucky". His God-gift earned him Colonel Jim Corbett's respect when he was eighteen. The royal game hunter, Colonel Jim Corbett from Africa, had met Lucky who was his gun boy when he was brought in to destroy the man-eater of Ranthambore. The Rajput Thakur Bahadur Rai, a close friend of the Viceroy, had been taken by a Bengal tiger. Jim Corbett presented the Viceroy's "condolence message" to the grieving Dharsink Bahadur Rai – the tiger, glazed-eyed and lifeless.

Years later, when Sir Douglas Hill contacted Jim Corbett to help him hunt the Sumatran, Corbett, suffering from a boil in the ear, pointed to the Tiger Wallah from India. A grand invitation, sealed with the insignia of the British Advisor of Negeri Sembilan, Malaya, was despatched to the hill country of Dehra Dunn. Enclosed, a return air passage on BOAC.

For Lucky Lakhvir Singh, now thirty, it was divine intervention. His God-given gift was turning into a sword in his own heart. The moment of truth had been a bloodletting orgy in Alwar with the Maharajah, Jai Singh, and his English guests. It ended with twenty-seven dead tigers displayed in shameless gore, and eight cubs, England bound as house pets. The debris of black bucks, chital and sambar ran into the hundreds. His God-gift smote his heart and began to eat into his bliss as he questioned, *'Prabu, Sublime One of the White Gyrfalcon, have I not pleased you!'*

Lying on his charpoy, searching the stars, he saw himself when he was fifteen. He was standing in the temple after he had killed the man-eater of Ghola. The tiger was feasting on the *dak* runners – postal employees – who jogged from village to village with only a bell hung to a staff. Tinkling and trilling, it was an easy meal for the clever tiger. Loping after the dak runner, gun cocked, he found the man-eater, waiting lazily in the sun. Without breaking his rhythm, Lucky Singh brought the big cat down as it got up with a smile on its face. The villagers assailed him with garlands and flowers, the temple bell clanging with the good news. Standing on roses, thorns embedding into his bare feet, he was the presiding deity, the pain in his feet nothing compared to the glory.

Now he felt only the tearing at his feet. He feared he had offended the temple god. What other reason could there be for this growing distaste for his raison d'être. Lakhvir Sher Singh was, for the first time in his life, afraid. He did not know anything else but the exultation of the kill. Then the invitation arrived from Malaya to hunt the Sumatran. A White Tiger. He had never seen one but his Indian soul, as old as the Ganges, knew it was written. *Sanjog*[127], destiny. The invitation was a pilgrimage to the god of his gift, the White Avatar.

Standing in the prehistoric Malayan jungle with fat leech anklets and bracelets, Lakhvir had an overwhelming sense of divine appointment. The lofty trees stood in eerie condescension as shafts of light began to float upwards in the primordial atrium. In a matter of minutes, he was stranded in total darkness. His senses kicked in to their keenest.

He knew he was not alone. And inexplicably, he knew *he* was the hunted. He braced himself, gun readied, as *it* brooded. Rarely skittish, something brushed his neck and he jerked around. There was nothing to focus on. At the same time, it was everywhere.

---

127   Sanjog – destiny.

Through years of practice he steeled his heart, quietly turning back in the direction of the camp. It was all he could do not to run. As he neared the camp, which was as noisy as a Chinese funeral house, he felt his chest contract, making him breathless. It was the same sensation he felt as a boy sitting in the car, approaching his grandfather's home in Amrita Nagar. Like a spring being wound up tight, ready to "twang" through the air when released, he would fly out of the car without touching the ground and vault into his Dada Ji's arms. Now Lucky Lakhvir felt the same tautness.

The Shikari quietly made a round of the stockades. The aboriginal trekkers were smoking cheroots, rifles in one hand. Without speaking, he communicated his unease to them. A shower of cheroots hit the ground as they cocked their rifles, eyes searching the jungle. Then, he headed for the Advisor's tent.

A Devi in white, with a river of black hair, caressed a harp, creating celestial sounds. Instantly Lakhvir knew she belonged to one of the tycoons. She must have been brought in when they went out for the fresh provisions. The Advisor, Bok and TK were sitting at a table covered with white English lace. It overflowed with silver girandoles, crystal glasses sparkling from lit candles and fine bone china. Conversation flooded in the fashion of pillow talk, words escaping in dribs and drabs. They were all nicely tired, ready for a kingly banquet before they turned in. It was clear they were waiting on Lady Hill.

'Ah Lucky, you're in time for tea', Sir Douglas purred. 'Was your little detour fruitful?'

'Good evening Sir... sincere apologies, but there a few things I have to attend to.'

'Oh, dinner's not for another three quarters of an hour. I'm sure we can wait, gentlemen? Bok...?'

Patriarch Bok, stout and robust with grey hair, was pinching some snuff in an onyx box to clear his catarrh.

'Yes, yes! The Chef will just delay the preparation of the Peking duck, and we're having cold soup, vichyssoise.'

'Teak...? Shall we wait?' Sir Douglas asked genially.

TK Abdullah's attention was on the girl. Lakhvir Singh knew she was his. It was in the girl's eyes. They were locked on TK's in a dream-like gaze. He had seen it so many times in the big cats he hunted, the bullet-ridden animal waiting for release. Abdullah could bend the girl anyway he wanted, she would meld into his demands.

'I can see that Stella's won herself another admirer,' the Advisor enthused, following the Shikari's gaze.

On the hunts in the past, Lakhvir had seen Maharajas lead young boys into their tents after all the guests had retired. He had averted his face to a depravity that made the animals tame by comparison, but there was something about the girl.

'She plays like a Devi. But she's a child,' he said, 'to be here.'

Teak Abdullah slanted a look at Lucky. Not one hair on the Tiger Wallah's face was sticking out. Like everyone else in the camp, he was fascinated by Lakhvir Singh's toiletry. Each morning, he would bathe in the cold stream nearby even though there were gallons of hot water. Returning with wet tresses hanging down to his waist, hair on his face in riotous disarray, he looked like the wild man of Borneo. With a tiny little comb, he would roll and twist his hair, tying it atop his head. Then a little tub of Fix-O teased the rowdy growth on Lucky's face into a super fine roll under the chin, twirled and tucked away by a string that ran to the knot on top of his head. Until the Fix-O dried, a fine ladies' hairnet would hold the beard close to Lakhvir Singh's face, as he wound on a black turban. The Tiger Wallah was stiff and starched in the sweltering jungle.

'I'm going to adopt Stella,' TK Abdullah challenged dismissively.

'Join us Lucky,' Sir Douglas said coaxingly, 'it will be...'

Lucky Sher Singh was no longer paying attention. His God-gift kicked in. The tiger was upon them and he waited for a shot to ring out from the stockades. Automatically he pulled his rifle off his shoulder and trained it into the dark recesses beyond the bamboo grave.

It's in the camp! he thought coldly. *Why aren't they shooting?!*

'Lucky?'

'Sir, the Sumatran, it's here! It's followed us back,' he said placidly above the dream sound of the harp. In the background the elephants were trumpeting their brains out. The smell of barbecued tiger steaks accosted the camp but the men around Lucky Sher Singh had dry mouths. They looked blankly at the Shikari.

'That's rather interesting, old chap.'

'You're sure you know what you're talking about?' demanded Patriarch Bok.

Teak snapped his fingers at his personal bodyguard. The man, a bulked up wall with eyes, immediately moved up behind him and fished out a revolver. Lakhvir's eyes slid like a blade, left to right, right to left. There was nothing in the shadows but the prickles on his neck were now running into the small of his back.

Arrogant one, he thought with disbelief, *walking straight into my camp.*

At the same time, the Tiger Wallah felt a grudging admiration at the tiger's audacity. The Sumatran was defying feline logic. Tigers only sought man's company when they were hungry. The White Sumatran had only just fed, the carcass of a rhinoceros had its unique paw prints all around it. And the bellowing gaur in the trap was also easy meat.

What's it doing?

The tiger was not stalking the camp for food. In his Indian soul,

Lakhvir Sher Singh believed the tiger was coming for him. It was *kismet*[128], his audience with the White Avatar, the Dada Ji of his gift.

'Sir Douglas, I believe' he said, breath rasping in his throat, 'we should...'

From the corner of his eye he saw the silvery moon glide and land with a soft sigh on the grass behind Stella. No one else saw it, and no one else heard it.

'... stay very still.'

It was a few seconds before they all became aware of the tiger standing behind the girl. In the moonlight it looked platinum white, almost like an illusion. The black of the jungle around the tiger seemed to expand and contract as the Sumatran's chest heaved, its head lowered.

It's not real, Lakhvir thought silently, easing his loaded rifle in its direction.

'My God!' whispered Sir Douglas.

'Shoot!' croaked Patriarch Bok, his snuffbox falling from nerveless fingers.

'The girl...' the Shikari said quietly, unable to take the shot because Stella was in the tiger's path. She had stopped playing. Eyes wide with fear she was looking at him and the gun pointed at her.

'Just shoot!' hissed Teak Abdullah venomously.

Then Lady Hill screamed, emerging from the side where the tents were. The tiger turned, and as it lunged, Lakhvir squeezed the trigger. Lustrous lamé leapt through the air, an impossible distance of ten metres and suddenly he was flying. Something wet and silky lashed him, ripping off his turban and he heard a mighty crash. When he got up on his feet again, the dining table was ripped in two, glass and china

---

128   Kismet – divine will.

everywhere and the lace tablecloth scrolling with fire. All around him there were screams of horror amidst a thunderous volley of gunfire.

'*Rimau*[129]! Rimau!'

By the time Lucky got to the stockade, four people were dead. One Tamil sweeper had lost his head to the tiger and two had been caught in the crossfire from the aboriginal trekkers. Three cooks were severely burnt from cauldrons of boiling water that had been over-turned. Scores were hurt and one trampled to death by the elephants in the pandemonium. As Lady Hill clung, trembling, to her husband, there was no doubt in anyone's mind, the hunt was over. The sweepers, some wailing piteously, were not willing to stay another minute in the camp. Only the night constrained them from leaving immediately. They huddled together behind a circle of drumbeaters, who thrashed their instruments frenziedly. A patrol of trekkers stood guard over them, while the Ghurkhas formed a human wall around the Advisor and his friends.

When Lakhvir Singh returned after checking the outskirts of the camp, Lady Hill extricated herself from her husband and ran to him.

'Lucky, my dear! My dear, you saved our lives.'

Before Lakhvir could respond, Abdullah shoved his bodyguard aside and eyeballed the Tiger Wallah darkly.

'You missed!' he berated bitterly. 'A waste of my money!'

Lakhvir Sher Singh felt a need to bash the man's head in with his rifle butt. Deliberately he turned. Stella was still on her stool, her white organza dress clinging to her legs. She had wet herself.

'The child should *never* have been brought here.'

'A crack shot would have got me *my* tiger,' snarled Teak Abdullah, enraged by Lakhvir's words.

---

129   Rimau – Tiger, in Malay.

'If Lucky hadn't been here, Eleanor would have been taken,' Sir Douglas said firmly, as he too stepped forward to clasp the Shikari on the shoulder.

Then for the first time, the Advisor noticed the red streak down the Shikari's face, shoulder and hairy arm.

'You're not hurt?!'

'No! ... no, I believe I hit the tiger.'

Teak Abdullah too, suddenly saw the blood.

'... tiger blood!?' he exclaimed in an incredulous tone, eyes widening.

Before Lakhvir could answer, the timber tycoon put out his hand and touched the blood on the Tiger Wallah's arm with his forefinger. Then he rubbed his finger with his thumb, almost relishing the texture, before bringing it up to his nose for a sniff.

'You're covered by the blood,' he said, envy loud in his voice.

'If the tiger is injured...' Sir Douglas asked hopefully.

Lakhvir Singh nodded in agreement.

'I will go in the morning with Anak. The camp must disband... the other trekkers will stay and see all are out safely.'

Nobody dared to argue with the turbanless Shikari. Hair flayed off his head, face congealed with blood, his eyes were red with unshed disappointment. He looked dreadful, like a voodoo doll that had been rescued from a witchdoctor's fire. Lakhvir Sher Singh knew he had met with the God of his gift. And it was waiting for him in the jungle.

20

FROM THE MAIN ROAD, gas lamps and torches blazed down to the Club and the adjoining field. Army trucks were unloading revellers from the innards of rubber estates and vegetable farms. Heading for the Pesta, boys jumped off with Tarzan cries and "yahoos". Those going to the Club were of a different coterie. They came in cars, impatiently tooting and beeping people out of the way. In the carpark between the Club and the *Padang*[130], Alistair could hear the uniformed Boy's Brigade, giving those heading to the Pesta an earful.

'Excuse me! Use the side lane. This is for Club members...'

'*Yinneh dei*[131]*!*... Vai soh (sic) serious *thambi*[132]??... Appy New Yer.' (sic)

The jocular placations from the interlopers were a clear indication that nothing was going to spoil the celebrations. Colourful clothes, jasmine flowers, red beetle-stained teeth and an accompaniment of spitting... It still shocked Alistair. The Malays and Indians, betel nut addicts, excelled in distance, while the Chinese hawked unashamedly. He felt a great urge to follow the stream of people spilling onto the

---

130   Padang – a field.

131   Yinneh dei – What's up?

132   Thambi – Younger brother.

Padang but he needed to get to the Club and debrief. He had just returned from Jelebu, where he had to readjust a boundary for a communist-free "white" village.

Several Muslim gravestones had appeared on a plot allocated to Chinese pig farmers. Laden with ancient maps of *mukims*[133] and land titles, Alistair headed for the malarial boondocks. Sitting on a mat, surrounded by odiferous farmers with twisted hands and black sullen toenails, he found out about the disastrous tiger hunt. In the shadows, the faces acquired harsh lines. Even though they talked in mellow tones, the pace like cows chewing cud, the conversation around the tiger gave the game away. Alistair realised the outward deference was only a mask. Hunched over blueprints, he was painfully aware of his neck and shoulder, vulnerable to a cruel Keris from behind.

'... plucked the head off the Hindoo, like a ripe papaya.'

'... just a warning. Tok spared the Advisor's wife.'

'... the Chinaman Bok, no respect or culture. How would he feel if we went to China and killed their dragon?'

'Clearly this is not his country!'

'If not for the Sultan, I won't sign this paper.'

'Abdullah, may Allah forgive him, destroying our forests for greed.'

'...and that *Bengali*[134] hunter, going into our jungle alone. Tok will teach him respect!'

Fortunately, his talent in speaking their language gave room for some bloodletting. It was a marathon five days. Gallons of sweet black

---

133 Mukims – subdivisions of districts.

134 Bengali – generic term for a Sikh Punjabi in Malaysia.

coffee kept the ruminating and rambling bearable into the nights. This was followed by a two-day march through a mangrove swamp which took them to the gravesites. And finally a "floral bath" over the graves involving prayers from the Koran. Then and only then, did they concede to having the land remapped.

Alistair avoided the main entrance of Planter's Inn where a constellation of medalled men awaited the High Commissioner. He took the door, which led into the boutique teahouse facing the sea. The oak panel doors, which privatised the tearoom from the formal Chamberlain Hall, had been dismantled. He sucked in his breath. The grand ballroom glittered with a six-tier chandelier and a hundred tables with tulle traipsing away like ballerinas. Tucked to the side, the Malay Regiment band played a Strauss waltz.

'Excuse me Mr Pierce.'

It was the Advisor's secretary, Captain Rutherford.

'Are there any last minute instructions?'

'Could you keep an eye on Sir Douglas's guests from the fishing village?'

Apart from the main table it was free seating. This was again, an order from Sir Gerald and seemed to result in a siege mentality on the part of the civil servants. Tables closer to the dance floor, in front of the stage, were already filled by the British. Instinct told Alistair that Ummah Ibrahim and his sons would be outside.

On the terrace, the mood was carnival, almost as if it had spilled over from the Pesta. Voluble male conversation interspersed with feminine laughter. The Headman, Ummah, arms folded over his chest, was chatting with a distinguished-looking Indian man. It was

Dr Azariah, the vet. Alistair walked over to them.

'Ismael, I didn't save your life. Prince did!' the Doctor said, chuckling.

'I've never used my catapult on dogs after that. I can't believe that I slept through all the fun.'

'You mean "trouble",' Isa said, his hand on Ismael's shoulder.

'If I remember, *you* started the trouble Isa. Ah, Mister Alistair, good evening.'

The sweet smell of 4711 Eau de Cologne rolled off them.

They must have used a whole bottle, Alistair thought.

'Alistair, I was just telling Ummah, I'm riding on Ismael's coattails. I only retrieved a bullet. He's the brave one!'

Quietly, a slim comely girl of about fifteen came up from behind the doctor and slipped her arm into his. She had a touch of gold to her tanned olive skin, with a waterfall of silky hair to her waist, and hazel eyes.

'Hello Sweetheart. This is my goddaughter, Mariam. Ummah you've met her before...'

Ummah's face beamed as he looked at the fawn-like girl.

'Yes, she saved Ismael's life. I mean the second time,' he said apologetically to Azariah. 'First time you operated on him, the second time she diverted the soldiers. Do you remember?'

'I remember him,' she said shyly, pointing at Isa.

'Isa, do you remember Mariam?' Ummah asked, as Ismael looked at his brother in amazement.

'Yes, Mariam... the soldiers wanted to shoot her,' Isa said, his face lighting up.

'We played with the kittens, you took one of them home...'

'Isa brought a kitten home... *Cinta*[135],' Ismael said slowly, looking at Isa then at Mariam.

---

135   Cinta – love (*pronounced chinta*).

'Ismael never got the chance to thank you... he was asleep,' Ummah said cueing his son.

'Thank you,' Ismael said obediently, putting his hand out for something manly to do, embarrassed at "being asleep".

Pressing into Dr Azariah, she coyly put her hand out. With the slightest of touches, she withdrew her hand, her eyes flicking off him.

'Thank you Mariam,' Ummah reiterated, this time not cueing his son.

To Ismael, it sounded as if his father was cueing him again because culturally, it was rude not to address the person by name, or title.

'Thank you Mariam,' he echoed automatically, as Isa looked on amused.

This time she laughed and looked at him in the face.

'You're welcome Ismael.'

'Here you are Mariam. I see you've found him! Azariah, good to see you.'

'Alvis...'

Adrian D'Alvisse was a gargantuan of a man. His petite Malay wife, Salimah or Sally, standing beside him, enlarged him further. Dark and commanding, he belonged to the distinguished D'Alvisse family. The Eurasian in his line had well and truly been compromised. He looked *Tamil*[136], not *Serani*[137], but nobody would have dared insult him or his family. Old man D'Alvisse, one of the few engineers in Malaya, had died building the Burma railway.

The D'Alvisse men had a signature pencil-line goatee beard. It was the Spanish touch. Ironically, through the Eurasian bloodline, he was Mariam's closest living relative. After the war she lived with

---

136   Tamil – Dark-skinned South Indians.

137   Serani – Local term for Eurasians.

him and his Malay wife Sally, in Seremban.

'Pa Cik Ummah,' exclaimed Sally joyfully, as she reached out for Ummah's hand. *'Salaam waalaikum.'*

Everyone knew Sally. She sold semi-precious stones in the Peninsula and she left no kampong unturned.

'When Mariam finishes school, she's going to help Sally with the business,' volunteered Dr Azariah, putting his arm around Mariam.

She hugged him back, smiling and half nodding. It was clear for all to see she adored him. Just then, a high frequency screech split the air, drawing grimaces. The Master of Ceremonies was at the microphone, all fingers and thumbs.

'Ladies and Gentlemen, please go to your tables and be upstanding to welcome His Excellency the High Commissioner of Malaya, Sir Gerald and Lady Edith Templer, and the Honourable Advisor Sir Douglas and Lady Eleanor Hill.'

'I've got orders to sit with Lady Hill. Mariam, I'll see you afterwards,' Azariah said. 'Ummah, will you be alright?'

'We're sitting here in the fresh air with our friends.'

'Come on! We've got a table closer to the dance floor,' Sally said to Mariam.

'Bye Isa. Bye Ismael,' Mariam said demurely to the boys who could not get their eyes off her, as she walked away with D'Alvisse.

Alistair glanced at the table where Ummah's friends were sitting. All Malays, Alistair recognised a couple of them. One was the Sultan's personal aide, a gentleman with impeccable manners whom he met at one of Sir Douglas's dinners.

Why did anyone think he needed our help? Alistair thought as Ummah took his seat, and he headed into the ballroom.

21

SEARCHING AROUND THE HALL he saw a table with familiar faces from the Land Office. Ashman Lahud was amongst them and he hesitated. Turning around, he saw a couple of British Officers and their English girlfriends sitting with several Chinese gentlemen and ladies. Fun and warmth emanated from the group. The chair immediately in front of him was vacant.

'May I join you?' he asked everyone in general, hands on the back of the chair.

The woman in the next seat looked up at him haughtily over her bare shoulder, flashing emerald eyes. Chestnut hair flowed in a finger wave to a clasp of white orchids at a delicate neck. Alistair realised he must have been staring because she lifted her hand to her décolletage as if to ward off his eyes.

'I beg your pardon...,' he said disconcerted.

'Why not, Ivy? Seeing as Cuthbert hasn't turned up,' said one of the British Officers.

'No, please, if there's someone coming...'

A debonair Chinese man of about thirty-five, stood up. He graciously put his hand out.

'Bok's my name... Bok Kai Seng.'

Immediately Alistair knew who he was. Son of Patriarch Bok, he was liaising directly with the Dunlap headquarters in London, making them offers for their rubber acreage. Dunlap in turn redirected the letters back to the Crown Office in Negeri Sembilan. His tenacity was displeasing the Sultans and Sir Douglas was handling the matter himself.

'... and you are Alistair Pierce, Project Manager of Crown Property and Personal Assistant to Sir Douglas,' finished Bok.

Alistair was not at all surprised that Bok knew who he was. There was something formidable about the Chinese man. From his accent it was clear he had studied in England but this was only window dressing. There was a spirit on the man that was as ancient as the Mongolian warlords he descended from.

'Ivy, I think we should show Alistair some of the hospitality we're famous for,' Bok said charmingly to the female.

Before anyone could respond, a hand reached out from behind and grasped Alistair's elbow.

'Mr Pierce, why don't you join us Sir?'

Alistair turned around to look into the face of a middle-aged man, with hazel eyes giving away his Eurasian bias.

'Roland Leembruggen at your service,' he said warmly, putting his hands on the woman's shoulders. 'I assure you that you'll enjoy our company more than my nieces and her friends.'

Guests from the next table erupted in hearty agreement. With light eyes and swarthy complexions, Alistair immediately knew they were his hockey team.

'Please feel free to sit where you like. The choice is beauty or wisdom,' Bok said slyly.

Alistair's eyes slid to Ivy. She looked at him challengingly and then turned her head away.

'He's welcome to the seat,' she said in a bored tone.

Alistair was completely taken aback. She was the first local, even though she was Eurasian, to behave with such haughtiness towards him as a British man. The two British officers at her table avoided eye contact with him, which was astounding. He had heard all their disparaging remarks about Eurasian girls.

'What do you call a Serani girl who's got English, Dutch or Portuguese blood?'

'Don't know... tell me!'

'A bitzer... she's a bit of this, bit of that, and all black velvet where it counts.'

'Watch out for their ancestry old boy. They're more Anglo-Saxon than we are.'

'... except for their shrimp paste and *debal*[138] curry.'

Her hauteur and the thought of Bok Junior taking shots at the Land Office all evening, decided it for him.

'Thank you Mr Bok, but I will join Mr Leembruggen.'

'Well done Sir, wise men have to stick together,' Roland said, barely suppressing his mirth.

The band struck up "Rule Britannia". Applause and cheers broke out as the main doors of the Chamberlain ballroom were thrown open. In strode a dapper Sir Douglas Hill, one hand in the pocket of a black dinner jacket. On his arm was a chiselled Lady Templer in a midnight blue dress, white bow over her boyish bosom. Behind them by five seconds was Lady Hill. Gone was the khaki-trouser huntress. Wearing a cream ballroom gown, her hair was held up by a diamante slide. The "oohs" and "ahhs" however, were for the man on whose arm she walked. He was not very tall but the cut glass green turban, with its defiant flounce and matching tunic made him stand out like a

---

138   debal – devil.

Maharaja. Lucky Lakhvir Sher Singh, the Tiger Wallah.

Finally, in walked the Supremo, Sir Gerald Templer grinning like a beaver. Light shining on a receding forehead, moustache standing out over the gap in his front teeth, he looked deceptively friendly. By his side was a fatherly bespectacled Malay man in a *songkok*[139] and a richly embroidered royal yellow sarong. It was Prince Tunku Abdul Rahman, who was leading the locals to demonstrate against the formation of the Malayan Union, which would delay independence. Sir Gerald was making a loud statement.

'Get ready to hand over! Your time is up.'

With "God Save the Queen" the VIP table was seated and without too many preliminaries dinner was served. Throughout the first course, Alistair noticed Roland Leembruggen clear his throat, inconspicuous as it was, and direct the boys to the right choice of cutlery with his eyes. It was awkward as the waiters hovered with decanters of red and white wine. The young men had already used them as water goblets. He kept his face in his soup as slurps escaped around him. Behind him, Ivy was singing in accompaniment to the Gershwin rendition of "Things are looking up".

> *'Bitter was my cup*
> *But no more will I be the mourner*
> *For I've certainly turned the corner*
> *Oh things are looking up*
> *Since love looked up at me.'*

'She's got a great voice hasn't she?' Roland said proudly, 'She takes after her Dutch grandmother.'

---

139 Songkok – a Fez (hat) worn by Malay men.

In spite of the warnings, Alistair had no doubts that Ivy Lazaroo was a thoroughbred. There was nothing Asian about her to look at and she spoke with a hint of an English accent. From the corner of his eye he watched her between courses, her food barely eaten, as she fashionably held an ivory cigarette holder.

Just before the end of the main course of Boeuf Wellington, Roland signalled over a waiter, who whisked away his half-eaten dinner.

'Don't stop boys... carry on. They're making me sing for my supper,' he said roguishly to Alistair, pulling out some paper from his coat pocket. 'I've been called to tell a story before sweets.'

The Master of Ceremonies made a timely announcement.

'Ladies and Gentlemen, His Excellency Sir Gerald Templer would like to call upon his friend, Mr Roland Leembruggen to tell us a story that has found its way to Her Majesty. Mr Lazaroo, if you would be so kind...'

With a heave, the Eurasian stood up, almost taking the table with him. Some of the glasses and cutlery jumped.

'Oh bother!' Roland cursed, as water splashed him.

'Uncle Rolly! It's only a spot of water,' Ivy said, as she got up quick smart, and dabbed at his coat with a napkin.

'My notes... they're all wet!'

'You didn't need any notes with the Japs,' Ivy spoke quietly, removing the paper from his hands, 'and you certainly don't need notes with *them*.'

We're them, Alistair thought mildly surprised.

He watched fascinated, as she propelled Roland forward, her shoulder blades the wings of a dove. He could smell her, tiger lilies with a hint of cinnamon.

As Roland approached the podium, there was a round of polite applause. It was mainly the locals who showed their appreciation. Many of the British had finished with their dinner and were ordering alcoholic refills. Chatter flitted as chairs were pushed back from tables, coats unbuttoned and trousered legs crossed elegantly. Alistair, too, pulled his chair sideways so that he could see Roland.

Just before he reached the podium, Roland had to go past the main table and Sir Gerald stood up. A handshake turned into a hefty bear hug. A little rustle of asides could be heard. Now everyone was paying attention.

'Thank you Sir Gerald,' Roland said over the microphone. 'Malaya's going to lose a good friend. Ahemm... I've been asked to tell a little story but I'm afraid I've lost my notes.'

There was general laughter as Roland, with the measured pace of an orator, picked up the glass of water on the podium, and took a sip.

'I hope you'll bear with an old man whose memory's been shot to hell...'

Sir Gerald retorted something back to him and there was a burst of hearty laughter from the main table. Alistair strained to catch what was being said.

'I'm sure you'll keep me on my toes Sir Gerald,' Roland said audibly over the mike.

A twitch swept the room at Roland's liberties about Sir Gerald's short fuse.

'Well, I'd better get on with my story...'

'When the Japanese soldiers marched into Malaya, I was in Malacca, at what we Eurasians call "Padri sa Chang"– Land of the Holy Fathers – Portuguese Settlement. Just prior to the war in July 1941, I was working as a stenographer in the War Affairs Unit. I used to overhear, mind you, it wasn't eavesdropping, that the Japanese were planning to invade Malaya. Well, there was a Japanese photographer in Malacca, so I thought I would get friendly with the fellow and he was more than happy to give me a book on how to speak Japanese. Very talented chap this photographer. He cleared out back to Japan in October 1941 and came back in December 1941 as a Captain...'

Alistair could see the side of Ivy's face as he looked in the direction of the podium. She was watching her Uncle with great pride, her chin cupped in the palm of her hand. His eyes slid down from the little gold wedding band on her finger, to her neck. Sensing his eyes, she turned and looked at him. He refused to look away and it was she who broke their gaze.

'I had this book on how to speak Japanese and I started teaching our children in Portuguese Settlement some basic sentences. I was going to face the Japs when they came... and, come they did! Marching straight into Portuguese Settlement. Well, the first thing I did was bow down and say, "We welcome you to our village." The children came rushing out with some sweetened rose water and that day,' Leembruggen declared dramatically, 'they put up a paper on the board outside our village - "FREE ZONE". Nobody could harass our children and women.'

Pockets of half-hearted applause broke out in the ballroom. Roland Leembruggen was walking on ice. "Collaboration" was the key word in most minds.

'Many of you have heard of the hockey team that played for the Imperial government during the Occupation. Well, I was the manager of the young Malayan boys who formed the Nippon National team!'

Now every eye was glued to him.

'Some have thought us... DISLOYAL but we were in a devilish situation. We didn't want to be dancing with the enemy but at the same time we were left to fend for ourselves. So we came up with our very own game plan, thanks to my nephew Bonny.'

22

"Japanese Navy bomb US base. Victory Imminent!"

Bonnifacio Lazaroo straightened up from over the chase of the press, satisfied with the typeset. He was responsible for the composition and imposition of the type but the message was dictated by Akiro Kabota. Once the process was at lock-up he was physically removed from the printing press. Only the Japanese personnel would operate the hand press of the *Malai Baru*[140] newspaper, which was installed in the hall of the King George the Fifth School.

It was yet another rehash of the Pearl Harbor attack. The bobbin holding the roll of paper was not seated correctly and Bonnifacio Lazaroo passionlessly slammed it into place. Picking up a rag, he wiped his hands clean. All was ready now for the inkbottles to be topped up and the press to roll. His job was done and he clattered the metallic type galley with his tools onto the bench as he walked out. The acoustics of the school hall, converted into an office, amplified the noise he was making in the graveyard atmosphere. The dozen Japanese civilians in blue overalls scurried silently. Instinct told him there had been an upbraiding,

---

140   Malai Baru – New Malaya.

even though he was not privy to their meetings with Kolonel Kabota.

Kolonel Akiro Kabota watched him from a little glassed alcove, a troubled man. The Head of Psychological Warfare sorely needed to unload but there was no one, not a single person, to share his growing fears with. While the JMA printed their own propaganda on the war in Europe, underground pamphlets plastered on abandoned buildings were telling a different tale. The true story, much to the horror of the top Japanese echelon. In every town where a goodwill hockey tournament was held, the pamphlets would surface one week later. It was a deliberate strategy targeted to undo the goodwill of his propaganda campaign. Kabota was beginning to dread the tournaments which had given him such personal ecstatic pleasure.

The occupation in Malaya was becoming farcical. Throughout the peninsula, discouragement had settled on his soldiers. Many were wandering around listlessly, leaving posts unguarded. They did not expect the war to have lasted so long and pined for their island homes. A dozen soldiers had disappeared after obsessive musings of an invasion from America. Kabota had to organise a bombardment of Japanese songs on gramophones and "messages" from the Emperor over a loud hailer on the fringes of the jungle. Only six soldiers responded, the rest, swallowed by the jungle.

Kabota looked malevolently at Bonnifacio. As a psychologist, he knew that with the passing of time, a bond between captor and captive, inevitably formed. It happened with the locals who were now cooperating and actively trading in the new economy with the Japanese dollar or *duit pisang*[141]. No one was going anywhere. They were all trapped, but the English man remained inviolable. For the

---

141   Duit pisang – banana money in Malaya because the Japanese dollars issued had the motif of banana trees on the ten dollar notes.

first time, Kabota felt that Bonnifacio was slipping out of his grip.

I wonder what he would be like if he knew his family is dead, thought Kabota sadistically, watching Bonny walk towards the guard to be patted down.

On his way home, Bonnifacio Lazaroo dropped in at the "Good Health" sports shop. The proprietor, Tan Chai Yee, was already closing the shutters of his windows. Balls hung like clusters of grapes in fishing nets, while badminton racquets lined the walls. The hockey sticks were tossed on top of a broad shelf in the rear end of the shop. On the shelf below, in line with the customers' eye, strung up like bunting, were bright yellow jerseys embellished with bloody red suns.

'Closing already... curfew,' Tan said, disconcerted to find an English man in his shop.

'I've come to exchange my hockey stick, the binding's coming off at the handle.'

'Tuan got a receipt?' Tan asked, peering out through the shutters nervously.

'No, are you new here? I remember the number of the receipt, it's *136*[142].'

'Who sold you these sticks?' Tan said quietly, rooted at the open shutters as Bonny walked up to the counter and plonked the sticks down noisily.

'Old shop owner, Lam Thye, said I could exchange them here if there was a problem.'

---

142   136 – a code for Force 136, a British World War II resistance movement operating in South East Asia.

Two soldiers who trailed Bonnifacio everywhere for the last three years, meandered into the shop.

'Why's the shop still open?' one asked perfunctorily as the other half-heartedly took his gun off his shoulder.

Both Tan and Bonny bowed down immediately.

'... new hockey sticks...' Tan blurted out, speaking to the soldier's feet, his shoulders tensed for a blow.

'I regret the inconvenience, but I've got to get the hockey sticks for the National team. There's a match in Ipoh,' Bonnifacio said in Japanese.

The soldiers lost interest in the two men, and started wandering around the shop.

'I've got some hockey sticks that you can exchange with,' Tan said, as he moved to the rear of the shop and pulled out a high three-legged stool. Climbing up, he foraged for a bundle of hockey sticks and threw them on some bales of cloth. Bonny picked up the new hockey sticks whilst Tan got off the stool. Giving them a quick look-over, Bonny nodded his approval.

'I'll take these sticks, but the next time I won't exchange them. I'll want my money back,' Bonny said sharply, as he tied them up with some string and slung them over his shoulder.

It had started drizzling. Steam rose from the macadamised road in the settling dusk. Dogged by the soldiers, Bonny went straight home to the sparse backroom he rented in the government yards in Brickfields, near the railway lines. He waited outside as the soldiers went in and had their customary look around. After stoking his little paraffin lamp, he "locked" the door by wedging a chair against the door knob. Then he latched the door leading into the kitchen and bathroom. He had to keep out the pesky worm-infested urchins who were his neighbours' children. At the same time, they were his best friends. Their voices would fall away whenever the soldiers

approached. Outside they were playing *"Kaunda Kaundi"*[143]. The curfew was more relaxed inside the ghetto-like government yards.

Sitting on the bed, Bonny picked up one of the hockey sticks.
He propped it upright between his legs, and pulled out a penknife.
Expertly he slipped the sharp tip of the knife under the edge of the
tightly sealed binding at the top of the handle. In a matter of minutes, he had peeled off three inches of leather. There was a thin hairline cut on the wood. Using both hands and a great deal of strength,
he unscrewed the top. Sticking his forefinger inside the hollow of the
handle, he carefully pulled out a roll of paper slotted firmly inside. It
was a poster. He got off the bed and spread it out, pulling the paraffin
lamp close.

*Allied Forces crush German resistance and capture Rome. Europe
invasion is on.*

Bonny Lazaroo lifted a clenched fist as his face contorted in a
silent scream. Then with a twisted smile he rolled the poster up and
reinserted it into the handle. Each hockey stick carried a poster.
Revenge was not sweet. It was powerful, and it made him tumescent.
Worm-like shame gave way to an illicit virility. He now looked forward to the tournaments and sitting in the same car with Kolonel
Kabota, who personally transported the hockey sticks as souvenirs for
the locals. It was almost erotic, Kabota with his hand fingering and
touching the hockey sticks.

Bonnifacio Lazaroo felt a forbidden pleasure.

---

143   Kaunda Kaundi – a game involving two sticks. A larger stick used as a bat and a small
one like a ball. A cheap game for children who gathered to play.

Part 7

1953 – NEW YEAR'S EVE
PLANTER'S INN - PORT DICKSON
BRITISH MALAYA

"What then did you expect when you unbound the gag that had muted those black mouths? That they would chant your praises? Did you think that when those heads that our fathers had forcibly bowed down to the ground were raised again, you would find adoration in their eyes?"

Orphée Noir – **Jean-Paul Sartre.**

23

IN THE CHAMBERLAIN HALL the guests were google-eyed as Roland Leembruggen paused dramatically on the podium.

'The truth be known, my nephew Bonny Lazaroo, was working for the British-led Allied Resistance Force 136. The distribution of the posters were our *own* psychological warfare to demoralise the Japs. Our boys in the National Hockey team, they risked their lives for freedom!'

This time the applause in the Chamberlain ballroom was thunderous.

'... but some of us died,' Leembruggen said, putting out his hand to stay the ovation. 'Bonny Lazaroo, my nephew, was one of them. Someone from the *MPAJA*[144] turned informant but he refused to give up his sources. His Majesty King George posthumously conferred upon Bonny Lazaroo the Order of the British Empire. His sister is very proud to wear it today... Miss Ivy Lazaroo.'

Quietly she rose to her feet and Alistair noticed the medal on her right breast as Sir Douglas got up and walked over to Roland at the podium. With a handshake, the Eurasian stepped back from the microphone.

'Ladies and gentlemen, the National Hockey team,' Sir Douglas

---

144   MPAJA – Malayan Peoples' Anti-Japanese Army.

said, looking over his horn-rimmed glasses at the faces in the banqueting hall. 'Boys please, up to the front! Alistair? Ahh, would you accompany Encik Ummah and his sons please?'

As Ummah, Ismael and Isa stepped up to the stage, Alistair's eye caught Ashman signalling him over. Short of being rude it was unavoidable. A cut glass with scotch and water was neatly put before him as he sat down.

'Alis, I took the liberty... scotch and ice, if I remember,' Ashman Lahud said warmly.

'I hope I'm not taking anyone's seat.'

'David's too busy being Master of Ceremonies,' a buxom brunette said with a flirtatious pout.

'Alis, you know Captain David Soames. This is his wife Babs... Barbara.'

Alistair was transported back to the cliff face and the yellow Sunbeam-Talbot nestling in amongst the banana fronds.

'And of course you know the others.'

Alistair was conscious of the bigwigs, from the army and navy. Through *Brave New World*, he had met William Bland, Secretary of War with his matronly wife, and Sylvester Smithers or Sly, the Press Officer. Leon Porter, the Advisor's physician had nursed him through his malaria. They were all familiar to him, save one.

'This is Maude MacKeerne, a friend of Babs from the Bridge Club,' Ashman said following Alistair's gaze.

Big boned and earthy, in her thirties, she looked as if she had stepped out of a croft. Her sequined evening dress could not disguise the fact that she looked like a horse breaker, in amongst well-heeled pedigree. Her hand, as Alistair took it, was hard. It was her eyes that disturbed him. Dark pools of bitterness, they were his mother's eyes.

'I'll only be able to stay until the boys get off the stage,' Alistair said to Ashman, as he raised his glass in a toast.

'I'm sure they'll be able to find their way home, wagging their tails behind them.'

'They *are* heroes, after all.'

Alistair noticed that Maude had two glasses of gin and tonic lined up in front of her. He looked away. On the stage Sir Douglas was handing out ribbons and certificates.

'Looks like every man and his donkey's being decorated.'

'Templer's treacherous you know. He's rubbing our noses in it,' Sly Smithers seethed, stubbing out his cigarette in the bread and butter pudding which had only just been placed in front of him.

Alistair was taken aback at his vitriol and incivility but no one else seemed bothered.

'He's making us jump through hoops, engineering this farce. They've all come crawling out of the woodwork tonight.'

Alistair averted his face to the podium, joining in the applause as the stage cleared. He was looking for his excuse to leave but Ummah and his sons were being convoyed to a side exit. Sir Douglas was on to the next of Her Majesty's friends.

'On behalf of Sir Gerald Templer, I would like to introduce Prince Tunku Abdul Rahman. His wisdom has been invaluable in our preparation for Malaya's Independence.'

'Excuse me, at this point a visit to the latrine is in order,' Sly said with a supercilious sneer, standing up.

'His Royal Highness the Prince and other young Malay leaders were being trained at the Syonan Koa-Kunrenjo in Singapore by the Japanese...' William Bland said half apologetically to Alistair, who looked appalled at the lack of decorum.

'I don't think there's anything wrong with covering your bets,' Ashman interjected. 'I hate to point it out but we did leave them to fend for themselves. I would have done the same.'

'I hear Templer's going to fight his own personal war with the communists when he leaves,' baited William Bland, smoothly changing the subject. 'He's linking up with the Yanks and chemical warfare.'

'He's gone native, just look at the people he's brought in tonight,' Babs said unhappily.

'Half-breeds and *rangatangs*,[145] that's the new Club requirement,' spat Maude, taking a big gulp of her drink. 'Excuse me, I need some fresh air.'

She had put away three shots of gin and tonic in the short time Alistair had joined their table. Her face was blotchy and she looked inebriated.

'I'll come with you,' Leon Porter offered chivalrously, getting ready to accompany her.

'No need! I can look after myself,' Maude said sharply.

To have accepted his offer meant that she was out of control. They watched her walk, in the way drunks walk, to hide their drunkenness. Gaze fixed on the door, she zigzagged in straight lines from table to table, holding on to the back of chairs momentarily. Alistair looked at Ashman.

'She's a friend of Babs. Her husband's run off with the domestic... one of the girls from the village.'

As coffee and liqueur were served, Alistair excused himself and returned to his table which was empty. He looked over at Ivy Lazaroo. The seat next to her was still vacant but she had put her little evening bag on it, with a silk scarf over the back. Several British officers were hovering trying to gain her attention.

---

145   Rangatangs – Orang-Utan. A dig at early forest dwelling humans, here linking them to primates.

Poor idiots, he thought, wondering why her fiancé had not turned up.

'Sir Douglas would like you to join his table for a drink Mr Pierce,' Captain Rutherford said approaching him.

The seating arrangements on the main table had changed like elsewhere. Sir Gerald Templer had uprooted himself and was doing the rounds introducing the Malay Prince, Tunku. Lady Hill and Lady Templer had Dr Azariah sandwiched between them. Lakhvir Sher Singh, in his cut glass green turban, was listening to Alice Azariah, his head bobbing from side to side.

'Ah Alistair, I'd like you to meet some friends of mine. Mr Teak Abdullah and Miss Stella Loh.'

A rotund man of about fifty, with a mole on his cheekbone, his wealth spilled over onto the gorgeous nymphet by his side. In a red Dupioni silk dress, with matching pearl necklace and earrings, she had on a white mink collar.

'I'm pleased to meet you Mr Abdullah... Miss Loh, I hope you're enjoying the evening.'

'I is enjoy, sank you (sic).'

'Stella will be working with Shaw Brothers in Hong Kong,' Abdullah cut in as he gyrated the glass balloon of cognac plugged in his stubby hand. For some absurd reason Alistair thought of an udder.

'I'm sorry the Sumatran got away Sir. They say it's an honour even to have got so close.'

'It was truly magnificent. I keep thinking I dreamt it and yes, an honour. Lucky had the beast in his sight, it was so close.'

'Total waste! The beast was worth a fortune...' Abdullah said rancorously.

'Couldn't *you* have gone after it, Sir?'

'The elephants were distraught, too unpredictable and we couldn't push the sweepers... I'm afraid the attack on the camp broke their spirits.'

'We heard the Sumatran may have been injured?'

Alistair became aware that Lucky and Mrs Azariah had stopped talking, and were listening, waiting for the answer.

'We don't actually know. Lucky went after it but he came back with a fever. Must have caught a chill.'

'You didn't catch malaria, I hope,' Alice Azariah asked maternally.

'No. But I couldn't get out of bed,' Lakhvir Singh said in a thick, scratchy voice. It was quite clear that he was struggling physically and emotionally.

'*Celaka!*[146] Just one shot away!' bemoaned Teak Abdullah.

'These things happen,' Sir Douglas said philosophically. 'And Lucky here saved our lives. I'm privileged to have met India's best tiger hunter.'

'I'll take Stella to see the chamber where the Japanese tortured prisoners,' Teak retorted dismissively.

As Abdullah and Stella turned to leave, Ashman Lahud walked up and neatly intercepted the teak tycoon.

'Mr Abdullah, Ashman at your service Sir. I'm going to be the new representative for Royce Bofors,' he said suavely, shaking Abdullah's hand.

'Royce Bofors... isn't Sir Martin Magnus the Chairman? Yes, I met him in Hong Kong,' Abdullah said thoughtfully. 'The company's going to do well, the CTs are your biggest asset here.'

'Get Lucky some fresh sea air,' Sir Douglas said quietly to Alistair. 'Teak threw a fine tantrum when the tiger got away... and he's not been himself.'

---

146 Celaka – a Malay curse word that can vary from 'damn you' – to 'disaster'.

On the terrace, the noise from the *Pesta*[147] spilled over to the Club. Alistair was surprised by the number of locals milling around the white fence as he and Lakhvir Singh stood companionably.'

'May I join you?' Roland Leembruggen asked, coming up from behind them.

'Yes of course,' Alistair said, as he made the introductions. From the corner of his eye he saw Ummah and his sons approaching him, and he knew instinctively that they were coming to check out the Shikari.

'Encik Ummah, have you had coffee?'

'... *Dah kenyang*[148],' Ummah declined patting his stomach politely.

Ismael and Isa edged to the side to get a closer look at Lakhvir Sher Singh who was chatting with Roland. The conversation at the forge surfaced in Alistair's mind.

'Encik Ummah, this is Mr Lucky Sher Singh.'

Without warning, Lakhvir felt the hair on his nape prickle with static electricity. Turning sideways he saw Ismael and in his shadow, Isa.

'These two young men, Ismael and Isa, they know the Sumatran,' Alistair said following his gaze.

'Tok Panjang Kuku,' Isa said quietly in English, 'Grandfather...'

'Grandfather?'

'Tok is the Grandfather of our... *Keturunan*[149].'

'Inheritance, ancestry-family line,' Roland said helpfully.

'Tok Panjang Kuku is our Spirit. He cannot be killed, the *Sardar Bai*[150] almost lost his life!' Ismael said emphatically in Malay.

---

147   Pesta – funfair.

148   Dah kenyang – already satisfied.

149   Keturunan – family line.

150   Sardar Bai – Sikh Brother.

'What did he say?' Lakhvir asked turning to Alistair.

'He says... er... Tok is their Spirit... the tiger almost killed you.'

The Shikari from Punjab looked at Ismael and then at Isa.

'What does the tiger look like?' Lakhvir Singh challenged.

'Tok is white except here... ,' Isa said clearly in English, tilting his head as he pulled his hair off his forehead. There was a patch, the size of a strawberry, criss-crossed with thick short white fur. A birthmark of sorts.

'You've seen it.'

It was clear the Tiger Wallah was struggling, as he stared at Isa, voice wavering.

'I went to look for the white one – Grandfather... I was so tired I shut my eyes for half a minute to rest...' Lakhvir Sher Singh said, in self-recrimination, almost weepy. 'When I opened them, the white one was looking straight at me. Grandfather... he could have killed me.'

'You came from far to meet Tok, not to kill him...'

'What are you *Puther*[151]?' Lakhvir asked quietly, leaning forward into Isa's face. 'How do you know this?'

Isa's eyes were liquid and hot, tiger's eyes. A knowing came upon Lakhvir Singh's face.

'You protect them!... and I... so many...'

'Tok does not kill for fun!'

Ismael's indignation was so loud that the Tiger Wallah looked at him and then at Alistair.

'Fun?' Lucky echoed as Alistair interpreted hesitantly.

'Tok, our Grandfather; he gives life where he can take it,' Isa said gently.

---

151   Puther – *son* in Punjabi.

'Yes...' Lucky nodded slowly, '... life.'

'Ummah,' a Malay man called out, 'we're going across, see you there.'

'*Permissi*[152], the boys want to visit the Pesta before we go home,' Ummah said apologetically.

'Lucky, they've got an appointment across at the funfair.'

'Goodbye my little Tiger Wallah,' Lakhvir said animatedly to Isa, a different man from the one who had stepped onto the veranda. 'I know what I have to do... a wildlife reserve. The Sahibs won't be happy.'

'Grand idea,' Roland said encouragingly, 'and don't worry about the Sahibs, they'll catch on.'

As they walked away, Alistair looked longingly at the Pesta across the road.

'Have you been to a Pesta before?' Roland enquired.

'No, actually I haven't. This would be my first.'

'Well then, we must take you across. Hold on a tick.'

Turning around, he scanned the crowd outside on the terrace for a "volunteer".

'Lucky, do forgive me. I didn't realise how upset you were and the boys meant no offence,' Alistair said, turning to Lakhvir who had settled comfortably into a chair.

'No! No, it was very good, like a healthy dose of *julab*[153],' the Punjabi man said contentedly.

'Uncle Rolly, Cuthbert hasn't arrived.'

Ivy Lazaroo had come up to talk with her Uncle. Alistair stood up dutifully but she did not acknowledge him.

'Are you sure he said he was coming?'

'Yes, he was coming up from Malacca.'

---

152   Permissi – with your permission.

153   Julab – a Punjabi concoction that clears the digestive system.

'Don't worry about him then, he'll get here soon enough. Why don't you take Alistair here over to the Pesta for a little look-see?'

'My shoes...' she said taken aback.

'Your shoes have seen you climb over gates after curfew, to go dancing. Off you go Alistair, I'll look after Mr Lucky...'

They walked in silence out of the Club, Ivy draping her shawl around her bare shoulders. Alistair waited until they were out of Roland's sight.

'Miss Lazaroo, why don't you just slip back and I'll go ahead alone.'

'It's quite all right, I don't mind a little stroll,' she said cagily.

'Miss Lazaroo, I really would prefer you to go back to the Club. It's clear this situation's been forced upon you by your uncle,' Alistair said, feeling a little angry.

'Mr Pierce, no one in the world could force me to do anything, especially Uncle Rolly.'

'I don't want to take you away from your fiancé. He might turn up.'

'Fiancé?'

'The young man you're waiting for...'

'He's my baby brother – Cuthbert. And he's the sole surviving member of my family.'

'Oh, I'm sorry.'

'I didn't just lose Bonny you know. My grandfather, parents and brothers, wiped out...,' she said flatly, turning away and walking across the road to the Pesta.

As she stepped onto the grass Alistair put his hand on her elbow to steady her.

'When my parents dashed after the British trucks... we didn't know where we belonged,' she said with a brittle laugh. 'Cuthbert's my responsibility.'

Suddenly he was back home in England. He was aching as he

leaned over the bathtub, desperately propping up his father's lifeless body in his arms. The water, blood.

'Would you like to go back to the Club?'

She stopped in her tracks, her face haunted and heartbreakingly beautiful.

'No, not yet. This is always a difficult time of the year for me,' she said, folding her arms around herself. 'You must think I'm a hypocrite, coming to the Club the way I feel... but the truth is I don't have anywhere else to go.'

'You're not a hypocrite, I think you're wonderfully honest and I'm sorry that I took it to be my right to sit where I pleased.'

'We are a very hospitable bunch, you know.' She was contrite, released by his words.

'All's forgiven if I can have a dance when we get back to the Club.'

24

THE PESTA WAS A totally different world from the party at the Club.

The potpourri of jasmine, pandanus and dried fish assailed Alistair along with the heart-pounding drums as they pressed into the crowd. Two Tamil men, in red turbans, wearing only cotton dhotis and beating tablas strung from their shoulders, weaved in and around a bare-chested teenager in the throes of a trance. The boy had a skewer through his cheeks with belled ornaments hanging on either side of the iron spike and a dozen of the same ornaments, hooked viciously into his back. He danced with abandonment, eyes fixed in a glassy stare, to the drumbeat as the bells tinkled and chimed.

'My God,' Alistair exclaimed. 'Is this lawful?'

'Haven't you seen this in the rubber estates?'

'No! He's not even bleeding, it must be mind over matter...'

'It's no different from some of the pagan rituals in England...'

'Like what?'

'The Druids with their ritual sacrifices and shamanism.'

'Ivy Lazaroo!'

A gangly young lad of about seventeen stood behind them wearing a priest's cassock. White teeth flashed in an ebony face.

'Dom! Dom Hendrique...,' Ivy exclaimed. 'What are you doing in Port Dickson? And why are you wearing a dress?'

'I'm a novice up at the monastery at Cape Rachado. My new name is Brother Benedictine.'

'Dom Benedictine, Uncle Rolly drinks that,' Ivy said hugging the youth who hung back as far as possible.

'Er... Ivy, the priesthood, it doesn't encourage males and females...'

'Why have you joined the priesthood? I thought you wanted to marry me when you grew up,' Ivy said pinching his cheek. 'Alistair Pierce, meet my cousin Dom.'

Alistair saw the procession winding its way up to St Paul's Hill with the relic of St Francis Xavier. Dom was walking at the back and the rickshaw driver's words rang in his head. *Become Roman Catholik, think they are Eurasian, Serani.*[154]

'So tell me,' Ivy demanded, 'why a priest?'

'To keep my eye on this kind of behaviour,' Dom said importantly, eyes on the boy in a trance. 'He needs exorcism.'

'We've all got demons. Give me one good reason. No nonsense now!'

'I wanted to Ivy,' he said simply, 'it makes me happy.'

She looked at him and her face softened.

'... and when you stop being happy you can always leave.'

Both Dom and Alistair laughed at the way she said it.

'Alistair, Dom used to live with us as a child in Malacca. We loved our moonlight fishing...'

'Except when Bonny caught us. Remember when we were playing in the ghost house in Praya Lane where Dicky's father hanged himself? He wanted to cane us,' Dom interjected. 'Big shot driving us around in Mr Travers's car when he came to Malacca.'

'Yes, he was,' Ivy said proudly to Alistair, 'he really was stellar.'

'From what I heard this evening, I believe you.'

---

154   Serani – colloquial term for Eurasians.

'The hockey team's over at the Club. Join us Dom!'

'I'm not dressed for the Club. I'm wearing sandals.'

'It's all right, Alistair could sign you in.'

'Er... well,' Alistair said, uneasy at the breach of protocol, 'we could give it a try'.

'If they object to my sandals, then I'll leave quietly. No fussing okay? Promise Ivy?'

'Okay, but I can go in and get someone's shoes for you. Cuthbert should already be there...'

Alistair had never met anyone like her.

'Are you enjoying the *Pesta*[155], Mr Pierce?' Dom asked.

'... it's all... em... quite interesting.'

Ivy tapped him on the elbow with her fan sharply.

'Why can't the English learn to speak the truth? You mean it's all rather overpowering... but you're such stoics.'

As they steered through the crowd, a man stepped up to them. It was Ummah, the Headman.

'*Anak*[156],' he said warmly to Dom, grabbing him by the shoulders.

'Hello Pa Ummah!' Dom proclaimed excitedly, looking around expectantly. 'Is my father here?'

'He's in the village, he's well. Are you coming to see us soon?'

'Yes, next week,' Dom responded almost guiltily.

'He knows you're a Pastorrr (sic) and you're busy. He's very proud of you. Mister Ali... Miss. *Sihat*[157]?' Ummah said politely to Alistair and Ivy by way of acknowledgement.

'There's going to be a cowboy film at midnight,' Ismael directed to

---

155 Pesta – fun fair.

156 Anak – Child.

157 Sihat – Hope you are well; a euphemism for hello, addressed to Ivy.

216

Dom over his father's shoulder.

'If we don't see you later, come for dinner soon,' Ummah said sincerely, before moving on.

'You know the Headman?' Alistair asked Dom.

'Everybody knows everybody in Port Dickson,' Ivy said quickly.

'It's okay, Ivy. My father is not well, Mr Pierce. Pa Ummah's looking after him.'

'Shall we head back to the Club then,' Alistair said, taking the cue from Ivy and changing the subject.

She nodded appreciatively and slung her arm through Dom's. Then she put her other hand on Alistair's elbow.

'We'll go back to the Club, get a table under the stars and have some fun!'

With a salute, the sentry blindsided by a white Tuan, allowed a shoeless Dom through the side gate that led to the terrace. Ivy, looking like the cat that swallowed the canary, went off in search of Cuthbert. All the tables and chairs closest to the terrace were taken and they had to walk further towards the beach where they found a free table.

On the beachfront, where the white paling fence stopped before the water, a little skirmish had broken out. Moonlighters from the Pesta were trying to get to the other side of the Club and as the tide came in, had started pushing against the fence. In places, individual planks had come loose, and the sentries were speaking in low urgent tones to the jaywalkers.

'Please don't walk this way, you've got the rest of the beach...'

'This beach is ours! We can walk where we please.'

217

'The Club is private property,' said one guard, waving a stick threateningly.

'Eh you Tamil! Go back to your country.'

In the end, the sentries sullenly formed a rough boundary along the beachfront. However, they could not stop the tongue-in-cheek barracking from a group, having a stickybeak. Several guests seated nearby were most irate about the invasion of their privacy from the rubbernecks.

'Why don't they go away?'

'They've got their own amusement across at the *padang*[158].'

'Nosey parkers.'

'I don't know why we don't just shoot them!'

This was from Maude MacKeerne, the woman who had been at Ashman's table during dinner. It was clear that she was tippled.

Alistair Pierce's toes curled. He turned to the curious onlookers. A handful of men stood out glumly from the crowd. They had black turbans and wore loose black tunics, sporting unkempt facial hair and beards. They were coldly surveying the party, faces dour.

'Dom, who are they?'

'Oh, you don't want to upset them! They're Pharisees.'

'Fanatical are they?'

'Al-Sijjin! The messengers and executors of hellfire and brimstone.'

'What message are you carrying?'

'Unconditional love. To lay down my life.' There was no hesitation.

'Sounds like war... unconditional surrender,' Alistair said lightly.

'I'm called to God! It is unconditional.' The pupils of Dom's eyes dilated and his face lit up, the cassock threatening to swallow him alive.

'I've found Cuthbert,' Ivy announced, less than pleased. 'He

---

158   Padang – field.

dropped in at the NAFFI ball to pick up Adele Nunis.'

'Adele! I haven't seen her since Peggy got married.'

'She's just a *Furiada*[159]. She's using him to get into the Club and meet white men.'

'She could do that at the NAFFI ball, she's very pretty.'

'At the NAFFI balls they are mostly army types. The men at the Club are a different kettle of fish. District Officers, Plantation Managers, Road Engineers...hmm... Assistants to the Advisor,' she said slyly. 'What do you think Alistair?'

'Oh, well, honestly?'

'Honestly! I expect nothing else,' she said provocatively. 'Why do you think we girls came here?'

'I don't know about the other girls but I think you came to the Club to get your pound of flesh,' he said with a straight face.

Her eyes flashed and she burst into laughter.

'What's so funny? Share the joke, sis.'

Cuthbert Lazaroo, a strapping lad, had Ivy's eyes. Tottering beside him was a cocoa-skinned young lady with corkscrew curly hair and brown eyes that closed when she laughed. She wore five-inch stilettos to catch up with his height.

'*O binagri Olanda!*[160] What did you do?' Cuthbert exclaimed, taking in Dom's vestments.

'Why shouldn't he? *Olah*[161] Dom. *Nos sa Sinyora!*[162]'

'Olah Adele! Hello Bertie.'

'You succumbed... didn't you learn anything from us?'

---

159   Furiada – a vain flighty good time girl - Kristang language.

160   O binagri Olanda – O vinegar of Holland.

161   Olah – Look at you.

162   Nos sa Sinyora – Our Blessed Virgin Mary.

'Ivy, you've still got apple cheeks from England. I should have gone for Teacher Training.'

'They're not from England, *Nona*.[163] What brings you here? I thought all your friends were at the Terendak camp?'

As they rabbited on, delectation tilled Alistair Pierce's soul. He had never experienced anything like it before. Brothers, sisters, cousins... they were quite mean, like children secretly pinching each other under the table. From the corner of his eyes he watched Ivy. She had unfurled her fan with one delicate move and was fanning her nape.

'Are you a Catholic, Alistair?' asked Adele, as she coquettishly sipped her cocktail.

'I was born into the faith.'

'Oh, you're not a Catholic then.'

'It's the one faith, isn't it?'

'We are Roman Catholics, not Christians!' Adele said, scandalised.

'I'm not,' chirruped Ivy, her fan suddenly still, 'and neither is Cuthbert.'

'Oh I'm sure Bertie is willing to convert,' Adele countered sweetly.

'Are you Bertie?' Ivy challenged silkily, prodding her brother in a most unladylike fashion, with her pointed shoe.

'What?'

'Are you willing to become a Roman Catholic, brother dear?'

'Don't joke! I was just asking Dom, why couldn't he have been a Protestant Padri, at least he can marry and not suffer.'

'Oh, I won't suffer,' Dom said sincerely.

'Won't suffer! You'll never be able to dance cheek to cheek with a sweetheart again. That's suffering.'

'It's a heart sacrifice our priests make, they're married to the

---

163   Nona – Missy or young girl.

Mother of God,' Adele said effusively.

'Who's that dear?' Ivy asked with a wide-eyed innocence.

'Oh Saint Jude have mercy,' Adele said picking up a medallion from around her neck and kissing it. 'Mary, the Mother of God.'

'You mean Mary, the mother of Jesus, the Son of God,' Cuthbert challenged.

'If Mary is the mother of God, and Jesus is the Son of God, then Mary's Jesus's grandmother,' Ivy mused wickedly, chewing the tip of her folded fan. 'Or is Mary the wife of God, if Jesus is God's son... And her son!'

'Look, we've got to examine this Mother of God theology,' Dom agreed enthusiastically, sitting forward.

'There's nothing to examine. Mother of God is Mother of God!' Adele said dogmatically, holding on to the medallion.

'Adele, have you got a Bible? Cuthbert asked patronisingly.

'No, we've got our pew books and that's enough for me!' she retorted. 'What do *you* believe in Alistair?'

All eyes turned on Alistair, and he instinctively knew he was bait.

'Oh, it's the chasm between heaven and hell I struggle with... Is there a grey area and who decides?'

'Purgatory!' Dom pounced. 'Whose soul are you worried about?'

'Oh no one's! Nobody's really. I'm afraid I'm stubbing my toes on some of the doctrines.'

'Where do you come from Alistair?' asked Adele.

'I'm from London, my mother's family was from Kent.'

'Ah, Chaucer's home,' Ivy said, her face lighting up. 'I enjoyed Canterbury.'

'Then you've been to England?'

'Yes, to Kirkby, Liverpool, for teacher training. But I couldn't wait to get out... Too cold in more ways than one!'

'My high cheekbones come from my French ancestry. Our family name Nunis can be traced back to a French aristocrat, Albert Nenor. The family crest was a black stag,' Adele said with great pride.

'That's interesting.'

'Alistair, have you been to Malacca? Have *you* seen our home?' she quizzed.

'Oh, it was just a flying visit but very enlightening. I couldn't drive over the Malacca bridge though.'

'You will love it. *Tia*[164] Joan Marbeck wrote a lovely poem, *The Cry of the Old Malacca River.*

> *"... No more that call from Chetty quarters,*
> *Why have they forsaken my muddy waters?*
>
> *A Portuguese Admiral, a dutiful Dutchman,*
> *Rubber from the East India Company*
> *And gold from Siam.*
> *Traders all and a babble of languages in unison.*
>
> *Pretty nyonyas*[165] *gossip on the bridge*
> *Coolies carry rice from anchored ships*
> *Rickshaws with sound of running feet*
> *And bullock-carts squeak on laterite streets..."* '

She looked adorable as she finished, tilted her head and rested her chin on her palm.

'How charming,' complimented Alistair.

---

164   Tia – Aunt.

165   Nyonyas – Straits Settlement female Chinese.

'We should go to Malacca for a river cruise,' she offered playfully.

He had to keep his eyes away from Ivy who was clearly irritated. The fan in her hand slapped the air furiously. She caught her brother's attention.

'Ivy, isn't the hockey team waiting for a dance?'

'I just needed some fresh air.'

'I'm really surprised you're out here, knowing how much you love to dance.'

'I'll dance when I'm ready,' she said testily.

'Do you like dancing Alistair?' Adele asked hopefully.

Before Alistair could answer, a loud bang startled them all. Maude MacKeerne, facing the beach had stood up violently, her chair flying back with great force. It crashed into the table behind her, causing a wave of alcohol and beer to swill over the guests. The exclamations of shock were quickly silenced at the woman's stark insobriety.

'You stinking tramp!' spewed Maude, swaying drunkenly.

The object of her agitation, her ex-maid, Aini, now her husband's mistress, was cutting across the beach frontage. Drunk as she was, Maude knew where the Malay minx was heading – a little motel beyond the Club where her husband was waiting. Stoked by the heat of gin, she lumbered down to the chain of human sentries.

'Slut!' she screamed, a glass of gin still in her hand. The sentries, unprepared for an incursion from the inside, broke ranks. For Maude, Aini was a red flag to a demented bull. Each time she saw her ex-maid, the girl looked prettier. Tonight she was in red sandals, a matching plastic handbag and a red and white polka-dotted frock nipped in at the waist.

Aini was taken unawares. When the big white woman lunged at her, cursing, Aini stopped in her tracks. The soft sand had also broken Maude's momentum and she came to an ungainly stop in front of Aini. The two women eyeballed each other like a mongoose and a rattlesnake.

'You stay away from my husband,' Maude hissed at Aini.

'Eh! I don wan your husban...(sic),' retorted Aini, hands on her hips, speaking English with affectation. 'He wan Ann!'

'Ann! You whore, who do you think you're talking to?' Maude MacKeerne snarled.

Jabbing her hand viciously, she splashed her gin into Aini's face. For a split second the girl was stumped, as Maude stood with her mouth curling in a triumphant smile. Then Aini moved.

'*Babi!*'[166] she screamed, as she hit Maude with her plastic handbag, kicking at the same time. Long black hair flaying, she looked like a harpy as Maude grabbed onto her handbag to ward off the blows.

'Leggo my bag, leggo (sic)!'

In an instant, the cheap plastic sling snapped and Aini, who regarded the bag as a symbol of her up and coming status, went ballistic. Taking off her sandal she started beating Maude on the face and shoulders, red earrings looping crazily. Deep in her pickled brain, Maude realised that she had unleashed a she-demon. She turned and ran for her life, back to the veranda. Aini chased her, hobbling with a sandal on one foot. She would have gone right up to the Clubhouse, if the security guards had not grabbed her.

'Your husband don wan you, he wan Ann (sic)!' she screamed over and over again, as they removed her.

The Club guests who had been seated near the beach frontage sat like stunned mullets. Those near the veranda, were shocked to see a white woman stumbling towards them like an ungainly bear. Mercifully she collapsed into a rattan chair, hair in disarray, sleeve

---

166   Babi – Pig in the Malay language. A filthy animal to the Muslims.

torn. Several young officers immediately went to her rescue, whisking her off via the garden, Maude clinging brokenly to them.

My God, Alistair thought, mortified.

'Leggo my bag, leggo!' a young shrill male voice imitated Aini.

'I kill you... *babi*, better run,' another mocked.

It had the black humour of a Punch and Judy marionette but the look on the black-robed Al-Sijjin blanched Alistair. They were gleaming like a murder of crows feeding on carrion.

A barrage of English phrases punctuated the air before someone started singing "London Bridge is Falling Down".

'Are we going to dance? I'm bored! Alistair, shall we?' Ivy said loudly as she stood up with the flamboyance of a Tango dancer.

Her gesture shook off the pall of humiliation cast over the Club guests. Immediately there were murmurs of agreement from people around.

'Come on Adele, let's go and show them what we can do.' With a flourish, Cuthbert pulled her out of the chair and twirled her around. Adele squealed skittishly, her peacock-coloured skirt filling out around her. Talking with a forced light-heartedness, other couples too started walking towards the Clubhouse.

She's amazing, Alistair thought gratefully, eyes on Ivy.

'I think it's time for me to get back to my cowboy movie, Sir. Thank you for inviting me,' Dom said respectfully to Alistair.

'Sir?' Ivy said dryly, 'It's a bit late for formalities Dom. I'm surprised you are not calling him *Angkel*[167].'

'It was my pleasure Dom, I'm sure we'll meet again,' Alistair said as Ivy slung her arm through his.

Dancing to the strains of Tommy Dorsey's "Stardust", Alistair felt

---

167   Angkel - Uncle in Kristang language.

the tightness around his chest ease.

'Thank you,' he said.

'What for?' she said, with the trademark prickliness he was beginning to recognise as armour to her vulnerability.

'For what you did back there, I mean, when the two women... for starting the dancing.'

'I love dancing remember,' she said with a selachian grin, 'and thank you.'

'For what?'

'For Dom... for flouting precious British etiquette and house rules... for walking in with someone who looks like a joke.'

She was holding his gaze now.

'I'm sure any one of those fine gentlemen at your table would have been more than happy...'

'Alistair, I look like one of them, but when it comes to the family – they run!'

The bantering was over.

'That's why I'm still here... dancing with you,' she finished pertly.

Part 8

1954
PORT DICKSON, BRITISH MALAYA

... plant the seeds of jealousy, incite them to deeds of blood, in countries that are independent and prosperous, enjoying the blessings of peace... that the Church might be the gainer in the end, for "without the shedding of blood no man can be saved."

Oath of Extreme Induction
– Ignatius of Loyola, Society of Jesus
1539

"I want to throw open the windows of the Church so that we can see out and the people can see in."

– Pope John XXII, Vatican II
1962–1965

25

THE SACRED HEART

For Alistair, the next season was serendipitous. The existence he lived before gave way to parties, excursions and high drama. Ivy and family were "his gypsies" and this time he was loath to let them pass him by. When Ivy invited him to join her on a river cruise in Malacca for the "Festa San Pedro", he found himself opening the back door of the car for Brother Dominic. Their chaperone! (It was Ivy's orchestration to stop tongues wagging until she had made a decision about him.)

On the banks of the Malacca river, people were releasing candles in flower floats, the river swirling with colour. Hundreds of little wooden statues of Saint Pedro lined the route, decorated with fishing paraphernalia, candles and rosaries. Flanking a green promontory, the silting river cajoled the boats laden with pilgrims, along with the flowers to bob against a manmade dyke. Here, a huge statue of Mary with open arms welcomed them, the flowers at her feet a glorious train. As Alistair, Ivy and Dom, who had assumed the role of a guide, debarked at the pier, a brisk trade was underway. An oligopoly of blessed Catholic sacramentals from rosaries, prayer books, crucifixes, blessed salt, medals and holy water were on sale. Whites and blacks, pilgrims who had come from other countries, were climbing over each other to buy spiritual indemnity.

'A charm... a prayer... a philtre from Rome, blessed by the Holy

Father himself to keep you safe.'

'Rosaries... the Holy Virgin, Mother who makes everlasting intercession....'

'Welcome to *Ephesus*[168], Mr Pierce,' Dom sang out, throwing his hands up with a flourish.

'Ephesus? ... you think?' Alistair said, still piqued at the arrangements.

' "Behold! *The Great Harlot*,[169]" ' Dom said loudly gesturing at the statue in mock drama. 'She will be overthrown and her merchants and her Kings, who committed fornication...!'

His words were cut off as Ivy "accidentally on purpose" opened her parasol in front of his face.

He's going to incite a riot, Alistair thought alarmed.

'If you're not careful you'll be stoned,' Ivy said icily, 'and we won't help you.'

With that she propelled Alistair on the walkway, which skirted the statute. Dom quickly fell into step with them.

'What's wrong with you Dom?'

'I've received another poison pen!'

'What? Do the Fathers know?'

Alistair knew what they were alluding to. When they went to the Club with Adele and Cuthbert, it was *the* topic.

Dom was receiving secret material, blasphemous and denigrating of the Madonna. It was coming in through the articles he requested,

---

168   Ephesus – An ancient Greek city mentioned in the Book of Revelation for having lost its first love for God.

169   The Great Harlot – in Revelations 17, she is a mystery woman who sits on a Beast and defiles the world, vowing to destroy the Christians.

for his Theology degree. Not everyone who was a Brother had the privilege of doing a degree. Spurred on by Alfonso's words ('Get a edecation (sic) boy, be a big shot one day!') he qualified with a grade one and five distinctions in his Cambridge 'O' Level results. Brother Dominic enrolled as an external student with Santa Maria College, at the Catholic University in Lisbon. When he was assigned to the dissertation, "The Madonna: Woman of the Revelation", it began. A little article swept through the floodgates of scholarship from Lisbon.

"Papal Heresy: Mother of God unscriptural."

A vicious attack on the Madonna, it was written by a Father Francois Sarbatini. The note attached said he had been mysteriously killed. He fell from a train on his way to the Vatican City for an audience with His Holiness, the Pope. When Dom went to the Holy Fathers at Cape Rachado, they confiscated the article, absolutely convinced it was an act of sabotage. They made him promise not to have anything more to do with the attack on the Church and advised the young Brother to move on with his thesis.

Not Dom Hendrique, son of Alfonso Hendricks, who was into conspiracy theories. He remembered the postal address for the publisher of the article, and a clandestine correspondence was established.

'You are touching the untouchable, Dom! I've told you, get out if you're unhappy.' Ivy warned, as they stood under the outstretched arms of the statue of Mary on the waterfront.

'...but I'm not unhappy! And there's more I can achieve from the inside. Alistair, just look at that! Do you know what's happening in those tents?'

'No ...!' Alistair said tersely. His eyes however, were on the white tents, their curtains flapping open and shut, with people lining up outside.

'They are paying to have their sins forgiven. Indulgences! And some of them are doing it with all their earthly possessions!'

'Oh, I say, that's a bit rich!'

'Pardon the pun,' Ivy said darkly.

'We should be chasing them out with whips! This is the exact spot, here! Holy ground. Right here. The Holy Fathers stepped off the *Flor de la Mar*[170] as it was shipwrecked. They logrolled on the wine barrels ... it was a miracle ....'

Dom Hendrique was, to say the least, an anointed storyteller, weaving Malacca out of the cloisters of history and myth. And like King Shahryar, Alistair began to fall in love, reluctantly conceding to their tryst à trois. Ivy drew him. They were alike, striking existentialist cords in each other's souls. He knew he could tell her about his father, there would be no pity, only a liberty.

When the moment came, it was one of the rare occasions when they were alone in the Club on the terrace, having tea by the waterlily ponds.

'Cat got your tongue,' she said lightly. 'I asked about your Father. What does he do?'

'He's dead... he committed suicide.'

'Why?' she asked quietly, eyes narrowing a fraction.

'He was depressed after the war. He was a bomb aimer... Dresden was one of his targets.'

'Your poor mother must have been heartbroken.'

'They didn't love each other. They only got married because I was on the way...'

---

170   Flor de la Mar – *Flower of the Sea*. A Portuguese ship which sank in 1511 off the coast of Sumatra, carrying a large treasure trove for the Portuguese king.

He watched her face, like a voyeur. She held his gaze, as the words sank in.

'Let me see what the stars say about your life,' she said, pushing aside her teacup and putting her hands out on the table. 'Have you had your palms read?'

'No, never.'

She took his hands in hers, and began to look at them with great interest.

'Ahh yes... there has been sadness and death. Hmmm... There's a season coming, a good season... aha, this line goes into the mound of Venus... that's your love life...'

'Where?'

They were both scrutinising his palm, when she pulled back suddenly and looked at him deadpan.

'They didn't warn you, did they?'

'About what?'

'Eurasian girls and palm reading... it's just an excuse to hold your hand,' she teased, giving her shark grin.

He started laughing, suddenly conscious she was holding his hands, palm on palm, her fingers lacing through his.

'You found him, didn't you?' she said gently.

'How...?'

'It's all over you... Bonny had the same look.'

'Guilt?'

'No. Responsibility. It's too heavy to carry, Alistair. Believe me, I know.'

'... doomed like Sisyphus.'

'No! Just roll it away... let the anger go.'

'I'm not angry...'

'No? Not with your father for choosing you?'

'Choosing me?'

'He chose you to pick up the pieces… clean up the "mess".'

Her words ran through him like a knife. In a flash he saw himself in the bathroom, kneeling beside the bathtub. It was an ocean of blood. His father, razor on the floor, was as white as the wall he leaned on, clean-shaven. He was trembling with exhaustion, holding his father upright, trying to keep a dead man alive, waiting for the ambulance.

He looked away from Ivy feeling his chest constrict.

'You can't blame her you know… for not loving him enough to save him.'

Again in a flash, he saw a pair of hands in black Chantilly lace, holding white roses at the funeral. He had refused to forgive her when she kissed him goodbye at the station. A boulder heaved in his chest and stung his eyes, as soundlessly, the pain flowed.

'It's alright, Alistair. It really is alright.'

They sat there quietly, she holding his hand as the evening cooled and the magenta waterlilies opened.

The monsoon rains smashed the laterite soil, haemorrhaging the land. As floods swept away homes and uprooted trees, Alistair felt the barricades of his life come down. The downpour left the earth pliant and fragrant with jasmine, as bullfrogs honked in soft crescendos.

Returning home jubilant from dinner at Planter's one night, he was surprised to find Ashman waiting on the porch. Ivy had allowed him to kiss her and as he lingered in the cinnamon and lilies from her embrace, his soul was open.

'Ashman! How good to see you,' he said warmly.

'Alistair, sorry to barge in like this.'

'Coffee or port, or both?'

'We don't have time. There's a meeting tonight at Planter's and Sir Douglas wants you there.'

'Sir Douglas! At this time?'

'The bids are up for British contracts. I know you've been er, a little preoccupied, but we've got less than three years before handover.'

'.... but I just came from Planter's, there's no one there!'

'It's down at General's Quarters.'

'Somebody's got a bent sense of humour.'

'It's got something to do with Feng Shui – appeasing the spirits, I think.'

His mind was a maelstrom of questions but he could not bring himself to query Ashman. When they got to Planter's, Ashman drove around to the side where the stables were located. In the shadows he could make out the Ghurkhas assigned to the Advisor, as he followed Ashman through the stablehand's annex. A door at the end led to a long corridor, lit by a stark bulb. On either side were rooms, stables that had fallen into disrepair but used as torture chambers in the war. They came to a flight of stairs, manned by an armed guard. At the top of the stairs Ashman knocked a little code on a door and a key turned.

GENERAL'S QUARTERS.

Walls burgeoned with leather-bound books and oil paintings of English armadas, as Victorian ceramics accessorised Chesterfield sofas. Several doors led to private rooms and Alistair knew one of them accessed Planter's internally. In the centre was a teak table for eighteen, on which lay a trove of antiquated documents. They were being delicately unpeeled, by a man wearing white cotton gloves, from the fine muslin separating them. Sir Douglas, also wearing gloves, was studying one of the leaves with a magnifying glass and was at the same time, engaged in a running commentary with a distinguished Malay man by his side. A mammoth three-dimensional model of the Colony, like an emerald Keris, lay on a side table. Outlining the rubber estates and tin mines, pint-sized roads and railways replicated the Colony's transport network. Several men hovered, placing little red markers on the model.

The room palpated with the verve of war-time operations.

Bonnifacio Lazaroo was in this room, Alistair thought, taking it in.

Teak Abdullah was by the liquor trolley and did not seem to be in any sort of hurry. Alistair had heard he had his sights on Borneo. By the side, Patriarch Bok and the young Bok were talking animatedly with several Britishers.

'Ah Alistair,' summoned Sir Douglas. 'Sorry to get you out so late ...'

'No need to apologise Sir, I wasn't in bed.'

'Look at these cessation deeds for Penang and Malacca. What mastery!'

Gold leaf framed the historical deeds, exquisitely flourished by calligraphy.

'Perfection Sir.'

'We had to bring these in from London. There are sovereignty issues... delicate matter, the Straits Settlement.'

'The monastery on Cape Rachado is going to bring us into conflict with the Vatican,' said the Malay man who had been talking with Sir Douglas.

'It's an age-old pillow fight between Isaac and Ismael... family politics.'

'As long as it doesn't turn into a crusade.'

'Bakhtiar, this is Alistair. He's one of my boys with the Land Office.'

'Call me Mr B. Land Office? The resettlement program was sticky business with the Sultans. They need their wings clipped. Well done!'

'The Colony's in mint condition Mr B. The communists are

cornered, you have the best education system in the world, and the economy's doing well...,' enthused a Britisher walking up to the table.

'We are very grateful.'

'Gratitude isn't going to keep her unsinkable. You're in sore need of advisors and consultants,' someone joined in with a thick South African accent.

Alistair winced at the brassy tone. Botham, who grew up in Africa, owned plantations in Kenya and did not suffer fools. He had run afoul of Templer for buying an armoured tank for himself in the communist insurgency and Templer had to send in a squad of Military Police to impound it.

'Mr B, thank you for including us in the transition committee,' Ashman Lahud said smoothly, head bent in deference, as he stepped out of nowhere.

All the Britishers there looked like they had clothes hangers stuffed under their shirts compared to Ashman's engaging demeanour. The sting of Botham's words was diffused.

'Ashman, we should think of starting our own arms development plant,' Mr B said thoughtfully.

The idea tumbled through minds like dice cast at a roulette table.

'I'm interested in a North-South highway,' the younger Bok interjected, cutting through their thoughts.

'We've read your proposal Mr Bok and it's all very ambitious... a highway of that magnitude runs into hundreds of millions,' another of the Britishers said curtly.

'Mr B will, with the incoming government, get us approval and your British companies will give us precious acreage!' said Patriarch Bok.

'We buy British equipment, and with British consultants, your good selves, we build a highway. It's in the bag,' Bok Junior finished.

'How can we be guaranteed of profits?' Botham asked patronisingly.

'The same way you know those bomb shelters that protected you in the war, your subways or undergrounds, whatever you call them, were financed from our tin and rubber,' Bok pointed out with a smile, displaying perfectly clenched teeth.

'Once I get my timber concessions in Sarawak, there will be enough money for all,' Teak Abdullah declared magnanimously.

'Only if I get *my gerrymander*, Teak,' Mr B said quietly, his eyes narrowing.

There was an edge in the conversation that made Alistair stare intently at the deeds to stop him from gawking like a schoolboy. At the same time, he wondered where the Malay Prince, Tunku Abdul Rahman was. His absence was curious because he was marked by Whitehall as the first Prime Minister after Independence.

'Alistair here, is someone I trust. He speaks Bahasa, and in Negeri Sembilan he's well known. I'm going to get him started on looking at land the government can gazette,' said Sir Douglas soothingly, putting his hand on Alistair's shoulder.

Alistair knew he was not in their league and was not fool enough to pretend that he was. Sir Douglas was securing his future with the new government. A hail of acknowledgements and interested looks pinned him.

'Ashman, get everyone a drink while I have a quick word with Alistair,' Sir Douglas said intimately, propelling him to the sofa chairs.

'Ashman's a very enterprising young man, you should run alongside him.'

'We're very different Sir. Ashman's a businessman.'

'And you're an idealist. Oh well, to each his own. And there will be lots of opportunities with the handover ... that is, if you want to stay.'

'Thank you Sir.'

'There's the Department of Agriculture in the incoming

government. With your expertise in agronomy... Mr B... Bakhtiar, he's a good friend to have. He's the Emperor-in-waiting.'

As Alistair walked out of General's Quarters escorted by Ashman, he felt almost light-headed. The Advisor's driver was at the car to see him home and as he and Ashman shook hands, neither said a word. It was larger than either of them. Just then, shouts rang out in the dark night. The sound of the breakers could not drown them. In the shadows the Ghurkhas moved, guns readied.

'We'll bring the boats in further up! The water's too rough in the village!' a voice called out in Malay.

'It's only the fishermen!' Alistair spat at the Ghurkhas to halt them.

They all stood quietly as the voices moved away. For some strange reason Alistair felt cold. The elation with which he had come home from the Club after dinner with Ivy, had vaporised.

Someone's walking over my grave, he thought.

'It will come up roses,' Ashman said reassuringly. 'Watch and see.'

26

COUNTDOWN

Cape Rachado. Twelve months later.

THE GREY-BLUE MONASTERY was an inspiring marriage of castle and fortress. Whilst big blocks of granite had breastworks of iron, the turrets were covered with bas-reliefs of crosses. There was a low bulwark sloping inwards with four emplacements for artillery. A rusted drawbridge, an antiquated romantic feature, softened her Amazon stature. High above the citadel flew the flags of Portugal, the Vatican in the middle and a third which looked strangely like the Jolly Roger. With a dagger and red cross above the skull and crossbones, it was the black flag of the Jesuit Order. On the flag were the words,

IUSTUM, NECAR, REGES, IMPIOUS.
IT IS JUST TO EXTERMINATE OR ANNIHILATE IMPIOUS OR
HERETICAL KINGS, GOVERNMENT OR RULERS.

Built by the Portuguese in 1520, it had been purchased by Ignatius of Loyola for Pope Paul III. Convoluted European allegiances and hostilities that made for strange bedfellows, had preserved it. Now however, the five centuries of privilege it enjoyed, was in danger. The British were making way for a Muslim government and the Catholic

Fathers could not trust the British. They would never forget the devastation of the Malacca Fort A' Famosa in 1807 by the English, who found maintaining the gateway to the East a tedium. The fort, eighty feet in width, with eight bastions and housing a Catholic Church, was ground into dust in an act of hubris. Ironically, the glory of Malaya razed by the brotherhood who fought the crusades.

From the Archbishops' solarium, the handwriting was on the wall. Red surveyors' flags and stakes littered the picturesque view of rolling green and blue seas. With independence, there were plans to build a mosque on the boundary of the monastery.

In the midst of this "threat", Brother Dominic's infidelity was uncovered. He had disobeyed their orders about not soliciting the slanderous articles on the Holy Mother. They unwittingly intercepted his mail when Dom was away in Malacca to bury his father who had drowned in Port Dickson. The Holy Fathers were disappointed but forgiving.

'It's the last Temptation... before his flesh falls away.'

'Brothers, we ourselves have been tested. Let us put on mercy.'

For the unsuspecting Brother Dom, who had taken Alfonso back to his home in Malacca, it was the most exhilarating week of his twenty years. The funeral awaiting Alfonso shocked Dom. The *Regedor*[171] had offered his house for the wake. It was grander even than old Louisa Goonting's send-off. Alfonso had a fifteen-piece band whilst the grand dame only had twelve.

'They did love Father,' Dom marvelled. 'If only Alfonso could see this.'

He was too immature to realise it was fear. Everything Alfonso had predicted, was happening. The subsidies for boats were being

---

171 Regedor – Headman of Portuguese Settlement.

pigeonholed and the fishing industry was dying. They were frightfully superstitious and did not want any comeuppance from Alfonso's spirit.

'There will be nobody to speak up for you,' Alfonso had sworn, 'and I will come back and spit in your faces.'

'We want him to stay away... give the bugger a good send-off!'

'Restless Hendricks's blood! Like the wind... haunting us.'

'... say the rosary for forty days, St Peter will take the ill wind out to the sea.'

'Get rid of the *Diabu's*[172] curses!'

When Brother Dominic got back to Cape Rachado, the Fathers summoned him immediately to a meeting, and gently challenged him on his dalliance with heresy. Emotionally charged by the show of support for Alfonso, he did not sidestep the Holy Fathers.

'It's a deception,' he argued sincerely, 'a terrible lie. The Madonna is going to take us to hell!'

The Monsignors were shocked, but they believed he was being irrational because of his father's death. They would pray and wait for Holy guidance for the young priest.

"Bapak borek, anak rintek."[173] Like father like son. Dom Hendrique was destined to relive Alfonso's mistakes. What his father did with the Kristang, he acted out with his "Brothers." If he had been ensconced in the Kristang community, he would have been clipped on the ear and hauled up with cruel remarks about Alfonso. It would have been a brutal awakening. Unfortunately, he was entrenched in an institution which had withstood and outwaited, centuries of denouncements. It would bury the likes of Brother Dom with doctrinal scholarship, and if that did not work, there was purgatory.

---

172   Diabu – devil in the Kristang language.

173   Bapak borek, anak rintek – The father is speckled and the child is spotted.

'She's the Mother of God, the woman clothed with the sun and the twelve stars from the book of Revelations ...'

'There are no scriptures, not one that refers to the Mother of God theology.'

'... it is a divine revelation, prophesied in the Magnificat ...'

'Prophecies will fail ... all things vanish,' Dom pronounced passionately, 'but the word of God will remain.'

They marvelled inwardly at his knowledge, and they covered him in love. He was only twenty *and* he had carnality on his side. (His ebony smooth skin was erupting with pimples.) For Dom, now that it was out in the open, it was time to put pen to paper with the Vatican in sight. Trustingly, he handed the letters over to Monsignor Aloysius, the head of the monastery, who secreted them away. The Fathers had to safeguard the novice from his own foolishness.

Six months down the line, the pimples on Dom's face had moved upwards to his forehead. They formed a thick band of painful blisters which he constantly worried and scratched.

'Too much thinking,' muttered Brother Pius, the fat kindly cook, watching him read and eat at the same time, alone in the huge spare kitchen because the other Brothers avoided him.

He had become pesky, hell bent on exposing the Holy Mother as a deception. He would ask for permission to pore over the old manuscripts and nervously they would give it. The next thing they knew he would have new evidence, scriptures to justify his theology. His cunning and brilliance would have been admirable if it had not been directed to the sacred heart of their faith.

At the same time, he was like a puppy, vying for their strokes of approval. It was a sorry state and the Fathers were in an emotional tug-of-war. They saw him as a son and he saw them as his family, but his blasphemy was polluting their ascetically-sealed hearts.

'The Holy Mother had other sons with Joseph… she was human, with desires, one of us.'

'Stop your filthy talk! Leave the sacred Virgin alone.'

Only when Brother Pius stopped short of murder did the Catholic Order intervene. The monastery cook tipped over a precious cauldron of cabbage and potato soup when he tried to ram a ladle down Brother Dominic's throat. Brother Dominic was summoned to the Catholic headquarters in Singapore for a meeting with Bishop Clementis.

'You need to find out if you're really suited for the call. We're assigning you to Malacca for six months at the Christ Church.'

He was not to minister, only "assist in the duties of house cleaning." The Holy Fathers did what had been passed down through the centuries, in castigating one of their sons. Social scourging. They leaked Brother Dom's "sin" into the community before he left for Malacca. A letter from Dom blaspheming the Holy Mother was slipped into the hands of Eric Sosa, a "third-class Eurasian".

The Sosa family were Tamils who became Catholics in the 1920s, as a direct result of the kindness of the convent nuns. Their firstborn son, who contracted lockjaw, was bathed, cleaned and loved upon by the Sisters of Mercy for three weeks. When he was raised from the sick bed, the Hindu family name changed from "Soosai" to "Sosa" which they adopted as the Kristang family hallmark. Accepted as poor relatives in the Eurasian community in Malacca, their profession as night-soil collectors, kept them socially inauthentic. They were not "called by the sea", and so remained peripheral.

There was no love lost between the Sosas and the Hendricks or Hendriques as they called themselves. The latter were as dark and as poor but the Hendricks were, according to Eric Sosa, "*Ta fazeh cuma ki omi!* Proud as shit."

The Sosas had an old bone to pick with Alfonso Hendricks. Grandmother Inez Tatiana's letters had made him an insufferable snob and quite cruel. The Eurasians who could not point to a generational blood tie, died a thousand deaths. He highlighted their parasitic status. With Brother Dominic's letter leaked to the night-soil man, the bloodletting began.

On his early morning rounds, Eric Sosa began to drop morsels of Dom's besmirching of the Queen of their hearts. Oh! It made his job that much sweeter, and the older Kristang ladies were finally gossiping with him.

' "A Jezebel"... his very words on paper. And he said, "Our Lady has other sons – she's just a woman!"'

The response from the *Abok abok*[174] was incendiary.

Nos sa Sinyora! Desah fuzilada lambeh kung boss Dom.

Our Blessed Lady! Let cursed lightning lick Dom, may he drop dead.

Dom justu-justu sa pai Alfonso!

Dom's exactly like his father.

Botah kastigu Dom.

Give him a severe beating.

...koza dimal kunisang.

So badly brought up!

O binagri Olanda! Bariga di stori Hendriks.

O vinegar of Holland. These tall-tales by the Hendricks.

When Dom's "sacrilege" looped back to the monastery through the confessional box, the stage was set.

'Holy Father... I have sinned.'

---

174   Abok abok – grandmothers in Kristang.

'What is your sin my child?'

'I want to pull out someone's tongue ... and Father, it's terrible, he's a Padri.'

'Why do you want to do such a cruel thing for my child, are you not a grandmother?'

'He's blaspheming Our Lady, the Holy Virgin. I may be a grandmother but she's *our* Holy Mother.'

'Forgive my daughter, let God defend his Mother... Forgive and sin no more.'

'Father, what am I to do? He's coming back to *Padri sa Chang*[175]!'

'Close the door my daughter, say three Hail Marys until you hear he's changed his heart.'

Through subtle manoeuvrings, the trap was laid. The endgame was Coventry, "Silent Treatment".

Unbeknown to the Holy Fathers, Brother Dominic was actually more brittle than they realised. He was beginning to suffer severe headaches coupled with vivid dreams. The tragedy of Alfonso's life was catching up with him. In his dreams, he would see Alfonso on all fours, looking under the old cupboard, crying tragically.

'Where's the box? Grandmother's box with the letters! Where the hell is it boy!? I know someone's stolen it. It's that traitor Terry Boudville... look again under the almirah. LOOK! Damn you. Damn all of you... Kristang thieves!'

The only ray of light Dom saw in the decision to being sent to Malacca was that he was going home. He was assigned to assist

---

175   Padri sa Chang – Land of the Priests which is Portuguese Settlement in Malacca.

Father Pintado with the duties at the Christ Church. Dom was ready to pick up from where he had left off at sixteen before he joined the monastery at Cape Rachado. His memories of his Kristang family were precious; home-cooked meals of devilled egg curry, fish sambal, and sago pudding with gula Melaka. All this, downed with peals of laughter and stories which had no endings, with a hundred exciting diversions, and the ubiquitous solicitation of oaths.

'Promise?! ...don't tell anyone else. Swear this upon Saint Bartholomew, only you know.'

Nothing prepared him for their cruelty. His first meeting with them was on Sunday at Mass. Throughout the whole service he stood with a foolish look on his face. It was like hiding a lolly in the mouth when picked by a teacher to give an answer. No one met his eyes but he put it down to the solemnity of the occasion, they *were* eating the body and drinking the blood of Jesus. After Mass would be the moment of bosomy embraces and pinches. He quickly cleared away the vessels used for the holy sacraments and came rushing out to the compound where they always gathered. They were gone, even Father Pintado. He could not believe his eyes. It was not normal unless there was a wake or a big party to prepare for.

It was a Sunday. The priests were always invited to one of the homes for lunch on Sundays. Innocent as a child, he reasoned that Pintado had simply forgotten to tell him. He pulled out a spare bicycle from the shed and cycled furiously to Portuguese Settlement. He would find the Reverend Father, and if he didn't, he would have lunch anyway. Sweating profusely in his black frock, he headed to the nearest house where children were playing outside, still in their Sunday clothes.

As if by magic, the children seemed to have invisible strings on them as they were yanked into the house. Puzzled, he pulled up outside the house, only to see the door and windows shutting hurriedly. Down the street like a domino effect, they disappeared. The only sound for a few minutes was door after door, and windows being jammed shut. And then an unearthly silence. Not even the dogs barked. The smell of pickled mango and fish curry, mingling with shrimp paste, hung in the air.

In a flash he saw it.

'Coventry!'

He turned quietly and cycled back to the vicarage, feeling bitterly humiliated.

'They're using the family to break me. They can wait forever! I'll show them.'

He didn't know who he felt angrier with, the Fathers or the family.

'.... I'm not hard up for their *fedeh*[176] *debal*!'[177]

That day, Brother Dominic did something he was not accustomed to. He "put on his best face". This was the Kristang euphemism for "*fazeh besta*", pretending not to know anything was amiss. For three months that was the pattern. Brother Dominic had no homes to visit or prawn sambal sandwiches packed in banana leaf sent to him. He lived off a constantly cooking broth of lentils, rice and mutton bones. He carried out his chores dutifully, staying out of the way when people came to the vicarage. During Mass and confession he kept his eyes downcast and, if he bumped into someone, he learnt to steel his reactions. With a little mumbled "sorry", and a quick about turn, he made himself invisible. Only the children watched him with a strange look on their faces.

What he found the hardest, were his midnight encounters with

---

176   Fedeh – stinky.

177   Debal – mixed meat and vegetable curry which is pungent.

Eric Sosa, the night-soil man. His duty was to open the gates to the churchyard for Sosa and wait with him for half an hour until he left. Ironically, he was the only one who would talk with him. It was a torment because Sosa was out for his pound of flesh.

'What happened to your father, boy? Too much *samsu*[178] eh?'

'If horses were dreams, beggars would ride. Hee hee hee. I still remember my English lessons. I was in the same class with Alfonso.'

'What happened to all that big talk? Your father promised us boats. *Ta fazeh cuma ki omi*[179].'

'Old man Hendricks's big mouth! Empty vessels make the most noise! Thought he was better than us, eh boy.'

'Sad, grandmother's silver box sitting pretty in India. Paid off all your grandfather's debts, eh.'

And it went on and on and on, every night.

Internally, Brother Dominic began to bleed. It was like the story of the little boy and the leak in the dyke. It began with a tiny drip. Initially he pressed the finger of anger over it, but soon he found that the wound could not be plugged up. Perhaps it was the years of knowing, that little children have, which one day finds expression as an adult. Some external pressure or circumstance that triggers off years of sublimation. Perhaps it was Rozie's running away, which he had subconsciously accepted as his fault. After all, many women leave their men, but which mother forsakes her son? And then there was the guilt of Alfonso's death; he had died utterly alone nine months earlier.

---

178   Samsu – cheap moonshine.

179   Ta fazeh cuma ki omi – pretending to be a "big shot" – a VIP. – (Kristang language)

Whatever it was, the wormwood of rejection and malice, swallowed him. He was a misfit who had been pitied, not loved all his life. The looks, the whispers, the silent nudges he thought he had escaped came flooding in, and he remembered things he should not have. Getting hand-me-downs while the other children were given new clothes, getting a slap when it was someone else's fault, and helping with the household errands while others went off to play first.

Four months into Coventry, Father Pintado came back one rainy Sunday evening after tea, to find Brother Dominic gone, and with him, the old metal trunk holding his books. Ten o'clock that night, hitching a lift from an army truck, he arrived at Ivy Pierce's door in Port Dickson. Chilled to the bone, in the rain, he was burning with fever.

'Dom? Dom! My God! What's happened? You're sick... Alis, quick!'

He slept almost all of the first week. That was the beginning of his breakdown. Anger had turned to sorrow, and sorrow to depression. He desperately wanted to hear from the family. They knew where he was because Alistair had contacted the monastery at Cape Rachado.

'Anyone come while I was asleep?' he asked constantly in the first weeks.

'Apologise and they'll all be making *kanji*[180] for you,' Ivy said darkly, as she sat on his bed and fed him congee.

'I haven't done anything wrong.'

'Yes you have! You've insulted God's mother,' Ivy said wickedly, while Alistair shook his head disapprovingly from the doorway.

'The Reverend Father said they would come by at the end of the week, once you've rested.'

'Rested! I don't know why you even bothered calling them!' Ivy said unhappily. 'Give them something to worry about!'

---

180   Kanji – rice or lentil porridge.

'It's basic good manners and Dom is still a Brother.'

'They're just giving Dom "the treatment". They do it all the time. They did it to Daddy when I was about nine, because he was a Protestant and didn't buy into this Mother of God business.'

'Did they?'

'Cold treatment for two years, but Daddy worked in Kuala Lumpur and wouldn't put up with their nonsense. He ignored them back.'

'And then what happened?'

'Oh, Grand-aunty Valeria had her hundredth birthday and everyone headed for Malacca for celebrations and we made up.'

'I remember that party,' Dom said brightening up.

'You were only about three Dom,' Ivy said, shaking her head. 'I don't think you were there, even if you were, you were too young to remember.'

'I remember! Your father gave Grand-aunt Valeria a gold brooch that he got from Portugal. It was shaped like a Spanish galleon.'

'How did you know that?'

'I *told* you I was there. I remembered because Father talked about fishing boats. I loved all the parties and I never wanted to go home at night. I used to love sleeping with all our cousins on the coconut mat.'

When they were in bed, Ivy turned her face into her husband's shoulder, and cried silently for Dom's loss.

'Alis, there was no home to go to. Rozie had run away and it was pass the parcel.'

'He needs to grieve, Ivy, possibly for the first time in his life.'

'He can't go back to the monastery. I want him to live with us.'

'Darling, you've got to let him go. Cuthbert lives on his own in Kuala Lumpur.'

'Dom's different, he's not like Cuthbert. Dom's like Bonny... they're dreamers and good and pure ...'

Alistair realised then that Ivy had Dom and Bonny linked inextricably. For two weeks she refused to hand Dom over to the Holy Fathers. When they came knocking, she would tell Ah Lan to tell them no one was home, but she made sure she could be heard laughing boisterously with baby Tatiana.

'Give them a taste of their own medicine!'

Dom, however, did not improve. Instead, he deteriorated with headaches that could not be alleviated with codeine, prescribed by Dr Kendrell when he made a house call. His forehead had a thick band of scaly skin, which looked like a snake coiled around his forehead, clamping his brain.

'I'm afraid I've never seen anything like this,' Dr Kendrell said, thickly, his tongue sticking to the top of his mouth. 'I think we'll take a blood sample and send it off to the new medical centre in Australia.'

At Cape Rachado, there was a dark cloud over the monastery at Ivy's manoeuvrings.

'He is patently hiding behind the woman and using her to fight his cause,' Bishop Clementis from Singapore surmised at the emergency meeting.

They were totally misreading Dom's plight and skittish that the Advisor's personal assistant, Mr Alistair Pierce, was getting "involved" with the crisis. Given the political climate, they did not want anyone to take "advantage" of their situation.

'Mr Pierce, the woman's husband said he's sick and is having nightmares and fevers. Even Dr Kendrell's unsure. They took him for observation for a week to the mental hospital in Tanjung Rambutan but the woman refused to leave him there.'

'It's clearly the work of the unholy one, and we shouldn't be surprised, all the things he's been saying about the Holy Mother...'

'We've got to act, before he takes it into the public gallery. The

Vatican team arrives next week.'

A delegation was arriving from Rome to discuss the sovereignty of church land in the Colony and a decision was imperative. Brother Dominic was a dangerous malcontent and nothing had worked, not even the draconian Coventry. He still refused to recant. They too were secretly shocked at his head bathed in bandages, oozing with slime. Painful as the decision was, they had no other recourse. Ex-communication! Two of the Monsignors came to inform Dom of their decision, but he was too sick to care.

And then a week later, Ummah the Headman came for Dom. There were no preliminaries when he knocked at Ivy's door.

Ummah ni mahu anak Alfonso, dia sakit jiwa. Ummah menyuburkan dia.

'I want Alfonso's boy ... His heart is sick. I will make him better.'

With that, he walked over to the swing under the flame tree, and waited. Ivy would have put up a fight, except that Dom wanted to go with the Spirit Guide.

'Dom, this is your home! I can't bear letting you go. Not like this.'

'I'll be alright Ivy. I'll be near Papa. He still has his house at the fishing village.'

'You're sick! You need a doctor.'

'Ummah will look after me. I'm tired ... I just want to sleep.'

Alistair was quite amazed at the grace she showed. Turning away she went to the kitchen to pack a basket of food. He found her weeping, bent like a ragged doll over a tin of custard.

'He loves custard, who's going to make it for him?'

'Ivy, he's got to stop being a poor relative and come into his own.'

Dom was bundled into the Ford Prefect Ummah had borrowed from Mr Sarjit Singh, the teacher, with Alistair lugging his books in his metal trunk. Ummah, smoking his fifth rolled cigarette, watched thoughtfully as Ivy scurried back and forth packing the car. Pots, food, blankets, pillows. And finally something that Ummah had never seen before, a hot water bottle. Then when they were ready, she turned to Ummah for the first time. In the porch light, she looked like a girl, not a mother. Thick chestnut hair ruffled, face downcast, her green eyes fixed themselves on Ummah. Her hands were ramrods on either side of her body, her palms flat against her skirt.

Dia adik saya.

'He's my younger brother.'

Ummah tau ... Ummah kenal Si-Bonny. Dia kawan Ummah, dia pahlawan Malaya.

'I know ... I knew your brother Bonny. He was my friend, and our national hero.'

His words freed her. She nodded silently, eyes welling with tears.

Part 9

PRE-INDEPENDENCE

1956 – 1957
PORT DICKSON - MALAYA

"Things fall apart; the centre cannot hold;
Mere anarchy is loosed upon the world,
The blood-dimmed tide is loosed, and everywhere
The ceremony of innocence is drowned."

The Second Coming – William Butler Yeats

27

FOR DOM, the days were a mirage of fire and ice, and he moved wraithlike through vistas of reality. Gathering herbs and barks that did not see light, Ummah made embrocations that burned and chilled simultaneously. When he dreamt, it was of naked women riding him in paroxysms of lust, their faces melting into his chest, only to suffocate as they punctured his heart with fangs.

Through it all he sensed someone standing over him, head in a turban, censer in his hands, whispering.

Then one morning, like curtains being drawn open, the heaviness lifted off. He came out of his season of darkness, and Ummah was there.

'...*pontianaks*[181]...', he croaked, clutching his chest.

'They will not trouble you again.'

Then he knew it had not been a dream.

'They wanted your soul. But it is over now.'

And it *was* over. It was as if he had been exorcised of his past and deep sadness. He no longer saw his father's rejection. The fishing village became home, and the fishermen embraced him. They saw it as a filial honouring of the man swallowed by their sea. Dom Hendrique became a regular at Ummah's house, with Ayesha heaven bent on fattening him up.

---

181 Pontianak – she-demons.

'Eat the bitter gourd Dom. If you've got worms it will kill them. You're too thin, like *lallang!*[182]'

Ummah was secretly grateful for Dom's presence, what with Ismael's growing disaffection. It would be a matter of time before Ismael turned his back on the forge. He was working powerfully with the hammer and the anvil, but it did not reach his spirit. Unlike Isa he was earthy, a hunter by nature and killing the Japanese soldier had whet his appetite. He was also distracted by love which left him pining.

Every fortnight, he took a two-hour journey by bus hoping to catch a glimpse of Mariam Serani who lived with her Uncle D'Alvisse in Seremban. He was representing Ayesha on the pretext of doing business with D'Alvisse's wife, Sally, who traded in batik and precious stones. Ismael came home with sarongs, which he promptly gave Ayesha to sell at the markets. Often, the day after his visit with D'Alvisse, he would be despondent. Ummah knew what was eating Ismael.

'It's time your mother stopped cooking for you boys,' Ummah said casually, one evening over dinner.

'Abang! I like cooking for the children.'

'Yes, we love Ibu's cooking...this *otak-otak*[183] is delicious, Bu.'

'If my cooking is not good enough...' Ayesha sniffed, getting ready to be upset.

'Your cooking is very good Ayesha, have I ever complained?'

'Who will cook for them if I don't?'

'Their wives...'

They ate in silence, heads bent over their plates, until Isa started snorting.

'I don't want to marry *the* Serani girl,' Ismael said hotly.

---

182   Lallang – A coarse, long weedy grass.

183   Otak-otak – a combination of seafood, chili and coconut steamed in banana leaf.

'Did I mention Mariam?' Ummah asked blandly.

'You've really got it bad Bro.'

'What are you looking at? *Ada utang ke*[184]?'

'I think it's time you went out and worked so that you can take care of a wife.'

'But, the forge?!'

'I've spoken with General Ghazali, at the Terendak Army Camp. He's willing to give you a job in the army ... as a Ranger.'

'It takes three to work the forge!'

'Your mother will help.'

'She's a woman...'

'There have always been female *empus*[185] in our *keturunan*[186], she will observe the same rituals of cleanliness.'

And so Ismael joined the Royal Military Academy to become a Ranger. A natural trekker, he led British soldiers in finding communist bases in the jungle. Guns and grenades paled the little slim Keris into insignificance.

A few months later, Ummah decided it was time to ask for Mariam's hand in marriage for his son. The memory of a seven-year-old, with Japanese soldiers pointing guns at her, was carved on his heart. He needed someone from the Catholic path to approach Mariam's Uncle Adrian D'Alvisse. He turned to Dom Hendrique.

Dom was decidedly better. Results of blood tests from Australia

---

184   Ada utang ke? – Do I owe you something?

185   Empus – Keris makers.

186   Keturunan – family line.

showed he had had encephalitis from a shingle virus. The ropey snake blisters around his forehead had dried up but he still tired easily, needing to sleep a few hours in the afternoon.

'It's good for a man to get married Dom. Is there someone you have in mind?' This was the typical Malay way of putting your hand around your head to touch your nose.

'No one would have me,' Dom laughed cynically. 'A death sentence, not to be able to go for Mass.'

'Maybe Ayesha could be your *Mak Endam*[187],' Ummah said loudly.

'Eshh!' she squealed from inside. 'I don't know about these things.'

'Actually I was hoping that you would be a matchmaker for Ismael,' Ummah said grinning as he lit a cigarette.

'Me!'

'She's *your* kind, a Katolic...Mariam Serani.'

'The Serani family executed by the Japanese in Penang?'

'Yes, Serani's daughter. I know you know the family. She lives with her Uncle Elvis. Ismael will suit a girl like her, such courage and a big heart.'

'Ummah, she believes in the one true God, Allah. She will not convert.'

'There is no need to convert for the true believers. Al-Shiddiq Allah. There is no compulsion, the Surah Al-Bakarah is clear on that.'

Unwittingly, Dom became Ismael's "Mak Endam". Bearing gifts, he arrived at Uncle "Elvis's" house. The D'Alvisses were dark giants, Eurasians with goatees and pencil-line moustaches, a conquistadors chevron. Adrian D'Alvisse was a son of the famous Hector D'Alvisse. Hector, an engineer, had helped lay down the railway

---

187   Mak Endam – An older woman in the kampong who specialises in matchmaking. She will approach the bride's family with a proposal and if it is accepted, the Mak Endam prepares the bride. From teeth filing to dress and jewellery; she is very important in a Malay wedding.

lines for the Crown Transport, which took tin and rubber to the ports for export. Taken to Burma by the Japanese to build the death railway, he never returned. Adrian was one of eight siblings caught up in an infernal battle for his father's considerable wealth. With the acrimonious settlement, the family was in tatters. Adrian had further estranged himself from the larger Kristang family by converting to Islam and marrying a Muslim. He was a black sheep in the Catholic community. The Church regarded his six children as illegitimate.

A hard-looking man, with hair growing out of his ears, he was not cruel but ruled with legalism. His "yes" was "yes" and "no" was "no", and the maxim he lived by – "neither a borrower nor a lender be", earnt him no friends.

Dom Hendriques's "marriage proposal" was timely. D'Alvisse's papers for migration to Australia had been approved, and Mariam was not in his plans. She had no documents, they were all destroyed in the war. Her life had been on a downward spiral since receiving her certificate of bravery at the Club from Sir Gerald Templer. The only man who loved her, Dr Azariah, the darling of the English circle, was killed in a daring communist attack. One shot. Clean through the forehead, it was a warning to the running dogs. The entire community mourned because he dispensed free medicine to the estate Tamils, poor Malays and Chinese farmers. There was a huge turnout for the funeral and that was the last time Ummah saw Mariam. Sixteen, in a hat and pinafore, she was crushed like a flower. Alice Azariah went back to Madras, and Mariam was left to the kindness of her only living uncle, Adrian D'Alvisse.

In the D'Alvisse household, Mariam stopped being precious. There was no question of a higher education, she was a girl. As far as D'Alvisse was concerned, the years that Mariam had lived with him were mutually beneficial. He had given her not only a roof over her head but had put her through sewing classes. It was his trade-off for Mariam's nanny services.

Mariam was out when Dom arrived. His reputation for being a heretic had preceded him. D'Alvisse carefully studied the man sitting in his living room. He was prematurely grey for a twenty-two-year-old, and looked in his forties. Speaking slowly to focus his thoughts, he pulled constantly on the trousers at the knees, as if they were a little constricting in the crotch. He was no madman, only a broken man. D'Alvisse's lips curled. He knew the malice of that breaking.

There were no doubts that the marriage proposal was serious. The gifts from the prospective groom glittered on the rattan coffee table. It was the traditional Malay *hantaran*[188] for a bride. A gold necklace with matching earrings, a pair of sequined shoes, and perfume, sat on a silver tray covered with red embroidered *songket*.[189] And for D'Alvisse, if the proposal was accepted, a watch, and a gold ring for his wife.

'It has been very hard looking after a girl who is not your own,' D'Alvisse said resignedly, to Dom. 'Mariam's a good girl but she's headstrong.'

'It's perfect timing! Mariam has been talking of wedding dresses lately,' Sally sighed, her eyes on the hantaran, hand over her heart.

'We want her in a good home Sally,' D'Alvisse said brusquely, 'don't put any romantic nonsense in her head.'

Dom shot a hurried look at Sally. She was petite and buxom, with freckles running down her neck into the top of her frock. She looked like one of the Kristang women from Portuguese Settlement even though she was Malay.

---

188   Hantaran – a gift sent to the prospective bride.

189   Songket – Fabric belonging to the brocade family of Malaysia, Brunei and Indonesia, hand-woven with gold and silver threads.

'Dom, stay for dinner,' she said huskily, lowering her eyelashes. 'I've cooked Addy's favourite... *Nasi Kandar*[190]. He works so hard and deserves a good meal!'

'Mariam will be back soon but yes, please stay the night,' Adrian said hospitably, the thought of a sumptuous dinner acting like a rabies shot. Sally was clearly an expert at soothing her husband's distemper.

Within the hour, Mariam came home with D'Alvisse's children. Light skinned compared to the dark leathery D'Alvisse, she had lost her European bias. She looked like a fair Sikh girl, with her long brown hair and light honey eyes. A shapeless yellow frock buttoned to the collar hid her figure. She could have passed for fifteen not nineteen.

'Children, Mariam, this is Uncle Dom.'

'Uncle, good evening.'

'Children, go and clean up. Marie, Dom's got something important he wants to say to you,' D'Alvisse said without beating around the bush. 'Come and sit down.'

Dom was chagrined that she was being thrust straight into such a serious discussion. Mariam on the other hand was unruffled. She quietly moved over to one of the chairs, and sat on the edge, her fingers intertwined on her lap. Out of impermanence she was prepared for anything.

'Mariam, I've come to see you for a very special reason. A marriage proposal. There's a family in Port Dickson in the fishing village where I stay. Ummah, the father, he wants your hand in marriage, I mean for one of his sons...'

Dom found himself tailing off, quite unsure of what to say next. The neutral expression on Mariam's face turned coy, as she purposefully

---

190   Nasi Kandar – a popular dish originating from Penang. It is steamed rice with a variety of curries.

took in the hantaran on the coffee table.

'Ismael?'

'Yes.'

'*You* know Ismael!' Sally chirped. 'He comes to buy my batik every month. You've caught his eye *sayang*[191].'

'Uncle Elvis,' she said cautiously, turning to D'Alvisse. She was making sure that she would not run afoul of his displeasure.

'It's alright,' D'Alvisse nodded his head. 'Aunty Sally says he's an honest young man, hard working. And he's a Ranger in the army.'

'They will take good care of you. I've lived there at the village for a year and they're like my family.'

'Were they the ones who took care of you when the people at Padri sa Chang...?' she asked quietly.

It pained him that she knew who he was but Dom was cut to the heart at the way she called the family, "the people". She was more isolated than he was.

'I've brought a gift from Ummah for you. He said that even if you said "no" he wanted you to have this for saving Ismael's life.'

Dom got up and took a red pouch off the tray. Mariam's eyes widened with a feathery intake of air, as her fingers locked and her back straightened.

'Even if I said "no"?'

'Yes, this is a gift for you, an *utang budi*[192], for saving Ismael's life. Ummah wanted to do it for your *bapak angkat*[193], your father, Dr Azariah.'

A tangible change came over Mariam. Her face opened like a child's and warmth infused her fine-boned features.

---

191   Sayang – Sweetheart, love in Malay.

192   Utang budi – a debt of gratitude and honour.

193   Bapak angkat – a man who becomes an adopted father.

'My father...'

'You won't get another proposal like this girl,' D'Alvisse cut in. 'You want the family, not the gold.'

'Family?'

It was one word but it filled the room. Her guard was down and she had betrayed her emotions.

'I've told you so many times Mariam, count your blessings,' D'Alvisse said sharply, feeling the barb.

'We can't take you to Australia but Addy and I want you to be happy... to be settled in a good home,' Sally interrupted hastily. 'It will make us happy.'

There was a pregnant pause as Mariam folded her arms. Then, as if her back gave way, she sank back into the chair, forlornly.

'I'll get married. Be happy,' she said looking down at the floor.

'Excuse me...'

Before D'Alvisse could convey his obvious disapproval, Dom moved. He went over to her chair and sat down on the floor at her feet. She was taken aback, sitting up immediately, smoothing her skirt over her knees.

'May I?' Dom asked gently as he presented a gold bracelet from the pouch. 'They will treasure you, you know. You and your father, Dr Azariah, saved their lives.'

She looked into his eyes for what seemed like an eternity. Behind him, Dom could hear D'Alvisse's agitated breathing. Then with a deep breath, Mariam held out her hand. Dom clasped the bracelet on and moved back.

'Do what they tell you, be obedient!' D'Alvisse interjected solemnly.

With a little squeal, Sally rushed over to Mariam to give the girl a hug. Mariam, however, was looking at D'Alvisse, her face clouding at his words.

'Ummah wants Mariam to do what she wants,' Dom said quickly. 'She's got a few years to decide.'

'What do you mean, *a few years to decide*?' D'Alvisse asked concernedly.

'If Mariam wants to go back to studying or do a business in batik, whatever she chooses.... Ummah felt Dr Azariah would have wanted that for you, Mariam.'

She looked at Dom for a few seconds as the words sank in. Then for the first time she smiled. Her fingers moved to the bracelet on her other hand and she began to play with it.

'Well, as long as the old man's happy,' D'Alvisse said with the finality of a hammer going down on an auction.

And so Mariam was to be engaged to Ranger Ismael, a guide with the Worcestershire Regiment, after Merdeka.

On Cape Rachado, the Catholic Monastery ruminated on Dominic Hendrique for months.

'Was Brother Dominic a mole?'

'Did he infiltrate the Order to start some sort of trouble?'

'What was his relationship with the Advisor's personal assistant?'

'Or was it simply demonic!'

Whatever he was, they had culled it and there were no regrets. In the larger scheme of things, Dom Hendrique was only a carbuncle on the backside of an institution as inflexible as iron. He was squashed and forgotten as the Amazonian bride of God fought for her seat in Malaya.

28

Two months before Independence, a "Tuan" was found dead at the Si-Rusa Inn. His Malay girlfriend, slashed in the face, was rushed to the hospital at midnight. Rumours blitzed a town starved of serious crime.

The Tuan was the geologist with BP, Fred MacKeerne, husband of the Club lush Maude. His girlfriend, "Ann", was Maude's ex-servant. The two women were hauled in, Maude under pressure of neutrality with the approaching independence, by PC Hoskins. Ann, five stitches to her cheek, was as distraught as a banshee. "Freddy" was going to take her back to England, she repeated in broken English. Maude, in the python grip of alcohol, smirked.

The Constable was investigating several possibilities. One, a domestic quarrel where Ann had been beaten, before she "did Freddy in", or perhaps Maude had poisoned Fred, ordering Ann's disfigurement. BP paid out handsomely to widows. Privately, PC Hoskins put his money on the wife. She was a disgrace, not to mention an ugly cow, but it would be unthinkable to swing a white woman in Malaya. Fortunately for Maude, the Malay girl, who was returning to the kampong after visiting Fred, was unable to identify her attackers, it was too dark.

It was a scintillating love story for the small-town folk. A crime of passion… two women fighting over one man.

> Your cheatin' heart
> Will make you weep
> You'll cry and cry
> And try to sleep

The "cowboi (sic)" song marinated the mood in Port Dickson. The case, to Police Constable Hoskins's disappointment, was solved without much ado. Dr Kendrell, the in-house doctor for BP, reported that the geologist, sweating profusely, had complained of shortness of breath and shooting pains down his left arm. The man had died of a heart attack. When Constable Hoskins had gone to the fishing village to seek witnesses on Ani's attack, his case downgraded from murder to assault, the villagers lowered their heads and played "silly buggers." They were not about to betray their own but they all knew who was responsible. The Al-Sijjin.

Living in a commune on the Field of Blood, their fanatical kin were harassing Muslim women with uncovered heads and calves. They formed vigilante groups and were patrolling clubs and rest houses for deviant Muslims. Head knocking, slaps, spitting and verbal abuse began to crop up in the sleepy hollow. The Imams turned a blind eye, the Al-Sijjin were brothers.

After Ani's attack an emergency meeting was arranged at Ummah's house. Ten Imams in white jubbahs sat around a tray of barely eaten yellow rice and beef rendang. They sat quietly sipping coffee noisily.

'They had no right to disfigure the woman,' Ummah said finally.

'You know what she was doing!' one of the men said unhappily.

'This is not our way.'

'She's gone away to the city. We know what she's going to do there…'

Silently they ached with a yet unnamed malaise that was raising its nefarious head in Port Dickson.

And it was larger than the Al-Sijjin. The demand for land for a new highway was stirring a rancour that seemed to have been buried with the "New White Village" settlement program. The voices of Chinese farmers clanged like ladles in woks at the marketplace. Even though many resisted selling their farms – precious land obtained by Templer – to the newly formed Highways Cartel, the lure of money was still a hook in the jaw for some. Age-old tensions and infighting between the different Chinese clans put the vegetable acreage at risk. Culturally phlegmatic, the Malay fishermen internalised their unhappiness, (the proposed highway skirted on Tiger Sanctuary) but the Tamils were the most frenetic at the ecological upset. Covering themselves with temple ash and wrapping amulets around their waists, they looked ghoulish.

'*Durga*[194] feeds in the jungle, where will she turn?'

'*Kali Matha*[195] comes, the Black One, the Mother of Death.'

Then the white Sumatran, Tok Panjang Kuku, struck. It was on the border of Tiger Sanctuary, at the site of the ground-breaking ceremony for the new highway. The Civil Engineer, Ken Williams, was getting the plot ready for a pompous Roman obelisk. The first Prime Minister of the nation would unveil the obelisk, offer up prayers and pour in a shovelful of gravel.

'This is the spot, boys… dig in!' Williams bellowed, stamping the loam rich ground. The Tamil Coolies, twanging with fear, looked at him, white-eyed.

'Start digging! What are you waiting for, you cowardly mongrels?!'

---

194   Durga – Goddess Durga in Hindu mythology slays demons.

195   Kali Matha – Durga is also Kali Matha, the Black Mother, goddess of death and destruction.

From behind him, Long Claws leaned out and charily wrapped his paws around Ken Williams. The maps were still in his hands, as the jungle wolfed him up, screaming.

It was a bad omen for the locals and there was a shroud of dismay amongst the District Officers. Two white men dead in two weeks. The Tuans frequenting the Club had their hunting guns in the car, hip revolvers loaded. Alistair only realised how unsettled he was when Sir Douglas sent him a discreet note to oversee the dismantling of the centrifuge and *Brave New World*. He hesitated! (The project had died several years earlier but the debris had not been cleared.)

Armed with a dozen soldiers, two trucks and a bulldozer, he made the assault. The bulldozer roared and grunted, as it pulled down the sentry posts and he was grateful for the noise. They were barely out of their vehicles when, to their utter horror, the door of the greenhouse crashed open. Out leapt the creature with a deep-throated howl. Alistair stood paralysed.

'Don't shoot...it's human!'

It was only Gila Thambi, the madman. Hair overgrown, blimped up with layers of rags he looked like the Tasmanian Devil, bred with an orang-utan. As the soldiers wrestled him to the ground, biting and screeching, Alistair's thoughts cleared. *How long has he known about the greenhouse?* As if reading his thoughts, Gila spoke, his eyes yellow with lunacy.

'I say chaps, take care of her for me, won't you? She's all I got!'

Every eye fixed itself on the filthy "thing", shackled. It was a cultured voice, English, with a touch of American, shocking in its descent from dignity.

'Too many war movies at the Pesta, Sir,' a soldier said brightly, turning away, but his tone was false.

How the mighty have fallen, thought Alistair, as he saw his father sick, unhinged before the suicide. For days he could not shake off a deep anxiety.

In the fishing village, the fire in the forge blazed late into the night, the anvil clanging against the pounding waves. Ummah had been commissioned by the Council of Rulers to make the Keris for the first *Agung*[196], of independent Malaya. With Ismael in the army, Ayesha took his place because she had no cycle of blood.

Overnight, Isa's lean frame filled with muscles and sinews that drove the forge. There was a gifting on him that magnified with Ismael's departure. He pressed deeper into the arts, mastering the alchemy of metals, melding and beating the iron into startling silver damascene. According to the rites of old, Isa's purity would yield a gifting on the Keris. It was a new dawning and a new unction of Allah's authority over the Golden Chersonese.

---

196   Agung – King in the Malay language.

29

THE SPOTTED DOG, as the Selangor Club was blithely christened, was not going down without a fight. The Club had resisted Sir Templer's frothing orders to go native. With excuses, from flooding to termites in the floorboards, "exploding" toilets, and very naturally after that, a fresh coat of paint for the black and white Tudor Clubhouse, they outwaited Templer who left in the middle of 1954.

The members were an unenlightened bastion of colonial diehards, with locals disqualified from membership. The Club reserved the rights to remove forcibly, a partner who was not European. The bigotry at the Spotted Dog turned in on itself at the exclusive men-only Hunter's Bar. No female hazarded to cast her shadow on the men brooding over their *Stengahs*[197]. Large upside pyramids in safari jackets, stained with sweat patches, they stood at the long bar opening onto the equatorial forest of Federal Hill. With loaded rifles propped against the bar, they watched the jungle with a blinkered fixation.

Before the war, a pair of tigers in heat, had crashed amorously into the clearing. Disorientated, the tigers gave the lucky devils at the

---

197   Stengahs – Half a peg of Scotch whiskey with a spurt of soda.

bar time to scramble for their hunting guns. The female was killed, a warning for the women at the Spotted Dog. After that, every man standing at the Hunter's Bar prayed for a tiger to be thrown quite literally into his lap.

However, with Independence a month away, they could no longer stop the birth pangs and gushing forth of Asian cries in the Club. The incoming government was insisting the *Merdeka*[198] ceremony take place on the oval facing the Moorish "Mahomaten" styled Sultan Abdul Samad Building, the centre of British administration.

The recalcitrant committee of the Spotted Dog spawned a plan. Now for all their foibles, the British as a people have a remarkable virtue. At best it could be described as a Promethean death wish. A cricket match between the English and the local team would be a show of sportsmanship. They were going to be gracious, but they would trounce the locals and leave them with red faces long after the "Tuans" had gone. A notice was posted in the *Malayan Times*. Prominent locals would be issued invitations subject to strict dress codes for the veranda and viewing gallery. For the man on the street, stands were erected on the oval.

It was a perfect morning for the match, the Club full to the gunwales with local leaders attending handover briefs. Cloudy with a sweet breeze rolling off Federal Hill, the Spotted Dog looked like barley sugar dropped in the sun. Locals like ants were zeroing in for a hit. In the viewing gallery, the male guests wore sports blazers, the ladies, hats and or gloves, all from Robinsons.

It was very la-di-da! Those in school uniforms were marched off

---

198   Merdeka – Independence Day.

to the sheds erected around the green, while the riff-raff and urchins lined the outfield along the main road. Hawkers had unloaded monster tiffins of local cakes and curry puffs, balanced on poles on their shoulders and were making a killing. Across the oval, twenty-foot flags of the new nation mounted the façade of the Moorish edifice of the British administration. The Club flagpole with the Union Jack cracked back defiantly.

On the veranda, guests were drawing raised eyebrows and sniffs from members safely lodged into the prime seats before the doors opened. The "oohs" and "ahhs" were, for the repatriating English, as rude as the release of flatulence in public.

'What darling tea cups.'

'Let's go the powder room, I hear it's got a bidit (sic).'

'Don't forget your camera!'

'How do they get these napkins so white!'

'I dying for some *rojak*[199] from the hawker stall.'

'Kumar, don't you dare shame me.'

'Egg sandwiches are so boring *lah*.'

'Sit down!'

'The cups are Royal Doulton Bone China. Here, it's on the underside.'

Those who missed out on the veranda, spilled hastily into the Pig and Whistle brassiere. Chairs being pulled and voices raised in excitement augured the death of British sobriety.

In the Cavendish mezzanine, Sir Douglas Hill, Advisor of Negeri Sembilan, was hosting "elevenses", and a game of billiards. He had handpicked local businessmen who wanted to buy up British shares in private plantations under ten thousand acres. The group would be whittled down to six for a private luncheon at the Coliseum Café.

---

199   Rojak – A sweet and savoury local fruit salad with peanut sauce.

Those who could not keep up with the "play" could retire to the veranda and watch the cricket.

Alistair, winding through miles of rubber estate between Port Dickson and the capital, a revolver on his lap, was one of the few Britishers to be invited formally to the cricket match. Actually, it was Ivy who had been invited. Several years earlier, Mrs Pierce's guests had been asked to leave the Spotted Dog. The committee was extending a reconciliatory hand. Ivy had flashed her sharky grin as she tossed the invitation aside carelessly.

'They still don't get it, do they? We don't *need* to be invited to what's ours.'

'I think they're being decent.'

'Decent! That's not how I remember it.'

He could not forget either. It was the unhappiest moment of his life with Ivy. An awakening actually. It was six months after they married and they were invited to Uncle Jolly Bein's hundredth birthday party in Kuala Lumpur. The fact that he was confined to a wheelchair did not stop "the family" from celebrating with dance and dinner at the Chinese Assembly Hall and the *Trez Amigos* from Portuguese Settlement were special guest performers for the evening with their "gypsy" classical guitars. Alistair and Ivy decided to make a holiday of it, setting off with Cuthbert and Adele.

It had been Alistair's suggestion to stop at the Pig and Whistle brassiere for pheasant liver pâté in orange rind and the tart rhubarb pie. They had just made themselves comfortable, when a committee member, in the club blazer, popped up next to Alistair.

'Sir, I'm sorry Sir, there's been an objection.'

'May I ask from whom?' Alistair asked, refusing to look around.

'Mr Harrow, Kingsley Harrow... it's your guests, Sir.'

Kingsley Harrow was the most insufferable hypocrite the Spotted Dog had for a member. Head manager of the Sime Darby plantations, he carried a bullwhip, and there were lurid stories of its use on the rubber trappers. Kingsley stopped short of being one of the misogynists at the Hunter's Bar because he liked his women, and he liked them dark. These were only rumours of course, except for the pregnant thirteen-year-old, whom he carried through a thunderstorm to Dr Azariah. The good doctor delivered a healthy girl with hazel eyes, who was given up for adoption in the north.

'It'll just be a matter of time before we get this white trash out of the club,' Ivy said loudly, getting up from the table.

There was pin-drop silence as Alistair felt the blood pounding in his cheeks.

'And you know what's waiting for them back home, nothing! No clubs, no drivers, no servants, no *tabek*[200] *tuans*[201]. We'll be here, enjoying!'

Alistair had never been so angry in all his life, not even when his mother had suggested putting his father in an institution.

'You had *no right* to disgrace me like that Ivy!'

'Disgrace you! What do you think happened to us?'

'*You* were not told to leave. You are my wife, and immediate family.'

'You don't see it do you? I'm not just your wife! I've got family.'

It was then Alistair realised, Ivy was never going to cleave to him. It was a symbiotic relationship, born out of a congenital need for endorsement of her European-ness. She thrived like an English

---

200   Tabek – A salute showing respect.

201   Tuan – Sir or Mister in the Malay language for white men.

rose only in the glasshouse of Malaya, and he was a suture holding together her antipodal divide.

'Excited?' Alistair asked, turning to Ivy sitting next to him in the car.

'A little nervous. You?'

'Not nervous ....'

'I hope we're not in for a big disappointment.'

Neither of them were talking about the cricket game. Alistair was meeting Sir Douglas Hill at the Spotted Dog. He had expressed his intentions to stay on in Malaya and there was talk of a new portfolio. What, he did not yet know. The trip would reveal all. For Alistair, there was no great wrenching or dilemma about staying on in Malaya. In a strange sort of way, he knew it the day he had seen his "gypsies" in Malacca.

His eyes flicked to the rear-view mirror to the third person in the back of the car, Dom Hendrique.

Blessed Trinity! he thought resignedly.

Dom was asleep, mouth open. He had come along because he needed to buy a shirt from Robinsons for Ismael's engagement. There was no trace of the ugly snake-like scales on his forehead. In the mirror, Alistair saw only a shadow of the owlish eighteen-year-old he had met at the club four years earlier. He looked middle-aged, his hair prematurely grey, and it was a sad face. "Family" or not Alistair liked the fellow.

Lobotomised his dreams... but they couldn't kill his spirit.

'Will you be involved with the obelisk ceremony for the new highway in Port Dickson?'

'I'm not sure with the new portfolio.'

'Lots of people are unhappy.'

'I suppose the death of two Tuans hasn't helped,' Alistair agreed, remembering the madman at the site of *Brave New World*.

'The Brits have reneged on Portuguese Settlement. It's back on the market,' Dom said quietly, from behind.

'What!' Ivy exclaimed, turning to the back. 'Who told you this?'

'Ummah heard it from Father Pintado.'

'Alistair, did you know about this?'

'No! We don't have jurisdiction outside of Negeri Sembilan. I doubt Sir Douglas would know as well.'

'The Crown's revoked her freehold status and made it leasehold,' Dom said, refusing to meet Alistair's eyes in the mirror.

'But why? They're leaving!' Ivy spewed in utter disbelief. 'Everything they touch turns from gold to dust.'

'It can't be as bad as it sounds, nothing ever is,' Alistair countered lightly. 'There's got to be a good reason.'

'It's been *our* home for five hundred years, Alis. Our matchstick houses may not look much to you but it's the only thing we have.'

'We'll have to do something about it Ivy,' Dom said, sounding drained.

'*You* must Dom. Your great-great-grandfather was Panglima Awang Enrique. We're dying, Dom.'

Something brushed against Alistair's heart. It was the same feeling he had had before he walked into the bathroom in his father's house.

At the main entrance of the Spotted Dog, two handsome turbaned Sikhs in uniform, saluted them. A smell of polish, leather and tobacco lingered in the reception where a young British cadet in white uniform greeted and registered them.

'If you'll wait here Sir, I'll inform Sir Douglas.'

The reception flowed out onto the veranda where half a dozen steps led down to the oval. The cricket game was in play. It was plain there was trouble on the pitch. Raised Asian voices, smarmy and at the same time nettled, carried clear as a bell into the reception. They moved towards the veranda. On the pitch, the local team of cricketers were gathered around the umpire. The English team, apart from the Captain, were standing with great composure at their positions on the oval. Clearly the umpire was being harried about a call, both from the Malayan players and the locals in the crowd, including those on the veranda.

'Is not chucking Tuan... iss not (sic),' whined a Tamil bowler.

Suddenly, the English umpire, clearly fed up to his teeth, turned and addressed the spectators on the veranda.

'Is there a doctor in the house?!'

It was a call for help, for reinforcements from his side, because the chance of a local doctor being there was too slim.

'What's going on Alistair? A bit of skulduggery?'

Alistair turned to see Sir Douglas behind them.

'Ivy my dear,' Sir Douglas said, as he kissed her on the cheeks and graciously put his hand out to Dom.

'I think there's some doubt about the bowler chucking the ball Sir. This is his second batsman out on a golden duck. There's a protest being lodged. He insists it's the natural curve of his arm.'

'I could hear it all the way up to the mezzanine, the Club's woken up finally. Fallen out of bed, actually.'

'It's the Battle for Malaya,' Ivy bantered slyly.

'Ehm...,' Sir Douglas said, lighting his cigar. 'I hope it settles down before the delegation arrives.'

'I'm a doctor!'

They turned to look. It was Dr Kendrell. He made his way off the veranda, down the steps and onto the oval.

'It's a pity you're not a betting man, Alistair, I'll wager Kendrell's going to make a career move.'

'I beg your pardon, Sir?'

'Smart man our good doctor, risky business getting onto the pitch. A man could get killed in more ways than one,' Sir Douglas said lightly.

'The bowler says his arm was broken as a young boy.'

The umpire spoke loudly in the name of partiality as he dialogued with Dr Kendrell on the oval. No one talked as they strained to catch the conversation.

'Any medical proof? Any witness? What about his parents?'

'There is no medical documentation!'

'The arm *does* appear to have been severely broken below the elbow and badly put back.'

'He says he's the High Commissioner's driver.'

'Oh!'

'Bad call for the Club team, I'm afraid!' Sir Douglas mused. 'That's Murali, Sir Gerald Templer's driver.'

'Bad luck Sir,' agreed Alistair.

Everybody had heard of Murali, Templer's driver. At twelve, his arm had almost been severed with a machete by the communists, to deter the Tamil labourers from working the rubber estates. Miraculously, it had been saved from amputation. Murali joined the Indian army and became a driver. When Templer looked for a driver, he wanted someone with a grudge against the communists. He chose Murali.

Dom sauntered over to the veranda to watch the proceedings from close up. The silence was amazing as Dr Kendrell examined the young bowler. Then very deliberately the doctor turned and addressed the spectators.

'I would like to confirm that Mr Murali has a broken arm, an injury from childhood. In my professional opinion, there are no rules being violated due to this natural handicap.'

There was an outburst of claps and cheering from the locals, as the umpire, with a black face, shook Kendrell's hand.

'Mark my words, Kendrell's going to be nominated for a *Datoship*[202],' Sir Douglas said admiringly. 'You know he's put in his papers for naturalisation?'

'No, I didn't Sir.'

'Well, I'm sure you're also wondering about your own plans. Let's go over there, shall we?'

Sir Douglas steered them to some leather chairs in a private corner of the reception area.

'I won't make a meal of it ...' he said, as he put his hand into his inner coat pocket, and pulled out a letter. 'I hope you'll be happy.'

Opening the letter, with Ivy sitting next to him, Alistair could feel the relief sweeping through him. Ivy gasped in delight.

'Head of the Rubber Research Institute! That's a great honour, Sir ...'

'The Institute has its facility in Port Dickson currently. Within fifteen years they'll probably relocate to the city. There's a huge laboratory and greenhouse on the cards.'

'Thank you very much Sir Douglas! We're very grateful.'

'Don't thank me my boy. I never forget a favour. Now I've got to get back to the boys on the mezzanine. Why don't you go and enjoy the cricket ... what's left of it with Murali and his golden arm.'

---

202   Datoship – Peership bestowed by the Sultans.

Part 10

ONE WEEK TO INDEPENDENCE

1957 – 24TH AUGUST
PORT DICKSON - BRITISH MALAYA

"The office of magician is very often hereditary. It is not so always, however, there being certain recognised ways in which a man may 'get magic'. One of the most peculiar is as follows:

To obtain magical powers (ilmu) you must meet the ghost of a murdered man."

Malay Magic – Walter William Skeat
Civil Servant - Straits Settlements
Malaya.

30

ONE WEEK TO INDEPENDENCE

'THE AL-SIJJIN ARE BUYING GUNS from the communists.'

'What are you saying, Ismael?'

They were eating their evening meal and Ayesha had gone to a lot of trouble. Lance Corporal Ismael, recently promoted, was home to oversee the building of a brick house for his bride-to-be, Mariam, in town. Also, Isa and Ummah were leaving in the morning for the Sacred Seat of the Ancestors in Tiger Sanctuary. The *Keris*[203] for the first King of the new nation was ready to be consecrated. Ismael's best man and matchmaker, Dom, had been invited to dinner.

'The Al-Sijjin are buying guns from the communists,' Ismael repeated, one hand on his hip, cross-legged on the mat.

'How did you find this out, Mael?' Isa asked dismayed.

'My contact in the Special Branch. He said the British intelligence knows.'

'Knowing is not enough. What are they going to do about it? The Al-Sijjin live on our doorstep. This is British propaganda.'

'The communists *are* desperate, Abah. They're not part of the new government, they want to destabilise the situation.'

'I don't believe the Al-Sijjin would have anything to do with the

---

203   Keris – a 12-inch sinewy stabbing sword which is part of the Royal Regalia.

communists. Mao Tse-Tung and Stalin are God haters!' Ummah said vehemently.

He reached out and picked up a pewter teapot to wash his rice and curry-stained fingers into a fingerbowl.

'Abang!' Ayesha protested. 'You're not finished?'

'The communists are God-haters but I wouldn't call the Al-Sijjin God-lovers, Abah,' Isa said quietly.

'God-lovers can do bad things,' mused Dom.

'But guns? They are believers, Muslimin.'

'British intelligence intercepted a sale up at the Thai border. Their ID cards showed they came from Port Dickson.'

'Ya Allah!' exclaimed Ayesha. 'Shame on our kampong.'

'We don't want guns in our kampong. I've seen what they can do.'

'Love's really affecting you bro.'

'We should meet with our Muslimin brothers, and talk with them.'

'*You* don't go near them,' Ummah said emphatically, pointing his finger at Ismael.

There was an awkward silence, as Ummah lit a cigarette. Dom noisily cracked a crab claw and Isa made a pretence of preparing a mouthful of rice. Ismael reached out with his free hand and poured a cup of coffee from the enamel pot for his father.

'I'm not afraid of them, Mael, but talk won't help.'

'You've been away a long time bro, you don't know *these brothers.* They don't want the communists, they don't want the British, they don't want a democratic government...'

'So what *do* they want?'

'The *Hudud*[204] Law!'

---

204   Hudud – Islamic law which mandates public lashing, stoning or execution and amputation of hands. This is relatively uncommon in modern times and is currently witnessed in Muslim nations such as Saudi Arabia and Iran.

'I'm not going to *Keramat Rimau*[205] to sanctify the Keris,' Ummah said abruptly. 'I'm going out in the boat, to seek Allah's will.'

They were all shocked, especially Isa, whose mouth was agape.

'What is it Abang? The Keris must be given to the Council of Rulers next week.'

'I know Ayesha, I know. The Spirit of the ancestors, the *Mahamulia*[206], will bless the Keris. Only I will not go, Isa will consecrate it.'

'Why Abah? The British Intelligence has everything under control.'

'Something is not right here,' Ummah said, forcefully knocking his chest.

'The spirit of death is hovering,' Isa agreed uneasily, fiddling with his rice.

'You're not talking about Tok,' Dom asked nervously, envisioning his walk back to his father's kampong house in the inky night.

'It's over the whole town like a shroud.'

'It's the new highway,' lamented Ayesha, 'it's cutting though our *semangat*[207].'

'I am going out to sea for three days to seek God's wisdom. Isa, you go to the sacred grounds of our ancestors and consecrate the Keris. You have seen me do it … I know you can.'

'Yes Abah.'

Isa's heart was flooded with a rhapsody of emotion. The first Keris for the first King of the new nation. It was the moment he had waited for. From childhood, he was told he was set apart, because he was born en caul. The tuft of white fur on his forehead below his hairline

---

205   Keramat Rimau – Tiger Sanctuary.

206   Mahamulia – Sanskrit for the Great and Worthy one.

207   Semangat – spirit.

was the seal. He was a descendant of the Illuminated One, the White Tiger, called to the Seat of the Ancestors.

'And what am I supposed to do?' Ismael demanded, peeved.

'You get ready to get married! Your *Mak Endam*'[208] Ayesha said appreciatively, looking at Dom, 'is more prepared. I like your hair, Dom. Did Missy Ivy do it? Very suitable.'

'You look handsome,' Ismael agreed.

And he did. Ivy had dyed his hair, hiding all the grey. Where before he looked forty, he now looked fifteen years younger. He smiled gamely.

'Mael, you and Dom go and sort out the house. I want a nice home for my daughter-in-law and grandchildren.'

'Not bad, bro! You get a new house *and* a new wife.'

'How's Mariam?' asked Dom.

'She's fine, a bit shy.'

'Do you speak to her in English or *Bahasa Melayu*[209]?' Ummah asked suspiciously.

'Why don't you speak in English?' enquired Dom. 'You always speak in Bahasa to Pa Alistair.'

'That is the language of this country! Pa Ali has to come up to our level. How is he? I hear he wants to become one of *us*, a citizen.'

'*Ta mau kalah*[210]', Ummah said baldly, shaking his head. 'He's always got to win... that's why he doesn't speak English to Pa Ali. But you can't do that with Mariam, Mael... Ismael?'

'I speak in English, Abah,' Ismael said rolling his eyes.

---

208   Mak Endam – an older woman in the kampong who specialises in matchmaking. She will approach the bride's family with a proposal and if it is accepted, the Mak Endam prepares the bride. From teeth filing to dress and jewellery; she is very important in a Malay wedding.

209   Bahasa Melayu – the Malay language.

210   Ta mau kalah – You don't want to lose.

'Good! Go to her level, I did with your mother.'

'That means he'll have to go up, another promotion!' Isa said wickedly. 'Corporal Ismael Ibrahim.'

'At least I have a *stone house* with a pump toilet!'

Before dawn, Ummah slipped away quietly in his boat. He would say his *Fajr*[211] prayers out at sea.

At home facing Mecca, Isa was on his prayer mat, eyes closed, hands lifted almost to his face. His head was adorned by a turban and the first light caught him in dust-spangled rays. Ayesha watched him from across the room. She felt a deep love stirring inside her where there should have been a womb. Her eyes turned to her hawkish elder son, also kneeling and praying next to Isa. Ismael had treated her with all the respect deserving of a mother, but it was with Isa she had grown up into a "Mama". She could see him holding out the conch to her on the beach when Ummah had asked her to marry him. Then he was a nine-year-old boy, not this noble-looking young man in front of her. Silently she thanked Allah for her family.

Isa finished his prayer and then turned to a red *songket* package before him. Opening it, he drew out an exquisite Keris, in a sheath of filigree gold. Reverently he lifted it to his forehead, and salaamed it. He was ready for the most important journey of his life, to prepare the Keris for a King.

---

211   Fajr – Dawn prayer in Islam. The first of the daily prayers.

It was the first night of Ummah's fast. He woke up in his boat out at sea from a dream that left his eyes wet with tears. He was carrying a gift to the throne of Allah in a huge box covered by a magnificent green cloth. When he pulled the cloth off, inside were hundreds of little hands cut off from the wrists, children's hands.

'Allah Most Merciful, Most Compassionate, Lord of All Kindness, you have called this Land for your honour, let not the Hudud slay your truth. Allah Most Merciful, Most Compassionate, Lord of all Kindness ...'

Over and over he prayed, the imprint of fiery Al-Sijjin gripping his mind.

IN THE DARKEST OF NIGHTS, Isa trembling with exhaustion, knelt before the Black Lenggundi Tree. Taking a bottle of water from his knapsack, he washed his hands, face and feet and put on a clean surplice before he lit a censer from his torch. Sandalwood and vespers of *Salah*[212] filled the air. The Black Lenggundi Tree, with huge sails for roots, gobbled up the light from the torch. Moving towards one of the yawns of the roots, Isa disappeared into the Black Lenggundi Tree, a halo off into the void.

In the tree, the light from the torch shivered up the insides of the trunk, lined with a resin, the colour of silver gums. Within the Black Lenggundi Tree there were three trees, each the girth of a Mini Minor, thirty feet high. Their branches twisted and intertwined into a majestic canopy. In the seventh generation as the three trunks coalesced, a new Lenggundi Tree would be birthed. Isa stuck the torch into the ground and put his palms together.

Salaam Walaaikum, o ye Three Great Kings,

---

212 Salah – Practice of compulsory prayer in the Five Pillars of Islam.

Guardians of the Seat of the Ancient,
In the Great and Terrible Day, One,
Your servant comes to seek your will.

From in amongst the three trunks at the base, a flame arose. It was a reflection of the torch in a little pool of water. Allah's tears.

Going over, Isa prostrated himself on his stomach and drank from the pool, cupping the water in his hand. It tasted cold and silky with an aftertaste, which was almost bitter. He knew the taste. Once a year from the age of eight when he was circumcised, he came to the Pool of Allah's Tears and drank. In a few minutes the "tears" would seep through his whole being and fill him with peace. When he first experienced it fourteen years earlier, he had been afraid. His limbs had become detached from his mind, and he found himself looking down at them, his thoughts bouncing wildly. Abah had *pujuked*[213] him to relax. It was Allah's Tears stained with heavenly visions. It opened the door to *Syurga* – Paradise.

Isa stretched out on his back and made himself comfortable. There was nothing else to do until the Ancients appeared to consecrate the Keris. He looked up at the eerie walls of the Black Lenggundi Tree. The reflection of the torch on Allah's Pool rippled over him like an other-worldly glow. The last thing he remembered were the white tigers coming out of the walls at him.

Out in the sea on the second day of his fast, Ummah was sprawled at the bottom of his boat. It was late afternoon and the sun cauterised

---

213   Pujuked – coaxed.

his eyes. Thirst had swelled his tongue and he struggled to pray. He could feel himself disengaging from his body as the boat rocked. Only his spirit lingered like a ghost, knocking on heavenly portals to be allowed in.

In the Black Lenggundi Tree, Isa sat cross-legged in deep meditation. The torch in front of him was lit, the censer smouldering and the Keris lay on the red cloth. Only his beating heart linked him to the world. His spirit was with the ancestors and he could see them. The Wise Ones, the Kings of the Earth and something else he had not seen before. In the middle of them all, the hoary White Tiger. The Ancient of Old. He was standing up on his hind legs, like a man! And there were voices.

> *Daulat Tuanku!*
> *Daulat Tuanku!*
> *Long Live the King!*

THE THIRD MORNING
Planter's Inn, Port Dickson

In the eye of the rising sun, the horses churned the surf as manes flicked red and purple in phantasmagorical beauty. From their nostrils plumes of steam stoked the air.

'Magnificent morning for a hunt Alistair,' Sir Douglas said, his eyes on the horses as he sipped his tea.

They were standing on the veranda of the Club, where a hunting party was gathered. It would be their last hunt as privileged civil servants. In a week, the Colony would no longer be theirs. The Advisor had organised a foray into Tiger Sanctuary for a dozen Englishmen on the three-day adventure.

'Frightful noise Sir.'

Alistair was referring to the dozen Boerboels across in the parking lot, going berserk with pent-up energy.

'Infernal, but it'll keep the tiger at a safe distance. It was good of Dutch to let us have them. This time next week, they'll be on a ship to Northern Rhodesia.'

'What about you Sir, when will you leave?'

'Not for another month. I hope those rascals out there won't tire my horses.'

The Advisor was referring to another privileged group of civil servants who had no interest in the hunt. For them it would be sun and sea with Sir Douglas's horses.

'Well Alistair, shall we? "Tally-ho" and all that?'

After the Civil engineer, Ken Williams, was taken alive while preparing the plot for the ground-breaking ceremony of the highway, a "firebreak" had been bulldozed through Tiger Sanctuary. Countless tigers had been cordoned off from the Sanctuary. The aboriginal trekkers had isolated a strong female and a gaur was strategically placed. It would be over in forty-eight hours – an easy hunt because they would use the cleared swathe to roll in on their jeeps. The Advisor was giving the boys "a treat".

Alistair was euphoric.

'You look as excited as a wet tea towel!' Ivy exclaimed, as he kissed her goodbye.

'What do you want me to do? Run around starkers? I'm delirious, honestly!'

'You could get killed... please run then. And remember what I said, "No bodily functions" near the Keramat.'

'What superstitious nonsense.'

'Cannot pass water! Cannot spit! Cannot *berak*[214]!' barked Ah Lan, the maid, as she cleared his breakfast. 'Make the Spirits angry... bad luck for everybody.'

Getting into the jeep with Sir Douglas, suddenly the blood started pounding in his face. It hit him then.

Somebody could get killed, he thought, as a thrill ran through him.

Ummah gagged, as he regained consciousness. He was under tons of water.

The boat's capsized, he thought, panicked.

Strangely, there was fire in the water. Without warning, he saw IT. He had never seen IT before, but he knew what it was the moment he saw IT. *D'Ajjal*[215]. An abomination to God.

'Oh Allah have mercy, is this the spirit over the town?' he heard his voice in his brain, as he recoiled in horror.

Kicking wildly to flee, something strapped itself to his foot and he felt himself being pulled backwards. The water turned bloody as he screamed.

'Abah, Abah! It's all right....'

He could not make out the dark face blocking out the red sun.

'D'Ajjal!' he croaked, clutching the figure in front of him.

'It's Mael! We've got you. Drink this.'

'... Isa...' Ummah wailed, thrusting the water can away, a nameless terror filling him.

'He'll be back this evening Abah. Drink!'

---

214   Berak – defecate in the Malay language.

215   D'Ajjal – the Dark Messiah, very much like the anti-Christ who will deceive the world.

31

A Keris for a King, Isa thought with pride, as he pressed the Keris in the stringed bag against his breast. He was standing outside the Black Lenggundi Tree and drinking thirstily from a bottle of sugared water he had brought from the kampong. He was not allowed to drink of the Pool of Allah's Tears again, and he needed his vitality to get home. When he had woken out of his deep meditation on the third day, he knew his task had been accomplished. There were hundreds of tiger paw prints impressed on the soft ground around him. It had not been a dream seeing the Ancient One. Abah would know what that meant.

The sun was up when he set out but it was dark because of the impenetrable primeval rainforest. It was an easier trek back having already cut a path through the jungle. After five hours of trekking, still in uncharted jungle, his trained ears heard a sound. Stopping, he cocked his head to listen above the call of the jungle. He could hear a faint drum rhythm. Moving towards it, the clamouring of voices sounded like a celebration, a charivari.

'It was around here that _Tok_[216] killed the engineer.'

Then he saw a little clearing where six men were huddled in a circle. They were chanting, yodelling and throat frogging, whilst one beat out

---

216 Tok – GrandSire Long Claws.

a rhythm on a tin drum. In their midst was a mandala with a cockerel and a baby goat tethered to a stake. In a flash, realisation gripped Isa. They were making an animal sacrifice on the sacred grounds.

'What are you doing on this Keramat?' he shouted, rushing forward.

The men whipped around, and Isa's heart quailed. Their faces were depraved, forearms slashed below the elbow, dripping blood. They were Chinese, Indian and Malays, none of whom Isa recognised.

'Look what the Goddess brought us!'

'I asked you, what you are doing here? This is our sacred ground! Our ancestors guard this place.'

'Yes, your *Datuks!*[217] They make people afraid to work on the highway. That's why we're here.'

As one of them walked over to him, Isa noticed the man with the tin drum, sitting cross-legged on the ground. He was dressed in a loincloth, covered with red ash, hair thick and matted. Isa knew he was a temple Medium. In front of him was a little altar of joss sticks, a machete, and several beer bottles.

'What have you got in here?' the man approaching Isa asked, reaching for the knapsack on his back.

Instinctively Isa pulled away, putting out his hand to protect the purity of the Keris on the stringed bag across his chest. It was the wrong thing to do. Immediately the attention of the man turned on the stringed bag.

'Give it to me...'

Isa knew then, that he had to get away from them. He turned to run but they were upon him. Bound and bloodied, he watched the Keris pass from hand to hand, the men salivating with covetousness.

---

217 Datuk – Forebears.

'Get your filthy hands off it! It's for the *Agung*[218] for Merdeka.'

'Why not a *real* sacrifice?'

The men exchanged glances.

'The cockerel will get rid of the ancestral spirits and we have the goat if the omen is bad,' someone averred, balking at the suggestion.

'Lottery numbers... human blood will guarantee that. And who says the Goddess didn't send him to us.'

'I want the Keris. It has power!' growled another.

'The Keris has a curse for those who don't own it. Get rid of it. If we take anything back, we've stolen from the Goddess.'

The temple Medium started chanting in a guttural tone and they turned and looked at him in apprehension.

'He says Kali hungers for her meat. Give me the Keris, I know how to use it,' a man with a white jellied eye, said decisively.

'The cockerel or the goat. That's what we agreed... Nothing else!'

'They've paid us... and we've taken oaths on our children!'

Isa listening first in unbelief, then in horror, realised they were talking about killing him.

'I beg you, don't do this wicked thing! There cannot be human blood-sacrifice on this Keramat... your children will be cursed!'

His words had an immediate effect on them. They were afraid.

'Let the Goddess chose! Bring him over...'

They hauled Isa up and stood him on the circle of the mandala in front of the Medium. Laying the cockerel on the ground, and without warning, Jelly Eye lobbed off its head with the machete. Blood showered in all directions as the cockerel, headless, struggled frantically. The decapitated rooster was handed to the Medium, who put his mouth on the neck and began to drink.

---

218   Agung – King of the country.

Isa's eyes overflowed with tears and he sank to his knees. Then abruptly, the Medium threw the cockerel into the mandala on the ground. Headless, it got on its feet and ran into the men who had cordoned it off. It fell over and fluttered desperately along the ground. The temple priest was chanting. The cockerel's demented dance was having a strange effect on the group of men. Bloodlust seized them as they watched to see how the cockerel would die, on its back or front, a portent on the success of the sacrifice.

Isa was no longer looking at anyone. Kneeling with his eyes shut, he was praying. With one supreme last effort the cockerel leapt high. Wings fluttering madly, clawing torsos, it scrambled over the wall of human bodies and escaped the mandala. The men looked at each other in trepidation.

'Kali Mata[219] wants the boy! She rejects the cockerel,' the temple Medium said, voice thick with lust. 'He's pure, untouched... use the Keris.'

The virgin forests screamed with penetration as the Boerboels tore down the weal of laterite, while the jeeps followed in constipated grunts. The experienced few, walked fearlessly with the "bait", the sweepers, standing between them and any tiger. Beating tablas and blaring trumpets, it looked like a bridegroom's party. Wearing garlands of marigolds, indemnity from their gods, the sweepers were so florid, no tiger could miss them. It was a feast for five dollars, a fortune for the indentured Tamils.

Alistair, in Sir Douglas's jeep, was grateful for the gun-bearing

---

219   Kali Mata – Mother Kali. The Hindu Goddess of death.

bodyguards hanging onto the sides of the vehicle.

'Ramsey wanted to bring the horses,' Sir Douglas said dryly at a civil servant hollering out gorilla calls. 'Highly strung creatures. Intelligent, unlike elephants....'

'They found the civil engineer, Ken Williams, over there, Sir.'

The trees in the direction to which Alistair pointed were strapped with bedraggled white ribbons. There had been a sad semblance of a funeral for the engineer a week earlier. There had been no body, only bits and pieces. His wife and daughter had tied ribbons and buried a simple white cross in the ground.

'I think we should pay our respects, if you could get Anak's attention,' said Sir Douglas.

Anak, the head aboriginal scout, with a series of jungle calls, brought the hunting expedition to a grinding halt. The other civil servants, unsure of what was happening, looked around nervously until the word filtered to them.

'The Advisor wants to pay his respects.'

They hung about silently, lighting cigarettes, the hole in a doughnut of sweepers. The dogs were less respectful and had to be slapped and scolded before their leads were strapped on.

Flanked by a handful of bodyguards as Sir Douglas stood silently, Alistair felt vulnerable amidst the lifeless ribbons. The seething jungle glowered at them. He also needed to relieve himself but Ah Lan's warning ran down his spine. They were some distance from the phalanx of drum beaters and through the din, Alistair heard a metal drum. So did the Advisor and Anak.

'Must be another hunting party,' Sir Douglas said, a little put out.

Before anyone could respond, a scream, magnified by frantic bird screeches pierced the air. Alistair jumped. Sir Douglas turned nervously to the scouts. Anak and his two trekkers stood like hounds, ears trained in the direction of the scream.

'*Rimau*[220]?' Sir Douglas asked, stepping backwards.

'*Bukan Sir! Suara orang. Permissi...*'

'No Sir! ... Human cry. With your permission...'

Anak moved like an arrow into the jungle, throwing an instruction to the other scouts. Silently, they nudged the Advisor back to the group, in as dignified a retreat as possible.

In the jeep barricaded by soldiers and sweepers, they awaited Anak's return. It was a good thirty minutes before the aboriginal came running back. Ashen-faced, there was blood on his hands, arms and chest.

'Good God! Is it a communist attack?' Sir Douglas demanded, fearing the worst.

'*Anak Bongsu Penghulu Ummah, dibunuh!*'

'The younger child of the Headman Ummah. He's been killed!'

Even before the interpreter could finish, Alistair was out of the jeep.

'Isa?!' he said, his heart failing.

'Yes Sir...Isa...Ummah's son, killed. A sacrifice.'

There are days in a man's life he never forgets. For Alistair Pierce, it was that day. His father's death had been cruel, but Isa's death sealed his humanity, worm like and fallen. Sir Douglas who was standing next to him, gripped his shoulder.

'Alis! It's not the lad I was approached about? The one Ivy's prepared for Kirkby?'

Alistair nodded numbly. He could see Ivy's face beaming, holding out the winter coat she had bought Isa as a gift.

'Anak said ... it's some sort of ritual appeasement ... for the highway project.'

---

220   Rimau – Tiger.

'Dastardly business. Damn and blast them! ... such promise.'

'We should never have touched the Sanctuary, Sir!'

'That's neither here nor there.'

'We were warned Sir...'

'Pull yourself together man and stop this maudlin drivel!'

They stood in an uncomfortable silence for a few moments.

'I'll inform his family Sir ... I think you should go on ahead.'

'One of the drivers will take you. ... I don't suppose you'll be re-joining us?'

'No Sir. Ivy will need some company.'

Heading for the fishing village, Alistair rehearsed a thousand ways to break the news to Ummah, but nothing prepared him for the hysteria. They were on the veranda and Dom was with them. Ayesha screamed and started beating her chest, before falling to the floor. Ismael rushed into the house for his gun.

'I'm going to kill the *haram jadahs*[221]. Every one of them!' he raged, emerging with his rifle.

'Mael!' Ayesha gasped, coming to her senses. 'I don't want to lose another child. My son, *buah hati Mama*[222], *jangan*[223]!'

Alistair was truly afraid. Ismael's face was contorted with hate, as his gun swung crazily. It was Ummah who stumbled in front of him and caught hold of the weapon.

'A gun is not the answer Mael.'

---

221   Haram jadahs – an extreme swear word which translates to "son of a bitch" or "bastards".

222   Buah hati mama – fruit of my heart.

223   Jangan – don't.

'Abah?!! This is Isa ... Our Isa!! Abah he never wronged anybody... Somebody must pay for this.'

Alistair looked at Ummah, face peeled red from the sun, lips bleeding. Ummah appeared shell-shocked, but Alistair knew that the blow of Isa's death had registered. His eyes were pools of pain.

'It is Allah's will, I saw this out at sea,' Ummah said brokenly, 'put your gun away.'

'Ummah?!'

'Listen to your father, Mael, if he said Allah showed this to him, who are we to question Allah Most Merciful.'

'Mael we cannot desecrate the Keramat. We are the Keepers of the Seat of the Ancestors. *Biar mati anak, jangan mati adat*[224]. If our Isa is no longer, let it be so but not our tradition.'

Driving back with Ummah, Ismael and Dom, to the site of the murder, there was very little conversation. They were racing the sun, which had begun its descent. As was the Muslim custom, Isa had to be buried by sundown and Ummah was going to bury Isa in the grounds of Tiger Sanctuary. Dom's presence was a comfort to Alistair who was struggling to stay buttoned up. Dom conducted himself in a restful manner, a legacy of having attended countless funerals. It was splendid the way he held out the canister of water for Alistair after pouring the dehydrated Headman a drink, offering Ismael a cigarette from Alistair's case, and nursing the bag containing a *kafan*[225] and Koran, like a mother.

At the site, Alistair was grateful to see that Isa had been washed clean. He was naked from the waist up and there was no blood on him. He looked asleep.

'Anak must have sponged him for Ummah.'

---

224   Biar mati anak jangan mati adat – Let the child die but never let the tradition die.

225   Kafan – shroud for burial.

Standing back respectfully with Dom, he saw Ummah fall on his knees and pick up his lifeless son.

'Isa! *Rezeki*[226] Allah,' the lament ripped through Ummah as the dam burst.

Ismael, who had hesitated, half-afraid to embrace the truth, threw himself down next to Isa. The sight of Ummah's tears stilled his own pain.

'Abah. Abah! Your tears cannot touch Isa.'

It was not permitted in their culture for tears to fall on a body. It would make it hard for the dead to pass over. Ummah was unable to stop but he turned his face into Mael's shoulder.

Alistair felt his control slipping and he needed to get away. He looked at Dom and Dom nodded.

'Let me pay my respects.'

Ummah had laid Isa back gently on the ground but not before he put his *songkok*[227] down as a pillow for his head. Dom went over to the body and stood there for a minute as he crossed himself and prayed.

'Ummah, we're going back. Is there anything we can do?'

'No, we will bury Isa at the Seat of the Ancestors at the Black Lenggundi Tree,' Ummah said quietly.

'But Abah, I am not initiated! I can't enter in.'

'It is time you are Mael. Isa will lead us ... he will be your guide. You have obtained the *ilmu*[228] through a pure man, murdered.'

As he went up to say goodbye, Alistair saw Ummah running his hands over Isa's torso. He was looking for something. He had assumed Isa's throat had been slashed, but looking at Isa's body there

---

226   Rezeki – my blessing from God.

227   Songkok – A Fez worn by Malay men.

228   Ilmu – the gift or illumination to qualify as a Spirit Guide.

was a two-inch gash under the right diaphragm. Ummah's fingers were on either side of the wound, pressing into the flesh.

What's he doing? Alistair thought.

'He's been killed with the Keris. I can feel the blade.'

'They used it wrongly. It must have broken off at the tang.'

'Isa broke it, by falling against the grain ....'

Sure enough, as Ummah pressed down hard, a metal tip could be seen just below the skin's surface.

'Use a cloth ... pull it out!' Ummah ordered Ismael.

Alistair felt quite ill, watching the blade tear out of the flesh it was embedded in. He knew he was going to throw up. Sweat had broken out on his forehead and his hands felt clammy.

'Excuse us Encik Ummah, we have to get back. Please accept my condolences again.'

'*Terima kasih*[229],' Ummah said looking up at him. 'And I thank Sir Douglas for his help.'

That was all he could manage before he rushed back to the jeep. With Ah Lan's warning ringing through his head, he crossed the laterite road onto the other side and promptly vomited. Dom found him there a few minutes later. As they made their way home, Alistair knew that a part of him was buried somewhere in Tiger Sanctuary with Isa.

---

229   Terima kasih – Thank you.

Part 11
PRESENT

1985
PORT DICKSON - MALAYSIA

Why write this book? No one has asked me for it.
Especially those to whom it is directed.
Well? Well, I reply quite calmly that there are too many idiots in
this world. And having said it, I have the burden of proving it.

***Black Skin, White Masks* – Frantz Fanon.**

32

'FIRST ISA... NOW DOM.'

Alistair sat funereally in a shawl under the frangipani tree. The cool morning breeze twirled white flowers around him.

'Five days now and they're playing wait and see...'

"They" was the Church. Alistair was waiting anxiously on a call from the Anglican Bishop who he had lobbied for a funeral service for Dom. There were rumours that Dom was a Muslim convert and they did not want a confrontation with the Imams who had jurisdiction over his body, if it were true. The situation was "too delicate", they said.

'Where's Jihad? Why's Ummah hiding him? I need to talk to him!'

Jihad had found Dom staked to the Black Lenggundi Tree and had come looking for Ummah, convulsed with hate. Dom had clearly triggered a trap and a bamboo javelin had lanced him through the heart. Port Dickson was hyped with rumours. One on hand, the stake wound was only a vicious fang bite. Contrarily, he was also the person masquerading as the vampire, filling people with fear. Yet again, an apostate bent on desecrating the holy sanctuary.

'Ummah sent him there ... he engineered this!'

Something soft brushed his hand, lying on his lap. Alistair looked down. A frangipani had fallen to his lap.

'Death flowers ... we shouldn't have touched the land!'

His thoughts turned to his hunting gun in his Malacca cupboard. *I betrayed them. Ivy and Dom ... and Isa.*

Ex-Kolonel Akiro Kabota sat impassively on the terrace at Planter's Inn, by his feet a Reebok bag, waiting for the taxi he had booked. He looked dispirited, his paper-thin skin cracked and sun-glazed but Akiro Kabota would have disagreed. He was feeling almost happy. After six days in the country, he was finally going to rid himself of the Keris and Bible he took out of Malaya forty years earlier when he was recalled.

The Keris, he knew, belonged to the fishing village. It had been found at the river bank after a Korean sex slave had been sprung from the barracks by locals. The village Headman had been impossible to find, even though he made half a dozen visits to the village. The Bible was the property of the Lazaroo family. The English man had written his name in under his grandfather's but there were no surviving Lazaroos in Port Dickson or Malacca, where he had gone. There was however, one man, an English man, who was related by marriage, to Lazaroo's sister. He had the address and had made a decision to drop off the cursed Bible and Keris at the respective residences of the two men. Up until now, he needed to see a face behind the articles he returned, but he was out of time. In two days he would be on the flight back to Japan, a free man.

'Excuse me Mr Akiro,' said Shanti, the Tamil receptionist of the Club, flashing her picket-fence teeth. 'Your taxi is waiting.'

'Grandy....'

Alistair turned and looked at the strapping thirteen-year-old loping across the garden towards him. It was Bonny, his grandson. Tatiana, his daughter, married to an Australian RAF airman, had flown in from Adelaide at the news of Dom's death.

'Bones ... darling boy ....'

Alistair's face lit up, at the shamelessly handsome face in front of him. Almost a six-footer, it startled Alistair to see the same uncanny flashing green eyes he shared with Ivy, and apparently, Bonnifacio Lazaroo.

'Ivy would have been thrilled,' he thought sadly.

'Is there a call for me?'

'Mum wants you to come in and have some breakfast.'

'Your mother says you enjoy rugby and surfing.'

They were walking towards the house, and from the side of the large garden where they were, they had a clear view of the front gate. A taxi pulled up outside the front gate and an Asian man got out. He walked over to the bell on the side and buzzed.

'Who's that Grandy?' Bonny asked.

Alistair looked in the direction of the man peering into the house, through the bars of the gate. He was unaware of them in the garden because of the big flame trees.

'Not anyone I know .... Perhaps it's for Ah Lan ....'

'I'll see what he wants,' Bonny said, scudding off to the gate.

At the gate, ex-Kolonel Akiro Kabota waited for someone to respond from inside the house. Feeling dry-mouthed, he palpated the bag hanging from his shoulder. The familiar item he groped for, fortified him. Bonnifacio Lazaroo's Bible – which was strange indeed because he loathed it! The answer to how the English man outplayed him was encrypted within its pages. Kabota had almost gone insane trying to decode it for the first few years after the war ended but it remained shut to him. He could not see the mystery, nor the person who Bonnifacio Lazaroo worked for and protected.

'Return the Gods you have brought here. They give us no peace,' the Shinto Priest's words resounded in his ears.

Standing outside Alistair Pierce's gate, Akiro Kabota looked intently through the bars into the house, to see if there was any movement.

'Can I help you?'

Akiro Kabota turned and stared into the familiar green eyes, unprepared for them in his waking hours. His mind went "click".

'Go to hell,' Bonnifacio Lazaroo spat, torn lip lifted in a sneer, a goop of blood and saliva popping like bubblegum.

Two soldiers were propping the English man up in front of Kolonel Kabota in the Field of Blood, next to Planter's Inn. Lazaroo was a bloody mess. His face was polka-dotted with cigarette burns, his fingers raw with the nails pulled out, and his body covered with welts from a rubber hose. The interrogation had started at the General's Quarters at Planter's Inn. Kolonel Kabota, who was in Port Dickson, had summoned the Englishman from the capital, Kuala Lumpur, for dinner at the General's Quarters. They ate their teriyaki steak in the cold way that was Bonnifacio's trademark.

'I had an interesting visit from a man ... Yap ... today,' Kabota said casually, watching him closely.

'Oh yes.'

'He says he knows you ...'

'I'm afraid I don't know him.'

'He said to give you this,' Kabota said, putting the Bible on the table between them.

Bonnifacio looked at it and for a fraction his eyes narrowed. Then he put his fork and knife down, wiped his mouth with his napkin and lay it on the table.

'I lost that a few weeks ago at one of the hockey tournaments.'

'It belongs to ...' Kabota said lifting the cover and reading the name, 'Jaffna Geoff ... your grandfather, who is a prisoner of war? I believe you have petitioned the Emperor for his release.'

'Yes, they are in Changi,' Bonnifacio said calmly.

'It says here he died in 1941 December ...'

'Did he?'

Bonnifacio looked at Kabota and for a few seconds neither of them said anything. And then Bonnifacio smiled grimly. Kolonel Kabota felt his legs cut off.

'How are you distributing the pamphlets?'

His question only made him more helpless because he no longer had any bargaining power with the English man. Outwardly emotionless, Kabota was in tribulation. The distributor of the pamphlets was the same man he paraded in his motorcade, like a trophy. He needed the names of Bonnifacio's accomplices, but after twenty hours of pulverising abuse in the torture chambers under Planter's, there were no answers. Kabota had to move the interrogation to the field outside because the English man had lost control of his bladder and his bowels, and the stench was stomach churning. Blood from Bonnifacio's lacerated lungs was also bubbling up. He had been force-fed a mixture of soap with caustic soda and from experience they knew the mixture had gone down his windpipe. In a short while his lungs would fill and he would drown in his own blood. Kabota knew time was running out.

'Who is your contact with the Allies? What is his name?'

Kolonel Kabota's voice was monotonous. Mechanically he took

off his glasses to wipe the droplets of blood the English man had spattered on them. With a poker face he played his last card.

'Tell me, and *your* hockey team will live.'

Kolonel Kabota was taking the biggest gamble of his life. To execute the young Malayan hockey team was to acknowledge publicly that he was a fool. Through the burning, Bonnifacio Lazaroo heard the words. A deep groan resounded in his chest.

'I will execute them one by one, until you tell me the names,' Kabota said seizing the moment.

For Bonnifacio Lazaroo it was the end. He had endured hours of being sliced and minced to arrive at this moment. His mind through it all was still functioning. It was his cursed gift. Bonnifacio took a deep rattling breath and Kabota tingled. The English man would talk. He took a step towards the man being propped up.

'Tell me ...' he persuaded, almost gently, '... the names.'

Bonnifacio gagged, the acid of the caustic soda, a burning coal in his throat.

'... the Emperor's ...,' whispered Bonny struggling with the words, '... team ...'

'What did you say?' Kabota said breathlessly, tilting his ear closer to the English man's mouth.

'... the Emperor's team ... hockey sticks ... gifts, pamphlets in the handles ...'

As the words sank in, Kolonel Kabota turned in pure disbelief, his face a mixture of a grimace and a smile. Bonnifacio's eyes, green and chilling stared at him, unblinking.

'... execute ... *your* team,' Bonnifacio said, mouth twisting, as blood frothed at the sides.

Akiro Kabota saw it in a flash. The English man loading the car, the hockey sticks to be given as gifts placed next to the Kolonel in the back seat, with his hand resting proudly on them. And the Emperor's team giving them away as goodwill souvenirs after the games.

'... my boys die ... Emperor's team dies,' Bonnifacio managed, gathering his strength for his last assault, '... you die.'

Kabota knew the game was over. Jaw set, with the muscles in his thin neck like cords, he pulled back from the English man.

'Kill him ... but slowly,' he said in Japanese, eyes locked with Bonny.

From the corner of his eye, Bonnifacio saw a soldier pick up the red-hot tongs from the fire they had lit. They had been threatening to gouge out his eyes and were ready to do it. The last hours of his life, would be playtime for the soldiers.

... *end it fast*, he thought desperately, not sure if he could hold out against the tongs. He had to provoke Kabota into action. He heaved for air.

'... Rukiyo ... your son ...'

In his wildest dreams, Kolonel Kabota never expected to hear his son's name on the English man's lips. For almost four years he had sat impassively by his side refusing to respond to his overtures at intimacy. Now when he was least ready, the English man was fingering him. It was almost obscene, touching him in his most private part.

'Poor Rukiyo... shamed your son....,' he spat loudly for the other soldiers to hear, the effort like a million needles in his chest. 'You won't have the honour of Hara-Kiri.'

He was looking straight into Kolonel Kabota's eyes, which were murky pools through his glasses. For a fraction of a second Bonnifacio wondered if his words had found their mark. All his life he had used his mouth, to survive his Eurasian family. Now he needed it to survive Kabota. Then he felt rather than saw Kabota's hand move.

'I win ...' Bonnifacio whispered, his bleak green eyes locked with

Kabota's. As the Kolonel squeezed the trigger of his pistol, he saw, for the first time, the lifeless eyes, light up like emeralds. Then Bonnifacio Lazaroo fell back, dead, eyes still open.

Refusing to look down at the English man with a bullet lodged in his temple, Kolonel Kabota strapped his pistol back into his belt. He stepped over the body and walked to his motorcar.

'Who are you looking for?' The green eyes bore into him.

Kabota blinked mindlessly. Bonny, on the other side of the gate went over to the handle and lifted it. Kabota's legs turned to water as the English man opened the gate. He took a step back ... then another.

'Are you lost?'

Kabota was unable to stop himself as he ran and got into the taxi, slamming the door shut. The driver started the engine and the vehicle pulled away.

'Who was that?' Alistair asked curiously.

'I don't know...' Bonny said puzzled, 'he was really scared.'

'Daddy! What are you boys doing? Bones, stop messing around and come in for breakfast!'

In the taxi, Akiro Kabota avoided the taxi driver's curious backward gaze. He could feel the sweat break out on his upper lip and his neck. He felt sick in the pit of his stomach.

'It's the English man's grandson ... only his grandson,' he repeated until he felt his heartbeat slow down. The fact that Bonnifacio was only twenty-two and unmarried did not even register. Without realising it, he was clutching his bag to his chest.

'Where to now?' asked the taxi driver after a few minutes.

The question forced Kabota to gather his thoughts. He was

314

dismayed the Bible was still with him. While the taxi driver waited for an answer, Kabota formulated his thoughts.

The Headman's house .... I'll leave the Keris there, even if he's not home.

33

'MAEL, WHAT SHOULD HAVE BEEN BURIED thirty years ago... it's come back.'

'I know Abah. Isa... Dom. Where is Jihad? We need to talk to him before things get out of control.'

Ismael was driving Ummah's ex-army truck that ferried the fish to the city markets. They were on their way back from Kuala Lumpur.

'He's not in the kampong and he's not in the city...'

'What was he doing there... in the Sacred Forest?'

'I sent him there...it's my fault.'

'Jihad, I mean.'

'I don't know Mael ... I wish I had never encouraged Dom to investigate the *Pontianak* - the vampire.'

'Abah we had no idea how desperate they were... *they are!*'

'... where are the photos? From Dom's camera?'

'...in the glove compartment...'

Ismael watched his father take out a wad of photographs and shuffle through them. They were from the camera Dom had borrowed from Alistair, which Ismael had recovered from the Black Lenggundi Tree. Ummah had insisted the film be developed in the city. He could not trust anyone in Port Dickson.

'Dom! Forgive me, Dom! Why was I so stupid?' Ummah lamented, as he struck his forehead with the photographs in his hand.

'We have to find Jihad; he's got to be somewhere. The Al-Sijjin will know...'

'Ya Allah! Sumatra!' Ummah exclaimed. 'The Al-Sijjin headquarters in Aceh ...'

'Use the walkie-talkie ... find out if he arrived at the jetty in Medan. Ask Priyanto, he knows Jihad.'

Ummah was already dialling in the frequency on the marine radio. It wobbled and warped as it tuned into the frequency.

'Calling Priyanto? Yanto ... Salaam Waailai Kum ... ni Ummah calling from Port Dickson. *Baik, semua baik. Nak tumpang tanya ... Si Jihad ada di Medan?* ... ahhh! When? ... Oh! Ok ... ok.'

With his face like flint, Ummah switched off the radio and threw it on the dashboard. He turned to Ismael.

'He went there the day after Dom's death ... I have a terrible feeling he had something to do with it.'

'We can still save him Abah... he's *still* our family.'

'Mael!' Ummah's voice was thick with anger. *'Biar mati anak jangan mati adat.* The child can die but not our tradition.'

Taken aback, Ismael was silent as he looked ahead. He almost jumped out of his skin as Ummah's hand fell on his forearm and gripped it.

'Mael ...' He turned and looked at Ummah. 'No matter the cost... you're a guardian of the Sacred Seat of the Ancestors now.'

'Yes Abah,' Ismael said quietly.

'Never forget! You paid for that with Isa's life ... you have obtained the *ilmu* - the illumination as Spirit Guide through a pure man, murdered.'

Mariam Serani, lay on her bed, in her *stone house* in the town of Port Dickson. It was already nine o'clock in the morning and she willed herself to get out of bed.

'Get up Mariam ... go and open the shop! Get up NOW!'

She was clearly unwell. Her eyes were red and puffy from weeping for Dom Hendrique. They were the two faces on the same coin, and one face had died in the Sacred Forests. She felt like retching each time she thought of Dom hanging from the Black Lenggundi Tree. Beside her on the bed was a yellow plastic bowl for the bile rising in her throat.

'Dom, *what* am I going to do?'

Mariam was desperately afraid. In her heart she knew Dom had been killed because he was found in the Sacred Seat of the Ancestors. He was a Serani, a Eurasian with Catholic *patongs* – idols. And no matter what she did to immerse herself into her Muslim family, nothing could change the fact that she was a Serani.

'I'm next ... I know I am! ...Allah help me. Where's Ismael?'

Mariam felt fear rise and hit the roof of her mouth. Clutching at the yellow bowl, she promptly threw up.

Ayesha was outside the forge. She was cutting back the brambly secondary growth from the jungle behind the kampong houses. The forge had not been used for about a year and the path to the door was overrun. From the day of Dom's death, she had undertaken a fast, eating only one skimpy meal nightly and she knew it would end when he was buried. Deprived of food for six days, she was feeling light-headed as she hacked away with her machete. Isa was on her heart. She had woken up in the morning with a dream of him, in the forge light-ing the coals. He had turned and smiled at her, his lashes half-lowered.

'*Ibu*,' he said. 'Mother.'

It smothered her heart, with unbearable love. She felt it was a premonition and she knew that she had to spruce up the forge.

'Adoi!' she exclaimed in pain, as a sharp thorn embedded itself deeply in her palm. Bending her head, she picked it out with her teeth, before spitting it out. Blood flowed freely.

'Hello?' a voice called out from the front of the forge. 'Hello....'

Whoever it was, had heard the noise of the machete chopping down the overgrowth. Ayesha walked around the forge, one hand in a fist as she pressed the wound, and the other still holding the machete.

The moment Ayesha saw Kabota she recognised him. Except for the colour of his hair, he had not changed. Instantly she was standing in General's Quarters. It was filled with Kolonels and Generals, brandy and cigars in their hands. He was in his uniform, commanding and handsome. Several Korean girls, dressed in silk kimonos had been ushered in for first pickings by the top echelon. She was petrified, unable to walk in the sandals and socks forced on her. They were only peasant girls from Korea who had been promised factory jobs in the Colony. Standing in a pretty row of cherry blossoms and butterfly prints, each girl was to step out, bow and then parrot off her name. This was to be followed by a phrase or rhyme in Japanese that they had learnt hurriedly. Kolonel Kabota pointed at her. As she stepped forward, she tripped. Her fate was sealed. She was given to the barracks. Three hundred men who soiled her body and her soul, day in, day out.

Ayesha floated towards Akiro Kabota. She felt her hand lift up the machete to bring it down. It was so easy. She had been doing it for several hours.

'*Ibu!*' she heard Isa call urgently, 'MOTHER!'

'Is this the house of the Headman?'

'Yes,' she answered from far away.

Kabota looked at the woman standing in front of him. She had a vacuous expression.

'I have something for him, is he at home?'

'No, he will be back soon.'

Akiro Kabota's pallor changed. Ayesha was unaware that she had spoken in Japanese. She had responded out of the depths of her matrix, a place that was locked away with the death of her womb.

I'm going mad, Kabota thought, not believing his ears. At the same time, the more he stared at her, the more clearly he saw it. Despite the head cloth, the unlined face was from his inglorious past.

'What do you want? We don't have any barracks here.'

The bag he was clutching fell to the ground from his nerveless fingers.

'I have to go,' he whispered with a pathetic little crunch of a bow that was more a reflex action than anything else.

'Get out of here!' Ayesha spat poisonously in Japanese.

Ex-Kolonel Akiro Kabota turned and fled.

34

UMMAH AND ISMAEL left the truck parked near the boats and were whizzing back to the kampong on Ismael's motorbike. As they pulled up outside his home, Ummah was perturbed to find the windows of the forge thrown open. There was a stack of undergrowth chopped and tied neatly with raffia in bundles. Ismael was also taken aback. The forge could only be opened with his father's approval. He switched off his engine and got off the bike. He had not planned to stop. He needed to get home to Mariam who was unwell.

'*Salaam Waalai Kum,*' Ismael called out upwards in the direction of the wooden house.

'Ayesha!' Ummah exclaimed, looking into the forge. 'What has happened?'

She was in a white jubbah and matching scarf, sitting cross-legged on her prayer mat. The floor of the forge had been swept, the fresh breeze plying through the window. In front of her, the Koran was open on a wooden frame and she was reciting prayers. Ummah and Ismael hastened around to the back where the door was. Something was seriously out of kilter. They stopped to perform their ritual purification, washing their hands and feet with a bucket of water there. From the doorway they could see a pretty arrangement of flowers at the furnace, and sandalwood graced the air. Ummah's eyes went to the bundle wrapped in red cloth, lying on the cold fireplace. They waited respectfully for her to finish.

'Ibu?' Ismael asked anxiously, going and sitting cross-legged next to her. He put his hand out and touched the pearl of a tear on the corner of her eye.

Ayesha turned and held his hand in hers. Then she lifted it to her mouth in a simple gesture of affection.

'Ibu ...' Ismael said overwhelmed.

She was not a woman who displayed her affection. It was Isa who had received the touches, whether to feel his brow, towel dry his hair or administer a sharp slap on his calf to get his attention. Ayesha found it difficult to show her love for Ismael because he was a man from the time she met him. She looked at the strong, middle-aged man by her side and struggled with emotions.

'*Mama ta apa Mael ... bersyukur sahaja. Mama punya rezeki besar.*'

'I'm alright Mael ... I'm just thankful ...my blessings are so great ...'

'What is this?' Ummah asked dumbfounded. He had gone over to the fireplace and opened the bundle. He was holding up the Keris that had been lost forty years earlier. He sank heavily onto his haunches.

'Our ancestral Keris! ... the one Isa lost,' Ismael said with disbelief.

'He was here .... The Kolonel from the Japanese barracks ... he brought it back with the *Injil*[230].'

They sat quietly as her words sank in.

'Are you alright?'

'Yes ... I am now ...'

Ummah picked up the Bible and turned the cover. He shook his head and a strange smile came over his face.

'*Allahyarham*[231] Si-Bonny.'

---

230 Injil – Gospel in Islam.

231 Allahyarham – the deceased.

'What's happening Abah?' Ismael asked bemusedly, getting to his feet. 'Dom... and now this!'

'The circle is complete. The time has come.'

'...that is why I opened the forge. I had a dream of Isa....'

Ummah had got onto his knees and was digging up the cold hearth with his hands. Both Ayesha and Ismael knew what he was looking for. Ismael walked over to the cloth where the Keris and Bible lay. He picked up the Keris and held it up carefully, salaaming it to his forehead.

'*Salaam Waalaikum*,' he said in deep wonderment. 'Our line will continue, Ibu.'

She nodded, her face filled with joy as the tears spilled over.

He put the Keris down and his hand ran over the Bible like a caress.

'He couldn't make Si-Bonny talk ...'

'Thank God for that Serani boy,' Ayesha said.

With an exclamation, Ummah reached what he was digging for. From under almost a foot of ash and earth, he pulled out a slim package wrapped in yellow cloth. Shaking off the dirt he placed it on the brick framework, where the flowers were. Opening it, there were layers of white muslin soaked with oil and spices, now stained red. Carefully, Ummah pulled back the layers of muslin until a twelve-inch piece of metal was exposed. It was the blade that Isa was killed with.

'Isa *buah hati* [232] Mama,' Ayesha whispered tenderly.

It lay on the muslin encrusted with red, not blood, but the rusting of the metals in the blade.

'You were right to open the forge. We have to re-fire the Keris ... both of them.'

'The blade of the ancestral Keris and the one made for the King ...

---

232   Buah hati – sweetheart.

smelt them and make them one ....,' Ismael said slowly.

'What should have ended thirty years ago when Isa died .... We have to finish IT!'

'Why Abang, what will it achieve?'

'The old Keris will have the blessing of the ancestors and the new Keris, the authority of the King ... and the blood of a Spirit Guide! *Steel and flesh become one!*

'Mael, you and your mother get started. I'm going to Medan, to look for Jihad.'

'Abang?'

'Ayesha, this is my *Seruan*[233] ... God completed me as a father, and a husband,' Ummah said with deep tenderness as he looked first at Ismael, then at Ayesha.

'Let God complete me now as his Servant.'

'What is your name?'

'Jihad, servant of God.'

'What is your Father's name?'

'I have no Father or Mother ... I am a servant of God.'

'What is your destiny?'

'Heaven, where seventy-two beautiful virgins await me in *Jannah*[234].'

'What is your purpose on earth?'

'To die as a martyr.'

'What is your name?'

'Jihad, servant of God.'

---

233   Seruan – Call, as in "called by God".

234   Jannah – Paradise in Islam.

'What is your Father's name?'

'I have no Father or Mother ... I am a servant of God.'

'What is your destiny?'

'Heaven, where seventy-two beautiful virgins await me in Jannah.'

'What is your purpose on earth?'

'To die as a martyr.'

'What is your name?'

'Jihad, servant of God.'

A bare bulb glared painfully in the stuffy cubicle, which was an old underground bunker. Originally housing Acehnese freedom fighters who hated the dictatorial Soekarno, it was now the headquarters of the fanatical Islamic group, Al-Sijjin.

Jihad sat upright, shoulders squared defiantly. His face was stony but his oily skin and red eyes gave him away. For the past six days they had put him through eighteen-hour sessions, to test him to see if he could withstand the weight of the mission before him. Woken up at five for prayers and without breakfast, he would be plunged into the daily drill of videotaped messages from Islamic radicals. In the dark bunker, images flickered on his face until afternoon prayers. Then the leaders would start their *ceramahs*[235] on the "infidels" and the great *Syaitan*[236] America. It was a vitriolic bloodletting indoctrination, which warped quotations from the Koran, to endorse the message.

The late afternoon would be the combustion of their doctrine. He would, along with other trainees, simulate a hostage situation that would climax with a jihad. And in the night after *Maghrib*,[237] a gour-

---

235 Ceramahs – Group discussions, usually held in mosques and madrasas.

236 Syaitan – the Devil.

237 Maghrib – The fourth of five formal daily prayers practised by Muslims. It is performed after sunset.

met meal – a teaser for the many pleasures awaiting him in heaven. It was all about the glorious rewards from Allah. Surrounded by the Apostles of Death, Jihad felt immortal. He was ready to discard his earthly body. His mission was fait accompli the day he killed Dom Hendrique. He had proved to the leadership that he would do *anything* to keep the holy grounds from desecration.

Jihad was no stranger to the Black Lenggundi Tree. Observing purification, he had found his way there many times but he could not find the irreverence to step into the Seat of the Ancestors. It was a consecrated place, like the *Kaaba*[238]. All he could do was prostrate himself and sleep outside the Tree of Life but rejection ate into his spirit. The fitful dreams he had were only shadows of *Syurga* – Paradise. The Spirit Guide had withheld his blessings. And his hatred for Ummah, Ismael and Mariam the kaffir, grew. With this poison pickling his system, he stealthily chanced upon Dom Hendrique, standing in front of the Ancient Seat. For the uninitiated, the Seat of the Ancestors was a death zone. Ummah had set up traps that would protect the Ancient Seat from wild boars and poachers. That Dom had made it to the tree ruined Jihad.

Uncle Ummah has given him the blessings.

Murder consumed him as Jihad brought his machete down on a vine that held taut a series of bamboo stakes. With a "twang" they launched through the air.

'*Allah hu Akhbar*,' Jihad screamed, as a stake punched through Dom. A good five inches in diameter, it lifted him up as light as a bird and impaled him to the Black Lenggundi Tree.

Surrounded by the leaders of Al-Sijjin, Jihad was calibrated for

---

238   Kaaba – It is the most sacred site for Muslims in Mecca where millions perform the Haj annually.

his mission. He was the new Guardian of the Keramat.

'What is your name?'

'Jihad, servant of God.'

'What is your Father's name?'

'I have no Father or Mother... I am a servant of God.'

'What is your destiny?'

'Heaven, where the beautiful virgins await me in Jannah.'

'Show us!'

Mechanically Jihad lifted his hand to his jacket and pulled it aside. He was strapped with sticks of dynamite. His hand moved to a rudimentary detonator, attached to the explosive and without hesitation pressed it. It was only a dummy. Jihad's red eyes were beginning to glaze.

Part 12

PRESENT

1985
PORT DICKSON - MALAYSIA

Glittering World
Meteoric flash
City of Glass
Ground to
zero.

"Great indeed is the skill and ingenuity of these white men.
But what a pity that a building as fine as this should be brought
low in an instant of time.
But now by the will of Allah it was no more. The old order is de-
stroyed, a new world is created and all around us is change."

Munshi Abdullah, 1810 – assistant to Sir Stamford Raffles
on the destruction of the Portuguese fort – A' Famosa,
in Malacca by the British.

35

As Ummah headed for Medan in pursuit of Jihad, boxing glove clouds began to stockpile over Port Dickson. By late morning the sun had a blackened eye, and withdrew its squinting gaze. The wind walloped the waves and thunder growled. In the forge, Ismael, stripped to the waist, gleamed. In his hands, two mighty hammers. In front of him, fired and red, the two Keris – a molten strap.

> *Assalamualaikum Maharaja Batara Besi,*
> *Peace be to you, Highness Avatar of the Iron*
> *Lend me your keys to the gates of Hell*
> *Seal me Shield me Sulaiman Star*
> *Anoint me now Paladin of the Palace.*
>
> *Iblis spawn of Sakti-muna*
> *I am who I am – Greater than the Magician's Magic*
> *I hold in harmony the Cradle of Creation*
> *Iblis cease and desist*
> *I am who I am – Sentinel of the Universe.*

Ayesha, wearing the black trousers and shirt in the tradition of the Keris makers, pumped the cylindrical bellows. She looked like a pugilist, hunched at the shoulders as the incantations seized her.

> *D'Ajjal Creature at the Navel of the Seas*
> *The walls of Kaf fall – Gog and Magog sieged*
> *Gerhana hides your lubricious lair*
> *We will seek and destroy Iblis heir.*

Out of the mortality of sinew and bone, Ismael rose. He was the Grand Craftsman of the Forge, the last outpost between heaven and hell. With a ferocious cry he heaved the hammers up and brought them crashing down.

> *Kun, kata Allah*
> *Be! sayeth God*
> *Bend me, form me Fiery Lance*
> *Hurl me flaming Avatar of the Iron.*

In the afternoon, a volley of lightning strikes strafed Port Dickson, but still it did not rain. Gale-force winds began to bludgeon the seaside town, ripping off corrugated zinc roofs and slicing them through the air like razors. Picket fences in the Chinese farms were sucked up like toothpicks, and the terrified pigs bolted for their lives. In the rubber estates, petroleum drums, used for holding water, slammed into the rubber tappers' quarters. The temple bell could be heard clanging frantically, as if an invisible hand was trying desperately to appease the Goddess.

At twilight, as doors and windows rattled, many in Port Dickson were afraid. Dom Hendrique was uppermost in their minds because he was still waiting to be buried. By morning it would be seven days, and in a parochial town like Port Dickson, that was the worst thing imaginable. He was a dead man, his soul ravenous for revenge.

At the Field of Blood where the Al-Sijjin lived in kampong houses on the fringe of the jungle, there was absolute mayhem. The pigs from the Chinese farms had found their way to the Al-Sijjin rice paddies and were wallowing in the mud. Panic gave way to religious umbrage, and then to hubris. Someone sent for a can of kerosene and the sacrosanct Muslim brothers set the pigs alight. Squealing red balls of fire ran helter-skelter, some into the sea, to finally collapse in a charred quivering mess.

With nightfall, the sky caved in and finally the rain!

It was angry and hot and torrential.

Before dawn the deluge had ceased and in the early hours of the morning, news of the wanton destruction of their pigs reached the Chinese vegetable farmers. Armed with cleavers, they headed for the community of the Al-Sijjin, who were equally incensed at the defilement and were waiting for them.

Ummah, returning from Medan, literally stepped into the affray. It had been a fruitless search for Jihad. The storm that pounded Port Dickson had unleashed in Medan earlier and kept him housebound. There was no need to go to Aceh to look for Jihad. His nephew was seen leaving in a motorboat for Port Dickson by one of the Indonesian fishermen. By sunrise, he took a boat from Medan to the jetty in Port Dickson. Heading for the Al-Sijjin commune looking for Jihad, Ummah intercepted the armed Chinese men in confrontation with a band of Al-Sijjin wielding machetes.

'What's happening here? This is my kampong! The first man who draws blood, every fisherman in this village will pick up a Keris against him. I swear this by God!' he shouted in alarm, heart beating violently as he threw himself into the incursion.

Immediately, he drew the attention of the group. They were prepared to kill each other in a two-way fight, but to contend with several hundred fishermen was not something they had factored in. The Al-Sijjin leader looked at Ummah with contempt and then with cold calculation, spat at the Headman. Spittle hit Ummah in the face and as planned, the gesture broke the restraint on the Chinese leader who knew Ummah.

'You have no respect!' he hissed at the Al-Sijjin leader, lifting up his machete to strike.

Twisting around, Ummah put out his hand and grabbed hold of the Chinese man's hand.

'Ah Tan! Stop! This is not the way to settle things....'

'There is no other way,' a Chinese farmer agitated. 'Fight and die!'

'There is *always* another way!'

'Another way? Another way! They have destroyed our livelihood,' Ah Tan said in disbelief, eyes red and hot with unshed tears, as he shook Ummah off.

'Your livelihood is *haram*[239]. We will die happily!'

'Ah Tan, we are friends!' Ummah gritted, latching himself to the Chinese leader. 'Do you remember the time you brought Swee Lan to see me? She was sick!'

Ah Tan was thrown by the Headman's aggression, looking blankly into Ummah's face. Behind him, the Chinese men were waiting for a signal from their leader.

'You came to see me! We saved her life. You carried her to my house, your Boy-Boy was six months old. The snakes!'

---

239   Haram – Illegal, polluted in the eyes of God.

Then, Ah Tan saw his wife, swollen with poison, lying on Ummah's veranda. She had disturbed a nest of cobras and had been bitten several times.

'Do you remember what you said at that time? What you promised? Do you remember?'

Instantly Ah Tan knew what Ummah was asking of him. The Spirit Guide had saved his wife's life with his prayers and his black snake stones, *batu geliga ular*[240]. He had been so indebted because there was a six-month baby at home, that he was willing to give the Spirit Guide whatever he asked for. Ummah had graciously declined the offer.

'Tan, I'm asking you *now* in God's name! Do not draw blood. This is a *Keramat*[241], the same Keramat that saved your wife's life.'

'We have nothing left.'

'This is my Keramat, what happens here is my responsibility. Take our fish and sell it. Use the money to buy new livestock.'

Gasps ran through the Al-Sijjin. The Headman was making redress for the filthiest of all creatures, an abomination in the Koran.

'*Murtad!*[242]'

Ummah's words were a balm on the Chinese men, cutting the ground off from under the Al-Sijjin. Outmanoeuvred, they were also conscious of being sieged by passing fishermen who had stopped on seeing Ummah.

Without warning, two army helicopters mowed over their heads. Ummah could see the gunners on the machine gun at the side hatch. *Something's wrong!* he thought. *In the town... something's wrong.*

240　Batu geliga ular – a manufactured stone of different alloys when placed against a snake bite will adhere and draw out the poison.

241　Keramat – Sanctified ground.

242　Murtad – Apostate in Islam.

36

IN THE TOWN, the storm had wreaked havoc, leaving the Sunday morning market struggling with the fallout. Tamil labourers from Town Hall hurriedly hosed and cleared zinc sheets, pieces of plank and cardboard mulch for the arrival of the overnight tourist buses from Singapore and Thailand. Some who owned stalls were themselves late, because of fallen trees and mud slides. The "King" of Port Dickson, Gila Thambi the Madman, was in his element as he prodded and poked the big bins, almost disappearing into their mouths, talking to his "many selves" in his pukka English accent. The Tamil hands exchanged glances, knowing better than to respond in any way. Even a glance could earn them Gila's unwelcomed attention.

It was on this morning that Alistair Pierce brought his grandson to the markets. He had been forced out of the house, after an earful from Tatiana.

'Daddy, what are you doing moping around?'

'I'm listening to the news darling. Did you hear, there's been a break-in at the armoury at Terendak?'

She knew he was waiting for a phone call from the Bishop's office.

'It's a Sunday, Dad, all the offices are closed. Everybody's at Church! Take Bonny to the markets, he's looking for some surfing accessories.'

'Like what?' he asked unhappily.

'Sarongs, necklaces, Tiger Claws! There's a Mini-Malaysia in the town square.'

'Mum, can I get a tattoo, a tiger?'

'Get me some worry beads. Daddy just get him out, it'll do you both good!'

While he waited on the debris around the market to be removed, Alistair walked over to the seawall, where exactly one week earlier, Dom had been sitting. Alistair sank down cheerlessly. He had no energy to do anything else as he watched Bonny happily scavenging for flotsam and jetsam on the reclaimed land.

'There's sunken treasure out here Grandy. After the storm I might find a doubloon or some pieces of eight,' Bonny called out.

What hope? So untouched ... Alistair thought dully, nodding his head at his grandson.

'Look, an old Indonesian coin, one thousand Rupiah! Is it true? Mum said Uncle Dom was a treasure hunter!'

'Yes. Yes, he was.'

'It's in *our* Portuguese blood you know, we discovered the world!'

Alistair had heard the words hundreds of times before from Dom's mouth but this time he *heard* it. His heart cracked. He had never seen, nor recognised Dom. It was the refusal to embrace "a bastard son".

'Grandy? Are you alright?'

'Hmm ....' he nodded, wrapping his arms to still the breaking inside.

'I'm going over to the Mini-Malaysia. I want to see the clock tower.'

Alistair could barely hold on as his grandson vaulted the wall and dashed across the road. Then he cried, mouth open, chest racking sobs. Abandonment swallowed him. Dom had slipped past him like a majestic galleon and he, not Dom, was the ghost. He had not been able to grasp the treasure that was Dom Awang Hendrique, Cabin Servant to Magellan.

I should have told Dom the truth about Tiger Sanctuary.

From the most inward part of his being, a piece of truth tossed up on the storm of his tears, and it stilled him. He was afraid that he had said it aloud, as he looked furtively over his shoulder. A tourist bus had just pulled in at the bus station and people were pouring out, bone weary. There were over a dozen white faces in sarongs with wilting flower garlands and it was clear they had come from Pattaya. From experience, he knew that some of them would wander over to the wall, to have a stretch and a cigarette.

I'll go and find Bonny.

He did not move. He was emotionally drained.

At the stalls, Mariam was dragging her feet as she unloaded cartons from her van to the stall. What should have been routine was a struggle. It was the first time since Dom's death that she had ventured out of her house. With Ismael holed up at the forge reforging the two Keris, she needed to keep busy.

" 'Mariam, come and have your tea before it gets cold.'"

She stopped and looked at the empty table from where Dom had called out to her one week earlier.

Stuffed into an ice box in the morgue. Hot tears stung her eyes. *Stop it Mariam! Don't let people see you being weak.*

It was the way she self-talked growing up. She had to survive being forgotten. Now she had to overcome a surmounting fear that she was visible. A target. She was guilty, by association with Dom, a Serani who had no business at the Seat of the Ancestors.

Don't show you're crying for Dom!

Immediately self-loathing filled her. She had never stood on shakier ground in all her life. The sense of danger engulfing her was the same feeling she had had as a child when the Japanese soldiers stormed into Dr Azariah's, her godfather's house. She looked at the walkie-talkie lying on the table and fought the urge to call Ismael, telling herself he could be asleep at his father's house. Feeling hollow, she turned back to her van.

Sitting a couple of tables from Mariam's stall, ex-Kolonel Akiro Kabota was having his last meal. His Reebok knapsack was on his back and a black briefcase on the empty chair next to him. In thirty minutes he would board the bus to Kuala Lumpur, and then take a taxi to Subang International Airport. He was scheduled to fly out of the country at midnight and would sit at the airport for eight hours for his flight, a minor inconvenience. He had discharged himself of the Keris and the Bible, and he could not *wait* to get out of Port Dickson and its demons, its *Yūrei*[243]. Still shaken by his encounter with the *ianfu*[244] and English man, he felt no remorse only terror. Strangely, he could smell the English man, the mingle of blood and bowel. He felt death was a hair's breadth away and needed to get onto his bus.

Coming back with more cartons, Mariam's heart almost stopped beating. Jihad! He was sitting at the very same table where Dom had sat.

What's he doing here? Ummah's looking for him in Medan. I've got to tell Ismael!

Jihad stared at her coldly, holding her gaze. Normally he would give her contemptuous looks before flicking his eyes away, but this time, she was the one to look away. There was something about him that set alarm bells off in her head. He usually sat with his body half-twisted, elbow on the table as he arrogantly appraised people coming and going. Now he sat upright and looked menacing, his hand on a

---

243   Yūrei – ghosts in Japanese culture.

244   Ianfu – comfort woman or prostitute.

black briefcase, like the ones the bank officers carried.

He was with Dom before he died, she thought and her stomach heaved. *Don't look at him.*

She turned her back on him and pretended to open the cartons. Her eyes were on the walkie-talkie but she felt afraid to pick it up. Intimidation was overpowering her. Furtively she slid the walkie-talkie into the fold of her jubba.

'I'm getting something from the van,' she called over her shoulder to her assistant.

Jihad watched Mariam scurry off, his hand on the black briefcase on the table. The "tick-tick-tick-tick" reverberating through his palm, made him powerful. It was beating with a rhythm stronger than his heart, and his fingers subconsciously tapped to the beat. It was the timer of a briefcase bomb, a token reward to assuage his personal vendetta, set to go off at Mariam's stall.

It was the debut outing of the Al-Sijjin sect, and the timing coincided with "Visit Malaysia 1985" with its precious presence of foreigners and dignitaries. Jihad's briefcase bomb was incidental. There was only one suicide bomb and one message: *Denounce the liberal "un-Islamic" Malaysian government and teach the western Syaitans[245] a lesson.*

Jihad had to be positioned at the clock tower, improvised to look like the old Portuguese Fort in Malacca. It was the ideal spot for hostage taking because tourists, with their silly maps and cameras, cheerfully trooped up to the viewing balcony. Jihad would demand for a television broadcast, and start killing one hostage at a time until a TV crew arrived. After a fiery speech on national television, he would detonate the suicide vest strapped to him.

---

245   Syaitans – Devils.

Jihad was poised to be martyred but he also wanted to hurt Ummah fatally, and Mariam was his lure. Ummah would come looking for him once the briefcase bomb went off.

His eyes took in Gila Thambi in the background, dodging the Council cleaners, and emotionlessly did a head count. He did not care that there were some Muslim believers; the innocents went straight to Heaven. Mariam was back at her stall, giving him less than fifteen minutes before the bomb went off. Carefully he put the briefcase on a chair and pushed the chair under the table, concealing it with the cheap plastic tablecloth. Without a backward glance, he got up and walked towards the clock tower.

At the Field of Blood as a vanguard of fishermen escorted the Chinese farmers away, a Norton Commando motorbike from the direction of the kampong came thundering to a stop. It was Ismael who had spotted his father.

'Abah, Jihad's in town! Mariam called on the walkie-talkie. He's sitting at her stall.'

'Let's go! Why the helicopters?'

'Someone broke into the armoury at Terendak. Guns and grenades were stolen. We're on red alert! Do you think Jihad...'

'NO! I don't know who broke into the armoury but it wasn't Jihad. He's been with a cell group for five days and he left Medan last night.'

'Something's wrong Abah. It's a *wayang*[246]!'

'The *Dallang*[247] emerges ... where's my Keris?'

---

246   Wayang – Show. Wayang Kulit – Shadow Puppetry.

247   Dallang – Master Puppeteer.

'I've got it but it's only just been set in the hilt. It's not ready!'

'It's ready! Give it to me, Isa tested it!'

At the marketplace, ex-Kolonel Kabota called for his bill at the tea stall. After paying, he picked up his Reebok bag and black briefcase and headed for the bus station.

Unbeknown to Jihad, and Akiro Kabota, Gila Thambi had been scanning the grounds of the market. Schizophrenic as he was, he was not a thief, looking only for discards. His eyes had fallen on the briefcase on the chair next to Kabota's and he had taken it in pictorially but he knew it was not a throwaway and turned his attention elsewhere. Ten minutes later, after Jihad and Kabota walked away in different directions, he ventured over towards their tables.

As he sniffed around, almost down on all fours, Gila Thambi saw Jihad's black briefcase on the chair, under the table, hidden by the plastic cover.

'Hello,' he asked surprised. 'What have we here? A toad in a hole.'

His words caught Mariam's attention, and she turned to look as Gila Thambi lifted the plastic sheet and pulled out the briefcase. In his deranged mind he saw a picture of Akiro Kabota with the black briefcase on the chair next to him. Gila stared at the briefcase in his hand, then looked up and around like a hound dog, to complete the picture in his mind. He saw Kabota walking away towards the direction of the bus station and the fact that Kabota had a briefcase in his hand did not even register. Mariam, who knew well enough to stay out of Gila Thambi's way, was cognisant that Jihad had been sitting where the briefcase was found.

That's Jihad's briefcase, he's forgotten it.

'Oh, I say good fellow,' Gila called out, bristling with "fast-for-ward" energy as he rushed after Kabota.

Akiro Kabota was standing outside the bus, looking into his Reebok bag for his bus ticket, when Gila caught up to him.

'Excuse me old boy, you've forgotten this.'

Ex-Kolonel Kabota looked up to see a black face with yellow pus eyes. The rotten smell from Gila's mouth punched him in the gut and Kabota tried to take a step back, but the lunacy in the madman's ravenous smile transfixed him.

Yūrei![248] *Goki Zoshi*[249], he thought.

And the bomb went off.

---

248   Yūrei – Spirit that seeks revenge for violent murder.

249   Goki Zoshi – Hungry ghost.

37

I'D BETTER FIND BONES before he gets a tattoo, Alistair thought, wearily swinging his legs over from the drop of the retaining wall.

Then the bomb went off. He fell backwards onto the pavers from shock. There was a daunting silence as the sky began to fill with a dark mushroom. Then the screaming started as burning singed his nostrils. He knew what it was straight away from the air-raids on London.

A bomb! he thought as cinders floated over him.

He struggled to his feet and took in one of the buses at the bus station, folded in two, emitting flames and black fumes. Strewn around the vehicle were several charred bodies, as people, bloodied and blackened, screamed for help. Out of the bedlam, a bus tyre hurtled towards him.

'Bones!'

Alistair started towards the clock tower, as overhead a helicopter whizzed in from the water with sonic tremors. Cutting across the road, Alistair saw a black military vehicle, a Volvo, parked on the side lane. A uniformed officer standing outside the Volvo was giving instructions into a walkie-talkie.

How did they get here so fast? he thought. *The raid on the armoury, they were expecting trouble.*

The tinted glass of the back window was down and he could see straight into the car. An army general was seated in the back and next to him was Ashman Lahud. They looked at each other in the very same instant as Alistair kept running towards the clock tower.

The walkie-talkie in Mariam's hand dropped at the carnage before her eyes. She was aghast as a human torch – a man on fire – came screaming towards the stalls. Something must have registered in his soul. He did a u-turn and ran towards the wall and sea. It was then she saw Alistair running. He was clearly in trouble.

'Pa Ali!' she cried out, grabbing his arm. 'Are you alright?

'Mariam? Mariam, my grandson...'

'Where is he?' she asked turning to the burning bus.

'The clock tower, he said he was going there...'

Without a word she locked her hand around his wrist and hauled him towards the market square.

When he walked away from Mariam's stall, across the square to the fountain, disappointment assailed Jihad. There were no great masses sitting around the fountain in front of the clock tower, his podium. Debris from the Mini-Malaysia had choked the fountain and water was overflowing. Two bleached blonde males with floral trousers sat on a bench, their feet up, out of the water's way. A young European couple was walking over from the bus station.

Jihad blinked in disbelief. The input of the storm had not been factored into the Al-Sijjin plan. Walking on automatic pilot to the clock tower, his eyes on the lookout, he thought he saw a face at the telescope. The countdown was on and it was only a matter of minutes before the briefcase bomb went off. He passed the European couple who did not stop at the tower but squelched their way to a stall for breakfast. There were barely three souls in the vicinity of the tower and a bead of perspiration broke out on Jihad's forehead. Stepping into the tower, he pulled out some padlocks and locked the outer grilled gate. Then he hitched up his long tunic, reaching behind for a Sten gun which was strapped to his back and armed himself. Swiftly he scuttled up the thirty-something steps.

In the clock tower, Bones, Bonnifacio Francis Ryan, was at the lookout, peering through the telescope, when the bomb went off. He instinctively lifted his head and turned in the direction of the explosion. He could see the bus station and a plume of black smoke reaching for the sky.

'Oh hell fire! A petrol tank must have exploded!'

Training the telescope on the burning bus, he did not hear or see Jihad slip up behind him. When Jihad saw the single white tourist on the balcony of the clock tower, relief coursed through him. The plan was still operable. There would be no hostage killed every hour because he only had one hostage, but the decision was made for him to kill a few of the people in the marketplace. He would aim for the tourists but if the locals died, *Inshallah*. It was God's will. Quietly he padlocked the inner grill door, before he let the lock fall with a harsh clang. Bonny jumped and spun around.

'Shhhhh...' Jihad said quietly, putting the finger of his free hand across his mouth. Then he lifted open the jacket he was wearing and Bones saw the dynamite strapped to his body.

'I die, you die! SIT DOWN!'

Bonny, a fresh-faced surfie from Adelaide felt his being melt down. He had never seen a gun in real life and intuitively he knew the bus explosion had something to do with the black-robed man in front of him. His legs gave way, and he sank weakly to his feet. Jihad opened his bag and pulled out one of several handcuffs, gesturing for Bonny to put his hands around the stem of the telescope and handcuffed him. With the youth secured and out of the way, Jihad positioned himself at the balustrade. Bones watched, mouth open, as Jihad pointed the gun into the marketplace.

In the marketplace, the bomb blast caused great panic. Early risers already trading, stood rooted in the exchange of money and purchases, whilst others were already running towards the bus station. There was one person who was totally undone by the explosion. Ibu Latah, as her name suggested, a victim of hyper-startle, jumped up like a jack-in-the-box.

'*Adoi*. Oh my God. *Lari!* Run. Run! Shoot the running dogs. Emergency, communist! Phone 999.'

Training the gun on the two blond tourists who were now standing uncertainly at the chaos around them, Jihad pulled the trigger. The shots like crackers ripped into the anxiety in the town square, and bodies began to drop. Women screamed, and pandemonium broke out.

'Get down! Get down, there's a gunman in the clock tower,' shouted an ex-army soldier in a booming voice.

In minutes the square was empty, bodies lying like red skittles, the dying leaving a trail of blood. Cowering behind stalls and under tables, no one moved. That is, no one in their proper senses. Ibu Latah, running helter skelter, was triggered into another level of hyper-startle. She began to prance around the two dead blond boys, chattering away.

'English. English! Get up! *Tora! Tora!* Hail Mary full of Grace, the Lord is with thee. Serani RIP. *D'Ajjal*[250] *tiba*[251]*!'*

From their hiding places, the people of the town watched her, spellbound. She was cherished the way people in sleepy towns love their familiars. The hairdresser, the dressmaker, the dhobi man.

'Rest in Peace ... RIP. Our Father who art in Heaven, Blessed is your name ...'

A short burst of bullets cut off her words. Her head hit the cobblestones with a loud crack. The running water from the fountain was turning pink through the square.

Mariam, with Alistair in tow, eyes on the lookout of the tower, saw Jihad with the gun, and Ibu fall. With a strangled cry she pulled back and dropped with Alistair, behind a tourist information booth in the square.

'Jihad amok! He's in the tower with a gun.'

'Where's Bones? Where's my Bonny?' Alistair asked faintly. '*Ivy* will never forgive me!'

Taking a deep breath, Jihad viewed the scene before him with a detached clarity. Overhead the helicopter hovered noisily, unable to descend because of the big trees and power lines. Putting his gun on the ground, he opened his bag and brought out a folded cloth, which he unfurled over the balustrade. The size of a double bed sheet, it was a banner for the Al-Sijjin. Securing the ends, he went to the wall opposite from Bones and sat down, knowing it would be a short wait before Ummah came to him. Bones was unable to take his eyes

---

250   D'Ajjal – the Dark Messiah, very much like the anti-Christ who will deceive the world.

251   Tiba – appears, arrives.

off his captor, like a mouse trapped by a cat. Next to Jihad, an empty packet of cigarettes and a couple of cans of beer had been discarded by tourists from before the storm. Jihad picked up the packet and held it out to the teenager.

'Cigarette?' Jihad asked mockingly.

'I don't smoke.'

'No smoke,' Jihad said, pursing his lip in mock surprise. 'Beer?'

'I'm sorry, I don't drink alcohol.'

'Good! You die, you go *Syurga* – Paradise,' Jihad nodded with approval.

'I don't want to die! Please?' Bonny begged, and started crying.

'Shhhhhh ...' Jihad said intimidatingly, reaching for his gun.

Bonny choked on his mucus as Jihad quietly began to reload the magazine, the banner flapping in the morning breeze. In bilious green the words "AL-SIJJIN" were emblazoned on the banner. Under the words was a chilling picture of a four-year-old male child in full Arab gear, armed with an AK 47. A message in Arabic, the Al-Sijjin manifesto, ran down the banner.

Kill the infidels even if we have to sacrifice our children.

Peeping up at the lookout from behind the booth, Mariam's womb contracted with longing at the face of the angelic dark-haired child on the banner. Of all the children she had dreamt of, there was not one she imagined as beautiful as this thick-lashed boy. For the first time, tears started flowing down her cheeks.

'Please don't die Bones... Please God, don't let Bones die,' Alistair whimpered by her side as he also took in the banner.

The helicopter, scattering paper like pigeons in the air, moved away and an oneiric calm rolled in. After a few minutes, people began to call out to each other.

'What's he doing? Is he still in the tower?'

'Keep down!'

'Where's the army?'

'There are soldiers in the helicopter! It's trying to land at the school field.'

Then with a loud roar a motorbike burst into the square, and as suddenly it choked as it hit a body. Ummah and Ismael were cartwheeled off the bike as it went hurtling on the cobbled square, making a jarring sound.

In the Tower Jihad got up with an impending sense of victory.

'Ummah! Mael! Over here!' Mariam screamed, galvanised by hope. 'He's got a gun.'

'Abah, are you alright?' Ismael asked as he pulled Ummah off the ground. Quickly they scampered to the stand behind which Mariam was taking cover.

'Pa Ali!' Ummah exclaimed, when he saw Alistair squatting against the wooden stall. 'Are you hurt?'

'My *cucu*[252], Bonny, he's in the clock tower.'

'WAN! Old man, I know you're there. Come out! I want to talk with you!'

Jihad's voice was like a raging bull through the square.

'I've got a hostage Ummah. I'll kill this white tourist if you don't come out NOW!'

Ummah crept forward and craned his neck. At the balcony, standing with Bonny in front of him, Jihad searched the stands for movement. On pure instinct Alistair got to his feet but Ummah

---

252   Cucu – Grandson in Malay.

pulled him down.

'My grandson!'

'Sit still! He wants *me*.'

Ummah's face was grim as he took his sarong off from his waist and began to plaît it into a turban around his head.

'Abah?'

Ismael's voice was thick, as he put a hand on his father's shoulder. Without unlocking his eyes from his son's, Ummah reached out from behind and pulled out the Keris in his waistband. He took Ismael's hand off gently and put the Keris in it.

'*Untuk Isa. Biar mati anak jangan mati adat, inilah semangat orang Melayu.*'

'For Isa. The child may die but not the tradition... this is the spirit of the Malays.'

'Abah!' Mariam whispered in protest. Ummah looked at her.

'Child, do you remember the time you saved Ismael's life? You were very brave! When, Isa and Mael rescued Ibu from the Jepun! Ismael got shot, remember! You must remember... Mael?'

Ummah pointed at the big tree behind the lookout that branched into the tower. Understanding dawned on Ismael and he nodded as Ummah turned to Mariam.

'Mariam?'

She looked at Ummah and then at Ismael blankly, unable to comprehend what they were saying to her.

'Mariam! We cannot do this without you, I need your help. You did it for Ismael with the Japanese soldier.'

'Abah ...' she choked, shaking her head in realisation.

'I wanted you in our family because you were so courageous. Seven years old and you were not afraid.'

'Abah, I am afraid! Please don't ask me this ... you don't know...'

'I *am* asking you Mariam. I see you. You have stood up to my kampong, you are strong ... it is the gift of the Serani.'

His words were a love spell and she looked at him wide-eyed.

'Loyal, unselfish and very courageous! It brought *your people* to this country. Daughter... have I asked you for anything?'

She knew immediately he was referring to her childlessness. He too had suffered the brunt of the town's reproach at her barrenness.

'Ummah, you old fool! Your time is up. *Coward!* I'm counting to ten. ONE! ...'

'Mariam,' Ummah asked, eyes warm with light, 'just like when you were a child, in your father's house. Dr Azariah's kitchen.'

'THREE!'

With a heavy heart Mariam nodded. Alistair could not believe what he was hearing. They were talking of rescuing Bones. Ismael reached out and held his father's hand in a salaam, before raising it to his lips in a lingering kiss. Ummah gathered him in a tight embrace.

'SIX!'

Ummah broke the embrace and cupped Mariam's face as if she was a child.

'Don't forget who you are.'

Mariam's hands were trembling as she held Ummah's hand to kiss it.

'Mariam,' Ismael said tenderly.

She turned and looked deep into her husband's eyes. She wanted to say something.

'Do you trust me?' he asked quietly.

'Yes Mael, I trust you,' she said without hesitation.

Ummah turned to Alistair. It was an open gaze, all recriminations gone. They were two old men who could no longer carry the past.

'You will have your *cucu* back. It's a good name ... Si-Bonny.'

'EIGHT!'

With a solemn *'Allah hu Akbar'* Ummah gestured for Ismael to move. Without a backward look, Ismael sidled around the sides of several stalls. When he was clearly out of the eye line of the tower, he broke free and made a run for the trees. The Keris was tucked snugly into the back of his waistband.

At the same time, Ummah stepped away from the stand and walked into the square.

'JIHAD! DON'T SHOOT! I'm coming out.'

'Come to the fountain,' Jihad ordered, feeling powerful.

'Don't shoot the boy. I'm here!'

Bonny, hands handcuffed behind his back, gasped in relief when the gun found a new target. Ummah stood in the square. The stamp of authority on him was undeniable, in his turban, loose tunic, and white beard.

'So old man, you've come to beg *me* for mercy.'

'Let the boy go Jihad.'

'You fool! You think you can still tell me what to do.'

'Let the boy go and I'll give you someone you really want.'

'You've got nothing I want...'

'Mariam!' Ummah's voice was like a thunderclap.

Jihad lowered his gun in disbelief.

'Mariam!'

Behind the stand Mariam hunched like a child, lifted her face. With a raggedy sigh she got up, and stepped away from the stand.

'Abah...'

Alistair sagged, in selfish relief, his head thrown back against the wooden stall. His eye line reached the roof of the two-storey shop-houses and he saw an extraordinary sight. On a balcony of the top floor, an army sniper in a bullet-proof vest straddled the balustrade. He had a headset on, his Lee Enfield trained on the lookout. He made a thumbs-up gesture to someone on the street as he adjusted himself on the iron railing. Alistair scrambled to look down the street between the shop-houses and stalls. At the corner, where the army Volvo was parked with Ashman and the General inside, a military official was standing next to it, talking into the headset.

Alistair's heart soared. Whipping around, he looked at the clock tower and saw that Jihad was still standing behind Bones. As Mariam walked up to Ummah, Jihad cursed, ramming his grandson with the butt of his gun, causing him to fall to the ground. Alistair frantically turned around to look at the sniper.

Shoot now! He's clear! SHOOT! he screamed in his mind.

38

SCALING THE HUGE TREE behind the clock tower was much harder than Ismael expected. He was not the teenager who had freed Ayesha from the Japanese barracks and the moss on the tree trunk was wet and slippery from the rain. He used his toes to latch onto nubs to hoist himself along the thick branches. Through the dense foliage, he caught a glimpse of Mariam walking up to Ummah. Then she was lost to him as he got to the branches behind the tower.

'Jihad! We will come up. Let the boy go! Mariam wants to pray for forgiveness.'

Jihad was ensnared. His hatred for Mariam overtook him as she stood several feet away from Ummah. They were too far to take down and the white tourist was a paltry price to pay for her. They would die with him but not before he made an example of Mariam.

'Send her up, I will let the hostage go when I see her. Then you come up! First take off her jubba, she is not a *Muslimah*[253].'

In the square, Ummah held his hand out encouragingly to Mariam.

'Child, look at me, don't look anywhere else. Take your jubba off.'

Slowly Mariam pulled the head cloth off, exposing her knee-length hair which was tied up in a crown braid. Self-consciously, she unbuttoned the outer tunic at both shoulders. It fell to her feet,

---

253 Muslimah – a female Muslim.

leaving her standing in her slim-fitting long dress. Instinctively her hand went to her stomach. Ummah's gaze was drawn by the furtive gesture. Her waist had thickened, her breasts fuller, her body was beginning to burgeon with life. He looked into her eyes and saw what not even Ismael knew. She shied away from his intimate gaze.

'The Keris Isa lost, has spoken truth...,' Ummah said, voice breaking.

'Yes Abah,' she said shyly. 'Our line will continue.'

'It's a very good day for our family, Ibu will be very busy with a baby.'

His words released her. It was a huge relief that someone else knew, and that it was Ummah. A grandchild was his blessing and there was no trace of fear on him.

'It will be well, have faith! Are you ready? Jihad, Mariam is coming up!'

'I am throwing down the keys for the outer gate,' Jihad responded as he flung a bunch of keys down and to the side of the clock tower. 'You stand where I can see you.'

'I'm not moving from here,' Ummah shouted back, putting his hands up in surrender.

'Get up and open the door!' Jihad ordered, giving Bonny a vicious kick. Unlocking his handcuffs, he signalled Bonny to the inner gate he had padlocked and threw the keys at him. Jihad's gaze went beyond the boy. He was looking down the stairwell. Then he looked over his shoulder down to the market square to ascertain Ummah was not sneaking up with Mariam. Ummah was standing in full view and he could hear Mariam's feet echoing in the tower.

Why aren't they shooting? Alistair thought in agony. *It's a clear shot!*

Mariam's face emerged at the metal gate and Bonny, who had unlocked the gate, looked at her stupidly. Jihad signalled Mariam in with the point of his gun to the corner where the telescope was.

'Put the handcuffs on! Ummah, you come up now and lock the outer grill!'

Shoot! For God's sake shoot! What are they waiting for?

Without warning, Jihad shoved Bones down the stairwell. Coming out of the tower, the traumatised boy took a step back in fear as Ummah walked towards him.

'Bonny?' Ummah's eyes widened as he spoke in English. 'You okay? Not hurt?'

At his words Bonny realised he was free. He started choking with sobs. Ummah put his hands on his shoulders and shook the teenager vigorously to fortify him.

'Your uncle Bonny, very brave man! A patriot, my friend,' Ummah said proudly. 'Your grandfather is there, GO!'

With that Ummah disappeared into the tower and Bonny ran as if he was being pursued. He threw himself into Alistair's open arms.

'Get down ...... get down! Let me look at you ...... You're bleeding.'

Alistair felt dizzy. Hands shaking, he took out his handkerchief from his pocket and wiped the gash on Bones's forehead.

'I'm fine Grandy, I'm fine.'

'He didn't hurt you.'

'It's nothing...what's going to happen to the people in the tower?'

In the tower, Ummah stepped out onto the lookout. His eyes took in Mariam handcuffed to the telescope stem. Unlike Bonny, she stood up. Jihad waved him over to his daughter-in-law.

'*Salaam waalaikum,*' Ummah said respectfully.

Jihad smiled cynically, refusing the greeting.

'What do you want, Jihad? Mariam is ready to repent.'

'She is a *murtad*[254],' Jihad spat venomously, 'and you have defiled our sacred grounds with this woman and that Serani Dom.'

'Did you kill Si-Dom?'

'He deserved to die. I will kill everyone who touches our holy places.'

'Jihad, what have you done?' Ummah exclaimed ashen-faced.

'You gave him access! It's on your head. The Serani was a kaffir! Like your Serani daughter-in-law.'

'Mariam is a believer, there are no idols in her life.'

'She is a Serani, she did not convert to Islam.'

'Jihad you know the Koran. The Surah al-Bakarah says there is no compulsion, *Al Shaddiq Allah*[255]!'

Ummah's words so outraged Jihad that he rushed over and hit Ummah with the butt of his gun in the face. Mariam screamed as the Headman fell to his feet.

'Abah!'

'Shut up you *Perempuan Sundal*[256].'

Jihad spun around and picked up the can of beer and thrust it into her face.

'Drink this, you're just a Serani whore! Like your family in Malacca. They like beer and dancing and their statues!'

The smell of the beer was too repulsive in Mariam's pregnant state, and she threw up. Cursing, Jihad stepped back. Ummah struggled to get to his feet, leaning against the wall of the balcony.

'Please Jihad...'

'You foolish old man, you're begging me for this worthless Serani infidel...'

---

254   Murtad – Apostate.

255   Al Shaddiq Allah – There is no compulsion in Islam.

256   Perempuan Sundal – Immoral Woman.

'Yes Jihad, YES! She's a Serani. You're right. She's a Serani ......
a naSerani. A NASERANI Jihad. They're Nazarenes, the People of
the Book.'

Through his rage the word registered and Jihad's eyes flicked to
Mariam. Ummah saw that he had his attention.

'What does the Nabi Muhammad say about them? The
NASERANIS. Do them no harm!'

Jihad looked at Ummah. Before he could say anything, a shot
rang out. In front of his eyes a red hole appeared in Ummah's chest.
He looked at his gun, shocked because he had not fired.

'Ya Allah,' Ummah muttered, as he reached out, and touched the
widening circle of blood on his chest, falling backwards onto the
balcony wall.

'Abah!'

Before the lament was even out of Mariam's mouth she had
swallowed it. She knew that he was mortally wounded.

> *La ilaha illa'llah*
>
> *Wa ashadu anna Muhammadar rasulullah.*
>
> *La ilaha illa'llah*
>
> *La ilaha illa'llah*

The words were already bubbling out of Mariam involuntarily, as
Ummah looked up from his red-stained fingers. Their eyes locked,
and for a fraction of a second his lip lifted in a quizzical smile. It was
the look of a father apologising to his child.

Mariam's face was infused with tenderness and she continued to
pray, her words now feathery, as if she were singing over a baby. Jihad
watched Ummah, mesmerised by the death throes closing in on the
Headman, a man whose end he had thirsted for.

Behind the stand, the shot had ripped off the euphoria that cottoned

Alistair and his grandson. Bonny knee-jerked nervously whilst Alistair crawled frantically onto his knees and peeped at the lookout.

He saw the Headman's bloody back in full view, and then the second shot blew off Ummah's head.

'Oh my God! Oh God!' he wailed.

'Grandy what's happening?'

'They've shot the wrong man!'

Teetering heavily on the edge, Ummah's fingers clutched wildly. With the second shot, he tipped over, and fell almost in slow motion. Mariam tried desperately to grab his coat through the obstacle of the telescope. It was futile. Ummah plunged to the square below taking with him the Al-Sijjin banner. Mariam collapsed at the base of the telescope, spray-painted with his blood. Jihad, who had come to his senses, threw himself on the ground and took cover.

Just before the first shot rang out, Ismael was hanging precariously from a branch. The huge tree ran up and behind the tower. Unfortunately, it stopped short by four feet from the walled side of the lookout. On the wall was a one-foot ledge on the level of the lookout and Ismael was getting ready to jump when the shot jolted him. He released the branch too soon and knew straight away it was a mistake. He thrust his hands out, managing to grab onto the ledge, ripping off fingernails, as he hit the side of the wall. Pulling himself up onto the ledge, he heard a second shot ring out. Pressing against the wall, from the corner he saw Ummah fall over to the square below. It was all he could do to stop himself from hurtling after his father.

Allah be merciful! he thought closing his eyes to the hot tears. He knew as a trekker with the Special Branch, the shot had come from the square.

In the tower, Jihad knew that his time was up. The fallen Al-Sijjin banner and Ummah's death signalled that. It would be a matter of minutes before the elite squad from Terendak stormed the lookout. He had been emotionally sidetracked by the Headman's presence but suddenly it was all clear again. He felt cheated that there was not going to be an audience but he also knew the plan was to detonate the suicide bomb. He was not to be taken prisoner.

'It's time to die,' he said to Mariam, getting himself into the kneeling position for prayer.

His words sobered her, cutting through her distress. She looked at him and for the first time saw the suicide vest strapped to him under his coat.

'You're a murderer,' she croaked contemptuously, still heaving. 'Allah will not receive you into *Syurga* – Paradise.'

He looked at her, eyes narrowed at her boldness, but he refused to react. He put his hands out and began to pray. He was facing Mariam in the direction of Mecca.

'Did you hear me Jihad? You are a child of D'Ajjal.'

Jihad was impervious to her. Mariam, however, was becoming calmer, her helplessness giving way to a cold anger.

'Abah was right. We are the People of the Book! The Prophet, *Sallallahu' Alaihe wa Sallam*[257], has sheltered us in the *Ummah*[258], and you dishonour his name.'

Jihad continued his prayer. Behind him, Ismael quietly mounted the lip of the lookout from the ledge. Mariam's eyes widened but he

---

257 Sallallahu' Alaihe wa Sallam – May the peace and blessings of Allah be upon him.

258 Ummah – The universal brotherhood proclaimed by the Prophet Muhammed extending to Christians and Jews.

shook his head in warning.

Alistair had his heart in his mouth when he saw Ismael on the ledge.

They're going to shoot him, he thought, panic-stricken, twisting around to look at the sniper.

Sure enough the sniper was taking aim. In a flash, Alistair got onto his feet, and ran towards the Volvo.

'Don't shoot! Don't shoot! He's one of us,' he roared at the top of his lungs, alternating between cupping his hands over his mouth and waving them about crazily to get their attention. 'HE'S ONE OF US! DON'T SHOOT!'

The man in the military uniform standing outside the Volvo was taken aback. But there was no mistaking what the white man running towards him was saying. The sniper on the balcony of the second floor also heard Alistair.

'*Jangan tembak! Dia anak kampung! Anak kita!*'

'Don't shoot! He's a child from the kampong. He's our child!'

Suddenly, voices taking cover in the vicinity of the Volvo, joined in, clearly angry.

'It's Ismael, Ummah's son. You've shot Ummah! You've killed the Headman.'

Alistair was like a cartoon character, flapping his hands and running backwards and forwards. He could not tear his eyes off from the lookout, and at the same time he had to stop the sniper. His behaviour to get attention had its desired result. People suddenly saw the military vehicle and began to surround the Volvo. A mass hysteria was beginning to manifest. The military officer said something into his walkie-talkie. Looking up, Alistair saw the sniper lower his gun. Then he ran back to the stand where Bonny was. He was sweating and shaking with adrenaline.

In the lookout, Jihad finished praying and opened his eyes. Behind him as he climbed over the ledge, Ismael froze. Jihad looked at Mariam dispassionately, his hand going to the little detonator hanging at his waist.

'I want to pray,' Mariam said coldly.

'What?'

'I want to pray, I want Allah to forgive my sins,' she said, and without waiting for his permission, closed her eyes and started praying. She wanted to give Ismael a few more minutes and she needed to hide from what was about to happen.

Jihad's pharisaical zeal, consumed by her uncleanness, condescended to her request. Her prayers, from the Al-Koran, were a communal prayer recited from the heart. Even though he watched her with a self-righteous vindication, the purity of the words overcame him. Jihad's heart, demented in its ideology, convinced him he loved God. He closed his eyes and waited for her to finish, the detonator in his hand.

Quiet as a tiger Ismael stepped up behind him. Silently he pulled the Keris out from behind his back, where it was tucked in his waistband. Ismael, hunter and soldier, could have broken Jihad's neck in a split second. Instead he unsheathed the Keris. It was in obedience to his father and the Ancient Ones. The Keris was endowed with spiritual authority. He salaamed the Keris and then turned it tip down. He looked down at the soft place on Jihad's neck above the left collarbone. It was the spot for execution by the Keris. The dagger was too fragile for an upward thrust. Going down vertically it would puncture the heart. One clean thrust, it was the way of the Master Craftsman.

He was a hair's breadth from the spot when Jihad turned and looked upwards at him. Ismael held his eyes as the Keris dived.

'*Allah hu Akhbar!*' Ismael shouted in a war cry.

The fear in Jihad's eyes flared and died instantly. He slipped bonelessly to the floor.

'Mariam,' Ismael said gently, kneeling beside his wife whose hands were still manacled around the stem. She did not stop praying. He looked around and saw the keys lying beside Jihad. He unshackled her hands. Then she opened her eyes, her face pale but serene, with no trace of the hell she had undergone. She looked at Jihad and then Ismael.

'*Ayahanda*[259]. Our Father...' she said with deep sorrow and tenderness, looking into his eyes. He turned his face into her shoulder and she put her arms around him.

From the square, Alistair searched the lookout but could see nothing. Turning to look up at the sniper, his heart stopped beating. The gun was trained on him. Something exploded as he felt a terrible pain in his chest.

---

259 Ayahanda – poetic word in Malay for father.

Part 13

PRESENT

1985
Port Dickson – Malaysia

*The end of all our exploring will be to arrive where we started
and know the place for the first time.*

T.S. Eliot

39

Alistair drifted like a mist, the rush of voices keeping him from sinking into a greater darkness.

I've been here before, he thought dispassionately, the voices echoing with déjà vu.

Then it came to him.

'Ivy's dying!' The cicadas shrilled.

The cancer was spreading like wildfire on her face and they were there to see the Spirit Guide. He could hear *him* whispering a little canticle that soothed. And Ivy was sitting beside him, on a slab that looked like a gravestone.

'Ivy, don't be afraid.'

She turned to him and the corner of her mouth lifted in her famous selachian grin. There was no trace of the mouldy, vile smelling cancer, her skin dewy like a baby's. Words trickled through his brain, they came from the Spirit Guide. In the thick of sulphurous fumes, Alistair saw him sitting at the end of the slab. Under him, the ground seemed to give way and a great annihilation rose up from the deep to meet them.

'It's the Beast.'

He knew *it* had come to claim him, the whispering voices, bargaining for him.

Om ... I am ... Om ... I am ... Om ... I am.

'I'm going to hell.'

The voices grew louder, pulling him back and he could hear feet scuffing in haste. He heard other sounds like hushed robes in the sacred corridors of a monastery and he thought of Dom in his frock.

'Get up Alistair!' hollered Dom in his ear. 'The hunt is on.'

He turned to see Long Claws looking straight at him, spectral and terrifying. Closer and closer he came, the White Tiger, head lowered, breath shuddery.

'Run Alistair!'

Dom grabbed his arm and suddenly he was running for his life. Fearfully, he turned to look behind, and GrandSire Long Claws, a white light, was almost upon him and Dom. It lifted its front paws to pounce, when amazingly the Tiger stood up. It was Isa. Alistair watched open-mouthed as Isa overtook them, and hot on his heels, followed the Tiger Wallah of Punjab, in his hands, a double-barrelled gun made of flowers.

'Sorry chappies, can't stop,' sang out Lucky Lakhvir Singh. 'I've found my *Atman*.[260]'

'Alistair, follow me!'

They were running like happy children, light and airy now. As they flitted through the jungle, there was no gravity and like a bird Dom lifted up, up, up and away.

'Dom wait ... Wait for me, WAIT!'

It was too late, he was gone and Alistair realised he was hovering. Looking down he saw a body, in a white shroud. Only the face was exposed. It looked like him. He needed to have a look and he moved closer. When he saw the pale white ghostly face in the bathtub with his veins opened, he started crying.

---

260   Atman – Sanskrit word for inner self or soul.

'Da! Da! Wake up!'

'Peace be to you,' the Spirit Guide said. 'I live, so you live.'

Through the mists he saw the white light get bigger and bigger. It looked like Long Claws. He could smell incense, and he could feel someone touching him. The pain in his chest eased out and he thought he saw Ummah. When he looked again, through tired eyes, he saw it was Ismael, wearing Ummah's turban. He struggled to keep awake but the comforting voice and warm hands swallowed him.

40

ALISTAIR WAS PROPPED upright in his own bed, under a blanket. He had suffered a mild heart attack. On his chest under his nightshirt was a poultice of herbs, eucalyptus and menthol, strapped on by thick plaster. It was a concoction made up by the Spirit Guide. Flowers and fruit burst out of a basket as sunlight poured into the room and a breeze teased the yellow curtains.

Alistair's face was grim. By his side, on the bed, sat Ismael and on his lap lay Alistair's camera. Strewn over the blanket were photographs. In his hand, Alistair held a few photographs.

'We found the camera when we went to investigate Si-Dom's death, it was at the Seat of the Ancients.'

'So this is what Dom saw ... before he died.' The last words were still hard to say. 'I know this man.'

'Tan Sri Ashman's driver. He was behind the *Pontianak*, the vampire.'

Alistair's eyes flicked to Ismael's face, questions racing through his head but he was afraid of the answer.

Don't go there Alistair, he thought, but somewhere in the marketplace when Ummah fell over the ledge, he had crossed his precious mental divide.

'So Dom *did* find out about his vampire, he solved the mystery,' he said, as he started to arrange the photographs in sequence.

Ismael reached out and helped him.

It was a brilliant morning, the jungle, lemon and lime throughout Tiger Sanctuary. Armed with Alistair Pierce's camera, Dom Hendrique waited at the kink in the North-South highway where he was to meet Ummah. The virgin rainforest had shrunk drastically from the last time Dom was there, near the spot where Isa was killed. Sitting side-saddle on his motorbike, he fiddled with the camera that was hanging from his neck. He had been waiting for twenty minutes and for Dom, that was too long. He was going to see the Ancient Tree! Ummah was honouring him beyond his greatest expectation, even though Dom was beginning to suspect there was a deeper agenda.

'Bring your camera, but no photographs until I tell you. NO PHOTOS of the Sacred Tree!'

That was the first inkling Dom had of mischief. Spirits did not cast an image on celluloid, but he asked no questions, not wanting to jeopardise the invitation.

The spot where he was to meet Ummah was a little green hollow just off the highway. Focusing his camera to take some shots, he noticed the fresh motorbike tracks in the soft earth.

'Oh no! I've missed them. That's Mael's bike, I must have got the time wrong.'

Without a moment's hesitation, he got onto his motorbike, and started following the trail into the jungle. Switching on his lights to see clearly, he rode, deep into the rainforest. The heartbeat of the jungle became stronger and stronger, but he was not afraid as he followed the faint track. When he saw the motorbike parked by a huge tree, relief flooded Dom. Ummah had briefed him on not taking the bike to the Black Lenggundi Tree. It was a sacred place, and furthermore, there were numerous traps set up for man and beast alike. As he pulled up alongside the motorbike, Dom realised there were two motorbikes and neither was Ismael's. Puzzled, he went over to them. On the ground, there was a plastic bag that had been dropped. Picking it up and shining a torchlight he had brought with him, he was surprised to see women's clothing. He looked around, totally befuddled.

The hills behind Tiger Sanctuary had been reduced to chaff by the highway. Huge monoliths of sunlight filled the green cathedral in which he stood. Dom had never seen such a glorious outpouring of savagery in his life. The towering trees had three or four terraces of flora and fauna cascading down on him. With a skein of vines and ferns, it looked like skyscrapers.

'Tiger City.'

He could hear the sound of water tinkling as it flowed down the terraces. Above this he could hear the distinct "chop-chop-chop" of wood. He knew straight away it was not Ummah or Ismael. He had been told there was to be no noise of any sort at Tiger Sanctuary. Only prayers were acceptable.

'Trappers!'

Pushing his bike out of the way, he concealed it, along with the bag of clothing he found, behind a tree. Grateful for the natural skylight, he cautiously made a beeline to the sound, the torchlight leading him.

And then God smiled down on him.

In the light of a couple of hurricane lamps, two men were struggling with something about the size of a large sack of potatoes. Moving closer, camouflaged by undergrowth, he was shocked. It was a dead pig. The men were trying to impale the carcass onto a bamboo stake they had stuck into the ground.

'Nab shot! They're desecrating the Sanctuary.'

Heart thundery in his ears, he took the camera hanging from his neck and started clicking. As soon as they succeeded with the pig, the two men, unaware of his presence, quickly packed up and hastened past him. After they disappeared into the jungle, he waited for a couple of minutes before he came out of hiding. Stepping up to where they stood, he held up his torch.

Dom's heart rose like a Hallelujah chorus. Before him was the Black Lenggundi Tree. It was an ancient leftover with roots like sails in a Spanish Armada. He had seen pictures of giant red trees in America with a road running through. This was the diameter of six lanes. There were huge dark yawns at the roots, like doorways. He looked longingly at them but it was forbidden to enter. Ummah had told him there were three Kings, three trees, like children in the womb. In the perfectness of time, they would knit together, giving up their sovereignty and become one. Then it would be a new dawning, a second birth for the Black Lenggundi Tree.

'Isa's buried here.'

Reverence dissolved him. He lay his torch on the ground and a "nothing" in the shadow of the Tree, he crossed himself in the Catholic tradition and prayed. Head bowed, eyes closed, eternity infused Dom Hendrique.

> *Our Father who art in Heaven,*
> *Hallowed be Thy name,*
> *Thy Kingdom come,*
> *Thy Will be done,*
> *On earth, as it is in Heaven ...*

When he finished, he reached for the camera strapped around his neck. Keeping his promise to Ummah not to photograph the Tree, he took only close-up shots of the pig, until the roll ran out. Stepping back, hands on his hips, Dom surveyed the scene before him. It was only then, the enormity of what he had uncovered, sunk in. A big smile broke out on his face. All his life he had chased dreams and glimpses of reality only to come home empty-handed. He lifted his hands heavenward in victory, glorying in the moment, as he envisioned his triumphant return.

'Ummah's going to love this ... and Alistair Pierce, you're going to eat your hat. Dom Hendrique, cabin servant to Magellan, *will* be presented to the King.'

And joy, like he had never known, bubbled up from deep within his Catholic soul as he started laughing breathlessly. He never saw Jihad behind him nor did he hear the twang of the bamboo that sliced through the air straight for his breast. He felt himself lifting off the ground and his life flashed before him.

LAUGHTER PEALED LIKE CHURCH BELLS around him. He was a toddler and Rozie and Alfonso were holding his hands and swinging him as they promenaded along the beach.

Spell Timbuktu boy.

Tim ... buck ... one TWO three.

Mama's clever baby.

Higher and faster they swung him, propelled by delighted chortles. Rozie's eyes were crinkling with contentment as Alfonso beamed with pride.

You know the answer boy –

Because You know the question!

Swing high, swing low, carry me home, he whooped. He was almost shoulder high and they let him go... Rozie's hand on her crimson lips, blowing kisses as Alfonso cheered him on.

And again, laughter caught him, this time in Bonny's arms. He was in Charles Lazaroo's home on Morris's wedding day. Bonnifacio Lazaroo was hoisting him high in the kitchen as all around him the disconsolate faces looked up at him with such great expectation. They needed something, and only he could give it.

Well, what do you have to say for yourself?

High... Higher up... lift the son of Hendricks. The Son of God. There's hope through the Valley of Shadows... Don't be fearful little flock...

As Bonnifacio tossed him heavenward to the light over them, Dom felt all his 'interrupted selves' fuse in a blinding realisation.

Our Father, the God of hope and peace... He's got us! Underneath are the everlasting arms. He felt his being melt, and his heart stopped in exquisite pain as he touched the face of God.

'What are we going to do?' Alistair asked brokenly, looking at the photos strewn on the bed.

'We will wait. The Police?' Ismael hesitated. 'It was Jihad who killed Si-Dom.'

Alistair watched him as he gathered the photographs. There was a deadliness about him.

'But Ashman's driver! It doesn't make sense. Why would Ashman want *Keramat Rimau*? He's rich beyond our imagination.'

'It's nothing to do with the *Keramat*, Pa Ali.'

'What do you mean?'

'They can get oil under the headland...'

'There is no oil!' Alistair interjected. 'I've studied the geology of Port Dickson and so have the other big oil companies.'

'Under the Sunda Shelf on Indonesian territory...' Ismael continued. 'They've discovered a new way. They're going to drill sideways. Like between Iraq and Kuwait. Billions of barrels.'

'What are you saying?'

'The fishing village and Keramat Rimau, they provide the shallowest access under the Straits of Malacca.'

'How do you know this?'

'Ummah's old contacts from the war, secret reports submitted to OPEC. They warned him.'

'Ashman wouldn't...'

'Tan Sri Ashman has important friends all over the world. It's not so hard to believe, after all, you came to our kampong with your secret plans.'

Alistair looked blankly at Ismael and felt his hands go clammy.

Ismael held his gaze, his face grave.

'It's politics Pa Ali,' Ismael said jadedly. 'It's all politics. People like Jihad are pawns. Tan Sri is only one face.'

'Who?'

'Anyone, everyone...the CIA, IMF, the Army?! The Minister of Defence? You have to ask why *my* father was shot and Jihad was not!'

As Alistair looked at him, the picture of Ashman and the General in the car flashed in his mind.

'The people in the marketplace told me what happened. How you stopped them from shooting me.'

'I didn't do anything.'

'I believe you said, *"He is one of us"*. Ismael a white man? You almost started a riot.'

'I want to thank you for saving Bonny's life. You and Ummah and Mariam,' Alistair said overcome with emotion, putting his hand out and clutching Ismael's hand.

'It was an *utang budi,* a debt of honour. Your grandson's uncle, Bonnifacio, he gave his life protecting Ummah. My father was the agent for the Allies when the Japanese were here.'

'I didn't know that.'

'If he had given my father up, the whole kampong would have been executed. Give this to your grandson. It belonged to Bonnifacio.'

Ismael pulled out the Bible and held it out to Alistair who took it.

'There are codes in there... my father used to communicate with Si-Bonny through the *Injil.*[261]'

Hesitantly, Alistair opened the cover page. Like a crouching tiger the words leapt out and seized him.

Unless a grain of wheat falls down and dies, it will bear no fruit.

Underneath, written in capitals, was Bonnifacio's name.

He started weeping softly.

'I changed the maps.'

Ismael looked at him, not understanding what he was saying.

'We doctored the boundaries of Tiger Sanctuary before Independence. I was with the Land Office. The highway cut into Tiger Sanctuary... People got scared and Isa was killed!'

Ismael was silent.

'I'm responsible. For Isa ... and Dom. I had my suspicions about the vampire but I was compromised. I should have warned Dom and told him the truth. He'd still be alive.'

'Pa Ali, no one has control over death, only God. We are only men. Clay.'

'... but I...'

---

261   Injil – Bible.

'All debts have been paid Pa Ali,' Ismael said gently. 'It's time to forgive yourself.'

They sat in silence for a while.

'Grandy,' Bones popped his head in and rapped on the inside of the door. 'Can I come in?'

'Seeing you're already in ...'

'I've got to go Pa Ali. I'll come back in three days to change the dressing.'

'Grandy, there are some men from the church to see you. They're wearing dresses.'

'He's just like his grandmother,' Alistair said proudly, as Ismael laughed.

41

THE SUN, SAYING GOODBYE like an affectionate grandfather, pinched the cheeks of the sky pink and orange. Alistair sat on the swing in his garden enjoying the bird calls. Bonny and Tatiana had returned to Adelaide after Dom's funeral and even though the house was quieter, he savoured his privacy.

> *An Englishman and his castle,* he mused. *I'll see them for Christmas. It's time to take Bones to Malacca and get to know the family.*

His thoughts turned to Dom's funeral. The Church had come forward to bury him, but it was after the fact. Dom was buried next to Ummah a week later. They lay side by side in simple graves at the Muslim cemetery in Tiger Sanctuary, facing Mecca. It had been Ismael's decision.

'Si-Dom was a true believer, a Muslimin.'

No one in the kampong protested and Alistair felt it was right. He missed Dom dearly and the evenings at the Club would be a shadow of the past but it was Ummah who had left him with a sense of diminution. It was the same loss he had experienced over his father's death. They had lived for something bigger than themselves.

'I hope Ismael turns out to be the man his father was.'

'Tuan, Tuan!' screeched Ah Lan, his old maid, rushing over. 'Tuan, the tiger eat two people!'

'Really?'

'The rich man, Tan Sri. Killed!'

'What do you mean? Which Tan Sri?'

'The Tan Sri, live in the English house, Tan Sri Ashman. Got three wives, many girlfriends *lah*.'

'When?' Alistair stood up, shocked.

'This morning, when he come back from his girlfriend's house. Stupid man! How many times must tell people. He stop to urinate at the Keramat, make the Grandfather Tiger angry!'

She had her own hilarious interpretation of events, but this time he could not laugh. It was too close to the bone.

'On the news just now, TV3. The Tan Sri's head eaten off, his body by the car on the roadside. His driver still missing ... no hope *lah*! Stop on the road early morning, sure stop to *kencing*[262]. Tsk! Stupid man. Tok Rimau eat him up! Make his Keramat dirty.'

Alistair felt cold in the soft balmy night. He thought of Ismael and saw his quiet deadliness and his hand went up involuntarily to his chest.

'Why you hold your heart?' Ah Lan asked, immediately. 'You feel pain?'

'No! I'm fine, just a bit shocked.'

'No need to be shocked, not your friend what!' she said tetchily. 'You come inside now. Dark already.'

Her eyes gave her away, as she looked furtively into the darkening corners of the garden. She was afraid of GrandSire Long Claws.

---

262 Kencing – to urinate.

'In a few minutes. You go on in. I just want to see the sun set.'

In the twilight, the sky over him was the *dupatta*[263] of an Indian bride. Flame red with gold embroidery, it held the promise of a celebration. Alistair sighed deeply. For the first time since Dom's death, he wanted to live, a little more.

In their little *stone house* in the town, Mariam was preparing the evening meal. Ismael was sitting at the table, his fingers drumming restlessly. She had washed her hair and it fell soft and clean to her knees.

'Be careful of your hair,' Ismael warned, as she moved across to the stove.

'Do you think they'll find his body?'

'They defiled the Keramat,' he said harshly.

'Are you alright?'

'I'm alright,' he said, guarding his emotions and diverting the attention away from him. 'It's Ibu I feel sorry for.'

'Abah felt she should come and stay with us.'

'*Betul ye?*[264] He said it's never good to have two women in one kitchen. It can get very hot.'

'We both won't be in the kitchen. Abah thought she would be busy with the baby.'

Her back was to him and his hands had stilled their drumming.

'When was this?'

'At the marketplace, when I took off my jubba.'

Ismael got up slowly and walked over to her. He stood behind her,

---

263   Dupatta – Indian headcloth.

264   Betul ye? – Really? in Malay.

not touching her.

'How come Abah knew first?'

' ... because he has eyes to see,' Mariam said, giving him a sideways sugary smile.

He felt the unspoken hurt and hovered uncertainly. She refused to turn around, and make it easier for him.

'You don't tell me so many things... I mean you always talk with Si-Dom. Really I don't mind, he's like your brother.'

'I don't have Dom to talk with anymore,' she said, her voice breaking, 'and I don't want to talk with you on the walkie-talkie with half the kampong eavesdropping.'

'Half the kampong isn't eavesdropping.'

'You always call me when the fishermen are around, or Abah or Ibu. Why do you do that?'

'I don't always call you when others are listening...' he said half-heartedly.

'Ismael Ibrahim, you're not good at telling lies. It's as if you have to show them you're the boss in the house.'

'Mariam ...,' he said, shame-faced, nose wrinkled. He took her hair from the base of her neck and began to wind it around his arm. She turned around and looked at him, enjoying the moment, leaning into him as her hair drew them closer.

'Do you remember the day we got married?' Ismael asked.

'You looked so fierce.'

'I was afraid of you.'

'Why?' she asked surprised.

'... because I did not believe you could be faithful. I was afraid, you were so beautiful. Too beautiful for a man like me.'

'*Yo sa Amor*[265],' she said tenderly, touching his face and smoothing his furrowed brow.

'You are the most faithful woman I've ever met. Abah showed me when he called you out at the marketplace.'

'You're going to make me cry.'

'And so obedient, not just as a wife but a *Muslimah*[266].'

He let her hair go and it stayed wrapped and pliant around his arm. He looked at it and at her.

'Even your hair is obedient,' he said wonderingly, making her smile. 'You are my *tiang*[267], my pillar. My house stands because of you.'

A gecko chirruped and ran across the ceiling.

'See, the *cicak*[268] has spoken, my words are true.'

In the quiet intimacy of the dusky night, she reached for his hand and gently laid it on her swelling stomach. With the first stars peeping through, they embraced.

From the fishing boats out at sea, Port Dickson twinkled with lights. On Cape Rachado, the monastery looked like a castle, the Al-Fuad minaret, a heavenly sceptre. The lovesick moon hung over the fishing village, the sea calm like glass. It was so still that the unwavering Olympic flame of the oil refinery burned brightly. Nothing could disturb the sweetness of the night, not even the distant "pppfff pppfff pppfff" of the military helicopter patrolling the coast off Sumatra.

---

265   Yo sa Amor – My Love in Kristang language.

266   Muslimah – a female Muslim.

267   tiang – pillar.

268   cicak – ghekko.

The lighthouse, ever vigilant, kept its eye on the fishermen, drawing them home safely after the midnight catch. And over the spice-laden land, the mellow strains of the evening Azan prayers fell like dew.

Allahu Akbar Allahu Akbar

Asyhadu alla illahaill Allah

Asyhadu alla ilahaill Allah

Asyhadu alla illahaill Allah Asyhadu anna

Muhammadar rasulAllah

I bear witness that there is no God but Allah

And Muhammad is the Messenger of Allah.

It was perfect, even if it was only for one night.

THE END

Epilogue

Dom Hendrique
1936 – 1985
KRISTANG POPULATION THIRTY-SEVEN THOUSAND

Jesus wept
John 11:35

'Why do you weep?' the goddesses asked the lake.
'I weep for Narcissus, but I never noticed that Narcissus was
beautiful. I weep because each time he knelt beside my banks,
I could see, in the depths of his eyes, my own beauty reflected.'

The Alchemist – **Paulo Coelho**

Acknowledgements

EVERYTHING IS A STORY

The Kristang Serani – my beloved Nazarenes

Mercy Thomas – I believe we were huddling at the Si Rusa Inn in Port Dickson thirty years ago, researching this book. It's done! Thank you for walking me in Truth tempered by mercy.

Shumi – your celluloid magic in 'Pak Agus' ignited my imagination. Grateful for 'ambulancing' me to church when I bled. You have been an 'Ummah' to me.

Esther & Frankie Tan – thanks for chewing both my ears off. And looking after me when all was lost.

Karam Kaur, Fay, Debra, Dorothea and Tippy – for those mad and wonderful evenings. Kami, love you.

Fay, remember that horse in that mystical misty night.

Ranita and Steven Bicknell – Good and Faithful. For believing, praying and your incredible support. Ranita, I can never forget all those hours typing the manuscript from pieces of paper cut and pasted together! And baby Saran who had to share her mummy.

Kesh Karam Veriah and Lang and Kabir – for your serendipitous find on "*Tiger-Wallahs*". Our hearts are knitted in Love and God.

Ravi Hari Jacques – for reading Part 1 and your clever suggestion of 'Chapters'.

My siblings who have encouraged me through my journey. You've known from the time I was three, when I was devouring all those story books **Arjan** bought for me – this is it!

Atma and Rajindar – thank you for England

Rabin Veer and Gee Eng – for the leg up on the Hillary step.

Sheila V Azariah – my best friend and biggest fan who has always believed in my dreams. For all those nights after **Dad** died when we used to lie in bed as children - and you listened to my stories.

Florence Jonas King who gave me my first glimpse of Mariam. It took my breath away.

Marina and Rahim – for your unconditional love, support and the wisdom of Horus. As beautiful inside as outside.

Danny Boy. Savin. Abby. Pan Ji Gurbaksh. Rani Ludher. Aunty May & Judy Fernandez. Naveen Raj. Zoe. Mashitah Shariff. Robyne Gaultier. Marion Lockyer. Martha Boer. Julie Ryan. Seema Edwards & Sunaina – for your prayers, encouragement and protection.

I owe you a debt of love.

Joan Margaret Marbeck – an authority on the Kristang and a gift to history for her exquisite contribution and collation in her book **"Ungua Adanza** – An Inheritance."** My book would have lacked authenticity without you. *Mutu grandi Merseh*

R Winstedt and WW Skeat for their profound research in "The Malay Magician" and "Malay Magic" respectively. *Terima Kasih* for honouring the Malay culture.

GC Ward and DR Ward – for the exciting exotic world in "Tiger-Wallahs". And pointing me to the wealth of my heritage.

My publisher Ann Castle for that cosmic connection when we "saw the other." Namaste.

Moira Elliott – My editor for her invaluable feedback, patience and joyous laughter. And that word "brilliant".

Margaret Sebastian – My Malaysian advisor and editor. Thank you for being my eyes.

Lynette Stapleton – bless your razor gift of words and an Atlas mind that can hold up the world of literature.

Jill Messner. Simon Couch. Gilles Lo Cascio. Ari Badaines. Nicky Lock – for keeping me sane and well.

Jill, I've got you as a character in a future children's book.

Michael Stone and Angel for gracing my idiosyncrasies with your patience and talent. New frontiers await you.

My Beloved Muslim family in England – Sayyah Jlelati, Aneez Ismail, Fatimah-Donna, Fradoon – and all the others in Malaysia, thank you for showing me the bounteous heart of my larger 'Ummah family', especially **Tuan Syed Nik Aziz** of Bank Bumiputra.
I fell in love!

The Kristang Familya – Ursula Ann Mitchell 1954–1967, who drew me into their embrace.

Vernon Adrian Emuang – my secret Agent.

Tan Sri Johan Jaafar – for launching my book and believing in it.

Dr Daniel O.C. Dr Phil Pringle. Rev Maggie Lowe – the Aaron & the Hur.

Richard Fowler from Liverpool – for the Hallelujah chorus.

Jason & Susie and Penny Chow. KH & Mui – for the jet plane.

My Darling husband Mark – *Yo sa Amor*. Words are not enough!

Finally Daniel and Caroline – hitch your wagon to the star that was over Bethlehem.

No greater love ... **Jesus**

First published in the UK in 2019
by Atlantis Books an imprint of
Little Steps Publishing
Uncommon, 126 New King's Road
London SW6 4LZ
www.littlestepspublishing.co.uk

A CIP catalogue record for this book is available from the
British Library.

ISBN: 978-1-912678-08-2

Printed in China

Designed by Angel Rae McMullan

10 9 8 7 6 5 4 3 2 1

This is a work of fiction.

Names, characters, businesses, places, events and incidents
are either the products of the author's imagination or used
in a fictitious manner. Any resemblance to actual persons,
living or dead, or actual events is purely coincidental.